The Perón Novel

Tomás Eloy Martínez was born in 1934 in Argentina. His first novel and first book of chronicles were published in Buenos Aires between 1968 and 1973. During the military dictatorship, he lived in exile in Venezuela where he wrote three other books, all of which were republished in Argentina in 1983, in the first months of democracy. Since then he has written *The Perón Novel* and *The Master's Hand*, followed by *Santa Evita*, which became an instant No. 1 bestseller when it was published in Argentina. Currently he is the director of Latin American studies at Rutgers University, New Jersey.

Santa Evita is also published by Anchor.

THE PERON NOVEL

Tomás Eloy Martínez
Translated from the Spanish by Helen Lane

TRANSWORLD PUBLISHERS LTD
61–63 Uxbridge Road, London W5 5SA

TRANSWORLD PUBLISHERS (AUSTRALIA) PTY LTD
15–25 Helles Avenue, Moorebank, NSW 2170

TRANSWORLD PUBLISHERS (NZ) LTD
3 William Pickering Drive, Albany, Auckland

Published by Anchor – a division of Transworld Publishers Ltd

First published in Great Britain by Anchor, 1998

Translation Copyright © Helen Lane 1998

Originally published in Argentina as *La novela de Perón* by Planeta, Buenos Aires, in 1991

© 1991, Tomás Eloy Martínez
© 1991, Editorial Planeta Argentina S.A.I.C.
© 1991, Grupo Editorial Planeta

The right of Tomás Eloy Martínez to be identified as the author of this work has been asserted in accordance with the Copyright, Designs and Patents Act 1988

A catalogue record for this book is available from the British Library

ISBN 1862 30040 2

Typeset in 10pt Adobe Caslon by Kestrel Data, Exeter
Reproduced, printed and bound in Great Britain by
Mackays of Chatham plc, Chatham, Kent

to Susana Rotker

If the reader prefers, this book may be regarded as a work of fiction. But there is always the chance that such a book of fiction may throw some light on what has been written as fact.

ERNEST HEMINGWAY,
preface to *A Moveable Feast*

We Argentines, as you know, are characterized by our belief that we always know the real truth. Many Argentines come to this house wanting me to sell a different truth as though it were the only one. And what would you have me do? I believe all my visitors!

JUAN PERON, to the author
26 March 1970

Contents

THE PERON NOVEL

1 *Farewell to Madrid*

Yet again, General Juan Perón dreamed that he was walking toward the entrance to the South Pole and that a pack of women wouldn't let him past. When he woke up, he had the sensation of not being in any time. He knew that it was 20 June 1973, but that meant nothing. He was flying on a plane that had taken off from Madrid at dawn on the longest day of the year, and was heading for the night of the shortest day, in Buenos Aires. His horoscope predicted an unknown adversity. What could it be, if the only thing he hadn't yet experienced in his life was the yearned-for adversity of death?

He wasn't even in a hurry to get anywhere. He was quite comfortable as he was, suspended from his own feelings. And what were feelings? Nothing. When he was a boy, he was told that he didn't know how to feel, that all he could do was make a show of his feelings. All he needed was a sadness or a touch of compassion, and that did the trick: he simply pinned it to his face. His body was always in some other place, where his heart's desires couldn't hurt him. Even his language was gradually becoming tinged with words that weren't his: boy, in a hurry. Nothing had belonged to him, least of all his own self. He had had only one home of his own in his whole life – in Madrid these last few years – and he was losing that as well.

He raised the curtain over the passenger window and sensed the sea below the plane: that is to say, the land of nowhere. Up above, yellow wisps of sky drifted lazily by, from one meridian to another. The General's watch said five, but there where he was, in that mobile point of space, no hour shown on a timepiece was really the right one.

His secretary had made him stay in the first-class compartment so that he would still be at his freshest when he landed and the crowd awaiting him would see him as the other Perón: the one of the past. He had at his disposal four reclining seats, several couches and a little dining table. In the semidarkness, he looked at his wife, passing the time flicking through a photo magazine: she was as tiny as a bird and had the virtue of seeing only people's surface. The General had always been terrified of women who went farther, making their way through to his non-feelings.

Just before lunch, the secretary took him for a walk in tourist class, where an entourage numbering a hundred men was traveling with him. He recognized almost no one. The names of governors, congressmen, trade union leaders were whispered in his ear. 'Ah, yes,' he greeted them. 'I'm counting on all of you. Don't go off and leave me all by myself in Buenos Aires . . .' He shook a hand here and there, until he felt a sudden stabbing pain in the pit of his stomach and had to stop to catch his breath. 'It's nothing, it's nothing,' his secretary reassured him, and took him back to his seat. 'It's nothing,' the General repeated after him. 'But I want to be by myself.'

His wife wrapped his legs in a blanket and lowered the seat, so that the General's slow-moving blood would in time brighten his mood.

'Daniel is such a good man! Have you noticed, Perón, what an obliging man God has sent us?'

'Yes,' the General agreed. 'Now let me get some sleep, both of you.'

The secretary's name was José López Rega, but on the first occasion that presented itself to enter into a more personal relationship he had solemnly asked to be called Daniel, since it was by that astral name that the Lord would know him when the apocalypse to punish humanity would come thundering forth. He looked like a local butcher: he was short and fat and his manner too forward. He alighted like a fly on every conversation, without the slightest misgivings about other people's tolerance. In earlier days he had made an effort to be likable, but not any more. He now boasted about his disagreeable nature.

As the General was taking his afternoon nap on the plane, López had tried a couple of times to measure the thickness of the air in the alveoli of the General's lungs. He penetrated it with his thought and patiently followed, from one alveolus to the next, the languid and labored passage of its currents. When he came across a snore in the General's diaphragm, the secretary became alarmed. He decided to mount guard, seated on the arm of the seat, helping the air to move by his strength of will. Meanwhile the señora, having tired of reading and rereading the account of a number of betrothals in Seville in *Hola* magazine, took off her shoes and allowed her gaze to lose itself in the landscape of pure steel through which the plane was imperceptibly moving.

The moment he noticed that the General's eyes were opening, the secretary had him get to his feet and walk up and down the center aisle. He folded the blanket, placed the seat upright and moved one of the couches over closer to the window.

'Have a seat over here,' he ordered. 'And undo the buttons of your pants so they won't be as tight around your waist.'

'What time is it?' the General wanted to know.

The secretary shook his head, as though the question had come from a child.

'Who knows? Two o'clock at a guess. We'll soon be crossing the equator.'

'So that means we can't go back now,' the General sighed. 'What you predicted for me is true, López. That one day I would be lying with my bones stretched out on the pampas.'

Perón had been preparing for two months to return to Buenos Aires: as soon as the military regime had acknowledged the Peronists' victory in the elections and was readying itself to allow them to take over the reins of government. 'Come back to your homeland straightaway. Settle in your own home,' hundreds of telegrams urged him. My own home? he smiled. In Argentina the only home is exile.

Spring had come early in Madrid that year. At the end of March, when he opened the door to the balcony outside his bedroom, there came from afar a smell of fried food and of doves that sufficed to make his body smack its lips over the past. The General held his arms upraised and there it was, all of a sudden: the cooing of the crowd. Thousands of doves shivered at the ritual greeting: 'Comrades', and cheered him as they waved photos of him and huge placards. Farther on, between the beds of roses and the towers of the dovecotes, alongside the sentry box where the Civil Guards sent by Generalissimo Franco were posted, were entrances to the Anglo-Argentine subway, which had begun to be built almost before his eyes, in 1909. Hadn't he walked through those quagmires, trailing after Granny Dominga Dutey, as they went to the Ministry of War to apply for the providential scholarship that would permit him to study at the Military Academy?

At that point in the past, the General's imagination always

refused to go on. He began to feel sad about what hadn't yet happened – I'll have to leave Madrid, I'll be too old to get around in the house in Buenos Aires they've given me as a gift. And in the sudden emptiness of his heart he discovered that he had time for happiness only when he had no country.

In those days in March he was assailed by the presentiment that he shouldn't leave. Every time he thought of Buenos Aires, his center of gravity shifted from his liver to his kidneys and gave him a sharp pain inside. The General said that these were apprehensions that were a portent of misfortunes to come, and that the only way of exorcising them was to watch a John Wayne film on television: the dust of Westerns that the damp air of Buenos Aires couldn't penetrate. His hands were still entangled in towels and tablecloths, and when even the bed linen was packed for the trip, his body still clung to the aura that objects left everywhere.

Amid all this confusion the last weeks flew by. He had a schedule of six to seven interviews each day: always with the aim of being the arbiter of some squabble between the rival factions that were fighting tooth and nail for power. He wrote a few letters, he spoke on the phone a couple of times a day (if it wasn't with the doctor in Barcelona who was treating him for his prostate trouble, then it was with the veterinarian: he had a family of female poodles that needed a great deal of looking after), and when he tried to take a stroll down the Gran Vía, as he often did in the past, he was no longer allowed to do so. If the Eternal Father were to make a habit of strolling down the street in plain sight – they said to dissuade him, resorting to his own maxim – people would eventually lose their respect for him.

Ever since the Peronists had won the elections, the secretary relieved him of all the petty administrative details: he chose those who would be received by the General and those who, after having spent time with him almost every day, from now on would never see him again. In both cases the secretary made his decisions on the basis of the aura of good or evil that people gave off and that he could discern as clearly as an odor. At night, he sorted through the mail that came in and destroyed the messages of no importance, so that the General wouldn't waste time. Often the only ones that survived his scrutiny were the electricity bills and the announcements of sales at the Galerías Preciados, which were of such interest to his wife.

Each day at dawn, the crowing of cocks woke the General. To his relief he would discover that it was not today yet: that it was taking a long time coming round again. He told himself this so often that 20 June 1973 almost went straight past him.

It was late, past 4.30, when the first cockcrow reached his ears. The General clamped his eyes shut and protested: 'The damned day is here already and it hasn't even given me time to get myself ready.' He sat up slowly, walked to the balcony and contemplated through the window the mist in the mountains on the other side of the balcony. He turned the radio on and, as usual, tried to tune in the news bulletins. He caught a few strange voices and a bit of music, but they escaped his attention, as though they had landed in someone else's ears.

The secretary burst into the bedroom, still in his shorts, turned the radio off and snapped his fingers: 'Up, up, the time has come! Up!' The General moved back to the bed again. He wanted to breathe the fresh air out on the balcony, but a sudden dizzy spell had disoriented him. He was pale. His flesh had grown flabbier and flabbier with the years, and now he looked like a sponge that was slowly sinking in the water. I'm a man who's being washed away, and that's the way they're going to get me out of here, he said to himself. Then he noticed that his pain wasn't coming from his body but from the sinister brightness that was climbing up the skirts of the plateau.

His wife brought him his breakfast tray. 'No butter on rolls,' the

General had ordered, in an inadvertent Spanish accent. 'All I want is some mint tea. The farewells have given me indigestion.'

He picked out a blue suit and dressed carefully. He drenched his handkerchiefs with the scent that he had used ever since the days he first met Evita and that would forever remind him of the phrase with which she approached him: 'You smell of things I like a man to smell of, Colonel: Condal cigarettes and mint drops. The only thing that's missing is just a bit of Atkinsons.' And the next day she gave him a bottle of lavender toilet water and he gave her a bottle of Cytrus perfume, 'to prove that we're engaged,' she had joked, with every intention of turning her joke into a reality. But the phrase with which Eva won him was another one, impregnated with odors so penetrating his memory could no longer bear it: 'Thanks for existing.'

Standing alongside the still unmade bed, his feelings again motionless, the General heard the trucks that were taking their trunks full of clothes to the airport go past the house, guided by the diligent secretary.

'What shall I wear?' his wife said, giving him a start, as she undid her hair curlers. 'Look: I left three dresses out of the suitcase.'

'You're going to have to put all three of them on, my girl. Buenos Aires is so far away that even clothes are tired by the time they get there.'

It was 6.30 in the morning when they went down to the porch, holding hands. From the street, on the other side of the iron gate, applause and flash bulbs harried them. Several reporters shouted at the General, urging him to make a statement, anything at all: just a word, to compensate them for so many days in exile. But both he and his wife merely stood there with their arms upraised and said goodbye.

In the courtyard of Moncloa Palace, Generalissimo Francisco Franco was waiting for them, in dress uniform. Three months before, he had agreed, finally, to receive Perón, after so many years of not acceding to his requests for an audience or answering his Christmas greetings. But then, as now, he had come out to meet him with an escort of admirals and knights of honorary orders, amid the banners of the Napoleonic wars and of the Moorish guards from Morocco, with a hand so limply extended to him that the General could shake only the knuckles of it.

'What's happened to Franco?' Perón couldn't help thinking as the Generalissimo came forward. 'I'm only three years older than he is and he looks as though they've taken him out of a bottle of formaldehyde only this morning.'

And at the same time the Generalissimo was saying to his aide-de-camp: 'Just look at what exile has done to that man. He's my age and he's a wreck.'

But on 20 June they looked each other over curiously, to see what new adversities had wreaked their damage on the two of them. It surprised them to find that everything was the same and that they hadn't realized that fact. They signed several protocols of friendship and left in a motorcade for Barajas airport. The highway was dotted with blue and white pennants wishing them a good journey. A squadron of mounted hussars was on guard, posted in a semicircle, at the entrance to the tarmac. The Generalissimo noticed the name of the plane.

'Ah, Betelgeuse, the dying star . . . An astronomer pointed it out to me in the skies of Galicia, when we were out fishing. But it was no use; I couldn't see it. There were thousands of stars hovering about just one point. There it is, the man insisted: Betelgeuse is almost a thousand times larger than the sun! But I couldn't see a thing. No way, nothing.'

'It was López, my secretary, who thought of the name. Because the intensity of Betelgeuse changes every five years, like a person's fate. When I get to Buenos Aires I'm going to send you a telescope as a gift, Caudillo.'

They moved closer to each other for the embraces, but at the very same moment both of them had the feeling that the other might disintegrate. Franco offered his cheeks.

'This country is yours, your home, General.'

'I only wish that were true,' Perón said.

Once the plane took off and was lost amid the parched ocher expanses of Castile, he asked them not to bother him and dropped off to sleep. His wife took his shoes off and began to leaf through the morning papers. It was so calm, in a semidarkness washed so clean, that if they closed their eyes they could imagine themselves still in the bedroom in Madrid, lulled by those turbines that seemed more like the gargles of an aged aunt. In just a little while, the General awoke with a start.

'What time is it?' he asked.

'It's now 9.30 in Madrid,' his wife replied. 'But in Buenos Aires it's still long before dawn. Up here there's no way to tell what time it is for us. You heard what Daniel said: this plane is flying in the opposite direction from time.'

The General shook his head.

'How the world has changed, my girl. God has everything all confused.'

The plane made a stopover in the Canaries, beneath a sun so white that even the landscape was blurred. The governor of the islands came aboard with a bouquet of ceramic flowers for the señora and a handful of medals that he hung, at random, around the necks of those closest at hand. Then, on tiptoe, he delivered a speech addressed to the wrong visitor, since it dealt with the General's winning strategy in wars in which he had not been even remotely involved. The ceremony came to a sudden end when a horde of flies invaded the plane and fell mercilessly upon those present.

They were a long time taking off. As the day wore on, once the plane had skirted a storm off Cape Verde, the General went to the toilet. He looked at himself in the mirror. He had deep circles under his eyes and gray stubble had suddenly appeared on his cheeks. He came out to get his shaving kit and the cotton balls he used for touching up the color of the stubble. Damn that gray, he said to himself. I must be feeling a really profound sadness for my beard to grow like this.

Several maps had been left on his seat, showing the courses of Aerolíneas Argentinas marked with dotted lines, the naval bases in the Antarctic, the railway lines abandoned since 1955. He unfolded the map of Buenos Aires. He ran his finger along the expressway that went from the factories in Villa Lugano to the Ezeiza airport, past high-rise housing projects, public swimming pools and planted stands of eucalyptus. He tried to figure out the exact location of the little dais he was going to be taken to in order to address the multitude. López had told him that almost a million people were waiting for him. Whole families were leaving their houses without locking the doors, as though it were the end of the world. A famous singer, who was still going up and down the highways to keep the pilgrims' spirits up, had gotten all worked up as he remembered the experience: 'A mysterious beam of light is shining down upon us! This is the faith that moves mountains! God is with us! God is Argentine!'

On passing from one hemisphere to another, the plane encountered violent turbulence and the wings shook. The pilots informed the General that the coast of Brazil could be seen in the distance and offered to take him to the cockpit. 'I don't really care to see it,' he thanked them. 'The only thing that Brazil has ever given me is troubles and bad luck.'

He wanted, however, to have the few friends he still trusted come sit alongside him.

'Bring them here to me right away,' he told López. 'It's grown late and we must ready ourselves.'

He agreed that the first ones to come should be the secretary's daughter and son-in-law, who often amused the señora by telling her anecdotes about movie stars. The son-in-law, Raúl Lastiri, was a clever devil, with a local reputation for being good at barbecuing and at scoring with cabaret girls thanks to a single coarse gesture; Norma, the daughter, was twenty-five years younger than her husband, but treated him with the condescension of a mother-in-law.

Between the curtains that led to the toilets the General made out José Rucci, the scrawny secretary-general of the General Labor Confederation. He was biting his fingernails, waiting to get into the toilet. Perón felt a certain affection for him.

'Son?' he called out to him. The skinny man cautiously poked his head out. He had a bushy mustache that moved up and down in time with his enormous Adam's apple. So as not to have one hair out of place, the whole unruly mop of it was plastered down with hair spray. 'Come and sit down. It is true that there are a million people waiting down there? When we land there'll be twice as many. What if they were to get out of hand?'

'Don't worry, General,' Rucci answered with self-satisfaction. 'We've taken over the airport and the entire area around the dais. I have thousands of faithful young supporters posted on the access roads. If there's any need, they'll give their lives for Perón.'

'That's right: give your life for Perón,' they heard the señora say as she woke up.

The General lowered his head. It was odd. Whenever he did so, time turned into water, draining out of his body. He lowered his head, and when he raised it, many things had happened in the meantime that he had no memory of, as though today's dusk had suddenly turned into a dusk at some time tomorrow.

An Italian who kept presenting the señora with fashion magazines and sunglasses came and sat down beside her. It was said that, before he died, Pope John XXIII had rewarded him by offering him his most virtuous confidences. The General himself often heard how the Italian joked with the cardinals of the Vatican congregations over the phone and spoke with Mao Tse-tung and His Holiness Paul VI without intermediaries, even at hours when they received no one.

His name was Giancarlo Elia Valori. He often visited the villa in Madrid, always zealously doing his best to secure a decoration for a certain banker friend of his, Licio Gelli, who was accompanying him on this flight to Buenos Aires. Gelli was a well-bred, gloomy man of few words. When he spoke with the General he had a ready smile, though he kept his distance, as if he were afraid he might catch the plague. Charmed by Valori, the secretary had guaranteed that he would get the decoration for his friend that he was after. But the General hesitated. 'The Grand Cross of the Order of the Liberator, Valori . . . Why is it you're asking for so much?' And the Italian insisted: 'I got the Church on your side, Excellency. Get Gelli on my side.'

Of all the bitter experiences and annoyances that the General had had to endure during the flight, none was as unbearable as the company of Héctor J. Cámpora, the President of the Republic. In the last three years, when he was his personal delegate and had no other obligation save to obey the General's orders, Cámpora had been faithful, discreet, marvelous. At times, as darkness fell, the General missed Cámpora and even gave him several friendly little pats on the back, not noticing that the President was not there but in Buenos Aires. But when he found himself head of state, Cámpora had lost out completely with the General. He took his role as President seriously: he played it too enthusiastically. He wanted to be popular. He was delighted that people called him 'Uncle': the leader's brother. Every time the General thought about such gross stupidities, he felt a burning rage.

Fortunately, no one had seen much of Cámpora during the flight. A couple of times, while they were still over Spain, he had tried to approach him: 'Are you comfortable, sir? Is there anything you'd like?' But the General gave him the cold shoulder: 'Don't worry your head, Cámpora. Take advantage of these last few hours to get some rest.' They had eaten lunch together in silence. For almost a week now they had not been on close terms. At times, Cámpora felt like asking his forgiveness, but he didn't know what for.

He was sixty-seven years old and his feelings were transparent: his every happiness lighted up his face like a candle. He was proud of his teeth and of his little hairline mustache that skated above his lips; his manners were as elaborately polite and gracious as a tango singer's. He carried himself with swaggering self-assurance, his shoulders younger than the rest of his body. But in the General's presence he became transfigured: the tremors that came from his heart made him bow so low from the waist that he looked like a waiter with a napkin over his arm.

When Perón sent for him, he had felt ill at ease, upset. On entering the first-class compartment, he noticed that the sun shining in the señora's eyes was bothering her and hastened to close the curtain over the passenger window.

'What are you doing, Cámpora?' the General reprimanded him. 'Leave tasks like that to the stewardesses. And do sit down. You've been socializing for hours now.'

The secretary ordered tea with biscuits. There was a long period of silence, or perhaps of confusion, until the señora inadvertently knocked over a pile of magazines with her shoe. It was like a signal. Perón stood up. Cámpora, who had managed to relax, tensed up again. They could all feel darkness coming on, in perfect order. With a look of profound sadness on his face, the General stretched his arms out.

'History has paid me back in full by now, boys. I have no other hope in life except to fire my last cartridges in the service of the fatherland . . .' He sighed. His voice suddenly changed register and took on angry overtones. '. . . fact is that every day people bring me news from Buenos Aires that alarms me . . . I hear that for no reason whatsoever strangers are getting into the factories and occupying them in Perón's name, evicting the lawful owners . . . I have had word that in the name of a Peronism that is not mine they are harassing and beating up trade unionists who have been most faithful to me . . . I have even been informed that they telephone generals, in the middle of the night, to make threats against their families . . . What sort of madness is this? The ultras are infiltrating our movement at every level, top and bottom. We are not violent, but we are not going to be stupid either. This can't go on! Disorder brings chaos; chaos ends in bloodshed. When we finally wake up to what's going on, we won't have a country left. There will no longer be an Argentina. Seeing how slow-witted we are, the military will start plotting again. And for good reason! But I won't be there to put a stop to them. At my age, no one sacrifices himself to die amid ruins. No indeed. I warn you that at the first abuse of authority, Chabela and I will pack our bags and go back to Spain.'

The secretary nodded emphatically, his lips copying each word the General spoke. Able to contain himself no longer, he burst out:

'These tragedies happen because you're too kind-hearted – because you didn't want to give the guilty parties their just deserts.'

'. . . And kick them out of the movement,' Rucci chimed in.

'Kick them straight out,' the General agreed.

It was at this point of the story that it happened. One of the pilots opened the door of the cabin, obviously distraught. He desperately pointed downward with his thumb. The words he was about to say must have already been almost out of his mouth, because he didn't know what to do with them when he saw the General towering above that conclave in all his majesty. He hesitated for a few seconds and swallowed them. The secretary took him by the arm and went off to the cockpit to have a few words with him in private.

'Now then, tell me what's going on.'

'The Ezeiza control tower advises us to land at another airport, sir.' The radio on the instrument panel was emitting hysterical whistles. The co-pilot, all excited too, answered the situation reports coming to him from the ground with drawn-out ooohs and aaahs. 'It seems that the dais where they're waiting for the General has been attacked. There's a lot of confusion. People dead, hanged, crushed in the stampede . . . The reports are horrifying.'

'Tell the General this minute,' López shouted, opening the door to the passenger compartments. They all turned around. Even Gelli, who was putting drops in his eyes, listened in amazement.

The moment the pilot began to tell his story again, the señora exclaimed in despair: 'Good God! How horrible!'

Valori, the Italian, hastened to console her, handing her a handkerchief drenched with perfume. The General meanwhile had not lost his serene sense of command for even a second. He wanted to know if the pilots had established communication with Lieutenant-Colonel Jorge Osinde, the head of the reception committee, and had received an estimate of the situation from Vice-President Solano Lima, who must have been feeling great distress at the terrible events at the airport.

Yes, that had all been done.

'We received the first news at 15.05: a voice message from Lieutenant-Colonel Osinde. It was a very confused communiqué. Shouts and screams could be heard . . . Someone who did not identify himself contacted us again at 15.23. Depositions were being taken from people who had been arrested, he said. And it was thought that it was a plot to assassinate the General.'

The señora could bear no more and burst into tears.

'*Distensione, distensione!*' Valori recommended, in a hysterical voice.

'And what do we do now?' The secretary buttonholed President Cámpora. 'Let's see if for once you can think of something!'

'At 15.32 we spoke with Doctor Solano Lima in person,' the pilot went on. 'He had just flown over the area in a helicopter. His advice was to rule out Ezeiza airport. He agreed with Lieutenant-Colonel Osinde, who is advising us to proceed to Morón. The Vice-President promised to call back. He wants to communicate directly with Doctor Cámpora.'

'And have they determined who began the whole thing?' the General asked.

'That is what we were told, sir: they now know who it was.' The pilot read some notes aloud: 'At 14.03 some three thousand people were seen on Route 205, advancing toward the dais, carrying posters of the Revolutionary Armed Forces and of the Montonero Guerrilla Movement. At 14.20 these individuals tried to break through the cordons of the security forces and invade the area closest to the dais, just at the foot of the bridge, where there wasn't an inch of room left. Since the security cordons held fast, the revolutionary militants opened fire. They used assault weapons with sawn-off barrels made in the Soviet Union. When the attack was repelled, exchanges of gunfire started all over the place . . . The number of casualties transmitted to us keeps changing from one minute to the next: fifty, a hundred, five hundred. It appears that the first-aid teams can't cope with the situation, and that a number of the wounded are being taken to the hospitals in Lanús and Monte Grande. The thing that is most horrifying . . .' The pilot was about to go on and held back. 'The details are too much for the señora to bear . . .'

'Go ahead,' she said. 'What does it matter now?'

'They have found several men strung up by the neck from the trees, at Ezeiza. Husky young men beaten nearly to death with lengths of chain are crawling along the airport runways. According to the explanations from the control tower, the people are enraged and have taken justice into their own hands.'

Exhausted, the pilot handed the notes to the secretary and

massaged his pounding temples with his fingertips.

'Here is one last message from Osinde,' López said. 'Everything is all set for us to land at Morón. He's waiting for orders from the General and from nobody else.'

'And what can I do up here, so far away, so helpless?' Perón lamented. 'All of you leave me alone for a moment.'

'That's not possible,' the secretary broke in. 'There's no time. We're coming in to Buenos Aires.'

The General squeezed his wife's hands.

'I had a premonition that it would be like this. They've been sowing the wind and now they're reaping the whirlwind.'

She nodded. 'The whirlwind.'

The General closed his eyes and collapsed in his seat.

'To return under these circumstances . . . how sad.'

'How terribly sad,' the señora echoed, shaking her head.

'Then there's nothing that can be done,' the secretary decided. 'There won't be a ceremony at Ezeiza. Have them disperse people once and for all. Get them cleared out of there any way they can. We'll land at Morón.'

President Cámpora felt that his moment had come. Was the General displeased with the way he was running the country? Well then: he would act as if he were Perón. He would exercise the power that had been handed over to him.

'No, sir,' he said, undermining the secretary's authority. 'We must go to Ezeiza anyway. The people have been on the road for days so as to get to see the General from close up. How can we disappoint them? There must be some way . . . We've been on this plane for more than twelve hours. It will cost us nothing to stay in a holding pattern till we solve the problem . . .' As he spoke he began little by little to feel unique, irrefutable, really in charge at last. He turned to the pilot: 'I'm the one who's commander-in-chief of the armed forces, damn it all. Inform Osinde that I am going to record a message from here, calming people down. And if the General is willing, he too will speak. That's right: two messages. Notify the radio stations to broadcast them nationwide. We need ten minutes, no more than that. Keep announcing over the loudspeakers that the General and Uncle Cápora will issue an appeal for peace. Then the whole thing will be over and done with, and we'll be able to land at Ezeiza.'

The pilot opened the door leading to the cockpit, intending to obey these instructions.

'Don't send any messages anywhere,' the secretary stopped him. 'Don't even think of doing that! There are thousands of irresponsible people killing each other down there because one irresponsible man up here had gotten them all excited. There's to be no taking gambles with the General's safety. If we land at Ezeiza, the crowd will be on top of us in a minute. They're all sick, they've all gone mad. Weren't Osinde's reports clear?'

All eyes turned toward Perón, awaiting a sign from him. A mysterious force brought them to their feet. Nothing happened: the General had fallen asleep. The señora stroked his hair, affectionately perhaps.

'Daniel is right,' she murmured. 'Daniel is right . . .'

'Do as I order, Captain,' the secretary said, raising his voice. 'Or perhaps you still don't know who's in command here?'

2 Arca's Comrades

Arcángelo Gobbi has slept only a couple of hours on this night of terror, frozen stiff inside his sleeping bag. Nonetheless, he still has enough force of will left to stand up and thank God for having reached the Great Day alive. He contemplates with devotion the photograph of the General that the stage designers have placed in the center of the altar where he is standing guard, on the bridge closest to Ezeiza airport. At dusk Perón will descend in a helicopter and will walk to the pulpit – suspended above the heads of the multitude – to deliver his sermon celebrating his return. Arcángelo will be alongside him, amid the honorary escorts. He now steps forward a few paces and lies down beneath the photo to gaze up at the sky. Dawn is about to break at any moment. If the wind were to blow down the enormous portrait framed in iron and wood, Arcángelo's body would be cut exactly in two. It is the impossible death that God reserves for the elect of His paradise alone.

He was assigned to guard, between two and five a.m., the improvised shelters at the Municipal Autodrome. More than thirty thousand people were sleeping there; the women in the pits, the men in tents flanking the circuit. When his buddy came to relieve him, Arcángelo felt frozen to the bone. 'There's a strong wind,' he warned his comrade. 'What kills you is the wind.' The transistor radio announced that the wind-chill factor at that moment was two degrees above freezing.

At five-thirty he had climbed back inside his sleeping bag on the dais. Another half a dozen men were asleep there: retired non-commissioned officers who, like himself, were going to guard Perón's life. Squads from the Trade Union Youth Group, he knew, were patrolling the area above and below the bridge, with their revolvers drawn. The night was going lazily by. Now and again a drum throbbed, a complaint was heard. Little by little Arcángelo relaxed in his sleeping bag. All of a sudden, he heard the Virgin calling him, and in his dream ran about searching for her.

He had survived because God is great. His mother had died of puerperal fever shortly after giving birth to him, and his father had had to leave him in the care of a couple of sickly aunts, who were also dying, of tropical diseases. He had no memories of his childhood except the stifling heat in a small dark room with a corrugated zinc roof and walls next to the produce market, in San Miguel de Tucumán, and the vision of some sparrows dying on the sidewalk in the scorching sun. He spent most of the day by himself, while his father was at work, far from where they lived, as a Linotype operator for a newspaper. And the only outing he ever had was the walk along the stations of the Cross in church.

At the age of nine, Arcángelo could neither read nor write. Measles and recurrent diarrhea paraded through him without anyone ever noticing. He cured himself the way dogs do: by licking himself and drinking a few little sips of water. Only when the neighbors gave his father a talking-to because he was letting him grow up like a wild child did the latter begin to bring home from the print shop some slugs of lead type that he used to teach Arcángelo his ABC. In a short time, he could read easily, but he read by looking at books in the mirror, with the words backwards. His learning was put to rights when he had to learn his catechism.

He took classes in doctrine twice a week in a Franciscan monastery, where they rewarded the best pupils with a cup of boiled maté and a roll made of wheat flour and chitlings. One day one of the children told how he had dreamed of Saint Clare. The teacher asked him what the saint looked like and what the diadem she wore was made of. 'I wasn't able to see her face because the sky hid it,' the boy answered, 'but her diadem is made of bloodstained pearls.' 'You saw her as she really is,' the friar said approvingly. And he let the boy into the refectory, so he could eat the chicken left over from lunch.

That same night, Arcángelo dreamed of the Blessed Virgin. He saw her walking about in a velvet cape, dressed the way she was on altars. At one moment in the dream, she stroked his hair and smiled sadly at him. 'Arcángelo, my dear Arca': those were the only words she spoke. When he told the friars his dream he had a terrible disappointment. Instead of rewarding him, they ordered him to write 'I will never lie again' a hundred times in his notebook. But Arcángleo wasn't intimidated and dreamed the same thing many times after that.

Toward the end of 1951, his father was out of work and decided to move to Buenos Aires with his son. They traveled for two days on a train that groped its way through deserts of dust. They covered their faces with pieces of wet paper, but even so they had to close their eyes to keep the thistles that were flying through the air from tearing their eyeballs. When they woke up on the third morning, they discovered that the horizon was suddenly filled on every hand with gardens and mansions. It was Buenos Aires.

A friend of his father's gave them a place to stay in a little print shop in Villa Soldati, near the Riachuelo, and got them jobs right there in the shop. At night, they unrolled a burlap mattress and stretched out alongside the gas burners of the Linotype machines. They sweated buckets. The air was so humid that they lived with their bronchi stuck together and a taste of lead on their tongues.

On Sundays they went with their friend to a temple at the Basilio School of Science, in the Calle Tinogasta, at the other end of the city. On the outside, the place was not at all imposing: it was a house with pitted plaster, wrought-iron grilles and a grubby garden. But inside there were signs of God everywhere. At the foot of the walls of the living room a baseboard of candles illuminated the photos of the spirits that were doing penance in the house. Don José Cresto, the evangelical director of the congregation, explained to newcomers that all the spirits were souls to be trusted and that they should not be afraid of them. A few months before, in June 1952, Cresto had won fame by protecting through his mental powers two German tightrope walkers making their way, blindfolded, across a cable stretched from the apex of the Obelisk to the roof of a building a hundred yards away.

But the one who really kept the temple going was Doña Isabel Zoila Gómez de Cresto: she made and sold good-luck scapulars with mica crystals from the Humahuaca ravine and kept track of the offerings made by the congregation, threatening anyone who gave less than fifty centavos with the fires of purgatory.

It was necessary to remain very attentive during Don José's sermons and trances, because his language, which came out all confused even under ordinary circumstances, became incomprehensible on these occasions; he didn't say *chaplain*, for instance, but *lapchain*, and not *Our Father who art in heaven* but *Our Fat Her who art in heather*. A skinny young girl with thin lips and pigeon toes was always around, obligingly helping Don José when he stumbled over a word.

At the beginning of each month Doña Isabel de Cresto gave a

party at which she served meat pies and lemonade at reasonable prices. Now and then, the disciples got hold of a record player and recordings by the popular singer Antonio Tormo. More often, they entertained themselves by competing with each other in singing contests and reciting patriotic poems by Belisario Roldán. One day they brought in a piano, and at Doña Isabel's insistence, the skinny girl played Beethoven's 'Für Elise'. She went at it with such a will that when she struck a wrong note she began the whole piece over from the very beginning, apologizing with a shake of her head. On another Sunday she disguised herself as a peasant lass and danced a *chamamé* with Cresto without finishing the number because the old man's body kept getting so far out of step that the onlookers couldn't help laughing.

Arcángelo, who was fifteen at the time, fell madly in love with the girl, without the slightest hope of a happy ending. She was about to turn twenty-four, and when asked if anyone was courting her, answered, with lowered eyes: 'No, no one. I only like mature men, and I always come into their lives too late.'

In the autumn of '54 the school went downhill. Many disciples joined the hosts of devoted followers of a fundamentalist pastor, Theodore Hicks, known as 'the magus of Atlanta'. Instead of calling forth the dead the way Cresto did, Hicks scared off ailments of the living in a soccer field, in full view of everyone. Perón even received him at Government House 'to see what the whole thing was about'.

One Sunday at the end of July Arcángelo was alone in the temple on the Calle Tinogasta. The moment he came into the room he smelled the piquant aroma of the spirits who were wandering about. There was one in particular that flew higher than the others, and was greeted by them with respect. Arca asked who it was. 'The soul of Don Carmelo Martínez,' Doña Isabel answered, showing him his photograph. Martínez had been an admirable employee of the Banco Hipotecario, who had passed on twenty years before and had been summoned forth so as to bid his daughter a last farewell. At that moment Arcángelo spied the girl with thin lips, praying on a prie-dieu in the shadow, with her arms crossed on her breast.

'It's been such a long time since I last saw her!' Arcángelo exclaimed, the words escaping him before he knew it.

'Such a long time!' Don José agreed. 'A certain Redondo, who is an impromisario, engained her to dance flanishes in the privances.'

'Señor Redondo, an upstanding impresario, engaged her to perform flamenco dances in the provinces,' Doña Isabel translated. 'A month on tour. She has now been invited to join Faustino García's operetta company, and next week, after the last performances at the Teatro Avenida, they're going off to Montevideo and to Bolivia.'

'I predicted it when she was a yangster: that dummy Isabel is going to take a header for fame.'

'Is her name Isabel too, the same as the señora's?' Arcángelo wanted to know.

'No,' Doña Isabel said. 'Her real name is María Estela Martínez Cartas. But since she didn't like it, she asked to borrow mine, which is more artistic.'

That night, his eagerness to see Isabel dancing in the operetta kept Arca from sleeping. He awoke with sweaty hands from applauding so hard in his sleep. He waited until Thursday, when there was a late-afternoon matinée at half price, and bought a seat in the peanut gallery at the Teatro Avenida. The performance was a fiasco. Isabelita was indistinguishable from the other singers in the chorus, and since she was so thin she was often hidden from sight by the trees of the stage sets and the tambourines of the leading lady. In the second scene, Arcángelo waited in vain for her to appear. He never caught sight of her onstage again.

Nonetheless, that was the last happy afternoon to come his way for a long time. His father was told that the government had expropriated the property belonging to the print shop and that he would have to move immediately. To top everything off, nature began to be so confused that the trees smelled of incense and maté leaves gave off whiffs of sulphur on contact with water.

One night they heard General Perón announce on the radio that he had declared war on the Catholic Church. Arcángelo's father did penance, kneeling on corncobs, so that Our Lord would restore the General's good sense of bygone years, but a few weeks later Perón spoke out in impassioned terms against the perversity of the clergy, allowed marriages to be dissolved and ordered brothels to open their doors.

Though the Gobbis' prayers for the reconciliation of the General with the Church proved to be of no avail, they at least wrought the miracle of getting them work. The neighborhood butcher introduced them to a printer on the Calle Salguera and rented them a tenement room near the National Prison.

It was there that Arcángelo again dreamed of the Virgin each night. Although he wasn't yet a full-grown man and every so often his voice turned high-pitched on him, he looked like an elderly man. He walked all hunched over and his whole face broke out in pimples. His eyes were the oddest thing about him, for they were ageless: they gleamed like great empty lakes, but they were set so close to the bridge of his nose that when he looked about they didn't appear to be focused on anything at all.

He had only to smile at women for them to feel threatened and turn their backs on him. Arcángelo, who had always been sensitive about being rejected, got even with them by dreaming about them. He invoked them the minute his head hit the pillow; they lingered in his imagination all night long, immobilized on metal stretch bands, begging him not to tear their vaginas to pieces with bottle shards or lop off their nipples with garden shears, but Arcángelo remained unmoved. He made them pay one by one for the hurts he had suffered when he was awake.

All of a sudden, the Virgin too appeared in his dreams. Arca saw her come down from the altars in her bare feet, with the Infant Jesus in her arms, and when he kneeled to worship her, she raised him up tenderly and offered him her breasts to suck: 'I have too much milk and they ache,' she told him.

After a time, the Virgin began to come without the Child. She appeared with her face veiled, with the ears of a consumptive. Her enormous breasts gradually shrank to the size of tiny withered pears. Arcángelo awaited her with such compassion that tears welled up from all over his body, even the soles of his feet. Once, when the Virgin drew nearer to console him, he dared draw the veil from her face. And though he knew, beyond the shadow of a doubt, that she was the Blessed Virgin of the altars, the features he saw in his dreams were those of Isabelita Martínez.

Months of disturbances followed. The General was overthrown and fled to Paraguay. Doña Isabel de Cresto was wasting away from an illness that the doctors were unable to diagnose, and Don José's sermons lost their power to attract spirits. Even Arcángelo and his father had to make an effort of will to attend religious services on the Calle Tinogasta, where things had gone so far downhill that the furniture did not smell of spirits but of mice and moths.

The Crestos received two letters from Isabelita Martínez: the first one was a sad postcard mailed in Antofagasta; the second, a more expressive one, came from Medellín, Colombia. Her life had not been easy. Instead of going to Bolivia, she had traveled up the coasts of Peru and Ecuador with Gustavo de Córdoba's Spanish ballet company. She worked in such wretched theaters that the impresarios usually disappeared with the box office receipts on the day of the opening performance, and the only way for the artists to pay for their hotel rooms and their meals was to take jobs serving in sleazy bars after the last performance of the night. 'We got so thin,' she wrote, 'that a German in

Guayaquil offered us work as extras in a film about shipwreck victims.'

They were finally hired to dance tangos in Medellín during performances commemorating the late Carlos Gardel, the famous tango singer and composer. Since they were the only natives of Argentina in the company, they counted on being a success and spent all their savings on improving their wardrobes. But only twenty people came to the première and four the following day, because in the theater in the next block they were showing, for practically nothing, the eight films that Gardel had made for Paramount and a Japanese singer who imitated his voice was causing a sensation in the restaurant at the airport.

The company split up then and there. 'Abandoned to our fate,' Isabel related, 'we had no idea what to do. Some of the girls went back to working in bars. Not me. I pawned my clothes and my old jewelry at the state pawn shop and began to look for work giving piano and flamenco lessons, hoping to scrape enough money together to buy a return ticket to Buenos Aires. But the Almighty came to my rescue. A very famous Caribbean artist, Señor Joe Herald, took me under his wing. I've joined his company as second ballerina. When rehearsals are over, we're going on tour. We'll be a week in Cartagena and then make our debut in Panama. What we dance is variety, not flamenco, but we're treated so well that I couldn't be happier. Señor Herald is like a father to me. He keeps me so well fed I'm afraid I'm going to get as fat as a cow . . .'

With the aid of Arcángelo, who could write in handsome printed letters, Doña Isabel sent Isabelita a very long letter in which she told her in detail about her ailments and lamented the impiety that had come over Argentina. She languished as she awaited a reply. Every afternoon Don José went out to meet the mailman, and when he came back to the house empty-handed, he consoled his wife with the same phrase: 'That dummy Isabel is working hand in hand with fame.'

When Doña Isabel's illness grew worse, Arcángelo visited her regularly. Sitting next to the bed, he would take her hand and talk to her about the bats that he had seen flying underneath the ceilings of the market, in Tucumán. He longed to tell her about his meetings with the Virgin but never dared to.

Doña Isabel died in September of 1956, refusing to believe the turn of fortune that had disrupted Isabelita's life. As she lay in her death-throes, Don José showed her photographs in a magazine in which the young girl, her looks ruined by her obesity and by a perm, appeared with General Perón in a hotel in Caracas. 'The mysterious secretary of the deposed tyrant,' the captions read. Doña Isabel leafed indifferently through the magazine and decided that everything it said was a story concocted to dupe its readers. Then she turned her face to the wall and forbade them to come bothering her again with the absurdities of this world.

Her grave site in Chacarita Cemetery, which in the beginning had a showy display of ceramic promises and wreaths with ribbons bearing dedications, fell into a state of neglect in almost no time. Only Arcángelo and his father went to polish the metal flower vases from time to time, but when Isabel's widower closed the temple on the Calle Tinogasta and undertook a mysterious journey, they too lost interest in these mementos.

The print shop became the one place that attracted them. Most of the Linotype operators were taking correspondence courses from the Rosicrucian Lodge, and Arcángelo convinced his father that they should take the courses with them. They thus learned little by little the language of sounds and colors and the movements of heavenly bodies.

Even at the end of 1957, when work at the print shop became exhausting, Arcángelo and his father chose to study doctrine rather than getting some rest. Before going to bed, they used to pore over maps of the sky and take notes on the endless discoveries being made at the observatory of the Rosicrucian University, in California.

Arcángelo feared that military service would interrupt his apprenticeship, and presented himself for the medical exam wearing an amulet. He was declared unfit for military service, due to scoliosis of the spinal column. One of the male nurses berated him for having presented himself at the barracks without his glasses. What glasses? Arcángelo said in surprise. He learned then that his right eye was myopic and his left astigmatic, and that he had always had a wrong view of the world.

At the print shop, which was called Paso de los Libros, he was put in charge of turning out almost all the leaflets being read in Buenos Aires at that time: the election publicity handed out by Arturo Frondizi and Alejandro Gómez, Father Benítez's pamphlets urging people to cast blank ballots, and even the secret orders issued by the labor leaders of metal and textile workers to their unions that had been taken over.

In March 1958, another Linoptype operator – also a Rosicrucian – was hired at the print shop. Though he had a fluty speaking voice and was hard of hearing, he had sung – he said – on a radio station in New York before serving as a sergeant in the Argentine Federal Police. He frequently corresponded with the heirs of the Theosophist Eliphas Levi and prided himself on his mastery of the Kabbala and alchemy.

His name was José López Rega. His manners were discreet in those days, but he was already well endowed with a capacity for resentment. He liked to spend his evenings playing *truco* in El Tábano, a club in the Saavedra district whose members came dressed in pajamas and wearing thong sandals. On Sundays he happily assumed his role of father and husband. He arrived early at the club with a hamper full of offal for barbecuing and took up his position in the shadiest arbor of the back yard. As he kept an eye on the fire, he played pickup games of soccer, always as a right back. As darkness fell, accompanied by a lousy guitarist, he murdered in his baritone voice María Grever's boleros and Agustín Lara's waltzes. And as an encore, but only when his listeners begged for one, he ventured out onto the slippery slopes of the sustained high notes of 'Granada', risking running out of breath at any moment.

His greatest pride, he claimed, was having reached middle age without owing anything to anybody. Before he was thirteen he had been hired out as a day laborer in the Sedalana textile mill. To compensate for this nasty trick of fate, he took night classes in solmization and recitative from a neighborhood teacher. In the summer of 1938 he managed to get himself taken on as a scullery boy on a merchant vessel. He disappeared for six months. When he came back, he told how he had sung over WHOM, a Hispanic radio station in New York, and was such a hit that an impresario offered him a contract to sing at Chico's, a nightclub on 42nd Street. He appeared only twice, since his ship was about to leave on the return voyage.

One of the *truco* players at El Tábano who was a student at the British Cultural Institute resolved to take him down a peg by giving him a test. 'Write down the name of that Yankee radio station for me,' he challenged him. López Rega wrote down the right name: WHOM. 'Of whom are you talking?' the would-be professor asked him in English, backing him into a corner. And to everyone's surprise, the Linotype operator came out with this enigmatic answer, also in English: 'I knew six honest serving-men/They taught me all I know;/Their names are What and Why and When/and How and Where and Who . . . Of whom am I talking?'

Arcángelo found out the rest of the story because José himself told it to him. Early one morning he surprised him in the shed drawing planets around Vega and toning down the deep purple of Betelgeuse with a watercolor wash in several shades of gray.

'As big a star as that and it's dying?' Arcángelo asked.

'It certainly is. But it's not dying by itself. I've already begun to kill it.'

From that day on they became inseparable. In return for the respect that Arcángelo felt for his powers, López adopted him as his disciple. Each day after work, behind the locked door of the paper storeroom, they pondered the perfumes that were the equivalents of the tables of the zodiac and the musical notes that corresponded to each letter of the Our Father. López sometimes took him to El Tábano and accorded Arca the privilege of sitting behind him as he played *truco*. During the bus trip back and forth, he used to show Arca his notes for the colossal compendium of esoteric astrology that he had begun to write, and lamented the fact that his wife – he called her Chiquitina – often interrupted his reflections to offer a comment on the gossip making the rounds in the neighborhood: 'Poor Chiquitina doesn't understand that I don't belong to this world.'

One night, as they were walking through the Plaza Alberdi, a few blocks from the club, López revealed to him that he had been on close terms with General Perón and the deceased Evita. Arcángelo heard the story in stunned surprise.

'In 1946 the Supreme Powers assigned me the mission of guarding the two of them in the presidential mansion on the Calle Austria. The Voices told me that all I had to do was have a look at them once a day, from a distance. I resolved to incarnate myself as an ordinary police officer so as to be able to put in eight hours of guard duty in the sentry box at the entrance. I don't know exactly why I was found to have committed a dereliction of duty. For a time, I lost my powers. I was transferred to the offices of a judge, where I did five years' penance. When I was promoted to sergeant, I was able to return to my old post. By then everything had turned into a catastrophe. Evita no longer wanted to have conjugal relations with the General: the only thing that interested her was caring for the poor. She came back from work at five in the morning, just as he was getting up to start his work day. On top of that, she was wasting away from a fatal illness and it was too late for me to be able to save her. On 4 June 1952, as Perón was getting ready to take the oath of office as president for the second time, I happened to be the one on guard duty by the stairs that led to the bedrooms of the presidential mansion. At dawn, Evita ordered her attendants to bathe her and dress her to accompany the General to Congress. She couldn't stand up, but she set all the servants to bustling about nonetheless. A group of doctors met together and refused to give her permission to go, but she didn't give an inch: she was stubborn; she insisted. And wept so hard it broke your heart. After a while her mother, Doña Juana Ibarguren, came in to see her. Evita swept her into her arms and wouldn't let her go. "Mama! convince Perón!" she said to her. "After today nothing matters! I want to see my people for one last time and die in peace!" I heard Doña Juana tell her no. That it was freezing cold outside with a wind that tore a person's eyeballs. When her mother left, the nurses locked the bedroom door. Evita fell into a rage, but her own exhaustion finally calmed her down. She moaned slowly, softly: "Why won't they let me see my people, my poor little lambs?" Then the house fell silent . . .'

Sitting on a bench in the Plaza Alberdi, López positioned himself in those memories as though he were actually creating them, getting them ready to happen: 'I made a terrific mental effort, trying to make her better. It was useless. I wore myself out. For a moment, I was afraid I'd faint. I got hold of myself and went up to the bedroom. I walked by a big mirror. I looked at my body and saw that on the outside I was hale and hearty, but that my insides were nothing but spider webs and dust. I went through the door. Evita was resting in the semidarkness. She sensed my presence, but wasn't afraid. "Put yout mind at rest, because today you will be at the General's side and receive the people's blessing."

"And how will that happen?" she said, intrigued. She had a nasty tongue and began to run everybody down: "These doctors . . . these no-account little generals . . . Nobody wants to let me go out . . ." I touched her. She had been a beautiful woman, but now she was no more than a breath of air. She weighed less than eighty pounds. I felt that her death figured among God's immediate plans. "Send for somebody this minute to come inject you with painkillers in your ankles and the nape of your neck," I said to her. "And have them make you a corset of plaster and wire to hold you upright during the motorcade with the General in the open car . . ." She held her hands out to me. I squeezed them. And from that day on, I never once went back to the presidential mansion.'

'And what did they say at police headquarters? Imagine: a story like that getting out!'

'Evita never told it to anyone. Or else the Almighty erased it from her mind.' López chewed on a few little leaves. He showed no visible emotion now: the sweat, the sandals, the toothpick in his mouth were again the same ones as usual. 'I immediately put in for retirement. I tried to get back on the radio station as a baritone and I even had my photo published in *Sintonía*, along with an article saying I'd make a good movie actor. What more can I say, kid? I had to give up those ideas. Otherwise who would have put food on the table? With a wife and a daughter you can't offer yourself the luxury of being a performing artist. I got caught up in my Rosicrucian studies, I set myself up in business with a little Linotype machine, and when I sold it, I invested the capital in the Salguera print shop. So you see: the Lord is with us.'

As they walked to El Tábano, Arcángelo felt like telling López that he too, in his own way, had had a slight connection with the General through Isabelita Martínez, the girl with thin lips. He preferred to say nothing that night, because López Rega introduced him to a kingdom of astral symbols and the next day spoke to him of books that had changed his memory. It was only many years later, when the secretary won the complete trust of the señora, that Arcángelo dared tell him the story in a letter.

Was it so long ago now: a whole lifetime? The darkness is rising in the distance, behind the water tower lookout. Lying stretched out on the dais, Arcángelo observes the disorders in the sky overhead. The images of Perón's two wives cover him with all the bed sheets that he was stripped of by his mother. The wind blows across the unreal photograph of Evita and blurs it with a puff of smoke. Arcángelo sees Isabel, on the other hand, multiplied in the countless newsstands and in the early morning processions: here she comes, smiling on the tops of buses, stretching and yawning on the pennants unfurled by Berazategui's Labor Union Youth Movement and greeting the people with arm upraised from the Red Cross ambulances. Isabelita belongs to everyone today but there is a secret strand of her person that only Arcángelo has any knowledge of: not the devotions that both have shared at the Basilio School of Science nor the breath of love that she should have felt that last afternoon, at the operetta at the Teatro Avenida. No. The Isabel Arcángelo treasures has never left his dreams: he has possessed her, smelled her, spied on her, extinguished her and lighted her with all the passing storms of his blood. But no longer, Arcángelo Gobbi. She is journeying toward reality today. She will remain as incomplete in you as the twenty-four-foot photograph of her that is still being put together, to the left of the photo of the General. Inside yourself she will be missing the same elbow, the plaited bun of the hairdo, the shoulder of the dress that they are starting to place on her.

And at this point Arcángelo lowers the curtain, because the orders that he has received from José López Rega must be complied with on that very dais, from the very moment – now – that dawn breaks.

3 *The Witnesses' Photographs*

What are the orders, then? First of all, to learn who Perón is: that is what the editor-in-chief of *Horizonte* had decided. What can a man of his stature be like? Zamora the reporter had worriedly asked himself when he was given the assignment: there is no way of finding that out in a month.

That's how much time we have: one month. The editor had backed him into a corner. Perón will be back any moment now. How are we going to appease the readers' appetites? With summaries of speeches, with an album of splendid photos like the ones published in the weekly *Gente*? The official Perón is a subject that has doubtless been squeezed dry by now. We must look for the other Perón. Tell the readers about the great man's early years, Zamora: nobody has come up with the real story so far. Paeans of praise, myths by the dozen, whole collections of documents, but the truth hasn't come out anywhere. Who was the General,

Zamora? Decipher him once and for all: rescue the words that he never dared say, describe the impulses that surely he repressed, read between the lines . . . The truth is what's hidden, right? Hunt up witnesses to his childhood and his youth: some of them are still alive, I imagine. That's the right track: begin there! The Perón that Argentines know seems to have been born in 1945, when he was fifty: isn't that absurd? A man has time to be many things before he's fifty.

Zamora had resolved the problem in the quickest and easiest way possible: by weaving together in chronological order the statements of some seventy individuals. He worked frantically, for twelve, fifteen hours a day: without stopping to think that life was going by. What would he have gained by living life?

The other reporters envied his success, the splendid final paragraphs of his articles, the intensity with which he described an important figure in two lines, but Zamora was certain he was a failure. His marriage for love was an intolerable routine by now, the poems he promised himself every day that he would write never got beyond the second verse, the unsavory feature articles he agreed to do for the money – so as to buy the freedom to pour out some day, unhurriedly, the novel that he was carrying around inside him – had thrown his youth permanently off track. He settled for a twenty-year-old's healthy cunt in a hotel room rented by the hour and a couple of assignments abroad each year. The swamp had already risen past his nose and it was too late to get out of it.

To be lifting Perón's veils little by little had been exciting at times, he admitted. He felt an unexpected pride in his work. But the editor-in-chief didn't share it: something more was needed, he told him. Haven't you read what the others have done? Two special correspondents in Puerta de Hierro, night and day, and two others constantly at Cámpora's heels. Look at this, Zamora: first-rate photos of his exile, year by year. And we're going to compete by coming out with this measly story and that's all? We'll lose, the way we lost the war. Maybe a full-page ad in *La Nación* and *Clarín*, how about that? The General as no one has ever seen him, the naked truth – what do you think, Zamora? A terrible idea, sir: it strikes me as pure shit. The truth is beyond reach: it's buried somewhere in all the lies – like God.

So that was how the idea of staging the story had come up – staging it, that was it: the editor-in-chief was enthralled by the word – with real-life characters. *Horizonte* will put on an opera at Ezeiza, *il risorgimento*, the resurrection of the past. We'll bring all the witnesses who can still move, Zamora; they can be the homecoming parade. We have to get going. What if, two weeks before, we proclaim them 'the heroes of yesterday' or something in that vein, in a special edition: how's that? Imagine: his schoolmates, his cousins, brothers- and sisters-in-law, all of them inextricably tied in with the mag's logo, kissing the ground of the fatherland with Perón.

Just before 20 June, the editor-in-chief secured López Rega's consent to gather the magazine's guests together in the lobby of the international hotel at Ezeiza. Osinde, the head of the committee organizing the celebration of the General's return, categorically refused to allow anyone access to the tarmac. And he let it be known that he was not happy about certain names: what was Julio Perón, the General's first cousin, doing on the list, when he was given to confessing in public that he was ashamed to be a relative of his? And María Tizón, his first wife's elder sister – why dig up stories from so long ago? He agreed that breakfast could be served to the guests and photographs of the group taken in the hotel, no problem. But to be frank, he preferred that they be kept away from the General – take them to the terrace of the airport and let them watch his arrival from there. I have room for ten persons on the tarmac, no more. You can put up a placard with the name of the magazine: but it'll cost you. Won't that do?

It'll be absolutely revolting, Zamora had complained. The glorification of the Argentine gutter press. The editor-in-chief was annoyed: get on the same wave length as this country, man. What good are your old-fogey sermons now?

Cousin Julio himself had hesitated for days on end before accepting the invitation. He already rather regretted having allowed them to worm an interview out of him. And even though he carefully pondered every word he said, his tone of voice and a number of involuntary sighs gave him away. He had twice turned down this chance for a rare encounter with his cousin Juan — because we haven't talked together since we were twenty, do you understand? And because he was never willing to answer my letters. What can we expect of each other, Juan Domingo? Let me think — what could we give each other?

The one who had finally persuaded him was his sister María Amelia, Frene's widow. She was ready and willing to go. She was counting on the explicit promise that the memory of her father, Tomás-Hilario Perón, would not be insulted: his suicide in a pharmacy on the Calle Cerrito still caused talk every once in a while. They are going to give us the photos they've discovered, Julio; the reports of the police experts. I'm going to go, if that's the price I have to pay to sleep peacefully.

Then I'll go too. I'll shake Juan's hand if he holds it out to me, but I won't say one word to him. It's his fault that I've been living like a recluse on the Calle Yerbal for five years, denying my name. That silence is who I am, and who is he to make me break it?

When Cousin Julio enters the hotel lobby, on 20 June at eight a.m., he notices that the other breakfast guests are ill at ease too. They sit on the edge of their chairs as they talk. Alberto J. Robert, the farmer, who grew up with Perón in Camarones, is chewing a wad of tobacco. And when he looks about, his blue eyes turn to flint, veiled by cataracts.

'I remember Perón's father, Don Mario, so well!' he is saying.

'He was very good at working lizard skin. We made reins, halters, muzzles together. And we hunted as well. Yes indeed. Days at a time lying in wait for guanacos . . .'

Are all of them supposed to tell their story? Cousin Julio becomes alarmed: he's already told his. Tell their story? No, not at all. Zamora comes over to greet him and reassures him. The guests are only talking with each other: they're sorting out who they all were in the General's past. Has Don José Artemio Toledo been introduced to you? He's a first cousin too. And his wife Doña Benita? They haven't seen the General for forty years.

He, José Artemio, is wearing a beret, and tips it in greeting. Benita hasn't taken off her three-quarter-length fox coat: her face is flushed.

'Ah, yes . . . cousins on which side of the family?' María Amelia asks, drawing her chair closer to Julio's.

'The Toledos,' Benita answers. 'José Artemio's mother and the General's mother were sisters. People have often asked how that could be: sisters with the same father and mother and different surnames. We don't know. It's hard to figure out relationships between people from that part of the country: Lobos, Roque Pérez, Cañuelas, 25 de Mayo. It's all just one world . . .'

The waiters have already set the table for breakfast. Zamora seats Captain Santiago Trafelatti at one end of the table and Señorita María Tizón at the other. She is wearing a pink tailored suit: she has heard – she laughs as she tells to it – that Perón is going to fly over Buenos Aires in a hot-air balloon, at dusk. And that he's going to go from avenue to avenue, greeting people. Maybe when he sees his old friends and relatives he'll invite them to go aloft. And why not ask him to? Captain Trafelatti, a former comrade-at-arms, doubts that the balloon rumor is true. Perón would never do such a thing – he suffers from vertigo.

Horizonte has left a folder with documents and photographs at everyone's place. The guests get all excited when they discover them. But not Cousin Julio: he doesn't let any of his feelings show, doesn't move a muscle.

He comes from a family brought up to hide their feelings. A year and a half after his father died, his mother, still in mourning, remarried, leaving the children in the charge of Aunt Vicenta Martirena. To put them to sleep at night, Aunt Vicenta told them stories that all had the same moral: 'There is always a feeling to fit every occasion. Choose the proper one and you'll be better off.' So they grew up learning to be better off, to say what their elders wanted them to say.

Señorita María Tizón has them pass from hand to hand an enlargement of the photo of themselves that her sister Potota and Juan Domingo had had taken alongside a Packard.

'. . . in the summer of 1930, during their honeymoon.'

'It was in 1929,' Benita Escudero de Toledo corrects her. 'I know the exact date they were married: 5 January 1929, at seven-thirty p.m., not in church but in a chapel at the bride's house that they set up just for the wedding, because Juan was still in mourning. Don Mario Tomás, his father, had died a short time before. Here are wedding announcements that prove what I'm saying.'

María Amelia is also going through the photos in the folder, and is touched. 'I can't believe it,' she says in Julio's ear. And then, in a louder voice:

'Thank you, Señor Zamora. I finally feel that it's been worth the trouble.'

The pictures she has received are, truly, such living breaths from the past that they seem to be ghosts, not photographs. In one of them, María Amelia is standing reading her primer, affectionately embraced by Aunt Vicenta. In another, she and Julio are playing dominoes, perched on velvet stools, against a background of opulent decor: with flowers, Greek columns and gold-fringed curtains.

'They were taken shortly before Juan Domingo came to live with us at Aunt Vicenta's school, isn't that so, Julio?' María Amelia says, eager to contribute information.

'No,' her brother corrects her. 'They were taken in 1900, the last day of the century. Look at the name of the photo studio: Resta and Pascale, on the corner of Corrientes and Rodríguez-Peña. The wax seal on the back surely shows the date.'

Although he has urinated before sitting down at the table, Julio leaves again to go to the toilet. For days the looseness of his sphincter has been tormenting him. To tell the truth, he feels that no part of his body belongs to him any more. He has seen his double chin tremble in the mirror as though it had a will of its own and stop when he looks away; his left shoulder also twitches when he's least expecting it. His urine is just as unpredictable. He keeps having the sensation that a drop of it is leaking out, but it's not: when he feels himself he's dry. And now he has somehow wet himself. And even though there's a fire in the fireplace in the lobby of the hotel, and an electric heater at his feet, the dampness has seeped through to his trousers and is making him shiver.

As though inadvertently, on leaving the table he has taken his folder of photographs along with him. He chooses the booth at the far end of the toilet, bolts the door, and after voiding the miserable trickle of urine still in his bladder, he sits down on the toilet seat.

There are three photos. He piles them on his legs, so as to go through them in order. For a moment he feels the precise flash of the instant at which they were taken. He sees the photographer putting magnesium powder in a pan and then covering his head with a black hood, sees the powder go off again in a dull flare, perhaps because it is wet, thus explaining the sepia patches on the plate: that is also why Granny Dominga does not appear in the background. And the images are gradually developed inside him, as in the acid bath of long ago. Juan and Julio are wearing their hair cropped very short, with only a hint of bangs. Both of them (and María Amelia behind, sitting with two of her schoolmates in wicker hammocks) are wearing white dusters. Though Juan Domingo looks intimidated, he is well-built and tough, because of those icy winds of Patagonia your father made use of to tan you like leather. I told you to smile, Juan, and you answered me that you hadn't lost your shyness yet: you'd only been at Granny's house for a week. They just left you there and you were inconsolable. That must be why your sadness shows through on your face. I, on the other hand, feel nothing: the magnesium has washed out the expression on my face.

The same thing happens here, in this photo they took of all of us in the third and fourth grade at the Polytechnic School at 2300 Cangallo. I am still aloof, already hollow-eyed from my presentiment of the misfortunes awaiting me, and you, though you're scowling, are nice and plump, Juan Domingo, with your hair parted down the middle and wearing a big bow on your Eton collar. Enriqueta Douce, the monitor, whom you can see in the center of the photo, wearing glasses with a metal frame, used to say that you were my vampire: that I was gradually disappearing so that you'd get fatter.

Ah, Enriqueta: of course! At the end of '48, she telephoned me to tell me how surprised she was that you had told one of your biographers that that school we attended was the International School in Olivos, that (you said) 'children from rich families' went to, and not our modest building with three or four courtyards, between Azcuénaga and Ombú, where even the herbariums and the maps were middle-class. Do you even remember Enriqueta, the niece of Don Raimundo Douce, the owner and director of the school? She insisted on contradicting you, that summer in '48. She sent a letter to you at the office of the President of the Republic to set right what you politely called your *lapsus linguae*, a momentary slip of your memory, though I warned her that she shouldn't: that to you the past deserves nothing but betrayals. Enriqueta, I said to her: Juan is that way about everything. He doesn't talk about his father's small farm but of his big ranch, and he told me straight off that his mother was the great-granddaughter of conquistadors, when everybody in the family knew that she was the daughter of a conquered Indian. A pen-pusher in the president's office answered Enriqueta in your name, Juan: he promised that at the first opportunity the *lapsus* would be corrected, and that you would invite her to the presidential mansion soon so that the two of you might share memories of 'the good old days'. It no longer matters that you didn't make good your promise, so that the poor thing never got to wear the dress she'd bought especially for the occasion. She's grown old so suddenly that she doesn't even know what the past is. But I on the other hand am annoyed, Juan, that you persist in describing yourself as a former pupil of the International School in Olivos and not of the Polytechnic School on Cangallo, and that the error is now perpetuated in all the biographies of you. You thus offered yourself not only the luxury of making up your own life but also of turning other people's lives topsy-turvy.

Isn't that what you've always done: taken your story from a dreary place to another more prestigious one, yet carrying all the characters in it with you on your shoulders? Aren't we your classmates, former pupils of a school we never attended? And on reflection: why is Don Julio Perón sitting here, in one of the hotel toilets, looking apprehensively at these old photos, if not because of another of those theological disorders that Juan Domingo causes in other people's life stories? Seven old men and women have turned their daily habits upside down so as to come bid you welcome. They'll make fools of themselves by embracing you while carrying in one hand the special issue of *Horizonte* that they haven't seen yet: the true story that Zamora has written based on the things they told him.

Although Julio had given no secrets away, and the interviews of him took no more than two hours in all, it was obvious to him that Zamora had pestered the others with the persistence of a horsefly. And he had worked several miracles: come up with certain time machines, pasts that went on flowing in a pure state.

For example: José Artemio Toledo and Benita Escudero preserved intact the first bedroom that Cousin Juan and his beloved Potota had occupied after they married, including her wedding dress. Amid the glass bottles in the bathroom the letters that they wrote to each other during Juan Domingo's absences – long ones – slowly faded, the ribbons around them still undone. And Señorita María, who so firmly resisted Zamora's charms? Didn't she end up offering him her diary, when the attention of the other Tizón sisters, who were watching her through the curtains, was distracted for a moment?

Only Cousin Julio, boring the reporter with his more and more languid monosyllables, had finally driven him away. But now, against his will, he has come here: to complete the cabal of seven witnesses. Seven because that's the number of sounds there are (Zamora said), the number of theological virtues and of capital sins. And because the lines in the triangle upon the square, which reflect the lines of the sky above the earth, also add up the same number: seven.

The last of the photos lying on his legs doesn't belong here, in this place of excrement. Profanation, insult. It is a masterpiece by the photographer E. Della Croce, that brings back to life a young man with big ears and eyes set close together, above whose forehead the first lights of death part violently. In astonishment, Cousin Julio notes that the plate was made two days before that young man, Tomás Hilario, his father, killed himself with cyanide behind the counter of a drugstore. And he feels as though a fierce animal is awakening deep within him: he hears the gnawing of the animal biting through to the last bastions of his breath, but since no one has taught him to suffer, Cousin Julio doesn't know what to do with the swipe of that fierce animal's paw, how to put out the fire of it, what pain will wipe away this tear. He has a thunderous fear but cannot say exactly what it is a fear of: are the lightning, the storms that are being unleashed now the past? Or are they, rather, the questions that the past can no longer answer?

4 *The Beginning of the Memoirs*

'I've belonged to others all my life, Cámpora,' the General is saying. 'How can you maintain that now, at the age of seventy-seven, I still don't have the right to belong to myself?'

Outside, in Madrid, the night of Saturday, 16 June, is cracking open: the lack of rain and the heat are shocking.

For at least fifteen minutes President Cámpora has been standing listening, with the greatest respect, to the General's reprimand. He is wearing the formal dress that he refused to wear even on the day he took office, and along with the blue and white sash across his chest, below the pocket, he has pinned a large Peronist badge. Perón, on the other hand, sitting sprawled in his easy chair at his desk, comes off second-best with the loudest outfit in his wardrobe: a red guayabera shirt, two-toned shoes and ice cream pants. He still has on his peaked cap. Every so often, a troupe of poodles leaps onto his lap. The General's mind is then completely distracted from Cámpora, and his thoughts scurry like beetles amid the dogs' curly fur.

'You've come to live it up in Madrid,' Perón berates him. 'In order to set an example, I have had to deny myself all self-indulgences: just imagine, I even pretend – and it's all on account of you – that I'm troubled by a fistula. You've come to hear and to deliver a bunch of speeches. To me, things like that are indigestions of the soul. Look at the poor country you've just abandoned: merely to have, as you put it, the privilege of coming to fetch me. Some privilege! The only thing I'm ever told about are factories in Argentina that have been occupied and guerrilla activities that cause unrest. You'd have fulfilled your duty better if you'd stayed to right these wrongs by governing the country. I gave you power. Use it. Why do I need you here, Cámpora? History has paid its debt to me. I'm perfectly capable of returning to my homeland by myself. I had set this week aside to look after my own needs, to think, to have some peace. But you took it into your head to bring a bunch of lazy louts with you who keep asking me for personal audiences: they want me to receive them one by one for an interview in depth. And there are a hundred of them! They phone at all hours, night and day. The neighbors are complaining because they can't get through on the telephone lines in the area. And they don't give me a moment's peace. It's as if you're doing it on purpose, Cámpora. As if you set this pack of hounds loose on me to intimidate me and make me not want to return.'

The President lowers his head dejectedly.

'You misunderstand my motives, General. I'm not the one who wanted to come get you in Madrid. The country has given me a mandate . . .'

There is a knock on the door. The dog that the General was still holding in his lap leaps down and slips and slides amid the furniture, barking.

'Come in, come in!' And a journalist from the Efe Agency

whom the secretary has by the arm is ushered in. Cámpora is surprised: hasn't the General ordered that no witnesses be present? And yet: 'Please sit down, both of you. Would you like some coffee?'

Annoyed, the President looks at his watch.

'Excuse me,' he says. 'I was just leaving. Generalissimo Franco will be arriving at Moncloa at any moment. I'm at least fifteen minutes late. I came in the hope that you could accompany me, General: but I'm resigning myself to the fact that that is not your intention.'

Perón throws his arms open. Once again – he explains with a look – Cámpora hasn't caught on.

'Do you realize now that it's not the country that's come to get me? The country would be in no hurry to get to the banquet at Moncloa.' And taking off his cap, the General turns toward the reporter. 'I was just saying to Cámpora that with all the upheaval and chaos in Argentina we can't offer ourselves the luxury of going all over the globe drinking champagne. That is why I must return to my poor country – so that everybody will learn to toe the line.'

The President has started to bow, as a sign that he is leaving, when the General's last phrase gives his heart back the dignity that has been so badly ruffled on this trip to Madrid.

'You're right, sir,' he answers, his chin trembling. 'You're the one who ought to be in command in Argentina.' He steps back one pace, takes off the presidential sash, and standing on tiptoe, tries to place it across Perón's chest. 'This isn't mine. If I accepted the sash of office it was to serve you. And since you are the owner of it, I am giving it back to you.'

The General does not lose his composure. Paternally, he frees himself from Cámpora's grasp.

'Please. How dare you drape a sacred symbol over my guayabera?'

And suddenly, with no transition, he feels an overwhelming

desire to be alone, as imperative as a cough. That's what happens in one's old age, he has been told: one's mood unexpectedly changes. Sadness is summer; irritation is spring.

He wants to be by himself. Tomorrow, perhaps not, but right now I want to be by myself.

He has López Rega accompany Cámpora to the entrance of the villa 17 de Octubre, where a motorcade of limousines and motorcycles is waiting for him with all headlights on. And he dismisses the correspondent from Efe Agency: the heat and hustle and bustle of moving are making my blood pressure fall through the floor, my boy. We can talk at length some other day – in Buenos Aires, doubtless.

He notes that the President, heading toward the gate amid the palm trees in the garden, turns around to wave goodbye to him. The General then interjects into the scene an enigmatic invitation, which his biographers, years later, will not know whether to attribute to a sense of guilt or to sarcasm:

'Come take communion with me tomorrow morning, Cámpora! And don't stay up late tonight – the mass is at seven o'clock!'

He too ought to go to bed now. Both Puigvert and Flores Tazcón, his personal physicians, have advised him that he should always retire before ten p.m. But how to obey them if his work is not yet done and he feels that time is running out? For months now the General has been denying himself the slightest distraction. Every once in a while Isabelita tempts him by calling him to come see *Captain Blood* with Errol Flynn on Channel One, or *Call Unicorn*, the most violent episode in the Cannon series. No, sorry: he must dutifully reread Lord Chesterfield's letters to his son Philip Stanhope, where he has found rules of proper conduct in polite society that he would like to impose upon his undisciplined Argentina.

'It's the end of time,' he is in the habit of telling himself when his mind wanders from the book. The millennium, the deluge, the angel's trumpets heralding the apocalypse? 'It's the end of your time, Juan,' his mother has told in his dreams of the South Pole: the vertigo into which all horizons will be plunged, the neglect in which all your ages will meet.

And therefore he must deny himself sleep, as has already happened in the last two weeks. He is correcting his Memoirs. Or, rather, he is in the process of locating himself in the Memoirs that López has written for him − for months now, the General has been seeing him hard at work transcribing cassettes and shuffling documents.

Only now does he realize, too late perhaps, that these Memoirs were the cross on the Peronist church that was missing. More than the tabernacles of his master classes on political leadership or compilations of his discourses, it will be the Memoirs that will allow him to indoctrinate the common herd through example. He had been wrong when he told his guide Américo Barrios in Santo Domingo: 'No memoirs: I'm allergic to them. If I were to write them, I'd get the idea that I was no longer alive. Let someone else write them.' López, then.

Indoctrinate, instruct: the idea obsesses him. The masses must steep themselves in his virtues, recognize themselves in Perón's past. In a way, he had already said as much in 1951: 'The masses do not think, the masses feel and have more or less intuitive and organized reactions. But who produces these reactions? The leader. The masses are the equivalent of muscles. I always say that it isn't the muscle that matters but the brain center that sets it in motion.' It was clear: his past must cause virtue to spring forth naturally from future generations.

Evita had already intuited this when she published *My Mission in Life*. The people need fables and feelings, not the heavy gray mess of doctrines which, much to his regret, he had tried to feed them on.

At his back, in the library, alongside the collection of maté gourds and sippers that has gradually accumulated in exile, are the folders with a fair copy of the Memoirs. He no longer recognizes himself in certain anecdotes: but the documents are there, and documents don't lie. López is right: old age has erased many things from his mind by now. How many times the real name of Potota, his first wife, has evaded his lips! What was it, what was it? Amelia, María Antonia, Aurelia, Amalia, Ofelia Tizón? Memory had been the most trustworthy of his gifts, and he was losing it.

At times, in an effort to revive it, López would show him photos with rust-colored stains and patches of sepia. He would point with his index finger to one of the persons in a photograph and challenge him: 'Who is this, General? Let's see if you remember.' And he would shake his head. 'I don't know, I don't know. That one there looks familiar to me, but this one . . . I've never seen this one . . .' The secretary would then uncover the other half of the photo. 'Look, General. Don't you recognize who it is? It's yourself in 1904, in 1908, in 1911 . . . Over here, on this other side, is your cousin, María Amelia Perón: the two of you lived together in the same house for almost three years . . .' 'Down in Camarones?' the General said, intrigued. 'No, not in Camarones. In the school run by Vicenta Martirena, your aunt.' 'Is what you're saying really true: that that María Amelia is a first cousin of mine? And who's this lad here, López? Let's see: who is that with such a dim look in his eyes?'

Now he wants to be by himself with those memories. He puts his glasses on, brings the pages closer to the light, and once again goes over the first paragraph of the Memoirs, which he has never been satisfied with: 'My father was the son of Tomás Liberato Perón, a physician who also had a doctoral degree in Chemistry . . .'

Why not take a step back, rescuing from the shadows of the Rosas dictatorship his Sardinian great-grandfather, who disembarked in Río de la Plata around 1830, and his Scottish

great-grandmother, from whom his father inherited the blue veins
in his eyes? I'm a melting pot of races, Argentina is a melting pot
of races: here is the mark of identity shared by the country and
myself. I am going to emphasize it. The General rummages about
among the documents that López has filed under 'Ancestors', and
taking notes from here and there, he rewrites:

> As far as I know, the first Perón to set foot in Argentina was a
> Sardinian shopkeeper, Mario Tomás. He carried a passport
> issued by the king of Sardinia, and with a recommendation like
> that he soon was given a helping hand by other Sardinians. He
> opened a shoe store, and soon prospered. There are those who
> say he got rich by selling boots to the Mazorca, the name that
> the police force of Buenos Aires was known by in those days. I
> am more inclined to believe that, as a good businessman, my
> great-grandfather must have lighted candles at all altars, without
> paying any attention to which saint was displayed on them.
>
> He had been in Buenos Aires only three years when
> he married, on 12 September 1833, a Scotch lass with blue
> eyes. The two spoke Spanish badly, and so in order to under-
> stand each other they doubtless used the universal language of
> gestures.

It's better that way. They have written him from San Juan that a
certain Pedro Perón appears in the list of transatlantic passengers
for 1823. Another Perón, one Domingo – could this be his great-
grandfather? – reached the port of Buenos Aires in 1848, on a boat
from Montevideo. The General decides to skip over these details,
so as not to detract from the clarity of his account. Nor will he
linger over the storm clouds of bankruptcy that in 1851 threatened
the family business, on which a bunch of moneylenders held a joint
mortgage. He halts instead to eliminate the adjectives with which
López has ornamented the following paragraph:

Of the seven children that the Mackenzie-Peróns gave to their new homeland, the most outstanding was Tomás Liberato, the eldest, born on 17 August 1839. The life of that [illustrious] forebear was full of honors. He was a senator in the national legislature, a member of Mitre's party representing the province of Buenos Aires; president of the National Hygiene Council, the equivalent of a minister of health, and a [heroic] Army officer, who served as head of the medical corps in the war against Paraguay. He was sent on a number of missions abroad, to France in particular, where he lived for some time. [He shed blood] He also fought in the battle of Pavón. In 1867, shortly before taking his final examination for his medical degree, he married [a most distinguished lady, Doña] Dominga Dutey. That grandmother of mine was Uruguayan, from Paysandú, the daughter of [noble] French Basques from Bayonne.

More than one historian sought to correct these data when the General gave *Panorama* magazine permission to publish them. They have said that his grandfather was a deputy in the provincial legislature in 1868 and not a senator in the national legislature. That for his selfless medical services during the yellow fever epidemic the Sarmiento government awarded him a fellowship, for just six months, to Paris. But he did not take part in the war against Paraguay: they have disproved this. He was unable to leave his post at the first-aid hospital improvised in Buenos Aires to receive the wounded. He was a distinguished doctor, but not a national hero. Why did the General insist on giving his grandfather false luster is his real merits were quite enough? Fits of megalomania, as one anonymous critic wrote caustically. Don't you remember that you yourself, when you were lord and master of the Republic, commissioned a biography of Dr Perón that was to be laudatory and at the same time respectful of the truths?

Why wouldn't I remember all that? And besides, what does it

matter? I don't see what difference there is between the portrait of my grandfather, which López Rega – I agree – has touched up a bit in the Memoirs, and the flesh and bones of reality. Damn it all: are the two of them essentially the same person or are they not? That passion men have for the truth has always seemed senseless to me. I have the facts on this side of the river. Very well: I copy them exactly as I see them. But who can guarantee that I see them exactly as they are? Someone has written somewhere that I ought to study the documents more carefully. Ha! Here the documents are, as many as I please. And if there aren't any, López invents them. He has only to lay a hand on a piece of paper to turn it yellow: he's told me so. He's gotten me so confused that when I look at a photograph from my childhood, I don't know if I'm really in it or if López has put me there.

But what I feel about the facts is on the other side of the river. And to me that is the only thing that matters. Nobody will ever know what Mona Lisa looked like or how she smiled, because that face and that smile don't represent what she was but what Leonardo painted. Eva used to say the same thing: mountains have to be put where a person wants them, Juan. Because wherever you put them, that's where they stay. That's what history is.

I never knew my grandfather Tomás Liberato. I do know that he suffered from insomnia and that in his last years, when he could scarcely stand up, he spent his nights cooped up among retorts and incense burners trying to tap the virus of insomnia. He got the idea that the virus traveled from place to place on the legs of locusts, so he boiled locusts and then distilled the water to analyze it. He left such a penetrating odor in that house that, when her first years of mourning were over, my grandmother had to move, because even new clothes, long afterward, still smelled of grasshoppers. I have no way of knowing if those stories really happened that way or not. But that's the way my grandmother heard them, and transmitted them in those words. If other truths exist, they're of no interest now. History will retain the truth that I'm telling.

All right then, General. You can now go on without qualms to the very moment you enter the Military Academy. Forget the embarrassing details. Suppress them. Blow them off these official Memoirs so they don't leave one speck of dust. All men have a right to decide their future. Why shouldn't you have the privilege of choosing your past? Be your own evangelist, General. Separate good from evil. And if you forget something or get it wrong, who will have the nerve to correct you? Let's read the Memoirs then, word for word as they appear in the fair copy of them that López has made:

The names of my maternal grandparents were Toledo and Sosa. As far as I know, all my forebears on that side were Argentine. It is stated somewhere that they founded the little fort of Lobos in the days of the Conquest. I am not certain. I only know that my mother was born in that town, among humble, hardworking country folk.

My father, Mario Tomás Perón, was destined for a more urban life, but chance made him a man of the pampas too. He was born on 9 November 1867. Of his two brothers born after him, Tomás Hilario, the older one, became a druggist. We used to call him 'the pharmachist'. I believe the younger one, Alberto, wanted to make a career for himself in the army: he was a captain or a major when he died.

(And what about your mother? López insisted. What was her date of birth? If we put in the birth date of one of them, it wouldn't look right to leave out that of the other. The thing is, I don't recall it, the General answered. We celebrated her birthday early in November. But the year, the year . . . Leave it the way it is.)

There are many different explanations as to why my father was led to work in the countryside. I know that he began to study medicine at my grandfather's insistence, and that at some moment he gave it up. I read somewhere that it was typhoid fever that made him break off his studies, but that wasn't what he told me: he simply said that he'd had enough of them. In 1890, a year after his father's death, he took over some land in Lobos that he had inherited and settled there, as a cattle rancher. I, Juan Domingo, was born in Lobos on 8 October 1895. My elder brother, Mario Avelino, was just a few weeks short of his fourth birthday.

Around 1900, my father sold the cattle ranch and the hacienda, because he said the estate was no longer countryside but the outskirts of Buenos Aires. He went into partnership with the Maupas Brothers, a firm that owned a vast stretch of land near Río Gallegos, on the Patagonian border. And he began all over again.

(Here there is something that's not at all clear, López Rega told him. His father went into partnership with the Maupas brothers to exploit land in Río Gallegos. Why, then, did he go no farther than Cabo Raso, over six hundred miles to the north? How should I know? the General answered him. Those are stories so far back in the past now that to me they seem to be somebody else's. The secretary shook his head: Rack your brain. I don't remember the story as being the way you tell it, General. How do you know? Perón said, intrigued. I know, López replied. Every time you drop a thought, I pick it up as though it were a handkerchief. I pick all of them up here, within these limits: the invisible pencil line that I draw around my body.)

My father was strict about everything that had to do with our upbringing. He used anything and everything to teach us a lesson. We nonetheless felt no lack of affection. We used to go out together to hunt guanacos and ostriches. He often laid into us with all his might, because moving across the Patagonian pampas on horseback held many surprises. We had eight greyhounds that chased the prey, but in order to keep up with them we had to gallop. Hard.

As a horsewoman, I give you my mother. She was an Amazon. And in the kitchen, no question about it: she handled everything with the greatest of ease. We thought of my mother as our doctor, our mentor and our friend. She was the confidante and the crying-towel. When we learned to smoke, we did so in front of her.

(Have I understood correctly what you asked me to do, General: bring out the masculine traits in the portrait of your father and your mother's feminine ones in hers? No half-tones, so as not to confuse the readers. Have I presented them in the way you want: as exemplary lives? López had asked him when he had finished the first folderful of rough drafts, as they were coming down the stairs from the attic as slowly as convalescents. It's fine, Perón had answered. Just the way I wanted it to be.)

The two of them shut themselves up in their retreat to read shortly before midnight. Isabel was asleep and the dogs were lying quietly in their baskets. In the beginning – had a whole year gone by? – they used to get together in the study – there where the General is now, going over each page. The wind was blowing straight out of an oven, just as on this night of 16 June. Outside, on the other side of the iron grille, the men from the Guardia Civil on watch thwacked the air with their flashlights. 'This is no place for confessions,' the General had said. And López: 'You're right. Listen to those flashes going off: the guards are taking pictures of us.'

They still hesitated for several days, moving with their papers and tape recorders from the dining room table to a little room hidden underneath the stairway. Finally, they dared to go upstairs to the only retreat there was in the house: what López called the cloister. It was on the third floor and had served at one time as a place for storing cleaning equipment. From here a little winding staircase led to the attic, where the General kept his war maps, floods of correspondence and the newspapers and magazines from his years of glory. But since the memorable afternoon in 1971 when his mortal enemy, President Alejandro Lanusse, had ordered that the body of Perón's second wife – hidden away for more than fifteen years in a cemetery in Milan under another name – be returned to him, everything about the house had changed. Evita was there. Her presence could be felt.

Isabel had had an architect widen the storage room, put a window in, carpet it and furnish it with two couches, a prie-dieu, and an altar piece with the portrait photographs of the deceased that had become classics. Upstairs, in the attic – now whitewashed, spotless, with air purifiers – she was there in her coffin: beneath the perpetual light of six red lamps, shaped like torches. Isabel had insisted that the body should be illuminated by real tapers, but the embalmer said that those dead tissues were immaculately preserved with no sign of deterioration thanks to certain inflammable substances. And he recommended that even the electric lights in the attic be protected against the risk of short circuits and sparks. Few visitors, all close friends, got as far as the cloister. And almost no one as far as the sepulcher: Evita's sisters when they came through Madrid, and Isabel on Sundays, to leave flowers for her. They had lined the doors of the cloister with velvet, so that not a sound could be heard. There López noted down the General's reminiscences, and the two of them read, in total absorption.

In the first months of work on the Memoirs, Perón would close his eyes and let himself go: he breathed out one story after another, and it was as if the room were full of feathers. At times, when he was himself again, he couldn't locate the secretary. His body was immediately impregnated with an odor of flowers and benzine. It's Eva – he would say – wanting to come down from the attic. And he would shake with terror. López? he would call up the stairs. He always found the secretary sitting in his study, diligently transcribing the recordings. Though López's face was lined from staying up all night, he kept the current of the writing flowing. He not only sowed the Memoirs with his own thoughts; he also incorporated in them stories that the General had omitted, ones that he, López, on the other hand had right at his fingertips: 'Read this page: why have we cut that summer out?' he would say excitedly. 'Think, General, go back in time. January 1906. They dressed us in black, and as if that weren't enough, they tied mourning bands around our arms. Aunt Vicenta and Aunt Baldomera took us, dressed like that, to General Bartolomé Mitre's funeral chapel: you and I walked in front; Cousin María Amelia and Cousin Julio followed gravely behind, holding each other's hand. Baldomera dared kiss the forehead of the great man. The rest of us went to sign the mourners' book, remember . . . ?' And the General answered, 'Now that you've talked about it, I remember it as though in a fog. But the only thing I see is the two cousins. I walked ahead by myself, elbowing my way through the crowds of people in tears. Buenos Aires seemed like a cemetery. We sweated buckets and the heat given off by so many flowers stifled us. And what were you doing there, López? How old were you?' The secretary never answered.

Perón found such incidents amusing, but in the mornings, when López's voice recited phrases from the recordings that had already been corrected: 'My father, Mario Tomás . . .' or '. . . dogs were my best friends . . .', he felt that a foreign body was trying to dislodge him from his own, and he would then cling to the stair rails so as not to lose his instinctive sense of self. 'That's how I take the best possible care of you, General,' López placated him. 'That's how I attract to my organism the ills that pass through yours.'

Now that he rereads the pages from the first days, Perón perceives how carefully the secretary has corrected the passages where he slipped up. He has come up with the real story – the one that ought to have taken place, the one that will doubtless prevail. With his mind at rest, he can now go over the following section of the Memoirs:

Everything changed when we reached the far south. Although the new ranch – called Chankaike – had been laid out in such a way as to withstand the cold, life was hard. In winter, the thermometer went down to twenty degrees below zero. The fight against nature was our daily fare, but all the adventures seemed to us to be of little consequence. We grew up in total freedom, subject only to the guidance and discipline of an old schoolteacher who took over our elementary studies.

Our usual refuge was two vast plains. The trade winds, which in that region blew at more than sixty miles an hour, diminished our enthusiasm for wide open spaces. When it was below zero outside, we were kept indoors. One time one of those terrible cold spells set in all of a sudden and my toes got frozen. When I warmed them, my toenails fell off. But God knows what he's doing. The nails grew back again, tougher than before.

Dogs, found in such numbers in the south because they are used to herd the sheep, were my best friends. Just a few of them can do more work than several ranch hands. The dogs left an indelible memory in my body: a hydatid cyst, now calcified in my liver, caused by a larval tapeworm I got from them.

After the terrible winter of 1904, my father bought two or three square leagues of land in the middle of the Chubut, at the foot of the famous basalt plateau. From Chankaike we went back north again, to Cabo Raso, and stayed there for a time, waiting for a house to be built for us on the new land. At the end of 1905 we moved in.

Though I saw very little of my father from then on, he made a very vivid impression on me. He was a man of bygone days, few of whom are left now. He was a commissar and a justice of the peace 'ad honorem' everywhere he lived: these were posts given to the settlers with the greatest prestige. My readers will understand, then, that my house was both a ranch house and a public office. He wielded his patriarchal authority from there, enjoying everyone's respect and friendship.

A concert of gargles, in the upstairs bathroom, profanes his reading. The General recognizes the din with which López Rega announces his rituals of personal hygiene on the stroke of midnight. Each gargle is succeeded by a discharge of mucus, and almost immediately thereafter, redoubled farts that allow the secretary to relieve his stomach.

Your stomach, General, López has corrected him. I don't have anything to do with that. It's winds that creep into you through your mouth and then use my body to get out. How is that possible? Perón has asked him. My digestion has always been perfect. But the secretary insists: the gargles are indeed mine. It is you who pass the other noises along to me.

March, 1904? the General thinks again. Something is wrong here. I was at school in Buenos Aires that year, but I also remember the famous winter that depopulated Patagonia in those same months. They are two memories that won't fit together. It's as if one of the two has felt out of place and has changed position. López reassures him. Things like that, General, aren't slips made by a person's memory but mistakes made by reality.

Was it in 1904 then? Or the following summer? He can still see himself arriving at the big rambling house on the Calle San Martín, with his hands stained purple from the blackberries. On his back was a knapsack, and hanging from his waist a pitcher around the bottom of which his mother had painted broom sedge flowers, so that the boy would never forget the land he came from. His grandmother greeted him indifferently. She offered her cheek for him to kiss, as she went on swaying back and forth in the hammock, and the two very stout aunts, with their arms akimbo, ordered him to go wash at the sink in the back yard. Was that really in 1904? The General strikes out the last sentence and writes a sketchier version in the margins.

But the teachings of my father and the old schoolteacher did not satisfy the hopes that the family had placed in me. I was obliged to journey to Buenos Aires, where my paternal grandmother would take charge of seeing me through elementary school. I went through the lower grades at my own pace and soon caught up with the others.

Yes, at that point he can pick up the thread.

The change was enormous. The little tanned, tough gaucho was gradually being transformed into one of the many lads who lived in the Capital. By the age of ten I was thinking almost like a man. In Buenos Aires I made my own way and my mother's skirts or my grandmother's did not have the same attraction for me as they did for other youngsters my age. I thought of myself as a grown-up and acted like one.

My grandmother was already well on in years. Hence I assumed her place as head of the family. That had an enormous influence on my life, because I therefore began to feel that I was independent, to think and to decide things for myself. I was not very studious or diligent. Sports were something else: I liked nothing better.

When I entered the Olivos International School years later, I took quite a liking to the little soccer field we had there on the grounds. It was one of those schools for boys from wealthy

families, with every convenience. At Olivos I went through all
the grades up through the third year, with a schedule of studies
that was quite out of the ordinary in that we were given a great
deal of freedom and responsibility. It was there that I first
started playing soccer. Those were the days of the famous
Alumni team, whose players we looked on as heroes.

Like every *ragazzo qualunque*, I learned the things I didn't like
by memorizing them; when it came to the rest, I used my
powers of reason. The usual teaching method depends more on
memory. And at the end of his life . . .

The General comes to a halt here. He has often gone over the next
sentence in his mind. But did he ever say it out loud? Is the
sentence really his or was it the secretary, reading his thought, who
set it down on the page?

. . . a man knows only as much as he remembers. A man knows
only as much as he remembers.

But the precise memory of things isn't what matters, but what
he gets out of it – what color he tints it.

When I finished the second year of high school at Olivos I
had to make a decision regarding my future. I considered taking
my father's advice and pursuing a career in medicine. In the
Perón family, this had been the predominant profession. They
say that my great-great-grandfather was a surgeon in Alghero,
a small port west of Sardinia. And my grandfather attained
fame and honors as a doctor. I was almost persuaded that my
destiny lay there. In the third year I began to go at Anatomy
hammer and tongs, since it was the hardest subject to master in
order to gain admission to medical school. But around that time
some pals of mine who had just enrolled in the Military
Academy visited me. They told me all about it and were
enthusiastic about how marvelous a life it was and how much

effort the professors put into tempering the students' characters. 'That's for me,' I said. And I discovered within myself the soldier that I have never ceased to be. I took the entrance exam in 1910. Finally, at the beginning of the following year I enrolled as a cadet.

Everything was in order, then. López had been able to cleanse the Memoirs of the dark stain of cousins and aunts that tainted them. By eliminating Vicenta and Baldomera Martirena, in whose home the General grew up, it was no longer necessary to speak of the first marriage of his grandmother Dominga. A widow who marries for the second time is not a martyr or an example to follow. The shadows of his cousins Julio and María Amelia had also vanished from the horizon. For what reason, López? In order to get around the shameful suicide of Uncle Alberto and thereby eliminate every weak point in the Perón blood line? Or in order to insist that he, Juan Domingo, was free and responsible from an early age, a real head of the family as he had written with such sound judgment?

'López!' he calls. Beyond the padded doors, to the right of the desk, the secretary is standing waiting for him, on one of the landings of the stairway. He is wearing a shot-silk dressing gown and smells of Lancaster cologne even from a distance. 'This chapter is very good, López,' the General says, rising to his feet. 'We must go on in the same vein. How do you feel about working tonight? The conversation with Cámpora has undone many knots inside me. He tried to put the presidential sash on me, can you imagine? As if mere gestures were enough to set the country to rights! I want to go into these Memoirs more thoroughly, López. Now that the dampness of the past has dried out, I feel like talking.'

'I'm all for it, General – for having you remember everything.' The secretary offers him his arm in the dark on the stairway; Perón leans on it. 'Take your time going up here. Relax. That's it, climb on up. Just one step at a time. That's it – now the next one. Hold on to the railing with that hand, to guide you. One, two, one. Concentrate on me. Keep climbing. Don't be afraid of the dark. I'm up here above, in the cloister, can you feel my presence?

5 *The Countermemoirs*

The fact that the house should be so silent when everything outside is in uproar has awakened Nun Antezana. Every time he encounters silence, his body has a presentiment of some misfortune.

And yet: what is there to fear? Diana is sleeping at his side and every last detail of Operation 20 June is under control. Bighead Iriarte has checked the engines and tires of the Leyland buses for the hundredth time, Pepe Juárez has cleaned and greased the stock of firearms, Vicki Pertini has worked with a legion of volunteer seamstresses to finish sewing the letters on the big posters – PERON OR DEATH, REVOLUTIONARY ARMED FORCES/WELCOME, GENERAL/ MONTONEROS ANSWER PRESENT AT ROLL CALL – and before going to bed he himself has made the rounds of the groups of militants from Berisso, Florencio Varela and Cañuelas. At noon on this 20 June, after marching from the traffic intersection in Llavallol, the columns of militants will reach the rearguard posted behind the dais, on the Ezeiza expressway. Then Nun will give the order to deploy in a pincer movement and take the first three hundred yards packed with demonstrators before whom the General will bring to an end his eighteen-year exile, announcing the birth of the Socialist fatherland.

How can the inside and the outside be so different? Here in the house nothing but sounds of breathing can be heard, as though something were in its death throes. Everything has been left along the wayside: fear, family, health, pride. Everything has little by little left him by himself to see the light of this dawn, to embrace this moment in history. But outside, outside: who knows what history is plotting at this moment?

Nun gets out of bed and lights a cigarette. He feels – impossible not to feel, however far away it may be – Diana's imposing body. She and this odyssey began at the same time. At the end of March, Nun had promised Perón himself to organize the breakup of the special assault groups and prepare them for peacetime. 'We must set up schools of preachers,' the Old Man insisted, and the deputy, Diego Muniz Barreto, passing through Puerta de Hierro, had proposed that Nun make Diana Bronstein his assistant: 'She's a first-rate cadre, Nun. A born organizer. They're wasting her as a file clerk in a trade union in Almagro.'

Muniz himself had introduced her to Nun in his offices on the Calle Florida, when they came back to Buenos Aires. From the moment he saw her, with her body hidden among the aquariums of tropical fish that the deputy collected, Nun felt his whole being fall into a daze, completely stunned. He was disarmed by that thicket of red hair that flitted about with the same sensuality as the piranhas, allowed himself to be overcome by the intensity of eyes that didn't go at all with the full face dotted with freckles, and lost his center of gravity when his gaze fell between Diana's breasts, whose turned-up nipples sniffed the sky.

She was the daughter of a Rumanian tailor who had married a

dull Polish girl after an exchange of letters. They spoke only Yiddish at home. Once she entered high school, Diana made every effort to unlearn that language: she wanted to disappear forever from the family's memories, to be born again as a pure Argentine. A logic professor gave her a thorough grounding in sex and in permanent revolution. After two years, he wanted to marry her. Diana was disappointed.

Since that time she had not allowed any man to choose her. She chose them, in the textile mills and the candy factories she infiltrated to indoctrinate the workers. Lying naked in bed, she would patiently read them Marta Harnecker's manuals and Che's diaries, tenderly induce them to pore over the biographies of Trotsky and Rosa Luxemburg, and then help them discover pleasures new to them with a wisdom that always surprised her. 'There is no reason why the revolution of the body should be at odds with the revolution of the people. If we poor people are denied everything else, why should we be denied pleasure?' she used to tell herself again and again so as to excuse the mad frenzy of her orgasms.

In 1972, a candy packer who went by the name of Angelote talked her out of her Trotskyite passion. The Fourth Inernational was – he told her – the last link in the chain of a Socialism that was not only anachronistic but a lost cause as well. In Argentina, all roads to revolution led by way of Perón. Diana was indignant, her intelligence decidedly offended: in the name of what ideology were they speaking? Perón was a prime example of opportunism, an underdeveloped imitator of Mussolini. The working class continued to trust him, true enough, but the work of revolution consisted precisely of exposing that imposture and of dethroning the trade-union bureaucracy that thrived in his service. Angelote held her in his arms and with unexpected authority ordered her to read John William Cooke; the letters written to Perón from Havana will put an end to your misgivings, it'll be now or never,

Diana my darling, history's about to come our way and I won't let you go without your having touched it.

For a few weeks longer Diana still had lingering doubts, until a group of guerrilla fighters in Trelew were slaughtered — a turn of events that she took to be an unmistakable sign of state terrorism — and the stormy wakes held at the headquarters of the Peronist movement finally made her make up her mind. She agreed to be a soldier for Perón so long as they allowed her to keep her critical independence: she wanted nothing to do with a cult of personality or with blind hierarchism. On the afternoon the guerrillas were buried she began to collaborate with a local underground leader from Almagro. Meeting Nun turned her into a full-time militant.

In no way had she granted Nun the privilege of seducing her. She was the one who between one day and the next, after resisting weeks of siege, phoned him and invited him to a hotel with rooms for rent by the hour for the mere pleasure of pitting her strength against that presumptuous body of his. The room they ended up getting smelled of sex. It was impossible that anyone had ever committed the error of making love for love's sake there. The bed had a canopy with plaster angels that threatened to fall off. The humiliating plastic mattress protector peeked through the darns in the sheets. The windows hidden by threadbare velvet drapes afforded a glimpse of the memorial monuments of Recoleta Cemetery. The minute they entered the room, Diana asked to have the light turned off. It was a revelation. Their bodies fitted together with no need for explanations, they went into the same accesses of shuddering at the same moment, and they came out headed for the same memories.

Diana began to live the story with a constant feeling of danger. She was afraid she was falling in love. She drew away from Nun out of fear and returned out of pity. She felt him to be at once so stout-hearted and so waiflike, so avid for power and so illiterate in love and in pity, that when he told her (always reluctantly) about one corner or another of his life, she felt like sheltering him with the foliage of her hair and lulling him to sleep on her lap, my poor Nun, poor little thing.

And it was true that Nun had grown up alone, in the care of nursemaids who stuffed him full of ice cream so he'd leave them in peace. His parents, who had separated before he learned to walk, settled the custody dispute by dividing him in half, having him live six months a year with one of them and six with the other, though when all was said and done he lived all year long with no one. All of a sudden, after endless periods of neglect, they would experience epidemic outbreaks of guilt and fight each other for the right to take him on a yacht trip on the Tigre or a weekend in Punta del Este. But once they managed to get their hands on Nun, their enthusiasm never lasted more than an hour. One of the few times they agreed on anything was when they decided to enroll him in military school. Nun was prepared for any misfortune except dogma and discipline. It took him a long time to resign himself to the torment of being roused out of bed before daybreak, forced to wake up under a cold shower and subjected to weeks of close order drill, cross-country marathons and practicing squat jumps. Little by little he learned that, in order to make others respect him, he must go to extremes: taking orders like a slave and giving them like a god. He began to train his body. He detested sports and yet he stayed at school on Sundays and spent his time pole-vaulting and weightlifting. Once a sergeant punished the whole class by making them stand in formation in a horse trough full of blocks of ice. Nun was the only one who got through the whole hour without fainting, out of pride and contempt for others' weaknesses. But he swore in his heart that once he was an officer, he would look the sergeant up and force him to undergo the same punishment.

At school he went by the name of Abelardo Antenaza and had a lively round face, which didn't go with the dopey chin, that had such a deep dimple in it that it looked like a scar from a bullet wound. During his first year, the English teacher sent him to the blackboard to write a list of irregular verbs. A few strands of sunlight came in through the window and landed on his hair. The teacher stood up and contemplated him. 'Raise your head, cadet.' Embarrassed, Nun obeyed. 'It's wonderful! You have a noon-face,' he said in English. 'What does that mean?' the class laughed. 'You have a noon-face,' the professor insisted, and then translated for the class.

From then on everyone called him by the nickname Nun. When they played soccer, the cadets on the rival team knew that by calling him that they could get his goat, and every time he came dribbling through their territory with the ball well under control, they had only to yell at him: 'It's getting away from you, Nun!' for him to inevitably miss his kick.

In the spring of 1969, when he was about to get his second lieutenant's saber – fourth in his class, but the best marksman – a chance meeting changed his life. At the wedding of one of his girl cousins he met Juan García Elorrio. Juan was an impassioned, brilliant, tenacious debater. He walked all hunched over and baldness brought on by neurasthenia had left him with a high forehead. He was editor of a leftist periodical, *Cristianismo y revolución*. He preached heroism and sainthood, but he couldn't imagine any other way of attaining those states save martyrdom.

From their first meeting, with his index finger pointed at the stubborn set of Nun's chin, García Elorrio cleverly catechized him. San Martín's army was being reborn in an invisible tide of new liberators, he said. They were young Peronists and Christians, ready to give their lives in a battle without quarter against the torturers of the poor, who condemned them to a slow death from hunger, illiteracy and disease. 'And who is the enemy?' Nun wanted to know. To Juan the answer was as plain as day. It was the illegitimate occupants of the fatherland: the invaders from within, the bunch of generals and admirals selling the country out to imperialism.

A memorable lecture by García Elorrio finally convinced him: 'The duty of every revolutionary is to make revolution,' Juan had explained, predictably but feverishly. 'And the duty of an upright man is not to close his eyes to the frightful violences from above, not to stand with folded arms. How could anyone remain unmoved by the example of the new martyrs whose names were Camillo Torres and Ernesto Guevara, our brothers in justice, our mentors in charity? They will live forever in the rifles of the anonymous guerrillas who are fighting throughout Latin America, in the rebel machetes of the peasants and in the avenging dynamite of the miners. In Argentina those martyrs bear the name John William Cooke and Eva Perón, for whom the one salvation of the fatherland lay, as it does for us today, in the revolutionary consciousness of the Peronist people . . .'

Illuminated from within, carried away by a heroic ideal that would take him in a straight line to rebelling against the values of his parents, Nun asked to be discharged from the Military Academy and went over to the ranks of the enemy. He made the choice with such determination that no one dared hold him back. In December he read in the papers of the demonstrations and patriotic oaths of his ex-comrades. In the meantime, he had organized his own junior militia and had had an interview with Perón.

He saw him countless times in the three years that followed. He came to the villa 17 de Octubre as spokesman for the most radical groups, always laying out some daring scheme for harassing the military dictatorship. Although his war plans seemed impossible to carry out, the General always approved of them. 'If you can count on the right people, go to it, Antezana. We don't want the regime to mistake us for a flock of penned sheep.'

And Nun went to it. With the same tireless imagination he

organized an attack on the sentry boxes of the presidential guard in Olivos, the blowing up of thirty-eight oil storage tanks belonging to Fiat and the launching of balloons that showered down on prison yards slogans to raise the morale of incarcerated militants: A FALLEN MARTYR'S STORY EARNS HIM EVERLASTING GLORY; ONCE BLOOD'S BEEN SHED ALL DEALS ARE DEAD.

In April 1973, a few weeks after the Peronists' triumph at the polls, Nun returned from Madrid with grave forebodings. He had found the General too anxious to regain power. Whatever might threaten that final glory kindled Perón's wrath. Revolution? Out of the question. He wanted to return to the fatherland as a man of peace. 'I will put out all fires with one breath and will show no mercy toward anyone who rekindles them again.' Nun had bet on Lenin and it now turned out that the winner was Kerensky. The alternatives are clear-cut, Perón had told him. We must choose between time and blood. If we want to get ahead fast, we need rivers of blood. I prefer that we walk ahead on rivers of time.

His greatest hope was that the military would again trust him: that they would respect his experience as a leader. And, hence, he would begin by imposing only mild reforms, changes measured out with a medicine dropper. 'Take a good look at me. Antezana: do I strike you as being a con artist?' No, sir. 'I'm going to teach Argentines that institutions are more important than revolutions. I have said more than once: I'm a toothless wild beast, a herbivorous old lion. I don't fool anybody, but there are many people interested in fooling themselves about me.'

In any event, Nun left the villa with the certainty that if the masses got out of hand and demanded a revolution, the General would not hesitate – as he had in 1945 – to rally round that flag. Whoever takes to the street first will have Perón in the palm of his hand, Nun reflected. It's going to be necessary to prove to him that the Peronists of 1973 are not as uncompromising as the ones in

1955, that the justicialista doctrine they preached back then has to set its sails to catch the new winds that are blowing.

At the end of May, on meeting with his lieutenants, Nun decided to rent a villa on the Camino de Cintura, about a third of a mile from the Ezeiza expressway, and direct from there the march of twenty thousand experienced militants who would surround the vanguard of the manifestation in a flanking movement and protect the Old Man with their slogans calling on the nation to rise up in arms.

One 3 June, a Sunday, he and Diana moved into that rambling, gloomy old house, sheltered by fog-emitting woods, and with an outdoor sink in the back yard, full of mud and foul-smelling rotted leaves. A week later Vicki Pertini and Bighead Iriarte took up quarters there too, bringing with them collections of maps and Peuser guidebooks to study the field of operations in detail, but Nun preferred that they practice their maneuvers on a sand table, as at the Military Academy, with little sky-blue flags to designate the faithful troops and black ones to indicate the enemy's hypothetical countermoves. When the great moment was finally close at hand, Nun called them together in the dining room of the old house and explained to them that it would not be easy for them to advance, but that that was their only recourse, the only method available to them. The dais was surrounded by strong Fascist contingents: on Route 205, a battalion of hardened police, elite sharpshooters, would thin the ranks of the revolutionary columns and keep them from advancing; on the flanks, in front of the security cordons, there would be the first-aid stations and the ambulances defended by die-hard supporters of secretary López Rega; to the north, the line of tank trucks communicating by radio with the control center at the Ezeiza hotel from which Lieutenant-Colonel Osinde would be supervising all operations; and the dais itself would be guarded by the most illustrious rightist thugs, the guardian angels of the cliques of trade union leaders and of Isabel the usurper: the Socialist fatherland would have to shoot its way through the hosts of the reactionary fatherland.

Squatting on her heels, Diana checked every detail in her own sketch book; absorbed in the task at hand, she distractedly lifted up her cascade of red hair, making the veins in Nun's belly heave and addling his brain. Vicki Pertini, whose senses were like a logarithm table – they were never distracted – quickly filled the silence by changing the position of the little flags on the sand table, as Pepe Juárez explained, in a toneless voice, that the ammunition they had stored up was more than enough for any defensive action.

Diana then reported on the strategy of harassment that she and her work team had agreed on. Between nine and ten a.m., she said, a small contingent from Lanús that went by the name of the Golden Throats would take up positions next to the dais, at the foot of the music stands of the symphony orchestra, and would fan out in groups of seven to ten people, remaining inside the three-hundred-yard radius. Around noon, when they had made contact with the contingents nearby, they would open fire with a soft little chorus, as if to temper the climate: *Come, comrade, we're off to Ezeiza, let's go/to welcome an old Montonero*, stressing – oh so innocently – the last word. And immediately, not letting the enthusiasm die down, a chorus from the shantytown of Berazategui, the Blue Rivulet, would back the Golden Throats, chanting together, at greater volume: *We'll make our countrymen Peronists/By making them Montoneros and Socialists*, over and over, till Perón flew in over national territory. Given the signal over their transistors, the Golden Throats would then launch an attack on the biggest sore spot of Isabelism: *There's only one Evita, you know quite well/So why bust your balls for Isabel?*, while the Blue Rivulet boys would let loose with their entire repertory of threats: *Very soon now we're going to see/The end of the trade union bureaucracy*. At that point we'd make our entrance with flags unfurled, the General would leave Ezeiza in a helicopter and head for the dais, and when we saw him arrive, from every corner of the compass the strains of the march that will never fade away will rise, the only possible ending for this glorious day: *We Will Triumph as One*. Puffing out their chests, the Golden Throats and the Blue Rivulet boys would then launch, in unison, into the revolutionary verse: *It was the resistance yesterday/It's the Montoneros and the ARF today/Going off with Perón, come from afar/To wage what is now the people's war*. How does that idea strike all of you? Meanwhile, thousands of doves will come flying out and the girls from the Evita Association will let balloons loose, the Old Man will open his arms from the dais and everyone will burst into tears, it'll knock everybody's socks off, and it'll be like a dream for him too.

The cigarette he has just smoked leaves an aftertaste of moss and beetles on Nun's tongue. Smelling Diana, seeing her lips chapped from the winter cold (she claims it's from life), Nun wishes that everything was already over and done with and that they had no other horizon in front of them except that of his confused, burning desires: to take their pleasure with each other and learn and unlearn each other so as to meet for the first time all over again. He still can't believe that they're here, together: a distraction on nature's part, an unrepeatable benevolence on history's part.

Nun's skin is still irritated from the bonfires that he has made the rounds of, before going to bed, in Cañuelas, Florencio Varela and Berisso. He has seen the comrades multiply on the outskirts of Llavallol, as though they were walking on mirrors. When he passed by a newsstand, in Temperley, he bought the afternoon edition of *Crónica* and *La Razón*, and a special edition of *Horizonte* dedicated to the General – 'Perón: His Life Story – The Man, The Leader – Documents and Accounts of a Hundred Witnesses' – in a plastic jacket and with a giant poster portrait of the Great Man, smiling like a warrior eagle.

When he got back to the house, he called to Bighead and Vicki to come down to the living room to have a look at that mercenary filth, but now, as he feels the slow fire of insomnia mount through his body, he leans over the pages of *Horizonte* and reads, disdainfully at first, then filled with alarm by the erosions that the hundred witnesses have left on the patriarch's biographical body. Someone has really seen this Perón who is a stranger to me, Nun keeps saying to himself. Someone has tattooed him with these stories: folding him back in time like a sheet, transfiguring him to match his own limits as a man.

And feeling that Perón is at last about to succeed him, Nun, that Perón will fall onto his conscience like a red-hot brand, he looks into these unexpected pages, as into the abyss.

1 *Identity of His Forebears*

Mario Tomás Perón was never to forget the spring of 1886, when he arrived in Lobos as he was recovering from typhus. The railroad station was still so new that the townspeople celebrated the occasion of the train stopping there by dressing in their very best, as for a Te Deum Mass. The young men in their late teens found a place on the platform at an early hour, ramrod-straight, their hair slicked down with brilliantine, their backs to the wind that blew the tips of their handlebar mustaches downward. The girl cousins strolled about arm in arm . . . sensing that the boys were exchanging flattering comments about them among themselves. In those days every betrothal owed something to the train.

Mario Tomás Perón, who was then nineteen years old, was tall, deeply tanned, heavyset, and little inclined toward conversation. His pride was the beautiful handwriting that he had perfected at the National Academy; his passion was horses, which he rode and cared for with the skill of a cowboy. He had arrived in Lobos in search of healthy air in order to recuperate from his bout of typhus.

Through his efforts to make him eager to practice medicine, his father had turned him into a horseman. Once a month, Mario saddled up a pair of chestnuts and went with his father to visit the towns of Roque Pérez, Cañuelas and Navarro, where his scattered patients lived. Since the sight of blood made Mario feel faint, he preferred to spend the time out in the open, with the ranch hands. Many years later, those rides on horseback would kindle in him an abiding fondness for botany and archaeology. When he arrived in Lobos he had in his baggage a herbarium of pampas plants and an essay by Cuvier on mammal fossils.

He was the eldest son of Tomás Liberato Perón and Dominga Dutey, from Paysandú, on the Eastern Shore of the Río de la Plata, whose family had emigrated from Chambéry in Haute Savoie. She was twenty-two years old when she married, at the end of February 1867. She was a widow, and her daughters from her first marraige, Baldomera and Vicenta Martirena, would have a greater influence on the life of the Peróns than all their blood relations put together.

Tomás Liberato was descended from a Sardinian, Tomás Mario, and a Scotswoman, Ana Hughes, who came from around Dumbarton. For at least four generations all the Peróns had the same first names, so that their mothers would always have a Mario or a Tomás to remind them of their husband, and because their lineage – Ana Hughes used to say – was transmitted not only through their name but also through the holy oil of baptism.

Mario Tomás was born on 9 November 1867, as an epidemic of cholera was breaking out in Buenos Aires. His father was too busy investigating the hygiene of the salting plants even to attend the delivery. In the years that followed, Mario Tomás saw his sons only when they accompanied him on visits to patients who lived a long distance away, the boys riding behind him with the saddle bags full of provisions and cupping glasses.

At the time that Mario Tomás arrived in Lobos, Don Tomás Liberato was wasting away, weak and listless. He spent weeks at a time cooped up in his laboratory, studying the habits of locusts. He didn't even realize that his eldest son had left home.

A little over a mile away from the main square of Lobos, along the highway, the bricklayer Juan Irineo Sosa and his wife, Mercedes Toledo, had been living since 1870 in an adobe and wattle hut that they had built with the help of neighbors. The floor was of beaten earth. In the beginning, they opened two doors opposite each other so that the air would circulate, but since one of the doors opened onto a disreputable back street . . .

All the banks of reality then overflowed simultaneously. Diana stretches and yawns and her fingers reach out toward Nun's back with the swiftness of a spider; he hears though he does not see the passionate leap of the eternal female, calling to him with all the voices of the animal kingdom. And at that point Vicki Pertini knocks at the door, timidly but urgently.

'Hey, can you two come for a sec? They're shitting bullets at each other on the bridge! The Faschos have grabbed the dais.'

Nun lays the copy of *Horizonte* aside. 'Hear that, Diana?'

She has heard so clearly that she can give an on-the-spot description of the scene, even in a voice thick with sleep: 'It's not even six in the morning yet, and the fight for the three hundred yards has already begun.'

But Vicki Pertini, as usual, has alerted them in vain. With his mood darkened by his cigarette and lightened by a bitter maté, Nun Antezana arranges in order the reports that continue to reach him from the presumed front line. He follows all the developments in his mind. The incident on the bridge has been nothing more than a skirmish between two small groups with no political affiliation. There were shots, true enough, and a man has been wounded – one of ours, one of theirs? No one knows his name. He has been taken to the Ezeiza hospital with a bullet wound in his gut. They are most likely operating on him. As for the rest, Vicki's fears have a certain basis in fact: a thousand henchmen of López Rega's and of the Trade Union Youth Movement have woven an iron braid around the dais. They have occupied a school, a hundred yards to the south, on Route 205. And they are blocking the access roads. Wasn't that what we expected? Yes, it was, Pepe Juárez sighs. But we hoped for a miracle: a mass attack of diarrhea or for Perón to give orders against such tactics. What should we do? We never have any luck when we're really up against it.

Bighead comes back from a patrol. We've got a following wind, he announces good-humoredly: Operation 20 June is proceeding at full sail. He has seen more than a thousand comrades marching down Route 3 with provisions of powdered milk and sacks of bread. They are wearing ski masks and ponchos, as though the festivities were going to last a month. Near La Salada, a mile and a half or so to the north, he has dropped in on an encampment of pampas herders who are improvising musical dialogues in the General's honor. I cleared out of there, he tells them, because it spooked me: for those guys time has stood still. They talk as though Perón had never left. And I came here asking myself what we're going to do with all of them, what country we're going to put them in.

They feel the day rising – falling – at last. Sun is pouring in from somewhere. Nun doesn't know how to control that light and orders them to make it go away – to close the windows for a moment. He assembles his general staff in the dining room, alongside the sand table, and decides to begin the long march now, this minute. Bighead and Vicki will take the Leyland buses to the Llavallol traffic circle; Pepe Juárez and the shantytown volunteers will follow them on foot, along the train tracks, to the Beltway. He, Nun, and Diana will guide the columns from Monte Grande and Cañuelas to Route 205. At noon, all of them will rendezvous below the water tower on the Calle Almafuerte, a quarter of a mile behind the dais.

Before leaving, they take a quick look at the ghosts photographed in *Horizonte*; they shrug as they linger over the photograph of an inexplicable document, turn a deaf ear to the witnesses who are undermining the Perón myth. And when they leave, the magazine stays there, breathing its last in the shadows, amid the make-believe cities on the sand table.

Since 1870, Juan Irinea Sosa, the bricklayer, and his wife, Mercedes Toledo, had been living in an adobe hut a mile or so away from the main square of Lobos. In the beginning, they opened two doors so that air would circulate through it, but since one of them opened onto a disreputable back street lined with brothels, Juan Irineo had to board it up. They had two double beds – mattresses stretched out on top of lengths of canvas – a couple of iron pots, a washstand with water pitchers and several prints of saints pasted on cardboard backing.

At one end of the room was Juan Irineo's riding gear; in the other was a small looking glass in front of which their two daughters combed their hair. Juana was the older of the two: she had been born on 9 November 1875 and had spent her childhood on the loose, astride a horse. She whiled away her afternoons drinking maté in the shack next door or nosing about amid the guitar-strumming in the general store.

Both parents knew nothing of their origins: they surmised that they were confused and complicated. There were too many Toledo Sosas, Sosa Toledos and just plain Toledos in the family, with relationships so unbelievably incestuous they beggared belief. Halfbreeds with blond hair, whom Juana called her cousins, would often pass through town. They put them up without asking any questions, not out of fear that they would lie about their origins, but because they might reveal a truth impossible to bear.

One biographer of the family presumes, with no documentation to support him, that Juan Irineo's parents came from Old Castile. Juana would tell her neighbors in Cabo Raso a different story: 'They were brought up near Guasayán, in Santiago del Estero. And as far as I know, they were of pure Indian blood.'

When Mario Tomás met Juana, in 1890, both of them were still in mourning for their parents. It was sleep that had done Don Tomás Liberato in. One fine day, after months of insomnia, a need to sleep overtook him in the middle of the countryside. He stretched out on his saddlebags on the bank of a small stream, and when he woke up, drenched with sweat, such a sudden, violent fever had come over him that death didn't even give him time to change clothes.

Juan Irineo's last illness had come as a sudden surprise too. On coming home from his fields one afternoon, he ordered his wife to tie his clothes in a bundle and prepare food for a long journey. 'Where are we going?' she asked. 'I'm going off by myself,' he said, and there and then, he vomited up a black water. 'Just look at what death has done to me,' he complained, as he fell to the floor with his eyes clouded over.

The daughters were left so helpless that they were forced to hire themselves out as servants in gringos' houses. That was where Mario Tomás met them. Juana charmed him at first sight. When she served at table at the Cornfoots', she treated guests more haughtily than the young ladies of the family. She had a round, Indian face. Beneath her bright little eyes were high, imperious cheekbones. Her nose, coarse and broad, and her large mouth, with its ready laugh, went well together.

Among the townspeople of Lobos there is a vague memory, or

rather a conjecture, that she was meeting Mario in secret in Las Garzas ravine. Many years later, one of Juana's cousins would compare their romance with the Hugo Wast stories that she had seen at the movies, although this time there was a happy ending and the seducer from a good family did not abandon the fatherless peasant girl.

Early in the fall of 1891, Juana discovered that she was pregnant. Another of her cousins, Francisca Toledo, told how the girl felt so bewildered by the disturbances in her body that she was experiencing that she mistook the signs that she was pregnant for liver attacks.

Mario Tomás was also taken aback by the news. 'If I marry,' he wrote to his brother Tomás Hilario, 'my poor mother is going to get terribly upset. People here have advised me to put things right with the girl by giving her a bit of money and then forget the whole thing.' But he did nothing: he let time go by.

The baby was born on 30 November 1891, with the help of Aunt Honoria and Cousin Francisca. Thirteen months later, on Christmas Eve, they baptized him Mario Avelino Sosa in the parish church. Mario Tomás, elated, asked his brother Tomás Hilario to come from Buenos Aires to stand as godfather.

Years of such profound drowsiness came over Lobos that even the dust, when the feather dusters brushed it off the furniture, fell back in place in the same pattern. In 1896 the first streets were paved with cobblestones and the sidewalks roped off. The rumor that there was going to be a war with Chile reached the town very late, after the peace protocols had been signed, and to celebrate that lack of news the Lobos Athletic Club organized sack races, cockfights and jumping contests, attended by three thousand people of the region.

The main street of the town was called Buenos Aires. The Moores had a house on it, with balconies on either side of the entryway, venetian blinds, a fig tree and a jasmine vine in the courtyard. At the end of 1891 Mario Tomás asked them to take him in as a boarder. They gave him the room on the right, on the street side, where he lived almost up to the day he left Lobos.

For several months, between 1893 and 1894, he worked as an officer of the law. Juan Torres, his closest friend, used to urge him to leave that job that he detested so much and set up housekeeping once and for all with Juana, a long way away from Lobos, so that people wouldn't go on tormenting her with humiliations and insults when she went to do the washing at the gringos' houses.

Indecisive by nature, Mario Tomás didn't dare cause scandal, but neither could he bring himself to drop Juana. At the beginning of 1895, she was pregnant again.

The news disheartened the good families in Lobos. Don Eulogio del Mármol, whom Dr Perón had asked to 'look after his son' removed Mario Tomás from the scene by giving him a job as manager of one of his ranches, Los Varones. The ladies of the town proved to be less kindly. They ordered their daughters to cross to the other side of the street when they spied Mario, and forbade them to mention his name at social gatherings. 'Nothing is as contagious as a bad reputation,' Don Eulogio's wife used to say.

Mario, meanwhile, enjoyed his solitude. Before the sun was up, he would head outdoors, take the horses out to graze, look after the crops and clear underbrush away. He promised himself never to trade that free country life for the life to which he believed he was predestined.

On 8 October 1895, as he was riding toward Roque Pérez driving a little herd of horses half broken in, some of the hands caught up with him to tell him that his second son was being born. He rushed back to the ranch at a gallop.

2 *The First Years*

On the leather thong bed where she had slept since childhood, aided only by Cousin Francisca, Juana had a far easier delivery this time than she had had when Mario Avelino was born. The Toledos had made preparations to welcome a girl. Even the diapers that Granny Mercedes hemmed had little pink ribbons. And Aunt Honoria, who had decided to give the newborn baby her silver earrings, prayed that God would miraculously change its sex because it was the wrong one.

The first photo taken of the baby, at five months, shows how much he resembled his mother: he had the same thick coal-black hair, a face with the same Indian features, eyes precociously immune to surprise. More than two years went by before he was baptized because his father wanted him to be named Tomás Alberto, and his mother Juan Tomás. Since there was no way to get them to agree, Aunt Honoria decided that they should name him Juan to please the Toledos, and Domingo after his paternal grandmother. On 14 January 1898, they took him to the old parish church, now almost in ruins, where Cousin Francisca and Juan B. Torres stood as god-parents.*

---

*In 1971, José López Rega revealed that Juan Domingo's birth in 1895 was really the beginning of the latter's fifth life. In his previous ones he had been Per-O, an Egyptian queen whose name means 'The Big House' and who ruled over the villages of the Upper Nile in 3500 BC; Rompe, the fish with a snout that is an electric sword and lives in the marine trenches situated to the east of Isla Desengaño; Norpe, a mastiff that bit Marco Polo in Cathay and paid for its disrespect by being poisoned to death with ground glass; and the Jesuit priest Dominique de Saints-Pères, who was Descartes's teacher at the boys' school of La Flèche and was killed by a bolt of lightning on the Perron estate, where he was the guest of his pupil. In 1970, Perón admitted that he had signed some of his articles with the pseudonym Descartes 'because the philosopher used my surname (Perron) and I should like to return the favor'.

As soon as Juan Domingo learned to sit up alone, his father put him astride a chestnut horse and took him for a ride across the pampas, teaching him the language of the animals, harvests and rains. Don Eulogio del Mármol gave him a dappled pony and entrusted him to the care of one of his ranch hands, the 'Chino' Magallanes, who was to teach the boy to ride at a gallop. Sisto (the 'Chino') was a rustic, childish creature, whom they kept locked up on nights where there was a full moon because he used to climb up to the tops of the windmills so as to take off and fly. But he had an unusual gift as a teacher: in a drawling baritone, he would explain the reason for droughts and the curious phenomenon of earthworms as though there were no simpler truths in the world.

Mario Tomás very soon grew bored with that sedentary life. At the end of 1898 he sold his riding gear and saddles, ended his relationship with Don Eulogio on good terms, and left with Juana and the boys for land owned by Juan Atucha, near Roque Pérez, where he leased a farm and several plots of pasture land. The house they had to live in and the isolation of the place was not at all to their liking. After three months they moved to the hacienda of a certain Dr Viale, who leased several acres of land to them.

In February – or perhaps in March – of 1899, Juana and Cousin Francisca were washing clothes alongside a well. Juana was seven months pregnant and the suffocating heat made her short of breath. Near them, Juan Domingo was catching toads and doing his best to train them with a willow rod. It was midday. The women finished wringing out the sheets and were hanging them on the clotheslines in the yard. 'If I take one step more, the baby's going to come out my throat,' Juana said.

Francisca, believing that her cousin was about to deliver, took her in to bed. She was about to place cold compresses on her head when she heard Juan Domingo give a cry. She ran, saw the willow rod on the rim of the well and realized immediately that the boy had fallen in. She thought she could make out the boy's body floating on the gleaming surface of the water. She threw the bucket in, trying to fish him out. On the second try she was able to rescue him. He was unconscious and full of scrapes and scratches.

Months of boredom followed. Mario Tomás spent his nights sitting up in bed, not feeling like sleeping and even less like working those fields that belonged to someone else. Juana, who knew how the bouts of insomnia in the Perón family ended up, was afraid that Mario too would be consumed by discontent. When she heard him wake up, she would light a candle, undo her braids and begin to mend the children's clothes as though it were the most natural thing in the world. And talking away about meals and ailments, she kept the man's mind occupied until he forgot his restlessness.

Juana and Mario's third son was fortunately stillborn. He was sickly looking, with greenish skin. Instead of eyes, he had two black eggs, without eyelids. They told Juana that she'd given birth to a tapeworm, and Aunt Honoria never wanted to tell where that evil fetus was buried. The same night it came into the world, Mario Tomás had a foreboding that someone was casting a curse on them. 'We can't stay here any longer,' he decided. 'I'm going to round up the livestock and head south with them.'

Doña Dominga's house was small and white, with a privet hedge around it. It was there that Mario met the Maupas brothers, who were distantly related to the Martirenas and were interested in making bigger profits from their ranches in the Chubut. They soon worked out a good deal. Mario would manage the property at La Maciega – in Cabo Raso, some 150 miles south of Puerto Madryn – would raise his own sheep and divide the profits.

In the spring of 1900, Mario Tomás began the insane journey to the deserts in the south, driving a flock of five hundred sheep. He left Juana in his mother's care.

During the year of involuntary solitude that followed, Juana the intruder took to staying for days at a time at the country estate of Ramos Mejía, pleading so insistently that Doña Dominga finally gave in. Juan Domingo caught chicken pox while there, and his grandmother relieved the itching with hot baths and talcum powder poultices. The little boy had not yet recovered when he came down with whooping cough, and that time it was Baldomera who treated him with a remedy used in days long gone, pushing him on a swing in the park before dawn, when the trees give off oxygen and the air turns blue.

In September 1901 Mario Tomás returned to Buenos Aires, and just as he had promised, on the 25th of that month he married Juana, without a nuptial Mass and without a wedding feast. She signed the marriage certificate in her sprawling, childish handwriting that she would retain into old age; he signed his name with a flourish underneath, in the form of a double ellipse. The last paragraph contained the words: 'The spouses recognized Avelino Mario [sic] and Juan Domingo, both born in Lobos, as their children.'

Two weeks later they embarked for Patagonia on the freighter *Santa Cruz*. The moment she spied the desolate shores of the Chubut and heard the wild winds blow, Juana clearly foresaw that the family would never leave those parts. In a letter to her sister María Luisa she recounted how Juan Domingo, on seeing the pebbles on the beach flaming in the ice-cold sunlight of October, amid flocks of seagulls, had asked her if those birds laid hot coals instead of eggs.

The Peróns disembarked in Puerto Madryn, alongside the railway dock, and waited for the train until the following morning. On one wall of the station there was a bronze plaque

with this ill-omened warning, written in six languages: IT IS 51
MILES WITHOUT WATER FROM HERE TO THE CHUBUT SETTLE-
MENT. When the train entered the sandy hills, it seemed to
them that the horizon withdrew beneath an enormous sheet of
rust and gravel, covered with plumes of tough scrub.

And it was like that as far as the eye could see. In Rawson they
secured a large cart and for a week blazed a trail amid the dunes.
Halfway to their destination a raging windstorm that raised
columns of sand, pebbles and dried manure suddenly overtook
them, forcing them to detour to skirt the deep ravines and steep
slopes. Juan was bewildered to see that in this wasteland where
the wild animals were constantly on the alert for danger, the
sheep went on grazing, their muzzles buried in the broom sedge,
indifferent to everything: the roar of the wind, the fits of fury of
the men and the threats from the sky above.

Mario Tomás had turned La Maciega into a prosperous
ranch, clearing it of underbrush and covering the water holes
after building wooden retaining walls around them. The ranch
covered almost fifteen square leagues, and had nine to ten
thousand sheep and the best house in the region: made of wood,
with a mansard roof, wood stoves and a bathroom with a tub.
Even the old furniture, with deep scratches from the ranch
hands' boots, was waxed and polished.

When the Peróns came to Cabo Raso, a Frenchman, a
widower, whose last name was Robert, was just settling in on a
ranch outside Camarones, about twenty miles to the east. He
arrived on horseback, having left Luján a year before, his
motherless son riding pillion, driving a flock of five hundred
sheep. The rigors of the journey had caused such depredations
that when he arrived all he had left were a hundred sheep and
the scrawny horse he was riding.

Alberto, his son, would recount how they lived in the most
profound desolation: 'We learned to talk to ourselves, so that at

least the sound of own voice would keep us company. Little by little we lost our human ways and began to imitate the behavior of the animals that inhabited those parts. We knew how to control our thirst, turn our heads to one side to avoid the dust and sense the fissures in the ground before setting a foot down.'

The Peróns and the Roberts became inseparable, so as to conjure away all that empty space. Camarones, the town – on the ocean – consisted of ten houses, a general store and the post office. A hotel was under construction in those years, but it soon went under, for the few guests who had sent word that they were coming couldn't bring themselves to get off the boat.

The visits of one family to the other lasted for many days. No one could offer himself the luxury of riding seven leagues in the morning only to have a chat and then ride the seven leagues back the same way that night. Alberto Robert has told how the Peróns would arrive at his house in a cart drawn by three horses, preceded by the bronco buster Pancho Villafañe, who would enter the patio at a gallop, blowing a bugle the way postillions did. Juana instantly took over the kitchen, made an inventory of the provisions and began to produce, in mysterious ways, dishes made of jerky that lasted exactly as long as the visit. Having been trained by the women of the Toledo family, she was such a good midwife that pregnant women used to come all the way from Bustamante Bay and even from Los Mártires Valley, a two-week journey, just so that Juana could turn fetuses about to be born feet first all the way around so that they came out head first, disentangle umbilical cords, and take a good look when the placenta came out to make sure there wasn't a twin still left inside.

Mario Tomás also had skillful hands. With time, his face had crept up toward his forehead. A wattle like a rooster's hung down from his chin. All his strength lay around his blue eyes, hooded by U-shaped eyelids.

By the time he was seven, Juan Domingo had already completed his apprenticeship in the handling of horses. He knew how to lasso, to gallop amid gorges and to clean wounds. Hunting guanacos was his greatest passion. He would post himself in the tree lookouts of La Maciega, observe the movements of the little herds in the distance and trace the plan for the next day's dawn attack.

As he would say later, those attacks were his dress rehearsals for war. The guanacos grazed in the ravines and the foothills, with their bodies blending into the ocher underbrush. Camouflage and speed were their only defenses. When he saw a horseman approaching, the lead guanaco would whinny to warn the females and the young of the herd, and took up with pleasure the challenge of a battle of wits with the hunter.

Nothing delighted Juan Domingo as much as disturbing them by sending them false signals, throwing stones at them or raising dust, far from the places where he had posted himself with rope snares and pitfalls covered with branches. He would enter the gorges and burst out onto the plain to take them by surprise, attacking the little herds from behind, or else come at them from the flanks, where the lead guanaco was often not quite as watchful.

In the spring of 1903 Mario Tomás foresaw a new run of bad luck coming his way. Frozen seas had delayed a letter from the Maupas brothers, informing them that La Maciega no longer belonged to them. Between April and May they had sold it to the Mittau and Grether Company, which insisted on hiring a new manager for it. He was given permission to stay on as an assistant, with the right to graze his sheep on the ranch, but not to share in any of the profits.

He was dumbfounded by the news. He tore up several letters reproaching the Maupas brothers and finally, at Juana's urging, plunged into a voluminous correspondence with the army unit posted in the region and with local ranchers, inquiring whether there were any plots of public land that could still 'be homesteaded for one's own profit'.

He felt his nomad instinct had atrophied. Yet even in those days, completely abandoned as he was, he refused to leave Patagonia. The justice of the peace who had just come to Camarones recommended him to a friend, Luis Linck, who had bought a piece of land in the middle of nowhere, some fifty miles west of Río Gallegos, in the territory of Santa Cruz.

The Peróns took up the hopeless challenge of taming those wilds. One day in October 1903 they boarded a freighter, and reached their destination on All Saints' Sunday. The trail is clear from that time on, for Mario Tomás began to record his impressions down on the blank pages of a *Cooper's Guide*, a farmer's almanac. Chary of expressing any of his feelings, he noted down only changes in the weather, the ups and downs of his health and the epidemics that afflicted the sheep. With neither precision nor enthusiasm he also recorded several courtesy calls to the neighboring ranch, Los Vascos. Only one intimate passage leaps off the page, in his entry for 25 December 1904: 'Tomás Hilario has been dead for four years now. May he rest in God's peace. May God have forgiven him for forcing the wishes of Destiny by his own hand. This is the fate of men whom women pay back by being unfaithful to them. And what would *I* do? What would I, I myself do?' It was the only moment in his life when Mario Tomás's handwriting went all to pieces.

The land they reached had been bought by Luis Linck at the end of 1896. Seven years later, the caretaker's house – the only shelter within miles – was falling to ruin. The snow had melted and frozen again on the surface of the kitchen table many times over, and even the floorboards had been ripped out by the axes of thieving woodcutters. The landscape on the other hand was superb. Around the house was a wide arch of hills, and, farther in the distance, amid the hollows and ravines, were clumps of icicles and enormously tall Chile pines. The ranch, Chankaike, covered twelve square leagues and occupied the vertex of the damp area between the forking branches of the Coyle River.

Mario Tomás hired a sheep herder, Peter Ross, turned the management of the ranch over to him, and with his help rebuilt the house that had fallen to ruins. He devoted many pages of the *Cooper's Guide* to rough sketches of a brand for the cattle, until he finally came up with one that he registered in 1905.

By then, Juan Domingo and Mario Avelino had already gone away, having left Chankaike between April and May of the previous year. They could write their names in a laborious hand, but nobody had taught them to read. Mario Tomás decided to entrust the education of both of them to his half-sister Vicenta, who ran a girls' school in the Calle San Martín, in downtown Buenos Aires, in a house that had long belonged to the family, and occupied the top floor, with Baldomera, Granny Dominga and the fatherless children of Tomás Hilario.

In the *Cooper's Guide* Mario Tomás has noted that no one was waiting for them when they docked at the port of Buenos Aires. Family in tow, he walked through the dock area and climbed up the Calle Corrientes to the city. All of them had a knapsack on their back, carried a cardboard suitcase and had a clay pitcher and a canteen full of water hanging from their waist, for the Peróns could no longer remember worlds that were not made of dust or people who lacked a ready source of drinking water.

When they were within a few paces of the corner of San Martín, Juan Domingo tried to climb over a wall to gather some mulberries, but he couldn't get over it and fell, skinning his nose on the plaster. A wan-faced gentleman, dressed in a black frock coat and a bowler hat, hastened to lift him up and wiped away the blood with an immaculate handkerchief.

Mario Tomás thanked him and told the gentleman his name: Perón. 'A member of the doctor's family?' the man wanted to know. 'His son,' Mario answered, 'but nobody can tell because I've become a country boy.' 'I'm from the country too,' the man admitted, tipping his hat to Juana, 'and you can't know how much I regret that nobody can tell that that's where I'm from.' Without further ado he cut off a branch of mulberries for the children and handed Mario his card. 'At your service,' he said as he took his leave of them.

Juan Domingo entered Aunt Vicenta's house with his mouth as purple as a heart patient's, and was not allowed to kiss his grandmother until he'd brushed his teeth. Before going to bed, he told María Amelia the story about the gentleman and asked his father to show everyone the card.

The girl kept that little card tucked into one of her school composition books. Years later, she saw the gentleman in the frock coat from a balcony on the Avenida de Mayo. He was riding by himself in a carriage, and the crowd was applauding him. María Amelia threw him a bouquet of sweet peas and, all excited, shouted with the others: 'Long live the President of the Republic!' But she didn't remember the card even when Cousin Juan Domingo, in 1930, joined a conspiracy to overthrow the gentleman, or when the gentleman died, in July 1933, and she herself insisted on walking in procession behind the coffin to Recoleta Cemetery, amid washerwomen in black mantillas who wept every step of the way.

In the jewelry box she inherited from Doña Dominga, underneath the wedding ring of her late husband and a medallion discovered among her father Tomás Hilario's clothes, on the night of the suicide, María Amelia still has the gentleman's card, faded now from being buried amid her school composition books for so long:

Hipólito Yrigoyen

HACIENDA LOS MÉDANOS

3 *The Terrible Revelation*

Two days after their arrival in Buenos Aires, when Juan Domingo awakened and discovered his parents had gone off without saying goodbye to him, abandoning him to the care of those severe ladies whom he scarcely knew, he fell into the depths of despair. As the inconsolable little boy kept weeping and pounding on the floor with his fists, Aunt Baldomera brought holy water from the Church of La Merced to sanctify his thoughts. Leaving her dolls aside, María Amelia tried to hug and kiss him. That only made things worse. Juan Domingo was assailed by the tremors of one possessed. When he went to bed he screwed up the sheets and then tore them to shreds. They had to lock him in his room and wait till he had finished giving vent to his wrath. In case he fell into another fit of fury, Vicenta and Baldomera hastened to drape cloths over the grandfather clock, the pride of the house, on the face of which were the figures of farmhands cast in bronze.

For two days and nights Juan Domingo's weeping racked his

cousin's heart. At one point, she woke up and knocked on his door: 'Do you want some water, Juancito?'

'What I want is for you to drop dead,' she heard him answer. 'I want all of you to drop dead.'

Time washed away these sadnesses too. In the afternoons, Cousin Julio went with Juan to catechism classes in the parish church of La Merced. Both of them served as altar boys on Sundays at the seven o'clock Mass. In the mornings they learned the alphabet in the school on the downstairs floor, Calle San Martín 458, the official name of which was 'Upper School for Girls, Section 7', despite the fact that nine of the thirty pupils were boys.

Since he was several years older than most of the others, Juan Domingo was the leader of their games. He invented high-speed multiplication races and memory exercises using paragraphs taken from their current text-book. Taller, stronger, fatter and ruder, he took advantage of Mario Avelino's passivity and Julio's precocious melancholia, and constantly bullied them and embarrassed them in front of the others by tripping them and hitting them behind the knees with a big stick.

In 1905, María Amelia noticed that Juan was doing contradictory things. All of a sudden he spent all the money he'd saved on buying her a doll, and when he gave it to her warned her: 'Every time you play with it, just remember that I was the one who gave it to you, you hear? *I* was the one.' And the same day, or the next, he spattered ink on her spotless school composition books. Aunt Vicenta excused his misbehavior, thinking that the passage of time would be the cure for it. Baldomera, however, unburdened herself of her apprehensions to Dominga: 'What can be happening inside that boy, Mama? Can it be the result of his being abandoned, of what he felt when they left him behind by himself? Or is it his nature, this temperament of a Spanish-speaking Indian he's inherited from Juana? Sometimes, when I take a good look at him, I have the impression that he must not have a drop of blood left in his body; it's as though it had been drained of feelings. But as soon as the boy realizes that I'm looking at him, he puts on a feeling as though it were an article of clothing: he gives me hugs and kisses, he seeks affection, he cries, he laughs for all he's worth. I've never seen a child like that, so dark inside and so aglow outside . . .'

Men are fated to be remembered for their excessive acts, not their trivial ones. In Juan Perón's case, the opposite has happened: the most famous incident of his childhood is irrelevant. The story that changed his life, on the other hand, has remained in the dark.

As for the first of the two, it will suffice to know that Doña Dominga Dutey had inherited from her husband the skull of Juan Moreira, a legendary gaucho who was shot down in cold blood by the police in the yard of La Estrella, a brothel, at the entrance to Lobos. And as darkness was falling, before the aunts lighted the kerosene lamps in the house in Buenos Aires, Juan Domingo and Cousin Julio used to scare the housemaids half to death by lighting the skull from inside with tallow candles.

The second story took place between February and March 1909. Fifteen months before, put to flight by the sub-zero temperatures in Santa Cruz and by certain misunderstandings with Don Luis Linck, the owner of Chankaike, Mario Tomás Perón had headed back north again, finally settling down about nine miles away from Camarones and three or four from the ocean, on public land that covered half a square league. All he had left to his name was a flock of a hundred sheep, almost all of them afflicted with mange, which owed their survival to the creosote baths given them by Doña Juana.

Mario Avelino, who had been brought back to Patagonia because he was suffering from an intractable case of bronchitis, was the one who hit on the name for the new ranch: 'Have we arrived where we were headed for, Papa? So this is what you called the future?' he asked as they took the furniture out of the cart, fighting the wind.

The house at El Porvenir – The Future – was built by Don Mario Tomás so halfheartedly and with so little concern for their comfort that the family came inside it only when it was time for bed. It was an adobe hut, with a doorway so low they had to stoop to pass through it. To the west there was a window that was only about a foot and a half wide, with flimsy wooden shutters. The couple's double bed was next to the entrance, to the right, separated from the boys' camp bed by a cretonne curtain. The farm tools and the saddles were kept at the other end of the hut. To eat in or to take shelter from the cold, the Peróns preferred the ranch hands' bunkhouse, where some obliging soul always kept the braziers lit.

Once a week, Don Mario visited the justice of the peace in Camarones, and after a long conversation about the epidemics raging among the sheep and the forays of the pumas, Don Mario lent him his fine handwriting to record the title deeds, sales of horses and births of humans in the official registers.

'I am gradually learning the duties of a judge,' Mario Tomás's next to last entry in the *Cooper's Guide*, dated 6 December 1908, reads. 'Romero has promised to leave me the post when he leaves here. I need to practice my penmanship more.' And the last one, two days later: 'The frigate *Quintana* is expected to pass by this way tomorrow, a mile or so out to sea. I am certain it is bringing Juan here on vacation.'

Each year, when school let out, Juan Domingo went to a great deal of trouble to get passage on a boat going south. He was obliged to wander about the docks of Buenos Aires for several days, asking whether this or that fishing boat would be venturing as far as the Golfo San Jorge and, if so, whether they would take him aboard as a passenger. Or else he would find passage on a merchant ship about to set out for Chile, sailing through the Strait of Magellan.

It was often rough going for the boats. Beyond the Valdés Peninsula no captain put his boat at risk by sailing close in to shore. And so the passengers got ashore as best they could. Juan had the good fortune to be picked up by a tugboat captain from Camarones who knew those waters and was skilled at avoiding the treacherous tides. But even when the passengers reached land their anxieties were not over. They kept slipping as they clambered up the rough gravel of the beach, and often a wave would catch them and knock them down.

As his father foresaw, Juan arrived on 9 December. His friend Alberto Robert was waiting for him near the dock with two saddled Percherons and went with him to El Porvenir, without even once getting his fill of hearing about Buenos Aires, where the trains ran like moles through the bowels of the earth and the carriages galloped along all by themselves.

Juan Domingo was three years older than Alberto and had nothing but scorn for him. Alberto admired him for his lynx's eyesight, his unbelievable strength and his way of insulting people. Sometimes, as they calmly rode along, Juan would unexpectedly dismount, saying: 'The last one down is a clumsy jerk.' Or else, teaching Alberto his vowels, he had him write: 'Mama is a *pata*, mama is a *peta*, mama is a *pita*,' and so on.

Although Juan was very good at hunting guanacos, he had to admit that Alberto was better still. The boy knew which stretches were full of holes made by rodents – that the horses' hooves could sink into so easily – sensed what path the guanacos had taken when the herd dispersed and what refuges the females ran to so as to hide their young. 'You've got the instincts of a dog,' Juan complimented him.

On a certain morning in February, or perhaps March, 1909,

Juan Domingo went with his father on one of his visits to Judge Romero. A scorching heat was coming down off the high plateaus. They were riding along in the sulky, not opening their mouths so as not to eat dust. Dropping behind, Alberto followed them on a dark brown mare. They must have ridden just a little less than a league when, as they crossed through a hollow, Alberto sensed the presence of a herd of guanacos nearby.

Juan Domingo went out of his mind with excitement. He had never been that close to so many of them together. What excited him most about this hunt was imagining the advantageous position he would have: hidden in the ditch, waiting impatiently to leap out and surprise the guanacos and then knock them over with a sudden lash of his riding whip. He pictured them, their every sense on the alert, wandering across the plain in search of the dark spot where death would blow them to bits.

But Alberto wasn't all that certain. Using signs, he pointed out the drawbacks: Juan would have to leap out of the sulky onto the mare's rump, crouching down, not making a sound, as Don Mario Tomás turned the sulky around and went off, without picking up his pace. And even supposing that the guanacos suspected nothing, they had to keep in mind that when they fled at a gallop there was no horse that could catch up with them.

They went ahead anyway. Juan leaped onto the mare as his father headed the sulky toward Camarones. For a moment, the boys waited, not moving a muscle, holding their breath. The wind favored them, blowing the rusty odor of the guanacos their way. All of a sudden, they heard the whinny of a female above their heads.

'Now!' Juan shouted, putting his spurs to the mare. And they rushed out onto the plain. A *chulengo* – a soft, defenseless baby guanaco – crossed their path. Alberto broke its neck with his whip. He did not have time to raise it again. At that sole lightning-swift lash, the herd fanned out and disappeared behind some sand dunes. One of the animals lingered behind the others, at a slow gallop. 'It's the baby guanaco's mother and she'll come back for it in a while. We'll wait for her right here, in hiding,' Alberto calculated. Juan refused: he was certain he'd wounded another of the herd. And he insisted on following its trail across the open plain.

They went on for about half a mile beneath a sun so murderous they felt as though it was inside their heads. Finally, from the top of a hill, they spied the herd. Juan dismounted, rifle in hand, and fell flat on his face. The knife-sharp edge of a stone lodged in his left arm, making a broad slash in it. The blood spurted into his face. He didn't give the slightest whimper, but his gun slipped out of his hands and that negligible noise, muffled by the dust, was enough to cause the herd to take fright and gallop off.

Juan Domingo was not concerned about the searing wound but, rather, about the amount of blood he was losing. He tore his shirtsleeve into strips with his teeth and, aided by Alberto, bound up his arm. But the blood kept flowing. The sound of their own voices frightened them. The wind, moreover, was seething with boiling clouds of dust. They couldn't gallop. The mare covered, at a walk, the league and a half back to El Porvenir.

When they arrived there was a heavy, unusual silence. They saw the sheep grazing in the distance. Some ranch hands were keeping watch over them, drinking maté, in the shade of a scraggy tree. They tied the mare to a hitching post and went into the kitchen, looking for help. There was no one there.

'Mama?' Juan called out anxiously. But the minute he raised his voice, the silence drowned it out. 'Where can my mama have gone?'

They looked for her in the ranch hands' bunkhouse. She

wasn't there. They ran toward the house then. They found the door closed but not bolted. Alberto pushed it open, quietly and politely. And what he saw was one of those images that can never be forgotten: the parasite that kept making his memory ache for years.

To the left of the door, stuck into the horse's tail that held combs, there was a white one, with a handle and wide teeth, that didn't belong to anyone in the family. To the right, on the double bed, he saw the naked forms of a man and a woman, bucking and rearing. The cretonne curtain had fallen in the furious skirmish.

'Mama,' Juan Domingo called out again.

Alberto turned around. And caught on the face of his friend a grimace of inhuman suffering. 'Mama,' he heard him repeat. He did not want to look at him. He heard Juan leave the house and go hide among the sheep pens. In a little while the sound of ragingly angry tears reached his ears.

Doña Juana ran out into the blazing sun and blowing dust with her braids undone. She had put a man's poncho on over her kitchen smock. Behind her, in the dimness of the bedroom, Alberto made out Benjamín Gómez, a herder, putting on his boots.

Juan Domingo's mother wanted to cleanse his wound, but the boy wouldn't let her touch him. He slowly washed the blood off by himself, as Alberto kept pouring more water into the wash basin. One of the bronco busters came to bind up his arm.

'I've come down with the flu,' Doña Juana explained. 'I started shivering all over, really hard, and Benjamín offered to put some cupping glasses on me and give me a rubdown.'

Juan Domingo shook his head. 'Mhmm, mhmm.' That was all he said. His mother worriedly turned to Alberto, hoping he would understand. 'I don't want the two of you going to Mario Tomás and telling tales. Don't upset him. Or Mario Avelino either. Men who talk about women's ailments find their balls rotting away and their dong going to pieces.'

The next day, with the slash in his arm still swollen, Juan Domingo put the riding whip and the gun away in the winter trunk, packed his knapsack, and without saying goodbye to his mother, rode off toward Camarones. He wandered about the town for a week, sullen and silent. He had no appetite for the food that Alberto brought him and spent his nights on a cot provided by the chief of police. That long penance ended when a freighter, the *Primero de Mayo*, anchored in sight of the port, in a calm, transparent sea, to pick up some bales of wool that it was to take to Buenos Aires.

It was the one time that Juan Domingo did not turn his head to say goodbye as he climbed up the gangway.

6 *A Party at the Villa*

'This isn't me any more,' President Cámpora says on the morning of Sunday 17 June, when he still has three, four days to wait before taking the General back with him to Ezeiza. 'I am not myself but the man that Perón has created.' Entire nights without a wink of sleep have furrowed his face with bad omens and failures. The circles under his eyes, which are less pronounced at festive moments, are now deep black pouches, as though there were something shameful hidden in them. He is wearing pajamas and a bathrobe in bright colors, somewhat the worse for wear from his restless movements. Drowsing in the armchairs of the bedroom that Franco has assigned him, overlooking the grounds of Moncloa Palace, several trusted advisers are keeping him company. All of them are exhausted. They have arrived in Madrid on Friday, the morning of the 15th, after a thirteen-hour flight, and Spanish protocol has given them no respite. Just the night before they have had to put up with two hours of speeches at the welcome banquet offered by the Generalissimo. They got to bed at two a.m. At four-thirty, Cámpora started summoning them, one after the other, seeking their advice. The meaning of the story he is telling is full of obscure, ominous clues.

Why has General Perón left us all by ourselves like this? Why is he humiliating us, snubbing us? Two hours before leaving Buenos Aires I asked him over the phone if he would meet us at the airport, if he would attend the banquets, if he would answer Franco's toasts in his honor himself or would rather I did. Don't worry, Cámpora, he answered me. Set your mind at rest. And then he didn't turn up anywhere. Most embarrassing. Franco was annoyed. And will the General be coming along? he kept asking. I tried to reassure him: He has promised to come. Let's wait for him for just a moment longer. But he never did show up. And later, when I asked why he had been so rude, do you know what the General's reaction was? He roared with laughter! What can I tell you? he said, clapping me on the back. I'm sick, can't you see that? And I answered him: Fortunately I see that that isn't true, General. I find you hale and hearty, thank God. Then he stopped laughing. I'm having one of those terrible memory attacks (that was how he put it). I'm in pain from the promises you made me, Cámpora, and then never kept. And these twelve years of Franco's treating me like a pariah, not even answering my letters: they're giving me terrible stabbing pains in my memory. Have I let you down, sir? I asked him. Tell me what I could possibly have done, so I can make amends immediately. He didn't let up on me one bit. Think, Cámpora, think . . . Who made you a candidate? To whom do you owe the presidency? If it was up to me, I wouldn't mind either way. But there are thousands of Peronists who are furious at you. They want to kick you out of office, rub out your sons . . . Ah, that above all else: they want to blow your sons' heads off with a revolver. And what shall I advise them to do? he asked me. I stared at him, not believing my ears. I felt as if an icicle was piercing me to the marrow. Advise them? What do you mean? I said to him. Order them to have pity on me, General. Order them? I can't. What would I do next if they disobeyed me? I'm going to try to persuade them instead. Keep calm, boys. Cámpora's a good man. Give him a little time to force his sons to resign and repent of his nepotism. Didn't he say himself that he's Perón's number one servant? Don't they call you my uncle, my most loyal supporter? I speak up for you, Cámpora. If I were you, however, my mind wouldn't be at ease. If just one Peronist thinks you're a traitor, then nobody can save you. The General spoke as if our fate was of no concern to him. I still don't understand it, I don't know what to do, I keep racking my brain wondering how we failed him.

'We're guilty of holding back too long,' one of the aides says. 'This is what I think: that the day after we took over we should all have resigned and offered Perón the presidency. That was what he was hoping: that we'd do just that immediately.'

Cámpora laboriously heaves himself out of bed. Sprawled out in the armchairs, the men he has kept up most of the night puff anxiously on their cigarettes. Every so often, to console their bodies, they ask for a little coffee: it is always cold by the time it arrives.

'We haven't held back at all,' the President says, shaking his head. He tries to smooth down his few strands of hair stiff with hair cream as he puts his slippers on. 'Our time ran out, rather, as we were trying to hurry him along. Come back, General. Come, we need you. As early as March, here in Madrid, I said to him: Sir, what if, in the speech I deliver when I take the oath of office, I announce my resignation then and there and call for immediate elections? What if I explain that I am only your representative and that the people have voted for me as such, without a single one of those votes being for me personally? That would be premature, Cámpora, he answered. The military would stage a coup the very next day. There's no danger of that, I insisted. Nobody likes the military. They won't have a consensus. But he stood his ground: Listen to me, Cámpora. I know my flock. When the military come out shooting and killing, your friends will be scared shitless. Not even the dogs will try to defend you. I asked him what to do: Shall I stay in office for a month, two months? You'll know the answer to that, he told me. That's why I made you President.'

They open the windows and the cold damp air creeps in. They hear insects waking up. But it is still night there inside, consuming them. Their throats feel dry. 'A whisky now?' one of the men suggests. 'No. It's out of the question,' Cámpora stops him. 'We must (or at least I must) take communion this morning.'

A woman in glasses finally dares to say: 'He tried to put you to the test, Doctor Cámpora. That's my only guess, knowing Perón. He thought that the minute you took over, you'd come to fetch him. On the q.t., behind the scenes. With the General at Ezeiza, a military coup would no longer be possible: nobody's going to stage an uprising against him. That's what he told you, between the lines. But you remained in office, played billiards in Flores, ordered the police to forget about repressing the people, had a shipment of corn sent to Cuba, signed the social pact between workers and management, raised wages and kept prices down. You did the unforgivable. You became popular. Perón could put up with anything from you except rivalry on issues of that sort. It upset his liver. And in one respect you disobeyed him outright, Doctor Cámpora: you let the guerrillas out of prison. Twelve hours after taking office, instead of flying to Madrid, you pardoned political prisoners. Hasn't anyone told you that the General was outraged when he found out? That he was heard to say: Cámpora is a numbskull. Even drug dealers went free. Don't you remember?'

'Yes, but I don't understand. I was obedient, loyal. I told him last night: General, in the name of history I swear that if I erred in any way it was because I obeyed your orders to the letter. And I showed him the diaries with the statements he issued in Lima on 20 December 1972. I remember them word for word. "The first measure that a Peronist government would take would be to throw the prisons open immediately; there are more than 1500 persons still behind bars . . ." Do you know what his answer to me was? That the worst of my faults was being obedient. That I didn't obey this order or that, but all of them, blindly. Of the seven senses that a man ought to have, the one you lack, Cámpora, is a sense of the right moment. He told me something else: that I misinterpret his hermeneutics.'

'And then you were expected to place the presidential sash across his chest and leave the cermonial staff of office at the villa,' a press officer points out.

'I tried to give everything back to him: even my first salary check as President. What other attitude did the situation call for? He told me that he was the one in command and I was to act accordingly.'

Suddenly birds break into loud song. The shadows dissolve into cockcrows and barking. They order coffee again, hot, freshly made.

'It's too late to go back and do things differently,' the woman in glasses murmurs.

'And what shall I wear now?' Cámpora frets. 'The General has ordered me to take communion with him at the seven o'clock Mass and I have no idea what I should wear. He'll make fun of me if I wear sports clothes. He'll say: Is that any way to respect the office you hold? And if I wear a suit, he'll be dressed in sports clothes. He'll say to me: Only you would ever think of getting all spruced up at this hour in the morning. I don't know, he disconcerts me more and more. Ask my wife what she's decided to wear. The General wants her to take communion too. Ah, a tailored suit. That's best. Discreet. With a hat? A mantilla?'

He collapses in an armchair, a nervous wreck. He carefully

inserts a cigarette in the mother-of-pearl holder with a filter that he always carries with him. And when he tries to raise it to his lips, he discovers that his hands are trembling. He has smoked a lot in these awful days. His hairline mustache has taken on a yellow tinge.

Never, in all truth, has Cámpora aspired to the blessings of fate that have come his way. In 1943, he was thirty-five years old and had become resigned to his routine as a dentist. His practice was in San Andrés de Giles, west of Buenos Aires. He was a conservative, but there were any number of people in town who believed him to be a radical. On account of these merits, the military governor decided to appoint him town commissioner.

Cámpora did an impeccable job. He dutifully took charge of the town's civic ceremonies, was moved each time the flag was raised, and administered with admirable honesty the few funds entrusted to him. On 12 October 1944 he ascended (as he put it) to 'heaven on earth': he met his leader.

He had been invited to an official opening of a hospital in the city of Junín. The guest of honor was Perón. When they were introduced to each other, Cámpora became effusive: 'You cannot imagine how much I admire you, Colonel.' And he took advantage of the occasion to ask him to honor with his presence the celebration of the feast day of the patron saint of San Andrés, on 30 November. From then on nothing stood in the way of their friendship. Cámpora encouraged the colonel's secret affair with Evita, and in gratitude she decided to adopt him. My gentleman-in-waiting, she called him. In mid-1948, Eva foisted him on the Chamber of Deputies as President. Isn't that going a little too far perhaps, señora? he worried. Don't think, Cámpora: just do as you're told. And Cámpora obediently accompanied her everywhere.

Years later, when Evita was dying of cancer, he once kept watch all night long at her bedside. As day broke and he was putting a damp cloth on her forehead, she affectionately took his hands in hers. Sit down, she said, using the familiar form of address. And for a moment, they gazed into each other's eyes. 'I could have been so many things in life, Cámpora!' (She was ice-cold. Her eyes were going blank.) 'A housewife, a woman who works a farm, a bit actress . . . And just look what I've ended up being. What do *you* think: where can that Evita be? In bed, dying – or happy, putting on weight, with a baby boy in her arms?' (Cámpora was frightened. He wanted to call a doctor.) 'Was it all worth it, do you think? I've no idea what's going on any more. I don't even know what day it is. Here in this bed, nothing makes any difference to me . . . Whether it's afternoon or morning, the whole bit.' (She made as if to get out of bed. And immediately fell back onto the bed. With a sigh she asked:) 'Tell me, what time is it?' And he, in his panic, answered, 'Whatever time you'd like it to be, señora. Whatever time you'd like.'

When Perón was overthrown in 1955, Cámpora was sent to a prison in the Antarctic. This misfortune accentuated his spinelessness. From his cell next door, John William Cooke recounted, in a letter dated 11 April 1957: 'Cámpora has promised God that he will never get mixed up in politics again. He spends the day praying and explaining that he's not a man who fights for a cause.' Later on, Jorge Antonio would tell the rest of the story: 'We made our prison break in the midst of a raging blizzard. Cámpora suffered so much from the cold that he was on the point of death. When he realized he was safe and sound, he raised his hand, gazed heavenward and said: "Almighty God, I swear that I shall never enter politics again!" And tears froze on his cheeks.'

For more than thirteen years being a mere nobody gave him peace of mind. He went back to filling cavities, making dentures, grafting new varieties of hybrid tomatoes in his garden in Giles. Around 1965 he dared, not without misgivings, to write to Perón.

The letter ended with a quotation from Dante: '*En la sua voluntade è nostra pace.*' The General immediately answered: 'Don't carry on like that, man, and as soon as you have a chance drop by Madrid. A friend awaits you here.' He made the trip a couple of times. Walking beneath the trees in Puerta de Hierro, the two of them spent the time recalling their past triumphs. Or rather, Perón did all the recalling, and the other confirmed that his recollections were true.

From then on, Cámpora felt that his life was changing. He was still his same self, the one he had been before, but life escaped him: like a horseman who sees his horse running off into the emptiness of the desert. He continued to play an active role in politics, but always on someone else's account, pushed this way and that by hands that were unknown to him yet ones he nonetheless trusted, for they were hands sent by the General. One morning in November 1971, López Rega telephoned him in San Andrés de Giles, asking him to come to Madrid at once. Perón had just dismissed his political representative, and wanted to entrust the post to Cámpora. Once again, he felt tempted to ask: Isn't that going a little too far perhaps?

So many things began to happen to him that he took no special notice of any of them. He bought a house in the city of Vicente López, just outside Buenos Aires, so that the General could live there when he came back. He fought to free the widow of Juan García Elorrio, the editor-in-chief of *Cristianismo y revolución*, of the charges brought against her. (Juan had died in a mysterious car accident; Casiana, his widow, was put on trial for publishing subversive documents.) He led protest demonstrations whenever a comrade, a popular militant, was tortured to death or mowed down by machine-guns. He confronted the saber blows of the mounted police and tear gas. He waxed eloquent. He launched more violent attacks on military oppression than anyone else. Young people hung on his arm. They went everywhere with him, protecting him, dragging him into the inferno of their battles. In his dreams, Cámpora found himself flying on a magic carpet: was that what history was? One night in June 1972, at the entrance to the hotel Gran Vía, he said in confidence to Nun Antezana and two other friends: It isn't all that bad that a man sometimes has to do things he doesn't want to do.

That year, in November, Perón came out of exile for the first time. He stayed in Buenos Aires for four weeks. Convinced that the military would not allow him to be a candidate for the presidency of the Republic, he chose Cámpora in his stead. 'I have assigned him that post because he is a man of unassailable loyalty,' he told the newspapers. 'Cámpora in office? Well, that means that Perón is headed for power.'

Around that time Zamora wrote an article in *Horizonte*, in such muddy, convoluted prose that nobody paid any attention to it. It alluded, indirectly, to Cámpora. Like everything he wrote, it was really an autobiographical reflection. The reader can ignore it. The novelist cannot.

Every individual, however ordinary he may be, however conventional his natural inclinations, resorts at one time or another to unpredictable behavior: behavior that, while it does violence to his intimate being, also reveals it. We all think we know who we are. None of us is able to foresee what he will really do. For what we do, however contrary to our apparent conscious will, is in the final analysis what we truly are. We are, thus, what we do, rather than what we think or say. Hence Cámpora is observing his acts in astonishment, trying to see if he recognizes himself in them.

The error of philosophy lies in explaining man in terms of what he thinks or perceives. Man is what he is: the tortuous or labyrinthine impulse that impels him to sketch out a life that seldom bears any resemblance to his life plan. Only by living do we know ourselves. Life betrays us.

'Hand me my gray suit,' Cámpora decides as he gets out of the shower. 'I'm going to take communion and I must be appropriately dressed.'

On the ride to Puerta de Hierro he is so exhausted he doesn't say a word. María Georgina, his wife, strokes his hands, raising his spirits. It is not yet six a.m. but the air is already unbearably hot. Once they go through the gate of the villa and walk on amid the dovecotes, they see the General's silhouette in the distance, on the edge of the little brook at the far end of the garden, playing with the poodles underneath an ash tree. He too, as luck would have it, is wearing a suit and tie.

'Have you heard the news on the radio this morning?' Perón says as he comes to meet them, one hand outstretched. 'Absolutely outrageous. They compared me to Don Quixote. They said that a president like you in Argentina is like Sancho Panza on the island of Barataria. Another commentator, on Radio Nacional, makes me out to be the Count of Monte Cristo, going back to my country just to get my own back for the dirt they've done me. And they interviewed an Argentine correspondent. Why can't I remember who it was? The fellow had the nerve to advise me (just imagine, Cámpora) to cut off your head. All that is of no importance whatsoever. They're people who talk to hear themselves talking . . .' Carrying the dogs in his arms, he led the way to the chapel. 'Come, let's go in. Let us make our peace with God.'

Shortly before nine, when the Mass is over, the villa swarms with visitors. In the General's study, playing with the ceramic horses that litter the desk, Giancarlo Elia Valori, *gentiluomo di Sua Santità*, adviser to the Greek colonels, whom Perón takes to be an intimate friend of Paul VI's, is waiting. Prowling about in Valori's wake, as usual, is Don Licio Gelli: disdainful, digging here and there into the accounts of the life of Bartolomé Mitre that adorn the library. Everyone in this house owes him a favor, Valori is in the habit of saying.

Between the anteroom and the dining room hangs a Goyesque collection of portraits: dethroned boxing champions, tango singers, the usual labor bosses and a couple of ambassadors in pin-stripe suits, like gangsters in the movies.

In the kitchen, Doña Pilar – Generalissimo Franco's sister – is hard at work alongside Isabel, deep-frying fritters. Salty vapors rise from below stairs. Perón will serve his guests an Argentine stew.

Feeling himself adrift from everything once again, Cámpora wanders aimlessly about the dining room. He makes out López Rega, behind the screens, eagerly examining the bunch of telexes sent to him from Buenos Aires. Every so often, a message disturbs the secretary. He then asks for a telephone and issues orders. The President does not know to whom they are sent, nor where. Nobody tells him anything.

And he wonders what he is doing here, how to escape from it all. He passes the time looking at the photographs in the dining room, which are soon – the following day – to be taken down and packed: the General on the balconies of Government House holding his arms out to the distant masses; the General parading on his horse Mancha; Evita in an elegant evening gown at the Teatro Colón. He sees himself in two of the photos, permanently smiling. Everything was clearer in that past: everyone wanted to be precisely what he was.

Suddenly María Georgina, whom he is holding by the arm, shudders. She hears the shadow of a malaise weighing heavily upon the house: something, she doesn't know what, a knife cutting through the happiness of these people. If the conversations were not so noisy, if in every corner there were not so many arms pushing and shoving, so many guffaws and hearty greetings, María Georgina would say that a cavernous lament was descending like a vapor from the moldings in the ceiling. Is it Her? The President's wife opens her mouth and immediately hides her astonishment behind her hands.

'Tell me. About Her . . . Isn't she here in this house, upstairs?'

Caught off balance, Cámpora looks at her.

'The deceased?'

'The corpse,' María Georgina nods. 'Isn't Evita still here, up in the attic?'

Cámpora gives a start.

'Shhh, woman. Nobody talks about that here. They don't ever show her. I don't know what they'll do with her. It's best to forget that there's a dead body in this house.'

Shortly after midday, the General – who had gone upstairs to rest – comes down, in a foul mood, to the gardens. He has had nightmares. When Isabel went to wake him up, bringing him a cup of tea, she found him moaning, drenched in sweat. A man who suffers that much from his dreams shouldn't ever sleep, she will sympathize, over lunch.

Doña Pilar, Valori and Licio Gelli find themselves seated together at the General's table. López Rega sits down with his henchmen at Cámpora's. From the very first day he was elected President, Cámpora has sensed the secretary's hostility. War will break out at any moment between the two of them and he presumes that the General, being forced to choose, will protect his, Cámpora's, enemy.

A Spanish journalist, Emilio Romero, has passed on terrible suspicions to him. López is trying to find a place for Isabel in the Government, and Cámpora will be (he says) the only obstacle.

If that is true, I am of little importance, the President countered. The real obstacle is Perón. Romero insists: she, Isabel, is taking it for granted that death will soon remove Perón from the picture. He is an old man, almost seventy-eight years old; he has only to be gently pushed. What I am about to tell you, Cámpora, happened in 1970. And I witnessed it first-hand. It was autumn. Several leaders of the metallurgists' union were visiting the General. As usual, Isabel served tea. A fat man, from San Nicolás I believe, imprudently mentioned Perón's age. He said that to him he looked much younger. That, at that rate, he would never die. We all sat there, frozen to the spot. As you know, Cámpora, one never reminds the General of such things. López broke the ice. He remarked that, unfortunately, all men are mortal; that that was of no importance to the leader; on the other hand, he wanted his doctrine to be immortal. Sometimes, López said, he needs someone to relieve him. Not a successor, but a relief capable of preserving the doctrine just as it is: in its pure state, without a single change. The union leaders thought that López was attempting to take Perón's place and were alarmed: Have you given any thought to who that man might be? Yes, the secretary answered boldly. I've given it considerable thought. Señora Isabel. No one can safeguard the doctrine of a man better than another person who shares the same blood. At that point Perón spoke up. Chabela, you say? Don't be such an idiot, López! There are no blood ties, thank God, between her and me. The secretary then resorted to his esoteric authorities: That's the law today, General, he told him. But according to Paracelsus and other wise men of old, the spirits of husband and wife gradually impregnate each other. Their blood streams commingle, like dyes. Perón sat there thinking. A year later, the military returned Eva's corpse to him. The political game became more complicated. And they called on you, Cámpora. The subject never came up again.

That's utterly implausible, Romero. I don't believe it. (The President has firmly discredited people's suspicions.) It is obvious to me that Isabel is acting in good faith. If López Rega is trying to use her, she'll refuse to go along. I've heard her say a thousand times that she's not interested in power.

Romero disagreed. The General's wife (in his opinion) is suffering from ambition. She is a hypocrite and therefore unpredictable. Up until now, we have all believed that López is using her. It's the other way around. It's López, rather, who is her pawn. When he's of no more use to her, she'll sacrifice him too. That hysterical little rat is pitiless. She has destroyed all her enemies. She has polished off even the General's most loyal followers. She has fattened on the flesh of elephants.

Cámpora has been trying for some time to ingratiate himself with both of them: with López Rega and with her. The last time, just two days before, he called the two of them aside, and begged them to trust in his loyalty as they would that of a brother.

'Has the General ever told you what he thinks of loyalties?' the señora asked.

'Many times,' Cámpora replied. 'I have heard him say that, after so many setbacks, he can tell at a glance who is loyal and who is a traitor.'

'That's true,' López confirmed. 'But he has also said that that is not enough. That the best way of making certain of a man's loyalty is by putting someone else at his side to keep an eye on him.'

'Oh, is that so? And in my case who is that someone else?' Cámpora feeble joked.

'The two of us,' Isabel said gravely. 'Daniel and I are the someone elses of all of you.'

This very minute, before the President's eyes, the spiderweb of that endless vigilance is showing what it is made of. As he eats, López, his glasses perched on the end of his nose, is constantly receiving messages: telexes, marked maps, statistics that are secret codes. The latest reports mention a conspiracy. Everything is still vague, mere shadows of rumors. One or two columns of Montoneros, he has been informed, are plotting to take over the dais when the General lands at Ezeiza. They will seize the microphones, demand the heads of several people (his in particular: they call him 'the sorcerer'), humiliate Isabel by chanting in unison that there was only one Evita and that she is irreplaceable, but above all they will demand that Peronism be turned into a revolution *moto perpetuo*, the Socialist fatherland. Are they really Montoneros? One of the reports suggests they are not: that they are, rather, members of the August 22 People's Revolutionary Army, Marxists of the Fourth International.

If there really is a conspiracy, a fire like that will have to be put out with blood. The General, López knows, can't be counted on in such a case. He will simply say, yet again, I do what the people want – not noticing that the people have changed. They must force the General to face up to reality, confront him (as the señora has insisted) with *faits accomplis*.

The secretary is certain that Cámpora is in on the plot. Young people have had him in their power for some time: they are manipulating him, they are incubi. Hasn't he cited Che Guevara several times in his speeches? A number of people have already passed the word on to the General: that Cámpora is fascinated by the Cuban model. That he would like to found Castro-Peronism.

Even in the presence of his enemy, the secretary acts as though he were alone. He demands that they get hold of a certain lieutenant-colonel for him, so that he can give him an order by telephone; that they hunt up police captain so-and-so, an expert in antisubversive tactics. They must unlash the whole pack of dogs, he decides, against the suspicious columns. They must find out the names of the leaders, search for their lairs with a fine-tooth comb.

The latest telex advises him that a regular customer of a bar in Monte Grande has said that in the confusion of his arrival, as he is making his way toward the bullet-proof dais, the General will be shot with a rifle with a telescopic sight. But the telex has a disappointing ending. The police arrested the bar customer. They put the screws on him. They did everything to him: a manicure, a permanent, a little dip job. They tore out his fingernails; they drove him mad with an electric prod, they held his head down in a tubful of shit. They could get nothing out of him. The rumor he was passing on merely reflected a collective fear; it was the delirium, pure and simple, of a drunk.

Don't let this failure discourage you, López recommends. Keep a close eye on Rodolfo Galimberti, who has a grudge against the General and is capable of any sort of madness. Have Robi Santucho followed; he hates us with a mortal passion. Have a search made for Firmenich, Quieto, Osatinsky: the minute we look the other way, they'll pluck our eyes out and eat them. And above all, find out what Nun Antezana is up to. He's the worst megalomaniac of all. The others think they're good enough to replace Perón. Not Nun: he's sure he's better than Perón. Get a move on! (López is in a lather now.) In the three days still left any sort of catastrophe can happen.

The thugs vanish from the table. And López, ignoring Cámpora, reads the telexes over and over, his cheeks bulging with potatoes and tripe. In the distance, underneath the ash tree, a blind harpist deflowers the waltz 'From the soul'.

The General's smile has come unglued with all his wanderings from one table to another. The only thing left of it now is a dark spot above his upper lip. A raven-haired Uruguayan lyricist insists on dedicating to him an improvised musical dialogue: 'Later on, when it starts to get dark,' the General shoos him away. The wine has gone to the guests' heads. Outside, on the veranda of the villa, boxers are milling about, botching up a tarantella. At Raúl Lastiri's request, Doña Pilar Franco essays a few flamenco steps. Shortly after six p.m., having downed the Argentine stew, President Cámpora finally goes back to Moncloa Palace. Norma, López Rega's daughter, bids him goodbye with the chilling words: 'Poor Don Héctor! They were so fond of you once and now they say such awful things about you!'

The sun is slowly setting. When the General tries to get up from his chair, he is unable to. His muscles aren't paying attention. To relax his body, he licks his thoughts. That relieves him. He manages, furtively, to walk to the house. He climbs the stairs, heading for the cloister: for the antechamber of the sanctuary where Evita is lying. The din in the grounds has made his lungs ache. But there, in this refuge, there is not a sound to be heard. He picks up the folder of Memoirs, the reading of which he has broken off the night before. He idly leafs through the pages. All of a sudden he pricks up his ears. And what's that? And that? Ah, it's silence entering the room. It is coming from the attic where she reposes, safe and sound in this world. Eva, the bird: what he now sees flying through the air is her muteness.

A little dust rains down. Is it she who is shedding it: dust, a pollen of nothingness on objects, a shower of dead leaves for no reason at all? What else could Evita shed if not the oblivion she bears, the many years without a thought, the dampness of the non-places where she has slept: closets, cellars, coal sheds, ships' holds. What is it that she is leaving in her wake – this silence, this oblivion? Nonetheless, the General envies that eternity: the glory that had already returned to this world, that has no need of anything from anyone.

But is that what he really wants? In bygone days, Perón used to believe that it sufficed to imagine the past vividly to be back there again, stained with mulberries and carrying a knapsack on his back, correcting the mistakes of yesteryear and giving the answers that failed to come to his lips at the time; he used to think that by breathing in, even if only for a moment, yesterday's good health, perhaps there might not be any sickness tomorrow. That is so difficult! The General has written. How does a person go about learning whether this feeling or that is the right one, the one that will lead to a simple understanding of what feeling itself, which we refer to by that vague name, really is?

The one thing that he has felt more or less clearly is fear, and he would like to unremember it, to state with certainty that fear does not exist now and so could not have (should not have) ever existed. It has not been the banal fear of death but of something worse: the fear of history. He has suffered at the thought that history will recount in its own way what he has said nothing of. That others will come to invent a life for him. He has feared that history will lie when it speaks of Perón – or that it will reveal that Perón's life has lied to history. He has said as much so often: a man is only what he remembers. He should have said instead: a man is only what others remember about him.

He also had a remote, even realer feeling – perhaps the only feeling with an odor and a sensation that he has ever known – the tightness in his chest when he went through the doors of the Military Academy, in 1911, the palpitations in his oesophagus, the trembling of his tongue. There was, he remembers, mud at the entrance. A sulky passing by spattered his trousers and he tried to clean himself off. He stood there with his hands smelling of horse dung.

In what words had he recounted that? 'I said: this is what I want. And I discovered within me the soldier that I have never ceased to be. I passed the entrance exam in 1910. At the beginning of the next year I enrolled as a cadet.' (The first two sentences are his. The other two are López's. They had recorded thoughts that afternoon; what afternoon was it that they had made the recordings? They were trying to understand the country from afar, they sketched flowers on a sheet of paper. Ideas like soap bubbles, General. And one day López suppressed them. They flew away, his pitiful bird-thoughts. He ought to have taken a firm stand. He ought to have ordered López to write instead):

In 1910, the desert still surrounded Argentina on every hand. It crept deep inside a person. I came from there: from the farthest reaches of the desert. From the Argentina that did not exist: we were wind in those years, clouds of dust. To prepare us for the entrance exam, they made us study Alberdi's Bases. *I learned in those pages that the best law for the desert is the one that causes it to disappear. To govern is to populate, I read. Let us get the better of the desert by making it disappear. I was still a schoolboy and I thought: The desert disappear? What an odd phrase! It's like saying, The best way to overcome nothingness is to do away with it. The best way of making no one exist is to decree that no one exists. In a word, an adolescent's clumsy ramblings.*

I took the examination on 1 December, just after finishing my third year of secondary school, and on 1 March I entered the rambling old building in the town of San Martín, in a very sparsely inhabited region. The streetcar line ended near there. Across the street was a general store. I was to spend three years there. I was only fifteen years old; it might be said that I was still a boy. It was then that my parents handed me over to the fatherland. And I grew up, I became a man, in the shelter of the fatherland.

I feel the past. I can see myself in those days. I feel the past within as though a film had got stuck in the projector. I see myself saying goodbye to Granny Dominga. Did I cry? If I did it was by myself on those first nights in the big sheds of the Academy. If I did, it was in silence: so that no one would know. I thought of my parents, also lost in the lonely expanses of the Chubut. When I was with them, I had been someone. And all of a sudden, I felt as though I were no one.

Many years later, when I saw a television series in which men from another planet mingled with the multitudes of this world, I realized that that was what I was from that time on: a transplant, a tree whose roots were forever severed by fate. An almost homeless being, with families gradually burning down and going out like candles, someone who learned only to give orders and obey. But not to feel. From my earliest years it was drummed into me that feelings were a weakness, something feminine, a quality of the soul that must wither away before it flowered.

I see myself sitting in the courtyard of the Academy, as an army barber cruelly shaves my head, down to the scalp, leaving me just one miserable tuft on top; I see myself wearing fatigues; I see the days ruled off in squares by regulation x and rule y. No one was allowed a kind word, a smile, a tear.

They put us cadets in with the enlisted men, in a big shed: 'the stable', we called it, beneath a zinc roof where the raindrops pattered. Reveille was at five a.m., summer and winter. We had three minutes to wash our face and five to line up, already dressed, in formation in the courtyard. We drank our maté boiled with milk and then we were subjected to very rigorous, implacable close order drill, in a little soccer field. I realized then that a man never knows how far he can push his body, the limit of that almost infinite power the body possesses. The fact is that we seldom try to push it farther, to the point of total exhaustion. A man feels that he exists only when his body begs for mercy. At other times, he doesn't even think: I am this person, I am here, here is a tiny dot that I call my place in the world. Later on I was told that a Jewish philosopher had had the same ideas I did, but no one could tell me exactly when he set them down in writing. Nor do I know whether he felt them the way I did, in my very own flesh.

Though life was very hard at the Academy, I was prepared for every sort of effort and sacrifice. The freezing mornings in San Martín seemed like a game to me compared to the ones in Patagonia, and after a time the daily trials of the soldier became a mere distraction.

We had leave only once a month, after Saturday afternoon inspection, and had to be back on Sunday night before ten. Serious misdeeds were punished by depriving us of this one leave: the most rebellious cadets were made to sit in the discipline room with their hands on their knees, from reveille till retreat, allowed to get up from their places only to go to the toilet and to eat.

The theoretical courses were given in the afternoons. We were taught history, natural sciences, geography . . . The curriculum was like the one for the last year of undergraduate studies. Compulsory military service had been established by law only a short time before, its intended purpose being to inculcate Argentine values in the millions of half-literate young immigrants who came to settle in our land. I remember that Don Manuel Carlés, who would later organize the Fascist militias of the Argentine Patriotic League, was one of my most learned professors. He taught us literature. In his classes, which were veritable harangues, he used to treat us as though we were already officers in command of troops. 'The Nation' — Carlés would say — 'expects you to redeem the uncultured, ignorant, depraved conscript.' His intention was to put us on our guard against the anarchists who had already wormed their way in everywhere and were turning our political life into chaos. The majority of this bunch of anarchists were foreigners. They had infiltrated the factories, were stirring up the workers with their bitter preaching, and Troy was on fire. In 1910 they provoked nearly three hundred strikes!

My father used to say that no Argentine is a hundred per cent Argentine until he founds a town or sows a field. One winter night, when I must have been seven or eight, he sat my brother and me down next to the wood stove. 'President Roca took the best land in this country away from the Indians and gave it to his friends,' he told us. 'The privileged who couldn't get land thus from the top, bought it for next to nothing with the complicity of the military. Mario Avelino and I will take care of the little land we have. Juan Domingo must join the army, to keep it from being taken away from us.'

Both my father and my grandmother wanted me to study medicine, but I never forgot those phrases (perhaps spoken in a moment of impatience or depression). Sometimes I think that my future was decided at the very moment I heard them. I made myself a career in the military not to get myself land — since I don't own any — or to found towns, which would have been more to my liking, but to learn to found men: to lead them.

Within me there was no economic calculation or coveting of material possessions of any sort. How could I have had such motives if a second lieutenant earned two hundred pesos a month in those days, the same miserable salary as a schoolteacher? With that amount of money a person couldn't even afford to rent a more or less decent place to live in Buenos Aires.

The ones who taught us the art of leadership were German army officers. When I entered the Military Academy, the Argentine army still went by the old tactics of General Alberto Capdevilla, based on French rules and manuals. But we were already equipping ourselves with Prussian rifles and cannons. We knew how to use Mausers and Krupps. The traditional kepi with which I began my studies as a cadet soon became the German helmet topped with an elongated cone, beneath which was the Argentine national emblem.

We very quickly adapted to the new order. We marched in step and the commands were barked out Prussian-fashion. It was not a question of thinking but of obeying. At times we were strongly inclined to rebel, but we forged ahead. For my teachers, the names of von Clausewitz, Schlieffen and von der Gorz were as great a legend as . . . let me see . . . the legend of Napoleon. In 1914, General José Félix Uriburu returned from Berlin, where he had been made a member of the Kaiser's personal guard. He came back with such a Germanophile fervor that we cadets called him 'von Pepe'. The same thing happened in the case of many others . . .

One of the finest impressions the Military Academy left me with was that of the camaraderie there, the sowing of a crop of good friends. I have kept up those friendships down through the years. Of the hundred and twelve cadets who received their second lieutenants' swords along with me, nearly all are dead now. There were only seven or eight cadets of pure Argentine stock. I was one of them. Since we lived apart from civilians, we ended up forming a family among

*ourselves. There have been those who have claimed that I never had
any other family, that the army was my only real attachment. And
what if it was? I made no distinctions between fatherland and
army. In 1955, a traitorous clique tried to deprive me of both. It forced
me into exile. It decided, by decree, that I was no longer a general.
That second part didn't matter to me. When all was said and done, I
was still Perón. That they left me without an army, on the other
hand, was a terrible blow to me: it was as if my family had
abandoned me. And my very first thought was: I'm like Argentina, I
too am fated to be a desert. They are trying to condemn me to
non-existence, to emptiness, to a vast plain where there is no one. To
being nameless, to having no past, to living without roots. The
dictatorship that usurped power in 1955 decided that, after that date, I
was a zero. I began to think things over then. Let's see where we're
going to put that zero: behind the decimal point, where it's worth
nothing, or in front. So they forced me to fight. And thereby did me a
great favor . . .*

*On 13 December I received my commission as a second lieuten-
ant . . .*

He should have been firm and ordered López to write in that very
intimate way: the family, the desert, just as he felt it. But the
secretary was thinking of history. Be more historical, General, do
you see what I mean? Put a little marble in the portrait. Don't
reveal yourself, don't let people get to know you. Grandeur is made
of silences. When have you ever heard of a great man coming out
of the toilet, pulling the chain, and parading about in front of
people in his underwear? What is family anyway? Blank it out in
your memory. You weren't like this before. You never used to ask
yourself questions, General. Don't do it now. Great men have
nothing but answers.

López is doubtless right. He's very sensible when he wants to be.
History has no need to know that I, Juan Domingo Perón, have

a right to doubts and hesitations, to a feeling of powerlessness. That at seventy-seven, I don't find any answer that's better than a good question.

Very well, the secretary has said to him. Question yourself, General. Put your guts on the table. I dare you. What happened to you on the night of the hazing, when you entered the Military Aademy? Remove that thorn that's so painful from your heart.

And he has not been able to. There are prisons of memory against which nothing prevails. The memories are quite comfortable there where they are, in their nest, dying down. How did you hide them, López? What did you throw over those shadows to hide them? Let's see, what page is it on?

I took my entrance exam in 1910. At the beginning of the following year I enrolled as a cadet. It was a tradition to subject plebes who had just arrived to a hazing, a rite of baptism known as a 'blanket tossing'. It consisted of inhuman beatings that shook loose the last remains of our civilian pride and, incidentally, toughened our spirits. Before I entered, a group of cadets had suffered the humiliation of being forced to crawl on all fours, naked, across the frost-covered courtyard; others had been hauled out of bed in the middle of the night and forced to climb into big basins of ice-cold water; one of them ended up in the infirmary, with a broken rib from the clubbing.

I was prepared for any sort of rough treatment. I obeyed the second-year cadets without a word of protest when I was in the first year, and the third-year ones when I was in the second. To train oneself to give orders, I thought, one has to learn obedience first. But the hazings seemed to me to be vicious cruelty. In June 1911, three months after I arrived, we plebes found out that the second-year cadets were planning to give us the beating of our lives. They intended to make us come off badly the first time we went on parade, the day of the pledge of allegiance to the flag: to leave us in terrible shape so we'd ache all over as we marched. At that season the cold was terrible. The temperature went way below freezing almost every night. I rounded up my buddies and told them: We have to put a stop to this cruelty. Let's ask the third-year cadets for help. And that was what we did. We formed a committee and began negotiations. Let's put an end to hazing once and for all, I proposed. So that nobody ever has a bad memory of the days he spent in this academy. They all agreed. That was my first political victory. We presented ourselves before Lieutenant-Colonel Agustín P. Justo, the assistant director, and once he'd heard our arguments he sided with us. Since then those barbarous rites have become a thing of the past.

(A man should not be what he remembers. He should be what he has forgotten. Like the story he has just read: it is not the one he is still carrying around inside him, burning into his brain like a brand. The words have changed their spots as they went from his brain to his mouth. Someone has raped them. López? Or he, Perón – his will to forget?

The secretary has also dared him to tell about the maneuvers they were made to endure near Concordia, in the summer of 1913. And the General has refused. I have nothing to question there in that past, he has said: nothing to answer.

And yet. Ah, the maneuvers, López reminisces. Some of us were predestined to die that year. Do you remember 3 December, General? At dawn we raised our camp at Ayuí. We thought we'd march a few miles along the Yuquén River, and then go on in trucks to the railroad station at Jubileo. But Colonel Agustín P. Justo refused to allow this: he said that the resistance of the human body could always be stretched a little more, and that the more distant the goal we set our bodies, the farther we'd get. He ordered us to advance on foot along a sandy road, several leagues from the river bank where the trucks were waiting for us. Justo had – I remember – a hyena's disposition. He had forbidden the hazing as inhuman, and now, with an icy smile on his face, he was torturing us.

As we began the march, two cadets fainted. The sun opened a mouth with a temperature of over a hundred. You had a swollen ankle, General. Every so often, I unlaced your boots and massaged it. There was not a tree to be seen, or any water holes, or even a measly little patch of green in that immensity of sand and cracked earth. There was a moment when it rained down birds . . . Did you see them, López Rega? Did you too go through that frightening experience? . . . I marched and marched, the secretary answers. Don't you remember? I was one of you: a Juan Perón. I saw how the sun clung to the wings of the birds and I said to myself, They're going to fall. I saw how the sun stabbed the birds in the neck and knocked them into the fields of sand. It's raining birds, you said. And I said, It'll be the only rain of birds we'll ever see in our lives. We were carrying backpacks that weighed almost seventy pounds, and some of our buddies collapsed beneath the vault of fire overhead. Keep walking, Juan, keep walking, you and I said over and over. I'm a foot soldier, walking is my job. We were among the first to arrive at Jubileo station. The train had been waiting for us for many hours. The General shakes his head – the maneuvers, the birds . . . we'll make a good-sized bundle of forgetfulness out of all that. Let's take pity on our memory, López. Let's not frighten it.)

I received my second lieutenant's commission on 13 December 1913. For a long time I kept in my wallet some newspaper clippings that described the ceremony very well, from the roll of drums at daybreak to the arrival of the Minister of War. And our military formation in the patio . . . And the speech by the director of the academy . . . And the infantry drills, on the field behind the building . . . Twenty years later I hunted for the clippings to show them to the Tizóns, my in-laws. And nothing but a yellow dust fell out of the wallet. The clippings had turned to ashes.

That summer I went, as usual, on vacation to Patagonia. My father had bought me three books as a gift, and he asked me to always keep them close at hand. They were the *Letters to My Son*, by Philip Stanhope, Lord Chesterfield; the Garnier edition of *Plutarch's Lives*, and *Martín Fierro*, by José Hernández. My father wrote an appropriate dedication in each book. In the one by Lord Chesterfield: 'So that you may make your way about in the world.' In the one by Plutarch: 'So that you may be inspired by these wise men.' And in the one by José Hernández: 'So that you may never forget that, above all else, you are an Argentine.'

I used Plutarch's magnum opus many a time when I taught Military History in the War College. Reading the biography of Pericles in it, I learned the gift of patience. 'Everything in its proper proportions and harmoniously' was the guiding principle of that exemplary leader. And that is the phrase I repeat to those who are over-ambitious and those in a hurry to get somewhere when they come to me for advice.

I know *Martín Fierro* by heart. There is almost no speech of mine where for one reason or another I fail to invoke one of its wonderful verses. When my father gave it to me, that was reading matter for country folk. It hadn't yet reaped the glory it won later on. More than the figure of Fierro, an army deserter, a gaucho on the run from the law and more or less a rebellious outsider – to the point that he even went off and lived with Indians – what impressed me was the common sense of Old Vizcacha, who passed on to the defenseless, unschooled gauchos of those days profound lessons on ways to survive.

Hernández describes Vizcacha as an old hermit: dirty, poor,

with a pack of dogs. If for nothing other than his poverty and his dogs, he's rather like me, wouldn't you say? A city-bred man can find nothing likeable about such a bad-tempered character. But I grew up in the country, and I immediately suspected that Hernández wanted to turn Vizcacha into a protector of the unfortunate, into someone whose language would only be understood by those who had had an education in suffering.

That is what I did. Anyone who reads closely the letters I wrote to my compatriots during all those years will notice that it is not to Fierro's complaints that I draw attention but, rather, Vizcacha's cunning. 'Man's primary concern/is to save his own skin,' I have recommended, because I know of no better psalm of blessing to offer life. And to round out the idea: 'Make friends with the Judge/don't give people anything to complain about;/and when he's about to fly into a rage/you must make yourself look smaller,/for it is always good to have/a hitching post to scratch yourself on.'

I had just turned eighteen when I was assigned to the 12th Infantry Regiment, stationed in Paraná. I was in command of the first company, with a complement of eighty enlisted men and ten NCOs. The barracks, near the gorges of the river, were a rickety compound, made up of enormous windowless sheds. It had been built to house Jewish and Italian colonists. When I arrived, it was known as 'Immigration'.

For the first time I discovered the wretched poverty into which our country was plunged. The farm laborers' children were raised like animals: exposed to the elements, unschooled. And the parents died in the flower of their youth, their lungs full of lesions. I saw mere lads carry sacks weighing a hundred and fifty pounds for nine-hour work shifts. I discovered that women contracted tuberculosis carding wool and cleaning up the dust in cigarette factories. What made the deepest impression on me was that they looked on the future with disdain. Or rather they did not look at it at all. They lived lives blind to time. Since the past was always appalling, they erased it almost instantaneously from their memory. So they attributed the good and evil that befell them to fate. Or better put: the good to providence and the evil to the government.

Absorbed in his reading, the General has forgotten that downstairs, in the gardens of the villa, the party is still going on. Voices, on the stairway, remind him of that fact. He hears them coming up the stairs, muffled, obscene. What are they saying? The man, who is drunk, is searching for a bed. The woman is putting up a struggle. If they have gotten this far, the house is already taken over, its skin infected, filthy with mange. Will no one come to stop them? The General is terrified. He hears the groping, at the door, just outside. They are trying to get in, searching for the handle. Will they have the nerve to violate his cloister? Don't they know that Eva, the bird, up there above, might awaken?

'Come down from there, damn you!' López's distant shout, coming to his rescue, reaches the cavern of the cloister. 'Come down from there and clear out of here!'

(It had to be him – caring for the bird, keeping her from profanations, avoiding them.) The General sighs. He relaxes. Standing next to the door, he hears the couple go away. He recognizes the voice of one of the bodyguards. And he recognizes the woman too: a poor foolish hussy. López chases curious interlopers out of the dining room, clears stragglers out of the bedrooms: 'Get a move on! Out of this house with you!'

Is there music? Once again, there is not a sound. How dark can it be outside? And how much of Madrid does he still have left to live through?

The General goes back to the folders in a thoughtful mood. A fly-shaped chip of plaster has landed on the page. (Have you come, so soon, to read me the past? She and I never used to speak of this.

It was painful for both of us. This is something from way back, bird. From before you were born).

It was the winter of 1914. The same day that we learned of the attempt on the life of Archduke Ferdinand of Sarajevo, I founded the Boxing Club in Paraná. I had always gone in for boxing with a passion, but in those days we fought blindly, with no technique. We didn't even know enough to bandage our hands. In one of the fights, I broke my knuckles. The metacarpal bones broke through the skin on top, owing to a bad punch I threw. The lumps can still be seen on the backs of my hands.

I spent many hours all by myself, looking at the river and whiling away the time studying the motionless map of the stars. It was then that my first doubts – metaphysical ones, let us say – surfaced. I asked myself, as in the dialogue between El Moreno and Martín Fierro: what is the substance of eternity, where is time headed, at what point in the infinite universe is the beginning of things and at what other point can we see the end?

I unexpectedly found some answers. It was late one afternoon, in December of that same year. The sky was so clear and blue that not even the birds dared leave a blot on it. I had sat down on a bench along the Avenida Costanera. All of a sudden, a black hole opened up on the horizon. I heard the hiss of a black flame. In a second darkness fell: the air was saturated with a smell of poison. It seemed as if the bowels of the earth were rotting. An enormous swarm of locusts had fallen upon the city and were devouring everything green. I remembered my grandfather, who blamed locusts for his bouts of insomnia and boiled their legs in retorts, searching for the virus that kept him from sleeping. I forgot the stench and the turbulence and stopped there on the bank of the river to watch them lay their eggs. I caught a female, tore its wings off so that it wouldn't fly away, and examined it closely: the hard shell of its eyes, the feverish antennae, the imposing mandibles. And I asked myself, If God is everywhere, as the Gospels say, He must also be in the heart of locusts. I tried to find the heart of the female, digging about with my tie pin. I looked and looked. There was nothing. I left the insect on the ground and walked off. I learned that afternoon that God exists only where there is good, and cannot coexist with evil. That answer has remained with me ever since.

At the end of 1915 I was promoted to first lieutenant. A few weeks later the 12th Regiment moved its headquarters to Santa Fe, on the other side of the river. Some of the men were billeted in the old Rural Society, which in those days was called 'The Fair'. The others (and I among with them) took refuge in the orphan asylum.

I then had the extraordinary good fortune of serving under one of the best leaders that our army ever had: Bartolomé Descalzo, who was a captain. He was my Socrates, the maker of my soul. I once asked him if the acts of our life and the date of our death were already written in the book of fate. 'Only our death is written there,' he answered me, 'because no one knows anyone who has died on the eve of his death. But life is another matter: a real man never allows destiny to make the decisions he himself should have made.' I have repeated these ideas many times. So many times that some people think they're my own. But they're not. They're Bartolomé Descalzo's.

Years of turbulence began. On 2 April 1916 there were democratic elections for the first time in Argentina. I had leanings toward Lisandro de la Torre, whose electoral stronghold was in Santa Fe, but I voted for Hipólito Yrigoyen, who represented a great hope for the popular classes.

The army was shaken by the anarchist agitations. On 9 July of that year, just as the parade for the centenary of Independence ended, an individual made his way through the crowd, and shouting 'Long live anarchy!' took a shot at the head of Dr Victoriano de la Plaza, who was soon to hand over the office of President of the Republic. Luckily, his aim was bad. The bullet ricocheted off a balcony of the Casa Rosada.

That should have served as a warning to Yrigoyen, who took office three months later. But it did not. His administration was greeted by a veritable fireworks display of strikes and social conflicts. It was only to be expected. Yrigoyen had aroused many expectations among the workers and peasants, and waited too long to fulfill them. He personally received delegations of railwaymen and textile workers – something that no president before him had done – delivered speeches against management, but then he folded his arms and did nothing to promote the reform laws that we were all hoping for. The masses lost patience and were roused to rebellion. Yrigoyen had been a victim, in the flesh, of the brutality of his predecessors and had no wish to put down the uprising by force. But neither did he have a guideline for controlling the situation. He was confronted with a battle-hardened anarchism, inspired by ideologues as dangerous as Malatesta and Georges Sorel, and imagined that people of that ilk could be kept under control by the police. And naturally they overran the police, as usual. Then Yrigoyen called in the army. We officers were disappointed by his ineptness, since on the one hand he refused to lose popularity by imposing the iron hand that was needed, and on the other ended up involving the army in unpopular measures.

Now that he is reading them, the General remembers clearly the inflection with which he dictated every one of those sentences, the unexpected hoarseness at the end of each of them, the feverish intensity with which he uttered the name Malatesta or Sorel and thought of Cohn Bendit and Alain Krivine: the Buenos Aires of 1917 was transfigured in his mind into the Paris of May 1968.

Those years of intelligence were ravages wrought by idealists, dogs of the soul, were they not? Through the disturbances they caused, they vastly diminished the grandeur of Yrigoyen, the glory of General de Gaulle . . .

He had dictated with rage what he is now reading with sadness. And he asks himself whether this afterwards from which he is narrating himself has not already destroyed forever the yesterday on which the events took place.

Captain Descalzo had an unerring instinct for containing excesses before they overflowed. In 1917 he brought us to Rosario to occupy the switch yards where the streetcars were parked, as a precaution against anarchist sabotage. In 1918, when I was transferred to the Estaban de Luca Arsenal, he said to me as he bade me goodbye: 'We are entering the dark, Lieutenant Perón. The most terrible storm imaginable is knocking at the doors of our house, and the President is either unwilling to hear it or unable to. In Europe, the war has ended with the defeat of the best army in the world. The anarchists are now training their eyes on us again.' His words moved me. 'I am going to ask a personal favor of you,' I said to him. 'When the time comes to confront that enemy, summon me. I want to fight at your side, sir.'

In Buenos Aires I had a heavy work load. My passion for sports, which never left me, absorbed my every thought. I practiced high jumping and pole-vaulting. I played basketball and soccer. But I devoted myself to fencing above all. In the 1918 army championships I won the gold medal for swordsmanship. My technique was flexible, as though I were using the foil, and my rivals couldn't touch me.

On 22 June snow fell in Buenos Aires. People poured into the streets, in a state of euphoria. I, however, was all on edge. I saw the pattern the snowflakes traced on the window panes and it set me to thinking that I was almost twenty-three. I felt the emptiness of time. I knew I ought to marry soon. I enjoyed my solitude, but I needed a lawfully wedded wife at my side. Officers are regarded more favorably when they have a home and fireside.

In those days we went to very few parties and would never have dreamed of making love to a decent girl. We often went to dance halls, but with women we paid to go with us. When one of us wanted to empty out his body, he hunted up one of those women and that was that. Later on, the brothels were closed down, and young men, instead of paying a professional to satisfy their needs, solved the problem by turning decent girls into whores. The men of my generation didn't go in for things like that: inside our own circle we were respectable gentlemen. Outside of it, we had a high old time and danced more than anybody else: in cabarets, however, with women who were for sale.

Many years later I wrote an article a few pages long in which I spoke of a stern general, who never took off his saber and kepi even in salons. A brazen little French girl asked him straight out: How do you make love? And the man answered: I don't make love. I buy it ready made. That was my view of the matter too. So that nothing would distract me from my military career, I satisfied my urgent needs as a male for a few pesos.

Captain Descalzo's prophecy was fulfilled sooner than even he thought. The anarchists trained their eyes on us again. The year 1918 had ended with several skirmishes during a strike in Pedro Vasena's metalwork shops. A number of workers, urged on by the anars, demanded higher wages and less strict company regulations. There were many who refused to go along with them and the movement was a failure, but the seeds of discontent were already sown.

On 3 January 1919 the high-wire act began. Vasena owned the

factory on the Calle Cochabamba, near the Constitución district. The warehouses were in Pompeya, a few blocks away on Riachuelo. There was always a stream of trucks going back and forth between the two places. Because of the disturbances, the trucks were being guarded by mounted police officers. On the morning of that 3 January, the strikers came unexpectedly pouring out of a vacant lot and fired on the trucks. A woman who had nothing to do with the whole thing was shot to death. On the 5th, the same thing happened: this time they killed a police sergeant. On the 7th, the conflict turned into a pitched battle: the anarchists attacked, the police fired on them and drove them back with saber blows. The end result was five workers dead and some twenty wounded. Yrigoyen wanted to solve the problem by reconciling the two sides. He ordered the Minister of the Interior to try to bring about an agreement between Vasena and the strikers. Pressured by the Government, the company backed down. It offered to pay the workers a twelve per cent raise and not to engage in reprisals.

But the broken crockery couldn't be put back together again with saliva. The deaths on 7 January served the anarchists as a pretext for rousing the entire country to rebellion. Di Giovanni, Scarfó, Miguel Arcángel Roscigna and many anarchists who were to become famous in the years that followed got their first taste of battle in these clashes. They were part of a very well-staged international conspiracy. So well-staged, in fact, that during that same week in 1919 the Spartacist revolts broke out in Berlin. With the death of Rosa Luxemburg and her comrade Karl Liebknecht, the matter was settled in a few days there. Once the movement lost its leaders, order was restored. Here, however, Yrigoyen continued to place his trust in divine providence.

It was a terrible summer. Buenos Aires was scorching hot. In the courtyard of the arsenal the only breeze was the one raised by flies on the wing. Even the horses kept whinnying out of nervous tension. The dead were to be buried on 8 January. The anarchists called for a general strike beginning on that day. We were all afraid that a catastrophe was in the offing. The police were ill-prepared and were going to be overpowered. The army found itself forced to intervene.

My job at the arsenal was to make certain that the troops had the ammunition they needed. I had a great deal of work to do, since between eight and ten regiments were quartered in the city of Buenos Aires alone. As everyone expected, the funeral ceremonies turned into street fights. More than six hundred people died. On 11 January the Government agreed to meet with the anarchist leaders and calmed everyone down.

The workers in the Vasena factory managed to reap a certain benefit from that tragedy: the company reduced their work day to eight hours and gave them a thirty per cent increase in wages.

But when wounds are deep, they do not heal overnight. They must be carefully tended to. My old professor Manuel Carlés founded the Argentine Patriotic League, which many young Catholics and nationalists joined. They had a contingent of shock troops whose chief mission was to keep the foreign agitators in line. They sometimes used violent methods, but they were well-intentioned.

The 1914 census showed that the country had eight million inhabitants, a third of whom had not been born in Argentina. Many vital industries were in foreign hands. In Patagonia, adventurers recently arrived from Europe soon began fleecing unwary native-born Argentines. To the north of Santa Fe, the English had an empire almost as large as their home country. It was called La Forestal. The profits they made lay in cutting down enormous stands of red quebracho, a hardwood tree from which they extracted the tannin. The concession, which stretched from San Cristóbal to the frontiers of the Chaco, covered more than five million acres. Within it were seven or eight towns where, I believe, some ten thousand men worked.

Everything beneath those skies was the patrimony of the English: the company stores, the water, the forests, the guards, the women. Luckily, the English paid little attention to the women; they lived in big rambling houses surrounded by golf courses and impeccable gardens, giving parties with famous musicians who came to that lonely domain directly from the Teatro Colón. I learned that in 1903 they had hired Toscanini's entire symphony orchestra, and that in 1915 (shortly before the tragedies that brought me to that part of the country) they put on a recital by Caruso. Our young Creole girls were too much for them. They preferred the love of their vapid English blondes.

In July 1919, the working population in the towns rebelled. They asked for raises and sanitary living quarters. La Forestal then organized its own army to put down the rebellion. They let dangerous criminals out of the prisons, put them in uniform and gave them arms. The tortures and murders began. To put pressure on the strikers, the owners cut off their water and electricity. Once again, the army had to intervene.

One Saturday during that July, when the hours on guard duty in the arsenal seemed more interminable than ever, I was brought a telegram from Captain Descalzo. His orders were to restore order in La Forestal and he wanted to have me with him. He had already arranged everything: my transfer and the appointment of my replacement. Lieutenant Perón could not refuse.

Descalzo put me in charge of a detachment of twenty men and sent me to the town of Tartagal, where some four hundred families lived. I have never forgotten those wilds. A person rode through dense vegetation and saw flocks of birds that covered the sky like spider webs. Along the path were swamps and little gleaming towers that looked like bonfires. They were anthills. In the distance were the quebrachos, from forty-five to sixty feet tall, with gnarled, twisted branches. And hovering above all that was a brick-colored dust that dried up every living thing it fell on. It was tannin. No one in those parts lives past the age of twenty-five. The English had eight- to ten-month tours of duty. The Creole hands could do nothing but endure that inferno till they died. The one with the highest wages was paid a hundred pesos a month, and was obliged to spend his pay in La Forestal's company stores, where a packet of maté cost two pesos fifty.

I arrived in the vicinity of Tartagal on a freight train. The locomotive driver pointed out a break in the forest to me and told me that the town was some four miles away. My men and I began walking. We couldn't have gone more than half that distance when I noticed suspicious movements among the trees. I ordered everyone down. The men began to zigzag along on all fours. I chose to remain standing, motionless, listening to the silence. All of a sudden, I heard someone, behind me, undo the safety catch of his Winchester. I kept cool. Descalzo had asked me to try at all costs to avoid a massacre. What to do? I made the only possible decision. I raised my arms and shouted:

'Halt! Halt! Come out, whoever you are! Keep calm. Nobody will do anything to you. I am an officer in the Argentine army and I haven't come to fight you. I want to help you.'

A group of peons in rags, with several days' growth of beard, came out of the woods and approached me apprehensively. They said that their water supply had been cut off and that they had no way of feeding their children. The company was refusing to open the only store in town.

I advised them to lay down their arms and trust me. Nothing is going to get settled here by resorting to violence, I told them. When all is said and done, the English in La Forestal aren't ogres but human beings. They probably have fellow-feelings of some sort. Let me have a talk with them.

I took the peons back to Tartagal, escorted by the enlisted men. I hunted up the manager of the general store, a young man named Sosa, and ordered him to sell his merchandise to the peons. He was deliberately rude. Without getting out of bed, he yawned and began to wipe the sleep from his eyes. The general store belongs to La Forestal, he told me, and can't be opened up without written authorization from the owners. I had to raise my voice: Obey my orders! I'll be the one responsible, in the name of the Argentine Army! The young man made a move to turn his back on me. The army doesn't mean a thing around here, he answered. The only authority hereabouts is the Forestal Land, Timber and Railway Company.

He may not have known how to read or write, but he spoke English like a lord. I got really hot under the collar. I drew my revolver. You open the store this minute or you won't live to tell the tale! That was how I got him out of bed, in his underwear. It must have been around eight in the morning. The sky was red.

I left three men to guard the lad as he gave out the supplies in the store, and went in search of the English with the rest of the men. They turned out to be two married couples. One of the men had a broken nose that had been mended. I suspected that he had been a boxer. I spoke to him of Jorge Newbery, González Acha and other big-name fighters of that time. He'd never heard of them. His world was English, and he lived in that remote quebracho forest as though it were a suburb of London. There are men who are unable to adjust to their time. Others can't adjust to their surroundings: that Englishman was one of the latter.

I invited him to box with me for a couple of rounds and he willingly agreed. In the back of the house was a recreation room, with billiard tables, exercise bars and weights. We immediately found a length of rope and set up a ring. The Englishman lent me a pair of boxing gloves and helped me bandage my hands. I asked one of my men to blow a whistle to allow us keep track of the time: a short toot to indicate the beginning of a round and a long one when the three minutes were up.

We began boxing. The man was a professional, and got in some vicious jabs. He backed me into a corner and landed a hard left hook on my ear. I stumbled and landed on the floor. I saw the frightened look on my men's faces and held out as best I could till the end of the round.

During the rest period, one of the boys said to me: No matter what, don't let us down, Lieutenant. That got to me. An officer of the Argentine Army cannot afford to lose in front of his subordinates. Much less if he's fighting against a civilian, and a foreigner into the bargain. I was blind with rage, but I controlled myself. In tight spots like that, a cool head and cunning are the only thing that can save us. When the fight began again, I kept my distance from the Englishman, took a couple of punches in the kidneys and began to move about as though I were dizzy. My rival was taken in. He moved in to finish me off and let his guard down. I saw my opening and threw him a hard punch in the temple. He was knocked out and fell to the floor. We did a countdown on him of more than thirty seconds. When he didn't come to, we threw a bucketful of water on him. His English wife began to cry because we had ruined her floor. But after a while we forgot the whole thing and made friends.

They invited me to eat with them: a tender cut of meat, but badly cooked, cold. As they served me dessert, I said to them, Let's see now, what difficulties are all of you having in improving the workers' lot?

They brought a supervisor to explain the problem. Certain points of contention were easy to resolve. The peons earned an average of three pesos a day and were asking for fifty centavos more: agreed. They worked between twelve and fifteen hours a day; they were asking for a maximum of seventy hours' work a week: agreed. They wanted overtime for Sundays: not possible. A week's vacation: not possible either. If he gave in on every point, they'd come up with new demands the next year, the supervisor said.

One of the Englishmen hinted that the company could be more generous if it weren't for all the anarchists who had infiltrated the workers' ranks. I asked them if they had proof of what they were saying and they showed me some files drawn up by the police of that province. They mentioned certain names: Litito, Ifrán, Vera, Lafruente and Giovetti.

I offered them a deal. If they agreed to all the workers' demands, which struck me as being legitimate, the army would take care of the anarchists. They embraced me with feeling and gave me their word of honor to respect the terms of the deal, in Tartagal at least.

I walked back to the general store, where half the town had gathered. I mounted a platform and told them about the talk we'd had. The women began to cheer. The men wanted to carry me on their shoulders. Noting that everyone was satisfied, I asked them to look after their future themselves and immediately turn in to the police any anarchists who tried to stir them up. The two parties signed an agreement. I served as witness to it.

That night, the peons staged an impromptu dance. I agreed to participate, providing that there was no alcohol. My men had to walk back almost four miles to the railroad and wait for a train that came by at seven in the morning.

When darkness fell, I turned up with the two English couples. Up until that moment, the representatives of La Forestal had never mingled with the peons. In the beginning, they all felt a little ill at ease, but I asked one of the gringas to dance and that lessened the tension. Unfortunately, there's always some fool who causes trouble and this time it was a man who'd brought some cane brandy and was passing it around underneath the tables. One of my men drank too much. He got tight and took it into his head to flirt with the wife of a foreman. The husband took out a sheath knife, ready to slit my man's throat. I saw his hand move and stopped him. No decent fellow deserves a prison sentence on account of a woman, I said to him. I ordered the soldier to be put in the army stockade, apologized to the gringos, and left.

A few months later the anarchists came back and started to stir up the workers again. La Forestal had to go back on the deal I'd gone to such trouble to get the Englishmen to make. It left the townspeople with no water again. I found out that an epidemic of chicken pox decimated the towns and that a worker in Villa Guillermina whose nerves were all on edge killed a conscript. The 12th Infantry had to put down the rebellion with machine-guns. There was a massacre. But I wasn't there.

I was promoted to first lieutenant and sent to Junior Officers' School on 16 January 1920. I remember that time as clearly as though it were today. I was happy, but didn't realize it because happiness is always something we have left behind. I set out for Buenos Aires in a state of tremendous excitement. I had such a lot of living under my belt that I thought I was on the way back. Who could have told me that I had barely set out on my life's journey!

The General leaves the cloister and comes downstairs to the other side of the frontier. Inside the house, fortunately, he never has a chance to be himself. What clings to the banister of the stairway, what glides across the rug, is not the General but his representation. That body slowly fits itself into the gestures he has invented for his person. When he reaches the bedrooms on the first floor, the smoke from the barbecued meat and the liveliness of the guests stop him.

What if he took off his shoes, turned on the television and finally tuned into his own oblivion? On Channel 2 they're showing a tearjerker, *People Will Talk*, with Cary Grant: it is the implausible story of a man named Pretorius who is a slave to his sinister servant. On Channel 1 they're showing the adventures of Nick Carter, that have so often diverted him. He is about to yield to the temptation. But he doesn't. The only thing he has left are a few strands of Madrid and heaven only knows if he has any life left. Resignedly, the General walks out into the garden. He sighs. And then he walks on, with the Perón smile on his face.

7 *The Cards Are on the Table*

'All men are born with two misdestinations,' Don José Cresto lectured the disciples of the Basilio School of Science when he returned from Madrid. 'One is the misdestination of what we are. The other is that of what we might have been. I have just been disabused of this latter discalculation at the hands of my namesake, López Rega.' His congregation at the temple on the Calle Tinogasta had thinned out in that winter of 1967. It was made up of pimply little servant girls with no sweethearts, and of rheumatic widows who came to converse with the souls of their deceased husbands. When the collection basket was passed, Don José now received only a few paltry pesos, which weren't even enough to keep him in cigarettes. He too was declining. So many years had stuck to his body that he walked about all hunched over, quivering, like a strip of flypaper. His tongue continued to be on bad terms with words: the ones he didn't get mixed up came out split in two. His life was nonetheless serene. He slept in peace. Changing his life frightened him.

His real misfortunes began, as always happens, with a piece of good news. In 1964, shortly after New Year, his goddaughter Isabelita sent him a postcard asking him if he wouldn't consider coming to live with her in Madrid.

You're very lonely, Godfather, and to tell you the truth I miss you. Every morning I tell Perón about the days when you used to read letters without opening the envelopes and knew how to heal people with a few little incantations. And Perón says just go ahead and bring him here then, bring him whenever he feels like coming . . .

To tempt Cresto, Isabelita sent him an open ticket from Buenos Aires to Madrid, and a touching telegram: 'The date is up to you, Godfather. We have our hearts already set on having you here.'

The word 'we' meant that the General was asking him to come too. That was what finally made Don José give in to temptation. Here, in Buenos Aires, he had his school of science half gone to ruin, the mass evictions ordered by the Government, the popular soup kitchens, the unfair competition from courses in Christian doctrine. There, in Madrid, history awaited him. Would a man as great as Perón allow the doctrine of the Basilio School of Science and the twenty justicialisto truths to be conjoined? Would it be possible for the two ideas, united in a marriage of true minds, to penetrate each other and succeed in attracting all humankind? Others besides John XXII, Mijita Scruchó, Meao Setún and Yon Fichera Kenedy. The future would belong to Cresto and Perón.

With the end of his pencil well moistened with his tongue, Don José laboriously composed the telegram announcing, finally, the change in his destiny. 'Leafing Thors. Meet rarepot. Josecristo.'

To her husband's amazement, Isabelita deciphered this to mean that they were to go get her godfather on Thursday at Barajas airport.

Perón disliked that slovenly individual with his long fingernails tipped with dark crescent moons. On the trip back to Puerta de Hierro he tried, nonetheless, to be polite. 'Chabela has told me that you know how to heal people with words. I am more or less familiar with the method because my mother too used it, in Patagonia, where there are so many people with no health care. How did you learn, Cresto?'

'Before I got my false set of teeth I obsessed it. Afterwards, I didn't any more.'

'It seems he lost the gift once he got dentures,' Isabel translated.

As they went along the Paseo de la Castellana and entered the Calle del General Sanjurjo, Perón said sadly: 'Here you have Madrid, Cresto. I wish you the best of luck.'

'I too. And I hope I meet up with that dunce of a wife of mine, who will most likely be searching for me all over the Uropes.'

'She'll come here, Godfather, she's sure to come,' Isabelita said encouragingly, squeezing his hands.

Disappointed by the visitor's ignorance, the General deposited him in the house as though he were a piece of furniture and from that day on lent him only his distraction. Cresto, however, doggedly followed him everywhere, though always at a respectful distance.

Cresto brightened Isabelita's life. At the slightest pretext she would throw herself into her godfather's arms, calling him Papa, and would sit in his lap for long intervals. After dinner, when the General had gone off to bed and the lights in the house were out, the two of them would go up and down the stairs carrying big lighted candelabra, in search of Doña Isabel Zoila's soul. Then, in a bedroom on the second floor, with the door shut tight, they would summon dead friends and subject them to sessions of questioning that sometimes lasted till dawn.

Inexplicable phenomena soon began to take place in the villa. There were sounds that came from nowhere and silences in which everyone spoke. One time the General opened a sideboard and a cough leaped out. Another time, in the middle of the afternoon, he heard the steps of the stairs groan as he set foot on them. One Sunday in summer, around ten p.m., the noises ruined dinner. Seated at the table were the General, José Manuel Algarbe (who was his private secretary at the time), Isabelita and her godfather. A gust of wind slithered beneath the tablecloth like a snake and made the soup get cold. Ethereal figures began chasing each other all about the house. Algarbe, who was possessed of rock-solid good sense, feared that it was an attempt on the General's life and got up from the table to call the Guardia Civil. When he picked up the telephone, a noise bit him on the hand and made a drop of blood spurt out. He then ran through the garden and got the guard at the entrance. The two of them then searched every inch of the house, from the coal cellar to the attic. In vain.

That night marked a violent change of mood on Isabelita's part. She became melancholy. She spent hours shut up in her bedroom, weeping over anything and everything. She enthroned on the night table a color photo of Doña Isabel Zoila, changing the flowers she offered it each morning. When autumn came, she again took up her habit of walking about with the lighted candelabra, with Don José following after, and summoning spirits. After so many efforts, as was inevitable, Doña Isabel Zoila came at her bidding.

She came to them in the form of a little blue wisp of smoke, warning them that they would not be able to question her about the future, because the dead are not permitted to lift those veils. She promised, on the other hand, to throw open the doors of the past to them. Isabelita wanted to know what paradise was like. 'Stifling,' the dead woman said. 'There is a bed filled with stars where the spirits spend their time hugging and kissing each other.'

'And are you startled by all the bedlaming?' Don José asked her. But the little blue wisp of smoke, growing wispier still, turned its back on them and disappeared.

When the godfather looked about for the General to recount the story to him, he found him very upset, with his mind elsewhere. 'Perón doesn't want to be disturbed,' Isabelita said to him. 'He's having forebodings.'

Visitors kept coming to the villa in a steady stream and whispered in little groups, going off into corners where Cresto couldn't hear them. The reason for all this secrecy soon came to light. The General had promised that before the end of 1964 he would return to Argentina, and as December approached, he was obliged to keep his word. Cresto saw signs in one of the visitors that made him suspicious. The latter was a man with a sad look in his eyes, hair plastered down with brilliantine and a crooked smile. His name was Augusto Vandor. 'Keep a sharp eye on him, General, because they're going to turn that pancake over,' Don José predicted, taking a glimpse into the future. Isabelita had to take him aside and beg him to be more prudent.

On Monday, 1 December 1964, Perón left for Barajas airport, hidden in the trunk of a Mercedes. The following morning, shortly before ten a.m., the flight he was on arrived in Rio de Janeiro. It was not allowed to go on. That same night, the Brazilian government – at the insistence of the Argentine foreign office – forced the plane to fly back to Madrid.

With that fiasco, it seemed to Cresto that the time had come for the General to move his queen. Certain oracles of the Arab Al-Mu'tamid, which he was in the habit of consulting in moments of confusion, revealed the following to him:

> To his hand we are a game of chess:
> If the knight checks, the queen saves the king.

Isabelita found that nothing corresponded more precisely to the General's fears than that hermetic message. Isolated in his Spanish exile, Perón felt that the reins of the Peronist movement were slipping from his hands. Vandor pledged his loyalty from afar, but kept dropping sibylline hints, especially when he spoke with the military, that the General was now lost amid the clouds of Olympus. Peronism needed a leader with his feet on the ground – himself, of course.

'What do you recommend, Cresto?'

The godfather replied sententiously:

'If the captain is not allowed to unscathe his sword, then he must unscathe his wheals.'

Perón resolved to make his move immediately. On 10 May 1965, Isabelita flew to Paraguay. She arrived with a letter from her husband to General Stroessner and the order not to set foot in Argentine territory, no matter what guarantees and temptations might be offered her. She behaved most discreetly: discovered by a news agency, she apologized for her Spanish accent. Someone asked her on the street if it was true that she was a devotee of spiritualism. 'It makes me indignant that people should say that,' she answered, stamping her foot. 'I am a militant Catholic.'

When she returned to Madrid a month later, tears welled up in Perón's eyes as he embraced her and informed her that that trip would not be her last.

'Next time, Chabela, you'll have to go to Buenos Aires.'

In the middle of August the villa got wind of the news that Vandor was meeting once a week with military leaders and conspiring with them to stage a coup d'état. An utterly duplicitous slogan born of those meetings was now circulating among the metal workers: 'To save Perón we must be against Perón.'

The moment, then, had come. For a month, the General gave Isabelita lessons in the art of leadership, assigning her each day a couple of sentences that she was to learn by heart. He stressed the importance of playing before everyone the role of 'the General's other self' and speaking in his name, always. At the beginning of October, when he felt that she was ready, he took her to the airport and said to her: 'Take care of yourself, my girl. If I lose you, I have no one else left.'

He had Cresto left. Now that he was alone with the General, Cresto refused to leave him for one minute, from sunup to sundown. At eight in the morning, when the master of the house was in the downstairs study preparing to record the secret orders to his tactical commandos and write letters which, in this case, demanded the most subtle words in his repertory, Cresto's silhouette could be made out, posted in an armchair on the other side of the curtains, and every so often it trumpeted its presence by hawking up phlegm.

Before Perón entered the dining room for lunch, whether there were guests or not, Don José was already there, with his fork in one fist and his knife in the other, tucking a food-spattered napkin under his neck. After Algarbe had left Puerta de Hierro, ten months before, the godfather's manner had become overfamiliar and crude. Since no one expresssed disapproval of his behavior, he gave free rein to his nature. He disliked washing himself, and wherever he went he left behind a rancid odor of fermented urine.

One night in December he outdid himself. The General had been invited to dinner by the journalist Emilio Romero. The two of them wanted to compare the alarming reports that they had been receiving from Buenos Aires and needed to talk with each other alone. Perón had prepared a couple of messages against Vandor and wanted to discuss them with the journalist:

Those halfwits believe that I'm dying and are already beginning to fight over my garments, but what they do not know is that the dead man is going to rise from his grave when they least expect it . . .

That was how one of them ended. And the other one began:

> We have no reason now to resort to half measures. I am going
> to be very clear: the personal enemy is Vandor and his camp.
> We must go at them full tilt, aiming our blows straight at their
> head. In politics you can't just wound. You must kill.

But the dinner with Romero was to be a fiasco. Around eight-
thirty that night, the General wanted to put Cresto off the track by
announcing that he felt sick to his stomach. He went upstairs to
his bedroom. He dressed furtively and walked through the garden
in the dark to the entrance, where a limousine was waiting for him.
When the chauffeur opened the door for him, he spied José
Cresto's scrawny body in the back seat. The only thing he could do
was take him along with him.

The old man devoured his food so noisily and butted in on the
conversation so indiscreetly that Romero preferred to leave sharing
confidences with the General for some other time. When he
finished one course, Don José announced the feat with a belch,
and prepared himself for the next one by accumulating gobs of
phlegm in his craw and spitting them out in the porcelain urn on
the mantle behind him.

Although winter fell like a whiplash on Christmas Eve and did
not temper its rigors until well into the month of February, Cresto
did not wish to deprive Perón of his company on his early evening
strolls. He would come outside with a toothpick in his mouth, and
as he trotted at the General's heels he would endeavor to describe
to him the landscapes of the beyond and instruct him in the
control of one's passions. What with the breathlessness brought on
by the walk and the pirouettes of the toothpick, nearly all these
teachings spouted forth badly distorted. Perón listened to them
with little interest. He had scant esteem for the old man, and was
of the opinion that he was as intelligent as a mare's egg.

Cresto then changed tactics and switched to a different level of cunning altogether. When Isabelita had to go to Buenos Aires, he gave her only one piece of advice: under no circumstances should she see her mother or her brothers and sisters, for she would be risking her life if she did. To Isabelita's misfortune, shortly after her arrival, her widowed mother fell ill with cancer and begged her, in the name of charity, to come visit her in the hospital. In desperation Isabelita telephoned her godfather to ask him what she should do. Don José again told her: 'You know that seeing her is not possible, not under any circumstances.' Months later, while Isabel was on a tour in the Chaco, the news reached her that Doña María Josefa Cartas had died with the hope that her daughter would at least attend her funeral. Again the answer was no.

Between March and April 1966, Cresto sent a strange letter, which appears to allude to the creation of a golem, to two disciples of his from the Calle Tinogasta. To this day, no one has been able to make head or tail of it:

My dere beleavers: I have had occazion to influze Life into Something far too great, perhaps superior to Me. But it is so great that it may carry me away compleatly and even grow round about me like the fat that anvelops the flesh, I have finished the Manwom and at any moment I espect the Manwom to tourn upon Me. It stands to reazon. Creating such Grandure has esasservated my devility. For I have given it all I had. and (S)(H)e refuses to acept that I am a Makr. (S)(H)e dosent evendare look me in the face, so my bronkias ake a bit. I am heeling myself by avoyding esternal clenliness which crashes so badly with internal clenliness. Well Godbye. Read this in the famly and then bern it becuz it promcomises me. Sined: Josecristo.

Meanwhile, in the undeclared wars against Vandorism, Isabel was using her name as an offensive weapon. I am a mother who is coming to the rescue of children who have gone astray, she said. And when she was advised to return to Madrid to save herself from an attempt on her life, she stubbornly answered: The only way they'll get me out of here is as a corpse.

In March 1966, Vandor tried to foist on voters as candidate for governor of Mendoza a local political boss who supported him. Perón ordered Isabel to go to Mendoza and put up the name of another candidate from there. For nearly a week, she toured the province in clapped-out cars, kissing babies and receiving letters for the General. Vandor's man lost.

Three months later, her mission now accomplished, Isabel returned to Madrid accompanied by a bodyguard and a factotum who had offered her his humble services without expecting payment. His name was José López Rega.

They had introduced him to her as a faithful dog, who could be trusted absolutely. The person who interceded on his behalf was Bernardo Alberte, a major who had been Perón's aide-de-camp. Alberte had often called on López Rega to print underground publications and pamphlets of the resistance in his shop on the Calle Salguero. And when he asked for a discount or was late with a payment, López clapped him on the back, hiding his concern: 'The day of recompense will come, Major Alberte, it will come. We'll let it all be for the cause.'

The occasion presented itself at the end of February 1966. At the General's behest, Alberte organized the security forces that were to travel with Isabelita to the provinces in Cuyo. Remembering that López had been a police sergeant, he included him on the list. In order that the señora would approve of taking him on, the two of them made arrangements for Alberte to introduce him to her during a secret meeting, at his house.

It took place at seven p.m. López had dug up the blue suit he reserved for neighborhood weddings. He was wearing a rosette in the lapel. When the señora entered, loaded down with packages and complaining of fatigue, López bowed to her, staring into her eyes.

'I am a messenger sent by Our Lord,' he said to her.

The witnesses heard no more. Transfigured, Isabelita asked to speak with that man alone and emerged from Alberte's study half an hour later with a diaphanous smile, looking rested, as though she were just waking from a sleep of many years. From that moment on, she allowed no one to keep the miraculous messenger from her side. And instead of calling him by the diminutive of his name, Lopecito, she began to call him Daniel.

When the time to return to Madrid was at hand, López asked the señora's permission to write to the General: it was necessary to tell him in advance who he was and why he was coming.

'It's not necessary,' Isabelita said. 'I have already done the requisite singing of your praises to him.'

'It is necessary. As with every annunciation, we have need of an angel. Tell the General that Norma Beatriz, my daughter, will present herself to him this Sunday with a letter.'

Perón was extremely surprised by the very long message brought him by a timid young girl, in a short skirt, whose features disappeared beneath a helmet of black hair stiff with lacquer. His attention was drawn to a few scattered paragraphs of the letter:

I am from a LODGE that is fighting for the advent of the THIRD WORLD,   exhaustively. THE THIRD WORLD will consoidate around three magnetic vertexes: in ASIA (Peking), in AFRICA   (or failing that Libya), and the tilted L in LATIN AMERICA. The work of ANAEL, a lodge that you recognized by greeting by that name our precursor, the so-called MAGUS OF ATLANTA, fifteen years ago now, will be completed when it begins functioning   the TRIPLE A, which is obtained by drawing a straight line from Lima to BUENOS AIRES and a second one from there to São Paulo

I was one of the first   BASIC UNITS   I occupied a humble confidential post at your side, General   presidential guard. You see how the LORD maintained 'royal capitals' round about you! I have studied the soul of human beings all my life   above all, high echelons of the occult hierarchies   The members of THE LODGE are up-right men   But everything is kept under close surveil-lance   I am taking personal care of your esteemed wife's safety   proven effectiveness and disinterest. I am determined to move when the SENORA's political affairs are better oriented organizationally   ISABEL PERON'S objective, which the Peronist leaders, in their eagerness to place themselves in positions that as yet they have not matured enough to occupy, have apparently forgotten

Respectfully yours.

When Cresto embraced Isabelita at the Barajas airport and affec-tionately stroked her hair, calling her 'dear daughter' again and again, he noted in her a certain distance that never turned into outright rejection. He sensed that the weight of his tutelage had diminished owing to the influence of the robust man with a veiled look in his blue eyes who was accompanying her. Don José was surprised that his goddaughter, so withdrawn by nature, enjoyed giving orders and accepting such tireless worshipful attention: May I carry your handbag for you, señora? Shall I get rid of the reporters for you, señora? Cresto noticed immediately that his rival's skillfulness surpassed his own. He would have to force him to leave the scene at once.

Before going off with the General, Isabelita asked her godfather to find a clean, inexpensive boarding house for López Rega, to wait for him while he tidied himself up and then take him to the villa to have a talk with Perón. See to it that the bill for his expenses is sent to me, she told him. We owe this man many favors and we must begin to pay him back somehow.

Cresto remembered a smelly boarding house on the Calle de la Salud, where lodgers were locked out after ten p.m. He spoke highly of it to López in the taxi: The owners are nonpeccable about talaphone calls and change the sheets every day, with the greatest of putrification.

He went on to sound López out: 'Are you thinking of bringing your family over?'

'I have left my job and family behind to serve the cause. And I shall do so with total devotion.'

Don José realized that it was not going to be easy to do battle with him. They arrived at the reception desk of the pension after climbing up the three flights of a gloomy staircase. With self-satisfaction, Cresto inspected the room, where strips of wallpaper were falling off from the dampness. The odor of many dead cigars emanated from the bedclothes. As he bade him goodbye there, the godfather lied that Perón had 'forboded' all visitors for a week, so as to be able to be alone with Isabel. Then, since it is summer, he said, they'll be going on vacation to the Guamarramas. They'll be back in September.

'Then I'm going to phone the señora to apologize for not visiting her.' López was annoyed.

'Do so if you like, but the General is going to be peeved at your impertinence. Don't you realize that it's been nine months since he's been with my goddaughter?'

When Cresto returned to the villa, he ordered the fourth plate removed from the dining table.

'This fellow is such an odd bird,' he explained to Isabel, 'that he called some cousins of his straight from the rarepot. Then he aksed me to taxi him to the Atocha railroad betraytion. And that's where I left him. He'll send you word when he gets back. That's what he told me.'

Such unusual behavior disconcerted Isabelita: López (or Daniel rather) had told her in confidence on the plane that his only family in the world were his wife and daughter, whom he was leaving out of love for the Peronist cause.

'I couldn't say,' Don José shrugged. 'I'm just repeating what he saw me.'

In any event, he continued to feel on edge. When the phone rang he diligently hastened to answer, silencing voices he did not recognize with a flurry of questions resembling a police interrogation. His forebodings kept him awake at night. To top it all off, his goddaughter kept scolding him because he didn't bathe, and when he tried to justify himself by offering his bronchitis as an excuse, she had the servants put him in a tub of warm water and burn eucalyptus leaves all around him, so as to purify the air. 'If my godfather refuses to undress, bathe him with all his clothes on,' she ordered. And for days at a time she kept her distance, eating lunch and dinner alone with the General in their bedrooms.

On 24 July, two weeks after López's arrival, Don José finally came up against the voice he was so afraid of.

'I want to know the General's address in the Guadarramas,' López said imperiously.

Without turning a hair, the old man improvised: 'What do you mean? It's a state sacred.'

'A state secret?' López corrected him.

'If you get my drift, stop bugging me,' Don José said, in perfect Spanish, as he hung up.

From the very night he arrived, López had not known how to deal with his anxiety. When he tried to make it go away, by taking it for a stroll through the arcades of the Plaza Mayor or distracting it in the dives on the Calle Echegaray, his anxiety stuck in his throat like a chicken bone and made him short of breath. He had never before experienced uncertainty, and now he was walking on it. He often remembered the Gobbis. They had told him that Don José had always kept Isabel's guilt feelings alive, that that was his way of keeping her attached to him. Guilt at not having ever finished anything, at not being anybody: not a piano or dance teacher, half Argentine and half Spanish, a political emissary one day and a housewife the next. She could never be a whole person without Cresto's help. For now she was nothing more than 'the wife of'. Señora Isabelita Somebody. The antidote administered by López Rega to instill a feeling of self-assurance in her had proved to be effective. You can do it, Isabel. I will make you value yourself for what *you* are. I will prepare you for the time when Perón is no more. Little by little: you can do it. And thus López's spirits had gradually ousted Cresto's spirits. But what was the antidote against the old man? That was the question.

One morning, sitting in the Sabatini gardens, López resolved to put magic aside and call upon logic. He put in a long-distance call to Major Bernardo Alberte. He described his situation to him and asked for his help. Three days later, Isabelita herself came looking for him at the boarding house.

From the very moment he met the General, López made up for lost time. How many tape recordings supporting the dock workers' strike does he want us to send to the tactical command? I'll have them ready for you by tomorrow. Are you behind in your correspondence? Give me instructions as to what you need to say, and I'll whip your drafts into shape for you. Is the señora going shopping? I'll go with her. You haven't received *La Razón* or *Clarín* for two weeks? I'll drop by Aerolíneas and check up on what's happened. He was tireless. He knew by heart the books that the General had written and sometimes surprised him by reciting sentences that weren't even set down in them yet, but would be some day. They will be, because you've often thought them.

He set to work in the villa before seven a.m. and left at night only after making certain that there was nothing left undone. He made every effort to be self-effacing and silent. He did not charge a cent for his services. He was the opposite of Cresto. Difficulties seemed to melt away before him.

In October 1966, he set up an import-export office on the Gran Vía. As an associate of an employment agency that operated in Bonn and Cologne, he sent housemaids and bricklayers to those two cities and received three per cent of their salaries for a year. He made no effort to recruit more than eighty peasants, but even so he managed to accumulate a small fortune. Since he was convinced that luck would come his way only if he paid his tithes to it, he always set aside a certain amount of money to have postcards with portrait photos of Perón and Isabelita printed, which he then distributed throughout the world.

At the beginning of November, López Rega began at last to breathe with the full force of his baritone's lungs. He left the run-down pension on the Calle de la Salud and moved to an apartment in the Salamanca district, where he secretly taught Isabelita techniques of spiritual transfusion.

Not everything turned out well for him, however. Sometimes, after a good session, as his pupil was preparing to leave, well trained now in the strategy of perfumes and the free will of colors, López – or Daniel, by then – would take a good look at the street through the curtains so as to make sure that the visit had gone unnoticed, and often he came across the clumsy silhouette of José Cresto in the coffee bar on the corner, with the corner of his eye trained on the door of his building. Without looking up, Cresto would greet him with a nod of his head or a gesture, as though he were there only to ensure that his presence would be noted.

One afternoon, in the garden of the villa, Isabelita decided to free herself of that worry: 'You know everything by intuition, Godfather. You will have seen then that my studies with Daniel are perfectly chaste. They offend no one.'

'You may have chased some specks of dandruff off them, but they're not pure,' the old man said, shaking his head. 'If that man is not tempting you by way of the flesh, it must be because he is tempting you by way of lambition.'

And he kept a close watch on them nonetheless.

November was a month when Madrid was in a contrary mood. It was hot even at night. López's senses were so aroused that in order to lull them he wrote his thoughts down and then placed the corresponding notes of the diatonic scale underneath each of them:

Of Two We Will Make One Indivisible and Eternal
La-Do-Fa-Re-Mi-Sol/Mi-La-Sol-La-Sol-Do

And he composed a series of frenzied letters announcing that the volcanoes of the Last Judgment, the surging waves of the Flood were imminent, and the precise mid-point of eternity at which Time simultaneously remembers itself and forgets itself was now at hand. Most of the letters were for his comrades at the Freemen's Rose. But often too, he wrote to the Grand Masters of the Quimbandas Orders, in Paris and in Porto Alegre, asking them to prepare to bear witness to his clairvoyance.

(I am accustomed to being afraid of what I feel within me, I hear this wind that has just blown through me and I whistle to it: You will not be able to bear this grandeur, wind. Prepare yourself. You will not be able to bear it. Sometimes I stay in my room and bleed, to relieve myself. Is this life? Is life the blood that I sweat from the soles of my feet? Villone, Arcángelo, Prieto, Piramidami, Cacho, Nilda, listen to me. I am a reality outside but within myself there is another reality that I cannot yet show you, a cloverleaf where the realities of all of you intersect. Will you believe that the heights on which I alight have spun around? No: I am a breath of air. They dictate in my ear that I am Good. And as for Evil, they order me: You, Daniel, exterminate it. Don't let it past.) On 16 November 1966, around midnight, he wrote his friends at the print shop:

I have succeeded in bringing the General to life again. He is as strong as a boy. Young. On several occasions I touched him deeply and felt the edifice shake.

My ant work is beginning, slowly, definitively.

I put off preparing the General. But this week I felt at last that I could speak to him forthrightly. Among other things I told him that the purpose of my journey here was not to accompany ISABEL or to take my ease in his mansion. That I have come in search of a final definition with regard to WORLD GOVERNMENT and will not leave without it. The General begged me to see to it that he would live long enough to finish institutionalizing his movement and then take his leave as patriarch and philosopher of America.

I left him open-mouthed. He immediately saw that nothing is hidden from the eyes of the LORD. That every goal can be attained. But I did not want to frighten him and stopped there. I went no farther.

You will understand, then, how difficult it is for me to go on being Lopecito instead of DANIEL. How greatly my patience is tried by not being able to exterminate once and for all individuals who are worthless. Jorge Antonio? He will die. Onganía? He will fall soon and once he has fallen he will be worth less than nothing. Cooke and Américo Barrios are already dead and have only to realize that they are. Vandor's death warrant is already signed. The finger of the LORD has traced a cross in blood on the forehead of Pedro Eugenio Aramburu, the tyrant who overthrew the General.

I must rescue ISABELITA and place her wholly on our side. I lie awake nights trying to determine the best path to prove that I was THE ONE who rescued her. I do not yet know whether to pass on to her the power of the WANDERING DEAD WOMAN or whether to leave her in the immaculate purity of her spirit. The LORD will know how to lead me to what is best.

The one who is interfering with my task is José Cresto, whom she introduces as Godfather. You must help me to drive him out of here. Before Valori leaves, have him denounce Cresto as an infiltrator sent by the sinarchy. A way must be found to identify him with Vandor or with some even more fearful enemy. I have never asked anything of you. But now it is your turn to act.

May the LORD shed his light upon you and be with you.

Even before the first letters promising to help arrived, López Rega contrived to involve Isabel in his war on Don José. On New Year's Eve, shortly after the toasts, he solemnly swore that he would offer her a power that not even Evita could have dreamed of: I will make you Supreme Queen, the Daughter of God and the Redeemer of the world.

She lowered her eyes and blushed. 'May Our Lord give me the strength to deserve it.'

Visitors often stayed on as dinner guests. When the table was set, Isabelita saw to it that there was never a place to spare for her godfather. And the one time that the old man tried to sneak into one, his goddaughter herself dissuaded him, informing him that a tray with chicken had already been brought to his room.

Don José tried so hard to ingratiate himself with Isabel that his bronchi miraculously improved. He took a sitz bath twice a week and then came downstairs to the living room, in his pajamas and slippers, smelling of toilet water, so that no one would fail to note his heroic hygienic exploit. But his heart told him that it was hopeless. Even the General spoke to him gruffly, which was unheard of in someone so remarkably courteous.

One morning, just before lunch, Don José came out of doors to sun himself in the park at the far end of the grounds. The heat was descending awkwardly, as though swathed in veils. In the distance the General's voice could be heard, dictating letters. The cooks hummed a tune from an operetta now and again. All of a sudden, he felt a sharp pain in his legs. He went over and sat down amid the roots of the ash tree and smelled a damp vapor that reminded him of Buenos Aires. For the first time he realized that he was alone, many miles from home, with no affection to turn to for refuge. The poodles, playing underneath the dovecotes, ran over to lick his hand. Don José hugged them to his chest so as to feel a bit of warmth and petted their curly heads.

'Let go of them, you useless old man!' a hoarse, broken voice shouted. The General came down the porch stairs in one stride and planted himself before Cresto: 'You useless old man! Leave the dogs alone!'

'I only wanted . . .' The godfather was at a loss for the right words to apologize. He heard the General pant with rage, saw his bloodshot eyes. He was suddenly afraid. He spoke, unwittingly, in a country accent: 'Didn't you see how they were licking my hands?'

Perón turned pale. His eyes went blank. Asthmatic, carried away by the weight of a dead tongue that was coming back to life in him after many years, he exclaimed:

'Clear out of here! Leave my mother alone!'

'My mother'? Cresto began to puzzle over the words. What did Perón's mother have to do with it? He soon found out. The name of the man that Perón had hated more than anyone else in his life was Marcelino Canosa. He was a peasant whom Doña Juana had begun living with a few months after being left a widow, when she was still in strict mourning. He was the same age as Perón, and when she spoke of him Doña Juana referred to him as 'my son'.

But Juan Domingo did not suffer on that account. He suffered because a mother like that could not be introduced at an officers' club.

As soon as López found out that that memory tormented the General, he got hold of some photographs in which Canosa, an old man now, was posing next to a large portrait of Doña Juana, and had them retouched so skillfully that the stepfather's crooked smile, his face like a fox's, and his hooded eyes matched Cresto's features, point for point. Once he had that deadly weapon in his possession, López Rega waited for the opportune moment to let it fall into Perón's lap, hinting (in the tones of someone who is horrified by his own suspicion) that Don José had taken possession of Canosa's spirit so as to bring it into the light of day at any moment.

Cresto was in Buenos Aires when he caught on to López's underhanded trick. He was lighting candles at the altar erected to a man who had passed away and suddenly felt the revelation. He spent the afternoon smiting his forehead: Was I that stupid? And did that mathemagician make me fall straight into a trap as simple as that? I understand everything now. From that day on, Perón no longer saw me. He saw Canosa. And he asked Isabel to get me out of the house at once.

They resorted to a ruse to get him out – a sign that they still feared him.

Although he had been born on 7 April, Cresto had always insisted on celebrating his birthday on 3 February, the same day as Isabel's. The evening before, at one of the stands around the Plaza Mayor, he bought her a rag doll dressed as a flamenco dancer and placed around the doll's neck an amulet filled with bits of mica from Jujuy, like the ones Isabel's dead godmother used to make. That night, after wrapping the gift in cellophane, he came downstairs to the dining room, feeling pleased with himself. Isabelita, who had been hiding behind the curtains, crept up behind him and covered his eyes with her hands, cozying up to him in a way that Don José had forgotten.

'Guess who?'

'Darling daughter!' the old man said, taking her hands away and turning around to give her a hug.

Isabelita wouldn't let him.

'Tomorrow is our day, Godfather, remember? I want you to come downstairs to have breakfast with Daniel and me. At eight, all right? I have a little surprise all ready for you.'

'And I have one for you, darling daughter! I have one too!'

Don José Cresto fell asleep singing softly to himself. At five in the morning he took a bath in eucalyptus water and put scent on himself from head to foot. Through the window, he saw birds diverting themselves in puddles of cold water, and a strange feeling came over him as the sun began to come up, yellower than ever, above the skyline of the high plateaus.

During breakfast he competed with the other José in the art of prophesying. López announced, with a frown, that he had glimpsed Isabel levitating in her bed above the crowds in the Plaza de Mayo, enveloped in a mourning cape and wearing the presidential sash. To Cresto, the vision seemed incomplete.

'In order to ascend, my goddaughter must do so over Evita's debody.'

'Ah, Godfather, heaven only knows where the military have put poor Evita,' Isabel said, pouring herself another cup of coffee.

'I don't know where they've put her now. But I do know where they're going to put her next. Right here, my girl – at the top of this house.'

Cresto wolfed down the enormous piece of bread with the crust removed that he had dunked in his milky coffee and when he felt it land in his stomach he hailed it with a belch. He then untied his napkin, stuck a toothpick in his mouth and made a move to get up from the table. Isabelita stopped him.

'Not yet, Godfather. Look underneath the tablecloth. That's where your birthday present is.'

It was an Aerolíneas Argentinas ticket to Buenos Aires on the flight that left that very same night.

'You need to take a little dip in your homeland, Don José,' López Rega said to him with a smile. 'They're complaining at Basilio that you've abandoned them.'

Although he suspected that they were about to deal him a low blow, the old man couldn't figure out which direction it would be coming from.

'Thanks, daughter, thanks,' he stammered, fingering the envelope from the travel agency without opening it. He projected his five senses into the tips of his fingers and finally caught on: 'The thing is, this is only a one-way ticket. How am I going to get back?'

López reassured him. 'And what an I here for, Don José? I'm the one who takes care of things, right? Before two weeks are out, you'll be getting the envelope, so don't be impatient. And who can tell: perhaps the señora will come in person to get you!'

But Isabel's mood had changed completely. She didn't even thank him for the rag doll or the magic amulet, and grudgingly offered her cheek for a farewell kiss, not returning his resounding smack or reacting to the tears in the departing traveler's eyes. And at the boarding gate, as she put up with a last embrace, she made a comment that filled Don José with foreboding throughout the flight:

'How can the death of Godmother have changed so many things? When we lived in Buenos Aires we were different people, you more spiritual and I more of the flesh. And little by little life has made it the other way around.'

*　　*　　*

Once Cresto had left, the atmosphere at the villa was more relaxed, as though a sneeze had relieved it. The General felt so rejuvenated that he began having coffee at the California Café again and strolling along the Gran Vía with his chest puffed out. Sometimes, out of sheer joie de vivre, he would turn around to look at the legs – and the feet, above all the toes – of the young Spanish señoritas. Isabel was seized with an irresistible urge to buy dresses, and when spring came she went to Paris twice, with Daniel in tow. López too began to feel full of himself. He wrote letters to Lyndon Johnson and to Leonid Breznev proposing that a Conference on Cosmic Harmony be held, presided over by General Perón and inspired by his famous speech on the Organized Community. Neither of the two even acknowledged receipt of the letter.

But at least Arcángelo Gobbi answered him. He wrote in capital letters, with the *a*'s and *o*'s only half-finished, as though a moth had eaten away their bellies. But there were so many blinding revelations in a few lines that only the Lord himself could have dictated them:

I must confess to you that for some time I felt resentful toward you, dear Daniel, because you went away without a word of warning. But now I understand the secret. And I am impressed by the heights that you have reached.

In accordance with your wishes, Villone asked Valori to begin the campaign against José Cresto. Valori, who already had one foot aboard the plane to Rome, promised to write to the General from there, presenting him with evidence against Cresto. And, if necessary, he will proceed to petition the Holy See to excommunicate Cresto.

I still have one remaining doubt in my mind, Daniel. I believe I told you that just after my papa and I arrived in Buenos Aires we began to attend a temple of the Basilio School of Science, in the Calle Tinogasta. The name of the spiritual director was José Cresto. Can it be the same person? A very kind-hearted girl, Isabelita Martínez, often went there . . .

So many things had happened in so few years that López Rega was surprised to have no recollection of Arcángelo Gobbi. Wasn't he perhaps that pimply-faced boy who walked all hunched over: the one who dreamed of the Virgin? Of course, that was Arcángelo. He could still see him in his mind's eye, suffering because Betelgeuse was in its death throes.

López Rega had discovered long since that the will to power is rooted not so much in what one does as in what one is prepared to do. That all power lies in the knowledge (he was about to say the resentment) of other people's weak points: their genitals, their temples, their past. Now that Providence had shown him a path that led unfailingly to the very depths of Isabel's past, why not take it?

That same afternoon, invoking the most lofty spirits that unite us and the noble cause that keeps us awake, he wrote Arcángelo.

I ask that you tell me in detail everything you have learned about the SEÑORA. That you hide nothing, no matter how trivial it may seem. Describe to me the changes of odor that you noted in her defecations, the duration of her monthly periods, the teachings passed on to her by Doña Isabel Zoila, the colors and perfumes that she preferred, the sort of clothes she liked to wear, what people in the neighborhood thought of HER. Everything. If you have any document, letter or diary in which she is mentioned, directly or indirectly, send it to me immediately. Find out whose girlfriend she was and what she liked to buy at the grocery store. What chitchat she exchanged with the baker. I stress once again: tell me everything. The better you fulfill this task, the more blessings and favors the LORD will bestow upon you in return.

The information that Arcángelo sent him far surpassed López Rega's hopes. He was able at last to reconstruct Isabelita's itinerary from Montevideo to Medellín and imagine what her fate had been between Cartagena de Indias and Panama, when she was the protégée of Joe Herald, the impresario whom she and Perón wanted to erase completely from their memories.

To encourage him in his practice of the virtue of loyalty, López entrusted Arca with increasingly secret, daring missions. He sent him to act as courier between the labor unions and the archbishop of La Plata, to infiltrate the cells of the National Revolutionary Army (which at the time was plotting an attempt on Vandor's life), and to convince the mystics of the Last Stretch of the Way that Perón was not the Messiah.

Late in the winter of 1972 he decided that Arcángelo was not mature enough to join the Order of the Elect. How could that lad be of use to them? Commissar David Almirón asked him one morning in Madrid. Was he an elite sharpshooter? Did he know how to disassemble a gun? He doesn't belong to that category, López answered. He's nervous, he has sweaty hands, his eyes go blank in the presence of a woman. But he is pitiless. He'll be of use. There are men with skillful hands all over. We need pitiless men. And that same afternoon, walking under the arcades of the Palacio Real, he reflected: I want him cruel, but without a thought in his head. Do you understand, Almirón? I want him totally committed to the cause. And I know who can tame him. Coba. Lito Coba is the man.

Once he returned to the solitude of his room, upstairs in the villa, López Rega wrote:

Arcángelo: You must go about getting your body's resources in shape. The General will return to the fatherland for the first time in the middle of November and we must defend his peace mission with our lives. The left wants to implicate him in their Judeo-Marxist project and then finish off ISABEL, the one obstacle standing in the way of its plan to finish off the Christian family in Argentina as well. Even though we have measured all of them in that bunch for wooden suits, we must sleep with one eye open.

On Friday, 6 October, Lito Coba will come by the print shop. You must ask for forty-five days' vacation. Lito will tell you what is expected of you. Obey him and trust in him as though you were trusting in ME.

Arcángelo must have experienced desperate fits of jealousy and periods of unrelieved depression before admitting that, if Lito occupied a rank superior to his in Daniel's hierarchy, it was because he had better prepared himself. Lito had angular features, a head of abundant brown hair and a blank though alert expression. He had an intricate network of important friends whom he had taken on a pilgrimage to Puerta de Hierro: bankers, cattle ranchers, directors of financial corporations and acting presidents of multi-national conglomerates. The General always received them with the same words: 'What reason can you have to be against me if you never had it better than when I ran the country? The poor were less poor then, and the rich richer.'

It was not these relationships of Lito's that most impressed Daniel, but rather his canny knowledge of alchemical science, the exactitude with which he repeated the numerical keys of Notarikon and interpreted Nostradamus's prophecies.

And at the same time, Coba knew how to control his body with the grace of an athlete. In the Olympiads held by the high schools he had excelled at pole vaulting and swimming backstroke. But he had weak eyesight and his record as a marksman was a disaster.

Daniel had taught him how to aim by ear. For months, Lito practiced shooting at moving targets with his eyes blindfolded, missing and beginning over again, until he learned to hear the movement of what could not be seen: to make out the scrabbling of caterpillars on the bark of trees. Shortly before Arcángelo joined the Order of the Elect, he gave a definitive demonstration, at the little farm in Cañuelas that served them as a hideout, of what he had learned from Daniel. He posted himself in a dark little hut, with a Beretta. From fifty yards away, Commissar Almirón released a dove and shouted: 'Here it comes!' Lito kicked the door of the hut open, heard the dove cleave the air like an arrow and blew off its beak with one shot.

From the moment Coba brought him to the farm, Arcángelo hadn't the least doubt that he would have to subject himself to the same rigorous discipline. With no complaints.

The rambling house in Cañuelas where he was going to live could be seen from a long way away, at the end of a tree-lined alley. It was pink, with a roof of red brick tiles and covered walkways like a monastery cloister. At the entrance was a tiled courtyard.

'Wait for me here and don't move,' Lito ordered him.

He stood there for half an hour. There was no breeze and the sky was the same color as the sun. Half a dozen heavyset men in dark glasses suddenly emerged from the bottom of a ravine and slowly made their way toward Arca. They all felt his flabby muscles. One of them listened to his heart through a stethoscope.

'Strip naked,' they ordered him.

Asking no questions, Arcángelo obeyed. A firestorm of pain swept through his balls. He fell to his knees. They stamped on the pit of his stomach, hit him across the nape of his neck with a board, held his head down in a tubful of shit till his breath gave out completely. He came to in the depths of a cess pit. Only a foul, feeble breath of air filtered in. There wasn't enough space for him to sit down or even to squat on his heels. His throat burned with a thirst that nothing could quench.

Hours, centuries later, when they fished him out of the well, the worst still awaited him. They taught him how to climb over vertical walls without a crack; they made him work out with rings and bars, and on a trapeze far above the ground. Every time he felt his muscles tearing, they shifted the place that hurt worst by applying an electric prod: to his gums, to his groin, to his nipples. They wanted him to learn to recognize in his own body the language that he would be hearing later in the body of victims. At siesta time, he practiced with Ithacas and Beretta rifles at the firing range, blowing burlap dummies and clay birds to bits.

On 15 November Lito told them that Perón had already reached Rome and on the following day would be on an Alitalia flight to Buenos Aires. Maybe a holy war will start this very night, boys. Lanusse's dictatorship wouldn't dare kill the General here, in his own country. Daniel has told us that. Daniel thinks they'll try to assassinate Perón in Rome, before the flight. We're the Elect, the vanguard, heaven's militia. There is only one of us who has not yet gone through the initiation rite.

'Arcángelo?' he called. A soft voice, as cold as ice. 'You're to strip naked.'

His eyes, as always, empty lagoons, Arca slowly removed his sneakers, his polo shirt, his blue jeans, and stood there in his socks. Lito stroked his balls with car grease and then moved upward, little by little, to his asshole. Part your legs, nice and slow, Arca. A fusillade of quicklime ravaged Arcángelo's gut, erasing in one fell swoop all his memories and opening wounds, oyster beds, wasps' nests, sewer drains in him. He felt one more push, and another. He heard Lito bellow, between panting breaths:

'Now you know what a macho dick is, you son of a bitch!'

And for an instant he imagined that they were teaching him how to hate the General. But almost immediately he dimly discerned that that wasn't it: that Daniel was there, speaking to him of heroism and martyrdom.

When, finally, Lito said to him, 'Get dressed now,' he felt the lash of humiliation. He looked at the faces of his torturers, one by one, and spat a gob of bile and blood in Lito's eyes.

'Long live Perón!' one of the Elect shouted.

'Long live Perón!' Arcángelo repeated, with his last remaining strength.

Perón arrived in Buenos Aires on 17 November 1972 and returned to Madrid almost a month later, by way of Asunción and Lima. Now, as 20 June dawned, Arcángelo hoped he was back forever.

He awoke below the enormous portrait photo of Isabel. The thought occurred to him that when she saw him again she wouldn't recognize him. In a few months, from afar, Daniel had turned him into something else: a hero, a person? Day broke. The black light of early dawn moved lower and lower. In one corner of the sky, Arcángelo saw (still saw) the specters of nature: sprays of comets, breasts of virgins, angels who tore out their palpitating hearts to offer them to the Lord.

And he felt that he too was entering history. That all that was the annunciation or the epiphany of a new era. And that Arcángelo Gobbi would one day read his own name in the pages of that era.

8 *Miles in Aeternum*

The pendulum clock in the international hotel at Ezeiza has not yet struck nine that morning. Heaven only knows if it ever will, Cousin Julio thinks as he sits at the breakfast table in wet pants with the photograph of Tomás Hilario Perón, his father, in his suit coat pocket. Heaven only knows whether at this precise point in eternity – 20 June 1973 – time no longer wants to move on and we'll all be stuck here forever, living this present, with Juan Domingo flying endlessly from Madrid and me with no memories but with no death either.

Can the hotel's pendulum clock be one that already existed in the past? On the dial, inside the crown of Roman numerals, the figures of farm workers forged in bronze are the same ones we saw at Granny Dominga's house. And next to the clock, on the mantelpiece, there is a little statue of a woman. It looks like the one that Juan Domingo and I admired at the church of La Merced, when we were Fray Benito's altar boys.

What was it like, Amelia? But how can you remember? Your senses have stumbled on the opera that they're broadcasting over Radio Nacional at this moment, and now that they've fallen, they can't get up. I can still see it, though. The dim light that came in through the skylights of the sacristy is the darkness – the very same one – that is falling across the pages of *Horizonte*, lying here alongside me on this hotel table. I am the adolescent Julio Perón and I am the elderly cousin: in all these years, the light hasn't wanted to move.

You must remember, Juan Domingo. You were chubby. The two of us had our hair cropped off almost to the scalp, with short bangs. Feigning innocence, you asked: 'Do you happen to know, Fray Benito, how Our Lady is different from other women? What I mean is,' you said, pointing to the little statue in the sacristy, 'do you know if Our Lady has muscles, bones and a belly like an ordinary mortal woman? If she goes to the bathroom?' Heaven only knows what ideas went through Fray Benito's mind. He stood there with his eyes riveted on you, as though you were a thread that was too thin and he had to pass you through a needle's eye. I was nearly thirteen; you were younger.

The priest picked up a handful of chalk and drew two figures on the blackboard in the sacristy. The one on the left was a woman's body sliced open lengthwise. You could see her intestines, the spongy tissue of her tits and the caverns of her privates. The figure on the right was an almost incorporeal lady (like the little statue), with her breasts and belly hidden by a sky-blue fringe.

You're big boys now and it's better if it's a priest who shows you these things, Fray Benito said. Tell me, Juan Domingo, what is this called? Innards, you answered. It's a woman's small intestine, the priest corrected you. Mortal women have a small intestine six to seven yards long – do you see it? – and another larger one that is over a yard and a half long, both full of excrement and foul-smelling fibers. What I've drawn here is called . . . (he hesitated for a moment) a vagina. It has two thick lips, with hair, that hold back urine. Underneath the lips is a tooth that's called a clitoris. Our Lady, however, is perfectly pure and has none of these stains that are the mark of original sin. She was born with a womb of clouds instead of flesh, and never needed to defecate or urinate. Her breasts appeared after she gave holy birth to her one and only son, but disappeared when the Infant Jesus no longer suckled.

Fray Benito's sketches left the two cousins so perturbed that for months they went in search of new revelations regarding female anatomy. In one of the shops in the Bajo district, an Armenian offered them, for fifty pesos, a book of vaginal marvels in which a person could clearly see (he told them) that Japanese women had slanted lips down there that matched their eyelids. Since they couldn't afford to pay that much, he refused to show them even one illustration. They spent thirty centavos, however, to look through the slit of a lamp to see a woman undress herself, to the strains of a player piano waltz. Juan Domingo got to see an Indian woman with outsize breasts and Cousin Julio an odalisque who covered her nakedness with her long wavy hair.

But when the odalisque finally gave a faint smile, something fell into Julio's memory: a stone from another time made ripples in the smooth surface of the water.

So that was how it was. The opera that María Amelia is listening to is interrupted. There is a long silence, a tremor within the silence, like the one planes cause when they cross the equator. And immediately, over the radio, a cavernous beep announces that it is nine a.m. Heaven only knows if the pendulum clock will strike nine again. It does: it chimes nine times. Time begins to move once again: it's gone by now. Sitting at the table in the Ezeiza hotel, Señorita María Tizón is diligently describing, in a little notebook, the marital happiness that her sister Potota gave Juan Domingo. She intends to dictate these impressions to the reporters this afternoon, after the General has left the dais. Captain Santiago Trafelatti is distractedly leafing through the special number of *Horizonte* – Perón: His Life Story – The Man, The Leader – Documents and Accounts of a Hundred Witnesses. A moment ago Zamora brought a whole bunch of copies. There are any number of them on the table now. The captain looks at the photos and, every so often, when he spots his own name in a paragraph, he stops to read: Santiago Trafelatti.

An announcer reports over the radio that the *Betelgeuse* of Aerolíneas Argentinas is flying over the Atlantic at cruising speed, with the distinguished General aboard. It is 9.02 a.m. in Buenos Aires.

The opera has alighted on María Amelia's heart once more. Isn't it incredible that they've chosen this morning of 20 June to broadcast over the radio the same opera that she and Juan Domingo heard at the Teatro Colón sixty-five years ago? Isn't it miraculous that I can hear it, still intact, between the sheets of cellophane of a memory that long? It was wintertime, as it is now – June 1917. The cousin slowly walks toward that night in her youth, one little step at a time. She listens.

I, María Amelia Perón, hear once again the starch in the shirt fronts in the orchestra, I see myself leaping over the puddles amid the crush of carriages, as steam and slaver come out of the horses' muzzles, I meet once more the full-length image of my body in the gilt-framed mirrors of the lobby – that green taffeta dress and fox cape of Granny Dominga's.

Everything is there again: the orchestra tuning up between the acts, the old ladies coughing in the semidarkness of the boxes, the theater's maternal chandelier that has hung its wet lights up in the dome ceiling to dry. I see the title on the cover of the program: *Manon*. And underneath it the composer's signature: Jules Massenet. I would say that the voices have the same tremolos as then. The one thing I miss is the tenor. It isn't Caruso who is the Chevalier Des Grieux now, here on the radio: he's not the same one as that night.

You went to the theater against your will, Juan Domingo. You'd come from Santa Fe bringing some documents from your regiment, and Aunt Baldomera begged you to be our escort. You had to put on your dress uniform. You looked like – Auntie said – Manon's cousin. But the opera bored you. You yawned, are you watching? At the high point, María Barrientos, the soprano, sang the aria that another woman is singing on the radio now: '*Adieu, notre petite table.*' Auntie and I stifled a sob. You hid your mouth behind a glove. Then Caruso appeared in his monk's habit. He was suffering. He bit his knuckles. He wanted to seek God, but couldn't banish the thought of Manon from his mind.

I found it heartrending. You, Juan Domingo, began to tap your boots with your saber. Manon came onstage, and throwing herself in Caruso's arms, cried: '*Je t'aime!*'

The house lights went on. You rose abruptly to your feet and told us that you'd wait for us outside, that theatrical lies drove you out of your mind – especially the lies of a woman like Manon Lescaut, who made fools of men in such a despicable way. You missed two acts, the best ones. Will you miss them again tonight and, as you get off the plane, will you tap your boots with your sword? '*Ah, mon cousin, excusez-moi! C'est mon premier voyage!*'

It is still early, but they interrupt the opera on the radio. A new breach of silence is opened. Suddenly, everything is one great roar: as if one's ear had landed in a pit of dying animals. We are broadcasting to the entire country from the dais at Ezeiza. National network. The entire country is here, awaiting General Perón. Listen, comrades!

'This is Edgardo Suárez,' the radio says now. 'I am speaking to you from the dais. I have come to bring you the watchword for this glorious day. Peace and order. Try not to waste your energies. It will be many hours still before the General's return. We must offer him all our strength and the expressiveness of our throats.'

A second voice breaks in: 'Let's liven up the celebration with some folk music. No more speeches.' The radio broadcasts sambas by Los Chalchaleros. And the deafening beat of drums in the distance. And the shouting of the vendors hawking their wares: Soda, soda, sandwiches! Get your headband for the General's return! Perón is coming back, get your headband! Buy *Horizonte*, the special issue of *Horizonte*! Buy your Perón cap, your T-shirt with the Big Man's picture, banners, buy the Peronist emblem, buy!

María Amelia turns toward the pages that Captain Trafelatti is reading, and catches a glimpse of a photograph of herself as an adolescent leaning against a boulder: a somber, sad, forlorn image of her future.

She picks up another copy of *Horizonte* from among the left-overs of breakfast on the table. She looks for herself and there she is again, smiling at someone, who knows whom, at the purgatories that are to come. And almost without meaning to, biting her lips, she descends to those antiques of life. She reads in its pages:

4 *The Manual of Obedience*

'For a soldier there should be nothing better than another soldier.'

Juan Perón
Constitution of the GOU,
Bases, March 1943

The year 1909 was the saddest in Juan's life. Between May and June, Don Raimundo Douce, the director of the International School on the corner of Cangallo and Ombú, decided that fifth-grade pupils would take a preparatory course so as to skip the sixth grade and go directly on to secondary school.

Juan and Julio, who were – by far – the oldest students in the class, could not refuse. Since they were too old now to sleep in their grandmother's house among so many women, they were enrolled as boarding students at the school. They ate their meals and slept there. On many Sundays they were alone in those big empty school yards because their grandmother, intent on getting her housework done, forgot to come get them. They spent the time playing juggling stones and handball. When night fell they wandered about the classrooms, lighting their way with a kerosene lantern, their imagination kindled by the enormous illustrations of invertebrates and dicotyledons hanging alongside the blackboards.

Sometimes Enriqueta, Don Raimundo's niece, took pity on the boys and visited them at school on Sunday mornings to heat their soup for them. Or else, after prayers, she went with them to the dormitory and there, sitting next to the door – always just outside it – she read aloud Jules Verne's descriptions of underwater voyages and expeditions to the Pole, till the boys fell asleep.

Just before Christmas an unfortunate incident occurred. The moment the school vacation began, Juan Domingo said goodbye to his grandmother and his aunts, announcing that he was going off, as usual, to look for a boat that would take him to Patagonia. Two weeks later a police patrol found him sleeping in a granary at the docks. When a sergeant woke him up by shaking him roughly, Juan said to him in a broken voice: 'Mama, mama! Where can my mama be?'

They took him back to his grandmother's, in the Calle San Martín. To excuse his behavior, he maintained that he had missed all the boats and had intended to stay at the docks until March, helping the stevedores and sleeping where the tramps found refuge. His parents sent him a couple of letters from El Porvenir. Juan Domingo refused to answer them.

Giving in to his Aunt Vicenta's entreaties, he agreed one day to occupy the bedroom he had had when he was a little boy, but only for the summer. He bathed in anti-mange disinfectant and allowed his lice-infested hair to be shaved off. His aunt tucked him into bed between linen sheets. And that first night, seeing that he was almost asleep, she felt such affection for him that she bent over to give him a kiss. Juan was on his guard, prickly as a porcupine. He pushed her away, his arms flailing: 'No woman is going to kiss me,' he wept. 'I'm never going to let a woman get her hands on me!'

It was around the end of January that Granny Dominga, after sending Mario Tomás and Juana a telegram to keep them from worrying, decided that only rigorous discipline could tame a grandson as rebellious as that. She read in *La Nación* that scholarships offered for military studies had aroused little interest that year, and that the army was preparing to recruit reserve officers to fill the vacancies. She made inquiries and found out that a middle-class boy, brought up to love his country, had excellent possibilities of receiving a scholarship if, on completing grade school, he passed a very elementary examination in language, mathematics and national history. All he would need – she was told – was a modest amount of pull.

She then sought help from several of the officials from the Department of Hygiene who often used to visit the house on Ramos Mejía, reminding them of the services lent the country by her husband, Tomás Liberato. One of them promised her to put in a word with Julio Cobos Daract, a professor of history at the Military Academy. One morning in April, getting her skirts muddy in the ditches that had been dug for the new subway, Doña Dominga presented herself at Dr Cobos's office, with her grandson in tow. She waited for a long time in the anteroom.

Cobos received her in an indifferent manner, standing up the while, and told her that if 'this strapping young man' got good grades on the entrance examination he could regard the scholarship as already his.

Juan Domingo was placed fifth among the applicants. In exchange for signing a contract that obliged him to serve as an army officer for a minimum of five years, he would receive free tuition and meals plus a salary of 200 pesos when he graduated with the rank of second lieutenant.

On 1 March 1911, when, his knapsack on his back, he entered the old ramshackle house that served as a barracks, Juan noted that he was being branded, though with the brand of no one: that he no longer existed as a person but only as an obedience, that his thoughts were breathing in the plural: I am no longer Perón alone, I am Perón and something less than that. I will possess what others refuse, I will become what others wish. I will learn the trade of obeying and of being nobody so as to practice it on others, against others.

Martín López, the officer who was the plebes' instructor, explained that until the end of the year they were to look upon themselves as 'featherless bipeds', the lowest echelon of a complex hierarchy. They were to obey the NCOs and the second-year cadets, accepting all orders, however inappropriate or cruel they might appear to them. 'There is no discipline without the blindest possible obedience,' he said. 'And none of you will succeed without discipline.'

The following day, when they were handed their uniforms, Juan Domingo learned in his own flesh the unyielding truth of those warnings. After reveille and breakfast, as they were waiting for the instructor in the courtyard, the cadets in the next higher class began to prowl about among them. One of them came over to Santiago Trafelatti and ordered him to take off his shoes. 'Stand on one leg, the way hens do. Let's see that heel.'

Trafelatti felt a sudden violent jab in the arch of his foot and couldn't keep from crying out in pain. The aggressor held up a bloody knitting needle. 'This mare has hoofs that are still soft and tender,' he said, doubling over with laughter. The other prowlers guffawed along with him. 'It's going to take us quite a lot of breaking in to harden this mare's hoofs.'

The plebes were ordered to line up in the locker room and were then handed their uniforms. Juan Domingo was trying on his field cap when one of the second-year cadets snatched it off his head and handed him his own frayed cap in exchange. Another one took the blouse of his fatigues away from him. A third cadet appropriated his trousers and ordered him to put on a pair of stiff balloon pants that smelled of horse dung.

Saúl Pardo, the youngest of the new arrivals, feebly protested. The sergeant who was distributing the uniforms ordered him to step forward one pace and stand at attention, naked. 'You don't like this, featherless biped?' 'No, sir,' the lad answered. 'Six hours in the brig then: because you're a pansy, a shiteater. And when you get out, I want you to like it, do you understand, hen?' An officer backed him up. From the doorway of the locker room he said: 'Engrave this lesson very clearly on your memory. Obedience is obedience. Obeying tempers character and stamps out pride. You who have entered this academy are worms. When you get out, if you do get out, you will be men.' And he ordered them to line up in formation, in less than five minutes, in the dirt-paved courtyard.

There was no other way to reach the courtyard except through a corridor twelve to fourteen yards long. The second-year cadets had posted themselves along it, awaiting the featherless bipeds with strips of rawhide, riding crops, lengths of rope and spurs. Juan resolved to cross the line of fire with the first group. He thought of the guanacos who ran zigzag, stretching and crouching to escape the blows. But wherever he moved, they got to him: he felt the tip of a riding crop lash his lower back, the teeth of a spur rake the nape of his neck, the edge of a strip of rawhide slice into his shoulder. He was in bad shape when he reached the other side, burning with the terrible suspicion that this would be repeated every day. One very small consolation allowed him to sleep without resentment or knots of pain. He had discovered that, as he was pretending to ward off the blows, he could deal a few of his own: sink his fingers into an eye, crack a tooth with a well-aimed butt of his head.

In the 'stable' the cadets were crowded together in eighty bunks with two tiers. Juan's was next to one of the doors; Trafelatti slept in the one above. A week after their arrival, shortly before retreat sounded, a group of ten to twelve featherless plebes managed to remain hidden in the dormitory while outside, in the courtyard, the others were going through another ritual punishment. Trafelatti, who had taken refuge behind some crates, saw Juan burst in, pale and panting for breath. He heard a harsh rasping sound that did not come from Juan's lungs but from a cavern farther down, and recognized the breathing that comes from fear. In the darkness, without abandoning his barricade, Trafelatti dared to ask him what was going on. 'I knocked out two of Pascal's teeth with one butt of my head,' Juan panted. 'And he's ordered me to come out and fight with him tonight.'

Pascal was the star athlete of the academy: a bear well over six feet tall and weighing some 260 pounds whom nobody had been able to stand up to in the gym for more than half a minute in the ring. His specialty was a left uppercut they called 'the Killer Punch'.

The fight began at midnight, by candlelight. A third-year cadet acted as referee. Twenty featherless bipeds stationed around the ring held the candelabra aloft. Juan Domingo was gnashing his teeth. With parted lips, still swollen from the butting they had received, Pascal was dancing in his corner, warming up his imposing set of muscles. 'Go to it!' the referee egged them on.

The giant feinted with a right. He moved about almost listlessly, as though he had left his strength in some far-off place. 'Don't let him fool you, Perón!' Trafelatti warned. Juan Domingo covered his face with his fists and tried to keep out of Pascal's reach, but the athlete's endlessly long arms were everywhere; his body overflowed the vast ring.

Suddenly Pascal made his move: he barely touched one shoulder of his adversary, but he gave the impression that he had dealt him almost a knockout blow. Then he concentrated on Juan's face: he gave him one punch after another, on the temple, the forehead, the mouth, effortlessly, at half-speed, moving backward, to the center, to the left, punishing every last vein in his opponent's body. Juan Domingo felt his gums rip apart, a molar fly out of his mouth, and heard Pascal plow open a furrow in his lip and make slits of his eyes. His temples pulsed like a bird's craw. Stop this slaughter! Trafelatti shouted, but Pascal shook his head: it still wasn't enough.

He withdrew to his corner and stood there motionless for a few seconds till he saw Juan Domingo catch his breath and move blindly toward him, seeking an opening so as to land a blow. Pascal was waiting for him. He danced around Juan with his arms at his sides, letting his guard down, with an animal rhythm that came not from his feet but from his neck. Perón martialed his strength, picked up speed and landed Pascal a brutal punch in the pit of his stomach. It was like battling a wall of steel. His knuckles creaked. The giant showed no sign of pity. With infinite disdain, with regret almost, Pascal slowly raised his left hand. Trafelatti saw with terror the lightning blow of that Cyclops' fist descending. Juan Domingo didn't have time to see it coming. He felt the earth shake and everything went black as Pascal's Killer Punch landed between his eyebrows; the world turned upside down.

Trafelatti washed Perón's wounds and put his battered bones to bed. According to the diagnosis of a male nurse he had cracked his knuckle bones, and he was missing three molars. They bandaged his hands. Nobody heard one word of complaint out of him. On 12 March 1911, around three o'clock in the morning, Trafelatti heard something moving stealthily in the bunk below. He leaned his head over and saw Juan Domingo, still weak and disfigured, bundling up his civilian clothes and putting them in his knapsack.

He was leaving. He was deserting. He was throwing up his scholarship, turning his back on his destiny. He was giving up being nobody only to begin to be nothing.

'You leaving, Perón?' Trafelatti managed to ask him.

At that moment they heard the footsteps of a patrol approaching the door. They were making the last rounds of the night before reveille. 'Get back in bed,' Trafelatti whispered. 'Get under the sheets with your clothes on. Don't let them see you like that or I'll be put in the brig too.' Juan Domingo hesitated for a moment and then dived into bed with his leggings on.

A man is not what he thinks: he is what he does. A country, sometimes, is what a man failed to do. Who will say that later on, in the old age of that night in 1911: Trafelatti, Perón? Neither of the two remembers it now. They mistake one word for another: fate, fake, mistake, Perón, alone, nation. Memory, history has knotted up on them.

After the fight with Cadet Pascal, Juan Domingo bent his every effort toward joining his identity to that of the army, toward disregarding the commands of his desires, toward obeying the most errant desires of his superiors. The real universe died. The Milky Way, his grandmother's pendulum clock, the streetcar bell, the memory of the melancholy Sundays as a boarding student at 2300 Cangallo: those accidents of reality turned for him into absolute nothingness. The only thing that existed was the army. And in that army, on one shore or another of its regulations, his person dissolved. In order to be obeyed he had to learn to obey. Yes, lieutenant, yes, captain, I will obey your every desirorder.

He became fast friends with Trafelatti. On weekdays they went out running along paths of gravel and soft sand together to strengthen their legs, and they competed with each other on the rings and trapezes of the gym to toughen their biceps.

Every so often the academy was visited by Teutonic knights, officers of the Grand Imperial General Staff who observed the teaching methods and offered advice on changes of pedagogy. It was rumored that one of those lieutenant-colonels, merely by virtue of being a Berliner or a Pomeranian, earned as much as the Argentine Minister of War. Juan Domingo was impressed on seeing from afar the imposing gleam of their spiked helmets. He caught a whiff of a certain air of aristocracy in their guttural, monosyllabic orders. If authority had a body, the Germans were the mirror that reflected it. In a few weeks discipline became as rigid as a post. Even the act of crossing one's legs involved a prescribed ritual. The old manuals of French tactical warfare were replaced by the masterworks of Clausewitz, Moltke and Schlieffen. When he was wearing his dress uniform, Juan Domingo's thoughts flowed in a different way. He strutted. He was not just plain Perón but Cadet Perón.

Getting dressed, taking a shower, eating, parading, reveille, retreat, mess: everything was predictable. How many young men were that fortunate? Even the hazings began to be a necessary horror. Beat me so that my body will be tempered. I am not who I am. How not to be proud of a difference like that?

Late in the afternoon on Saturdays, when the bugle call

dismissing them for the weekend sounded, Juan Domingo and Trafelatti busied themselves pressing their uniforms and talcuming their groins and their armpits. Before going out they would take a look at themselves in the mirror of the officers' club, proud of those garments that set off their body contours so elegantly: the hussar's jacket with frogging and braided epaulets, the colored stripes down the trouser seams, the French kepi.

They would take a streetcar and ride though damp slums that smelled of dung. Near San Martín station, at the door of a bar with little red lanterns and papier mâché flowers, monumental women downing beer and plates of polenta were always posted, exposing chalk-colored flesh and toothless mouths, shrieking with laughter, shrill as birds. The corporals and sergeants spoke highly of the skill with which those women, for a mere fifty centavos, could explain in their exotic languages all the joys of being confined to quarters by love. The cadets were forbidden to have anything to do with them because if they so much as brushed against them they would contract an incurable disease, which could be relieved only with baths of permanganate and red-hot needles in the urethra. Being invulnerable, Pascal had dared to take care of his needs with them many times and had even seen photographs of them from earlier days, when they still had all their teeth.

Juan Domingo and Trafelatti sought less crude diversions. They went to circuses in the neighboring towns, Santos Lugares, Tropezón or Munro. As soon as the ringmaster saw uniforms arrive, he improvised a welcoming ceremony. The trombone orchestra played, off key, the overture from the San Lorenzo March. The clowns put on an act in which a French sergeant gave cadets orders: 'Marrch, on ze double, you,' whereupon they would humiliate him by answering, in a German accent, 'Ve vill not obey, you *Franzose*.' The lights dimmed.

The drums rolled. The trapeze artists bowed. And after some rheumatic numbers on the trapeze, the lights went out and a spotlight revealed the ringmaster. Ladies and gentlemen, esteemed cadets, the storm is abating because the performance is about to begin. The trombones essayed a tune that did its best to sound like country music. Two gauchos, knives bared, leaped from the stands into the ring. The beam from the spotlight turned red. One of the gauchos gratuitously insulted the other. The one who had been affronted sought the audience's understanding: his offended honor was calling for vengeance. They began fighting. The author of the insults lost his knife. The other gallantly allowed him to recover it. The scene was repeated, the other way around: this time the bad gaucho, amid arrogant bursts of laughter, slit his rival's throat. And then took to his heels, running without stopping, but always remaining in the same spot. Suddenly all the lights came on. Army troops appeared: hundreds of soldiers leading a couple of old nags by the halter. Imagine the dust and the flags, ladies and gentlemen, imagine the cowardice of the treacherous gaucho caught by the nation's armed forces, look at him begging for mercy. Shall we let him go free? Noooo! To jail with him then. The circus is Circe.

Proud of his insignia, of his cape, of the rosette crowning his kepi, Juan Domingo applauded. *I am Perón, the cadet. I am the Army.* And the show ended amid clouds of blue and white smoke, a splendid night.

On Sundays, he and Santiago slept in late. Dripping with brilliantine, they went to show off in the atrium of the church of San Martín. They pretended to admire the young ladies' hats so that they in turn would feel free to admire their uniforms. When Mass was over they strolled about the square and stopped in front of the bandstand where the firemen were playing the popular waltzes of the day. They listened gravely and then left, ramrod-stiff, one hand resting on the pommel of their saber and the other clutching their gloves.

In May 1911 a merciless cold spell descended on Buenos Aires. At dawn the fields were white with hoarfrost. Braziers had to be set up in the plebes' dormitory. All of them had chilblains. Trafelatti's ears were blistered. And what was more, the plebes were tense, their nerves on edge. On 9 July they were to parade before the stern German inspectors and they still had not mastered goose-stepping and changing the position of their Mausers as they marched.

In June the thermometer went down even lower and the continual wind ruined their target practice on the firing range. It was around that time that the second-year cadets hatched a plot to give the plebes a hazing so heretical that it buried the memory of their previous sufferings and left forever implanted in them the dogma of obedience.

It was Pascal's idea. Up until then hazing had been a routine game whose rules the victims knew by heart. It lacked surprise. From then on it was to be a rite. Its violence could be refined to whatever point they liked. No matter what happened, the officers would look the other way. They were the ones who spoke of the hazing as a process of Darwinian selection, thanks to which idlers and weaklings were weeded out of the army. 'That is what creates an esprit de corps,' the Minister of War had said in earlier days, implying that the corps of the spirit was created in the same way.

As the cold became even more severe, the second-year cadets allowed the plebes to relax and forget the cruelty of the hazings. At times, before retreat, they ordered them to carry boxes of stones through the courtyard, or made them strip naked and get dressed again within one minute. But that was all. Life became monotonous. Without the fear of punishment, practicing for the parade was a bore. On 28 June the temperature stayed at freezing all day long and the experts predicted that it would go even lower before dawn the next day. Pascal decided that the time had come to carry out the rite.

The plebes ate dinner at eight, played cards and went to bed at ten. Juan Domingo and Trafelatti went, as usual, to look for the NCO who was giving them boxing lessons. Oddly, he was nowhere around. Around two in the morning, dressed in their fatigues and wearing spurs, the second-year cadets burst into the plebes' dormitory. Everything happened at once: they turned the lights on, yanked the plebes' bedclothes off, ordered them to line up in formation, naked, alongside the bunks.

'Into the courtyard, cadets, into the courtyard!' Pascal shouted. 'We're going to give you a fifteen-minute riding lesson!'

In a daze, Trafelatti fumbled about for a blanket to cover himself with before going out into the cold. They caught him at it. One of the older cadets, lagging behind, looked his frail little body over from head to foot. And took pity on him.

'Put on your undershirt and socks. And get out there, on the double!'

Outside the cold shattered the air. In the semidarkness of the corridors, the plebes gingerly picked their way across the tiles, as though they were walking on red-hot coals. A few of them had managed to throw a blanket over their shoulders; others had on woolen socks. They were all shivering, feeling helpless, their noses running. A spokesman asked for a truce. Why not wait till after the pledge of allegiance to the flag?

'We're going to catch pneumonia, sir. Something catastrophic may even happen. We're not questioning the order. We're going to obey it. But we would like you to postpone it till some other time . . .'

Pascal gave a guffaw. 'Is the cadet afraid? Is he cold, poor little thing? Take the leap, soldier, and learn what courage is!'

A pudgy second-year cadet with a slit eyebrow, who did

everything he could think of to toady to Pascal, announced that the featherless bipeds would graduate that night and be quadrupeds.

'You're to line up in parade formation. But on all fours. Each of you will be ridden by a superior. At a walk, a trot and a gallop. Not too fast and not too slow, any of you. Anybody that falls waits in the arcade, rests for a minute and starts all over again. Have you got that straight?'

Juan Domingo was just a little over fifteen at the time. He weighed less than 135 pounds. He had furtively kicked his blanket along as far as the hallway, but even though he finally managed to put it around his shoulders, he still felt sharp pains in his freezing balls. Taking refuge behind a column, he tried his best to escape notice. He sensed that Pascal was keeping a sharp eye on him. He saw him adjust his spurs, button the neck of his cape, hitch up his belt. He heard him come his way, lumbering like a great bear.

'Take off your blanket, Perón. I want to mount you bareback.'

Trafelatti also heard Pascal's order. He saw Juan Domingo obey without a protest, and saw to his amazement that all the others were obeying. He silently thanked his lucky stars that that towering hulk of a man had stopped at Perón before he got to him. 'He's going to break his back,' he thought, knowing that he was never going to forget that thought.

The plebes were ordered to form lines three yards apart. Behind each line the cadets who were going to mount them readied themselves.

'Reins!' the chubby cadet shouted.

Pascal made Juan Domingo bite down on a mouthful of iron, with braided ropes at each end of the bit.

'Featherless bipeds, on all fours, maaaar . . . !' The crust of ice covering the courtyard shattered.

'Cadets, mount! Forward maaar . . . at a walk!'

Juan Domingo closed his eyes. He felt the unbelievable weight of his torturer on his back. He felt the whole planet doubling him over. The palms of his hands passed over a razor-sharp ridge of ice. The sting of the blood pierced him. Almost immediately, the cold anesthetized it. Pascal's spurs dug into his lower back; he smelled of grass, of horse. He moved on.

I must obey, he told himself over and over, I must obey. I am a man, I can do more than I can do.

Pascal urged him on with the riding whip. All right, colt, we're going to trot! And Perón, crawling with all his might, went on telling himself: I'm a man, I'm going on. He ran out of breath. Alongside him, the other bipeds were milling about in a pack, panting. That drove him on. I'm not giving up. You won't make me give up, you bastard. Are you giving me an order? I'm obeying you. Am I a horse? Yes, sir, I'm a horse, whatever your will forces me to be. A lash from the rawhide strip sent a shudder through his legs; the insatiable spurs dug into his backside. I'm still here, I'm still going.

He never knew at what moment his torturer let him go. Whistles began blowing, signaling trouble. Somebody was weeping. The guards' boots resounded in the hallways. The last thing Juan Domingo saw were ice-cold, bloodstained sheets, on which his body was falling asleep.

The next day the plebes did not assemble when reveille was sounded. Their knees were a mass of bleeding flesh. Juan Domingo's elbows became infected. Dark-colored sores appeared on his hip. He fell ill with fever. One day went by, then another. Santiago Trafelatti began practicing for the pledge of allegiance to the flag again, and he, Perón, wasn't able to. It took him longer than anyone else to recover.

Colonel Gutiérrez, the head of the academy, ordered a summary investigation, but since the plebes refused to violate the cadet code of silence, the cruel cavalcade of 29 June remained unpunished and therefore unremembered. Like all the others, Pascal was assigned the duty of making night rounds at the infirmary. He walked indifferently up and down the rows of beds, paying no attention to anyone. They were all equal now: they all bore a cattle brand.

The closer Juan Domingo came to making himself become a zero that was less than zero, the more the Argentine Army became his universe, his reality, the envelope of his self. It was the future, the only one possible; it was his body, tattooed now with obedience, incomprehensible now without his uniform; and as it was necessary for him to suppress his past, the army completely filled the place once occupied by the past.

The plebes pledged allegiance to the flag on 9 July and paraded, a bit battered but jaunty nonetheless, past the German inspectors. There then followed months of routine. Obliged to choose their branch of service, Juan Domingo and Trafelatti opted for the Infantry: field officers, educators of the plebs. They imagined that the battles of the future would not be fought on horseback but hand to hand, after endless marches.

They were subjected to field maneuvers that lasted forty days, in the vicinity of Córdoba, and to the north of Concordia, Entre Ríos. They were convinced that they alone embodied the fatherland. The miracle of *esprit de corps* was coming to pass. For a soldier there was nothing better than another soldier.

In those months Juan Domingo began to practice his new signature as a soldier. He signed himself only Juan Perón, slanting the J to the left and the P in the other direction, as if they were two trees lashed by opposing winds.

Finally, on 18 December 1913, he received his second lieutenant's saber. Of the 110 cadets who graduated, Juan Domingo ranked in the middle platoon, *uomo qualunque*, 43rd: the same number as the year in which everything would begin all over again. He was assigned to the 12th Infantry Regiment, in Paraná. Trafalatti, who finished near the tail-end of the class, got the assignment he had asked for, in Tucumán.

That last afternoon the heat was unbearable. Juan Domingo, sweating in the cape of his dress uniform, went back to Granny Dominga's by train, past suburbs rusted by the sun. One of his classmates, Saúl S. Pardo, had unexpectedly given him an album of photographs and newspaper clippings as a gift. In it Juan Domingo found his own face as a child in 1911, saw Pascal raising the flag, came across Pardo's bewildered gaze. And he lingered over the last of the clippings:

LA ACCIÓN, PARANÁ, 10 DECEMBER 1913

Disastrous Ending of Maneuvers

The cadets of the Military Academy, who camped for a month on the property of Señor Soler, north of Concordia, returned to Buenos Aires yesterday in a physical state that has brought criticism from their families. In July 1911, a number of complaints were presented to their superiors by cadets of the class of that year, charging that they had suffered humiliation at the hands of their superiors. It now appears that those responsible for this mistreatment were high-ranking officers.

Letters sent to this newspaper, the signatures of which we have been asked not to publish, state that after the practice maneuvers, simulating actual battles between Blues and Reds, all of which were successful, on the third of this month the Infantry company raised its camp on the Ayuí and readied itself to bivouac on the bank of the Little Uquén, and then go

---

on from there to the Jubileo train station. The assistant director of the Academy, Colonel Agustín P. Justo, ordered that this distance be covered on foot, despite the fact that the day that was dawning gave signs of being stiflingly hot. The infantrymen marched through sandy terrain and many of them, unable to withstand these rigors, fell unconscious from heat exhaustion and sunstroke along the way, and therefore army trucks and an army first aid unit had to be called in . . .

At his grandmother's, they uncorked a bottle of cider and Aunt Vicenta gave an impromptu speech asking God's blessing on the fortunes of the brand-new officer. The following morning, Cousin María Amelia added another clipping to the album.

LA RAZÓN, BUENOS AIRES, 18 DECEMBER 1913

Annual Celebration at San Martín School

The same bright sunshine, or perhaps even brighter than in years past, reached . . . [et cetera]. When the drumrolls ceased, and after a brief silence, Señorita Mercedes Pujato Crespo, president of the Pro Patria Association, uttered the highest praise of the Argentine Army, and then pinned on the blouse of Cadet Sergeant Eduardo Pascal Malmierca, the most outstanding pupil of the year, the highly symbolic gold medal . . .

A telegram from Don Mario Tomás urging him to come to Camarones marred the festivities in Juan Domingo's honor. In 1910, his father had inherited the post of justice of the peace. For several months he went each day from El Porvenir to Camarones. Worn out by then, he left the farm in the care of Doña Juana and Benjamín Gómez, and installed himself in the little sheet-metal building where the town magistrates administered justice.

In October 1912, with no explanation whatsoever, he gave up everything: El Porvenir and the pleasures of fine penmanship. He decided to look for another farm in the deserts of Patagonia, and to populate it all by himself, if that were possible. He dreamed of a city with battlements, crisscrossed by empty avenues, with a single inhabitant. He then summoned Juan Domingo to secure his son's approval of his dream.

Mario Tomás waited for his son near the docks, with a saddled Percheron. As they embraced, they were overcome by a feeling of sadness, as though the echo of some misfortune had left them with a lump in their throat forever. As they rode out to El Porvenir the father barely said a word. He sat straight in the saddle, though he allowed his head to droop. He mentioned the dream in vague terms. It seemed to Juan Domingo that, rather than venturing forth in search of a new life, his father wanted to invent a city in which all his past lives would be lost.

He found the farm in a run-down condition, as if it were readying itself to be abandoned. The sheep were suffering from another epidemic of mange and his mother had put off shearing them in the vain hope of curing them. The sheet-metal siding of the house was rusting away since no one had attempted to repair the damages. Even Mario Avelino, who in the past would put on jasmine toilet water to receive his brother, greeted him distantly, his mind elsewhere. His mother said that her first-born son had spent so much of his time amid guanacos that he had become a creature of the wilds.

Juan Domingo advised them to sell El Porvenir before the buildings came tumbling down. He had heard (he told them) that west of Camarones was a gravelly high plateau, with water sources that no one owned. By changing the course of the streams and digging irrigation ditches, that land could, perhaps, be made fertile. Someone had baptized the plateau with the name of a medieval utopia, Sierra Cuadrada. Why not try there?

'It sounds like a good place for a man by himself,' his father reflected.

'You've gotten that one idea into your head,' his mother said. 'Building a city for just one man.'

'And why not build three cities instead, Papa?' Juan Domingo encouraged him. 'Three cities for three persons.'

'I must explore the terrain first. I'll go up there tomorrow,' his father announced, taking off his boots and getting into bed with all his clothes on.

At daybreak the next morning he drank a couple of matés, filled a sack with hardtack and separated a relay horse from the herd. He did not want anyone to go with him.

'Are you sure of what you're doing, Father?' his younger son asked him.

'I've been sure of only one thing in life and now I don't trust even that. Let me go now. I'm setting out on a penitential journey.'

Don Mario Tomás wandered about, totally lost, for a hundred days. When he returned, in April, he said that he had come upon the minarets of a holy city in the middle of the desert, on the other side of the Chico River, after crossing hills of salt. He wanted to leave his bones on that expanse of pampas. He agreed to sell El Porvenir to one of his ranch hands, loaded the trucks, sent Benjamín Gómez off with the flocks and waited till the rains abated. Then he left the coast forever, even poorer than when he had arrived.

Juan Domingo waited only a couple of weeks for him. In Camarones he boarded a navy cargo ship and went all the way around Tierra del Fuego, pulling rank as an army officer to secure passage. He saw several icebergs from a distance. He heard the lament of the ice in the narrow straits. And on hearing of Amundsen's and Scott's expeditions to the South Pole, he too began to allow himself to be attracted by the idea of making the journey there. He knew that the two men had left the Ross glaciers at almost the same time, in the spring of 1911. Scott, the Englishman, had counted on useless ponies to get him there. Amundsen took sled dogs with him. The two of them, however, had reached their goal on foot. Scott, held up for over a month by unfavorable winds, found when he finally arrived an ironic little note from the winner, alongside the odious Norwegian flag.

Aboard the cargo ship, Perón saw some of the photographs that Herbert Ponting and Lieutenant Henry Bowers had taken before the calamity that wiped out everyone. He saw the silhouette of the sailing ship *Terra Nova* on the rim of a vagina of ice, saw the terrifying mushrooms of the Berg Castle in the light of dusk, spied death in the faces of Scott and his four companions, it too disoriented by the emptiness of a blank sky.

They traveled on foot, Perón reflected. Willpower alone allowed them to reach a limit that no Argentine foot soldier ever attained. Might I not be the first, hoisting aloft the name of Perón and freeing my father of his penance? As he sailed in polar seas, he dreamed of the Pole. He imagined it as a volcano looming up behind a series of ice fields. He saw himself skirting glaciers and triumphing over towering ranges of ice. He walked and walked. He made his way amid peaks of foam frozen stiff, descended along cadavers of icebergs, was pierced through with sharp arrows of stalactites. And yet he went on. Finally, bloodied but invincible, he discovered the doors opening onto the goal, the volcano in the distance. But his mother was waiting there for him and would not let him past. Each time the dream began again, his mother planted herself in the very same place, with her braids undone and a man's poncho on her walking stick.

On 12 February 1914, Juan Domingo wrote to Pardo:

Lieutenant, I don't want to put off any longer telling you that I took a boat and went wandering about the channels of our Tierra del Fuego. You would have to see for yourself how fantastic it all is. Some young hands aboard the ship showed me photographs taken when Scott came to those parts and lost his life there. I'm told that Amundsen, Scott's rival, came through Buenos Aires not long ago. I think that as good Argentine infantrymen we ought to organize the same sort of expedition. What do you think, kid?

Everyone in the family was well when I left Camarones. We had a splendid shearing. My mother and father send you special greetings. With my best wishes to your family, and a hug to you from

Juan Perón. Second Lieutenant

He sent the letter from the 12th Regiment in Paraná, where he was serving as an instructor of enlisted men. The Archduke Franz Ferdinand was soon to meet his death in Sarajevo. The Great War was preparing to drown history in blood: Juan Domingo would truly realize that only much later.

He allowed himself to be involved in years of non-thought. His interests lay in outdoor games, the reasons of the body:

what he would call 'contradictions of one's musculature'. He would often feel that his tendons were pulling him in one direction or another, tearing him apart, as though they were other bodies locked in endless combat, commanding and obeying each other. Now and again, he found himself plunged into periods of indifference, of lassitude, of pure nothingness. Even at those times he threw himself wholeheartedly into every sort of athletic endeavor: he played soccer, practiced boxing and excelled at fencing.

The inevitable happened: he was seen in Villa Guillermina and in Tucumán, some hundred leagues away, at the very same time. He began to be unable to find places where he had to be. And at the same time, he came across places along the way that he would never go to. It took him a long time as well to discover the explanation for these changes. He was just over twenty and the duplicities of chance or history were not of particular importance to him. He didn't know that a man whose spaces have changed can lose his center of gravity at any moment.

9 *The Hour of the Sword*

A leader of armies is not made by decree.
A leader is born, his head anointed with the oil of Samuel.

> Alfred von Schlieffen,
> cited by Wilhelm Groener in
> *The Testament of Count Schlieffen*,
> 1926

Leaders are born, not made . . . and the one who is born anointed with enough oil of Samuel needs little more in order to lead.

> Juan Perón,
> *Political Leadership*,
> 1951

This cannot be the work of chance. What instincts of the body have been unleashed, what portents, for all my ailments to have hastened to awaken me, just now, when in just two days more I'll be returning to Buenos Aires? They perhaps want to bring me news. Perhaps they're concerned about the approaching battle. I have led my armies from afar for eighteen years. I don't even know what the surprises that battle fronts hold in store for a man are like. Don't allow my hesitations to see print, file them safely away, so that my enemy will never know of them.

At four-thirty a.m. I suffered a sudden attack of stomach cramps and shortness of breath. I woke up in a sweat. López brought a tranquilizer. Those are tricks a person's body plays, General. Why pay any attention to them? You look as strong as a stallion to me. Go back to sleep. He said to me: Throw off those aches and pains in your sleep.

But I wasn't able to. My heart boiled. I felt a sharp pain. I had an urge to go to the bathroom. When I sat down on the edge of the bed my legs creaked. They had turned to ice. López! I called. Help me piss. He slung me over his back. Don't you see how well you're walking? Like a young boy! he kept saying to me to reassure me. In the bathroom I voided a few miserable drops. My bladder was swollen, my prostate was bothering me, my whole body was full of urine. And yet none came out: just a few fucking drops.

And now it's 18 June. In a few hours I'll be leaving all this. Dawn is breaking. At least I have the consolation of knowing that what I've experienced here is staying right here. That time is not rotting my memories away. One can take them from one place to another, underneath one's feet, held in a close embrace in the depths of one's body. Is it possible to do the same thing with places? What do you think, López? To look through the window in Buenos Aires and have Madrid out there – the cool dry climate, the palm trees, the little dogs frisking about beneath the poplars. Ah, that would be another story then. Just imagine. If I could go out of the house I have there, on Vicente López, and step out into the shade of the Paseo del Prado, there where I'm so fond of taking a stroll: if that were Madrid, in what a different frame of mind I'd be leaving here!

Now, hearing the sun breathing outside, the General feels that his ailments are subsiding. He sees how the walnut trees, curled up tight, are suddenly putting forth feathers. With relief, he goes out to take a turn about the garden at López's side. He listens, distractedly, to the latter's litany of gossip. That Cámpora stayed up till all hours in the flamenco club and gave out carnations to the female dancers. That at three in the morning he ate barbecued meat in Tranquilino for breakfast. That they're probably waking him up at this very moment to visit an industrial exposition. That's enough of that, man. I don't want to know any more. We'll fritter our lives away on trivia like that.

The sun, which has been steadily clambering upward, suddenly lowers itself on Perón and dazes him. Hey, López: the steam of summer. Look at it moving among the plants. And that noise! It sounds like an army of ants. Let's go take refuge in the house.

Since there won't be any visitors this Monday, and the servants are airing the reception rooms downstairs, the General suggests that they go to the cloister and concentrate on the Memoirs. How much do we still have left, López? What period have we gotten to? I'd like to leave here without the weight of all that hanging over me. And you wear me out, man. You're making such slow progress.

At the foot of the stairs the racket of the clocks striking eight startles them. Isabel, still in her dressing gown and with curlers in her hair, is rushing back and forth between the bedrooms and the attic with a string of maids. She has already packed the bedclothes in the trunks and she still must pack the dishes. With all the commotion yesterday there was no way in the world to finish the job. Pilarica Franco, the last guest, left just before midnight. What a mess! Daniel? Come on upstairs, slowly. Look after the General for me. Don't get him all out of breath. Hey, where are the two of you going? Why so much time in the cloister? Why are you so fond of dark places? Come on, stay here. Doesn't the coolness of the bedrooms appeal to you?

On the last bend of the stairway, the General comes upon some patches of wind that are always lurking about there. For a long time now they have been trying to find out where those drafts come from: whether from the cold chamber, which keeps the temperature of the sanctuary at a steady level, or from the creature lying upstairs who, when she sighs, when in the middle of the night she gives one of her pitiful non-sighs, she leaves trails like bubbles. Cold-flies, the General calls them.

Just feel that, López: those drafts. The house is already turning inhospitable on us. It's just like the dogs: it barks when its master goes away.

They finally go inside the cloister. The secretary intercalates sheets of paper from one folder with those of another as though he were shuffling cards. Whether history moves from there to here, or whether it doesn't – that doesn't alter the consequences. Let's have a look, López: what have you done? The General looks around for a lap robe and covers his legs. Take turns reading with me. I must rest my eyes and my voice. Where were we? At a point where we were hesitating, sir – Do we cut out your reflections on military life or do we leave them just as they are? They're lengthy. And technical. We might leave the reader asleep by the wayside. What do you think, López: that I'm going to eliminate the very matrix of my doctrine? Everything comes from there, from what I say about the military. How is it that you haven't noticed? The rest isn't me. Perón comes from there. He's the *troupier*, the pedagogue of leadership, the palace strategist. The only thing I really know well is how to lead. And you'd have me not say that. Have me proceed like a monkey, by way of anecdotes, swinging from branch to branch. Not at all. I don't give a damn about readers. Let them fall asleep. Let them retreat to their hothouses and turn a deaf ear. I want it to be perfectly clear. I refuse to go on unless I explain what sort of soldier I was. Do you understand?

I understand:

Every soldier must know that his job is to handle men. To lead. Leading is an art, and as such it contains a theory, which is the inert factor in art. But the vital factor is the artist. Anyone can paint a picture and carve a statue, but a Pietà like Michelangelo's or a Last Supper like Leonardo's would not exist without them. Anyone is also capable of leading an army, but if what is wanted are battles that are masterpieces like those of Alexander the Great or Napoleon a general must be sought who has been born in the same way, anointed by the holy oil of Samuel. A leader is not made by decree. He is born. Like true artists.

Those are the same words that we've repeated so many times, sir. That is why I'm hesitating. We wrote them down that way in that first book – let me see the complete title. Ah, here it is: *World War 1914: Operations in East Prussia and Galicia, Tannenberg, the Masurian Lakes, Lemberg. Strategic Studies* – without changing so much as a comma. Later on they appeared in all your speeches and classes on leadership, copied word for word. And in your declarations to the press. And inevitably there were people who followed the trail we left. One of them said that in the beginning, when Perón quoted Napoleon and Schlieffen, he used quotation marks, provided footnotes, supplied bibliographical synopses. And that later on we forgot our obsessive concerns regarding such details. That we simply appropriated whatever famous phrase we had at hand. I think we ought to change now, look for other words for the same idea. To be more nationalistic. To act as patrons of our own countrymen. Not go on and on about Leonardo but talk about Quinquela. What do you think, sir?

The General is utterly opposed. Argentines don't even know who Schlieffen is, López, and in time they'll forget what Napoleon said or didn't say. They'll ask: Whose phrase is that? Ah, it's the General's! And that'll be the end of it. Don't worry, man, nobody will dare stain my reputation, even breathe the word plagiarism. The one thing my poor country has left is Perón. It has me, and that's it. I am Providence, the Eternal Father. Stop talking nonsense, López. Go on.

Within the range of my ambitions, my first priority has been to do good, and as a corollary of that, to do good to those who are most in need. I have never been able to explain to myself a love of one's native land apart from this human concept, just as I fail to understand the grandeur of the fatherland without a happy people. I prefer a small country of happy men to a large nation of wretched men. I understand those who work only for themselves. What is more, I justify them. It seems to me only logical that they should receive the material benefit of their efforts. But I understand much better those who work for others without expecting the least recompense.

Perón and Jesus Christ one single heart, López discovers. It seems to me to shine forth. To be possessed of a perfect cellular tonality. And the General, removing the lap robe, sighs: It is my sermon on the mountain, López. My hymn of beatitude.

Each time I think back on my life's journey I regret nothing. I have no reason to. I have always been able to sleep with an easy conscience. They have reviled me, they have heaped the nastiest insults upon my name. They have even tried to kill me. Nothing has upset me or been of concern to me, because I answer to my conscience alone. And I am at peace with it.

I had no other vice save cigarettes, and even today's sunshine has not been able to rid me of it. I smoked Caftans, Condals, whatever came to hand. I have also tried Ombús. I have no idea what they were made of. I remember only that my lungs heard the word Ombú and took off at a run.

I can boast of having been a good company commander. Of the 110 men I had under my command, I had one named governor of Buenos Aires, and made ministers and ambassadors of the others. All of them were humble but loyal. They would have given their lives for me.

Those were days of great turbulence, of profound ideological change. The storm of immigration had died down and both in the pidgin Spanish spoken by the Italian immigrants and in the unfailing plates of ravioli on Sunday we began to assimilate the gringo influence. A farce by Armando Discépolo, *Mustafa*, convinced us that in the end the mixture would produce a 'strong race'. Nonetheless, Buenos Aires was a nest of tenements. Women who clerked in stores, seamstresses and schoolmistresses earned barely enough to eat. In the factories female apprentices were paid twenty pesos a month, and a pair of cheap shoes cost fifteen.

Eminent visitors were shown, naturally, a very different city. Prince Humbert of Savoy, the Maharaja of Kapurtala and the Prince of Wales, all of whom arrived at almost the same time, during Alvear's presidency, saw nothing but sumptuous palaces. No one took them to see how the Russians auctioned off women in the brothels down by the docks. I myself saw a little fifteen-year-old Polish girl who had been gulled into coming by promises of marriage, sold for a silver bracelet and two hundred pesos. Instead of showing them the slaughterhouses, where suffering filled the air, the royal visitors were shown the Rural

Society's champion bulls, which never shit anything but eighteen-carat turds.

One episode left its mark on my mind for the rest of my life. It was the speech that Leopoldo Lugones delivered in Lima, on the centenary of the battle of Ayacucho. It caused a tremendous ruckus between the liberals and the conservatives, who reproached him for his admiration for Mussolini, but it gave us young officers quite a bit to think about. We began to be aware that the army had to be the country's compass.

The politicians were corrupt and, fortunately, hadn't the slightest contact with us. To keep us apart from the corruption, General Agustín P. Justo, the Minister of War, asked President Alvear to issue a decree forbidding military personnel from engaging in party politics. Our world was the barracks, but within the barracks were the symbols of the fatherland. It was our duty to keep watch over them.

Leopoldo Lugones was a splendid exponent of those ideas. In Lima he said . . .

I had a terrible time finding that speech, General. I had to go search for it in the library on the Avenida Calvo Sotelo. But here are the sentences you wanted.

. . . 'For the good of the world, the hour of the sword has struck once again. Pacificism, collectivism, democracy are synonyms of the same vacant place that fate offers the predestined leader, that is to say the man who commends because of his right as a superior, with or without the law, because this right, as an expression of power, is one with his will.'

Read it aloud again, López. It is worth it. It was the first time that a civilian hero rose up to say to us: Soldiers, take power, it is yours by nature. Others have done so in these latter years. But they are no longer heroes or anything else. They're crafty devils: vicars of foreign companies. Tatters are all that is left of that glorious army. Look at the generals. They're scared to death. They all tremble at the mention of my name. They stripped me of my title, my uniform, and now they don't know what to think up next to keep me from taking my vengeance. Would you like your back salary, General? they ask me. Would you like a statue of yourself in the Campo de Mayo? They're a pitiful bunch of kids. They're afraid I'll leave them without their daily rations. That's all that matters to them: their daily rations, the good life, petty privileges. I know them well. I had to give a tranquilizer to one of them who came here. I won't do anything to you, man, I said to him. History has paid me back in full. Don't confuse me with the Count of Monte Cristo. If your conscience bothers you because you did wrong, that's not my problem.

They're badly trained people. They immediately start pulling strings. And to cap it all, they're ungrateful. Look at what they did to poor Lugones. An honorable civilian, a true orator. He spent five years pounding on the gates of barracks. Take power! he kept preaching. Take power, once and for all! And when we finally did, in 1930, what was he offered as a reward? A job as a schoolteacher. That was a mockery. Lugones went downhill. I tried to talk with him at the Círculo Militar, where we fenced together. I found him very distant. He was in torment on account of personal misfortunes of some sort. He was courteous to me. We agreed to meet. But the next day he sent me a note postponing our meeting. From then on, every time our paths crossed he'd say to me: We'll get together later on, Perón, later on. I understood. That meant never. His trials and tribulations had made him inaccessible. Not long after that he killed himself on a cruise up the Tigre . . . But enough of that. Let's go back to the other part of the speech he gave in Lima. Why don't you just go ahead and read it, man?

'The nineteenth-century constitutional system is outdated . . .'

That's it exactly. What I said in my message to Congress, in 1948: that the Argentine Constitution was a museum piece. Lugones was right. It wasn't possible to go accepting a law dating back to the era of horse-drawn wagons . . .

'. . . The army is the last aristocracy, that is to say the last possibility of hierarchical organization we have left amid demagogic dissolution. Only military virtue attains, at this moment in history, the superior life that is beauty, hope and strength.'

I was one of the few officers who appreciated the vast scope of Lugones's plan. But I was only a recently commissioned first lieutenant. What could I do? Power was too far out of my reach. My one aspiration was to receive my diploma from the Graduate War College and marry a decent girl who would meet with the approval of my superiors.

In the middle of 1925, after spending several months in Santiago del Estero, recruiting applicants for posts as NCO's, I asked to be assigned to the War College. Once again I was following in the footsteps of my mentor, Major Descalzo, who had been given the chair of Organization at that institution. I took the examination and passed with honors. When I was admitted, I felt that life was beginning all over again. If a person lives only once it's as if he had never lived at all. There is no other way of really living except to begin it, without waiting for it to come to an end. To keep continually beginning it.

Sit still, López. Just read and don't think so much. What are you looking for in those photos, man? Why are you scattering that pile of dead leaves all about? They're spaces that have been left blank, sir. The Memoirs that you've sent to purgatory. Look at this. Class notes, 1926. And this: the label from a pack of cigarettes. Mezcla, the blended-tobacco brand you really smoked. And these blurred accounts: receipts for the rent you paid on a bachelor pad in the Calle Godoy Cruz, with six other officers. Have a look at the photographs: there's a sadness that casts a shadow over them. You smile at the camera and yet it looks as if you were going off somewhere. You gradually disappear, turning more and more sepia-colored. I've also laid aside memories that hurt you. Look here at the summer of 1925. When you arrived at the family farm, in the Sierra Cuadrada in the Chubut. Your father, already nothing but skin and bones by then, had no other distraction except his flock of grandchildren. Mario Avenino had married Eufemia Jáuregui. They had four children: the second one, Tomás Domingo, bore the name that they stole from me. I realized that my father was suffering from a possibly fatal illness. With the greatest of difficulty I persuaded him to come back with me to Buenos Aires, to find doctors to treat him. Linger over the photo, General. Look at the barren plateau where you lived, buried between dark stone pyramids. And here, the labyrinth of irrigation ditches your mother gradually dug with the help of the hired hands. The gate, the sign: 'La Porteña Ranch'. Can you see the memory? I see it all, López, as though it were today.

When the doctors in Buenos Aires examined your father they didn't allow him to go back home. He was being eaten away by arteriosclerosis. The poor old man could barely walk. We had to buy a little house in the Calle Lobos almost at the corner of San Pedrito, south of the Flores district, and move in there, with Doña Juana. She returned to the Chubut, General, for the shearing. But only for three weeks. And then after that, how diligently she kept watch at the bedside of my old man! We knew that it was hopeless. Don Mario Tomas's body, that I had once thought was eternal, grew thinner and thinner and vanished little by little.

It was around that time that you met Potota. Do you remember how you met? How do you expect me to remember? It was so long ago! It might have been at a family dance, in Palermo. Let me think. It was, I believe, at a party at the Círculo Militar. I hear a waltz. I asked María Tizón, Potota's sister to dance. And after that I asked her. We talked about movies. I heard her play the guitar.

Her name was Aurelia, General. She was the sixth daughter of Tomasa Erostarbe and Cipriano Tizón: he was the owner of a photography studio and a militant in the Radical Civic Union. Because she kept such jealous watch over her daughters, Tomasa was known as Señora Eros Estorba, an anagram of her name suggesting her fears of the baleful influence of love on their lives. Potota was the shortest of all of them. She had an odd voice, hoarse but well pitched. A broken register, like Eva's voice. Don't keep lining up my memories in front of me, López. Be quiet. Recount my life as though it were a Harrods inventory. I'm not the one to blame, General. It's the blanks that you want to leave in your Memoirs. Can you touch the blank? Can you smell the silences? Aha, López. That's what I'm after. Put an end to these parentheses, once and for all. Have Isabel tell us when lunch is ready. And meanwhile, keep reading. Go on with the real Memoirs.

My studies, which doomed me to a sedentary life, made my body flabby. I put on weight. Till the scale showed over 190 pounds. After our courses were well under way, General Alexis von Schwartz, a brilliant professor of military fortifications who had served in the Imperial Russian Army, arrived at the War College. After class, I used to walk about Palermo with him. We would talk together about Moltke, Jomini, Clausewitz and other theoreticians of war. But when we took our leave of each other, he always used to say to me: 'No one is as great as Count Schlieffen.'

Books by Schlieffen were not easy to find in those days. The *Revista Militar* published only separate articles that whetted my curiosity. Schwartz passed on to me a work having to do with the battle of Cannae, in Italian. I devoured it in a single night.

In the beginning, the nearly endless number of strategic plans that Schlieffen had drawn up in the course of his life puzzled me. Later I became intrigued by the fact that one plan frequently contradicted another one that had been worked out for the same campaign. I thought: This can't be merely by chance. It corresponds to an original conception of war. I saw signs that Schlieffen was a genius and that even after his death no one understood him.

We see how year after year, despite the fact that circumstances remained the same, Schlieffen organized concentrations of forces at points that he had previously left undefended. He laid out a strategy, defended it as unbeatable, and then almost immediately laid out a new one that would have the effect of demolishing the previous one. At the same time he demanded that his officers prepare a battle plan A, and a battle plan B, that would be completely the opposite of A, but at the same time equally perfect. What was the point of those apparent paradoxes? Ah, that was the secret of his greatness! Even when it came to dogmas that he set forth as unbreakable rules, such as the one that states that one enemy must be wiped out before turning one's forces against a second one, Schlieffen was disconcerting: he also advised fighting on all fronts simultaneously. His first commandment was offensive combat. Attack, always attack, even in the face of superior enemy forces.

Almost everything I know today I learned back then. And I applied it to politics. Clausewitz regarded war as a continuation of politics by other means. To me, precisely the contrary is true: politics is a continuation of war by other means, but with the same tactics. Years later, when I was reproached for an irritating phrase, I could answer, in surprise: How could I have possibly have said that, if on such and such an occasion, I stated the contrary? No one can hold me responsible for a single idea that does not take its opposite into account. With the Church, the army, petroleum, agrarian reform, special formations, the freedom of the press. I have always espoused two attitudes, two plans or more, two doctrinaire lines or more: owing to my nature, which is averse to all sectarianism, and to the fact that I am a leader. I cannot go about measuring things with the yardstick of one and only one dogma. That was Schlieffen's greatest teaching.

I have preserved in my files every explanation of reality: those that constituted a positive view of things and also those that constituted a negative one, since both would serve me sooner or later. Of course, that play of opposites cannot be put to use if one is willing to do things any old way; on the contrary, very clear lines of thought must be followed, which the leader must not stray from under any circumstances. Mine are summed up in three apothegms: political sovereignty, economic independence and social justice. So that neither rich nor poor lack anything. So that there is equal opportunity for all.

In the blackest moments of my life, when my adversaries brutally attacked me, confident of the superiority of their forces, I answered by attacking. Attack, I told myself. And I thought of Schlieffen. Attack, and something will be left.

Reading was not the only thing we did at the War College. We were also obliged to make long reconnaissance marches across rugged terrain and conduct geodesic surveys on the border. The ones that I was assigned to carry out in the Andes, between Mendoza and Neuquén, left me with eyes that hungered for nature. I was not Mohammed, but the mountain came to me. The mountain was moving closer and closer to my destiny.

My thirty-third birthday was approaching: the age at which men conduct their most profound examination of conscience.

Certain things were already clear: the fatherland was my life, and the army my path to serving it. The most enlightened officers tried to end the country's fatal dependence on agriculture and livestock production alone and demanded that President Alvear organize national industries managed by the military, beginning with the steel industry.

Under Agustín P. Justo, the Minister of War, the army had become an extremely important factor in the exercise of power. He was the one who pulled the chestnuts out of the fire each time that there were disturbances of the peace in the provinces, the one who repressed the attacks on private property in the Chaco in Santa Fe and on the wool-producing estates in Santa Cruz. And what did we receive in return? Crusts of stale bread! Only Justo's tenacity forced certain increases in the military budget. The anarchists killed a lieutenant-colonel, and all his widow received was a telegram expressing the Government's condolences.

By now we were fed up with words. It was a time of drastic changes. We were the only ones who were offering a new overall plan for the country. And we were the only ones who could carry it out. I thought that the healthy forces of the fatherland would soon be knocking at the gates of the barracks. And that it was our duty to prepare ourselves.

I remember the day that Yrigoyen was elected president for the second time. It was on an afternoon in April. The rainy season was beginning. I went to Lieutenant-Colonel Descalzo's home and watched the street from the balcony: the people hurrying about, the voiturettes, the trees with yellow leaves. I felt that everything presaged an enormous sadness for Argentina. I said to my mentor: 'This country will no longer be the same when Doctor Alvear is gone. Politicians are a dying species. Yrigoyen will be head of state, but we military officers will be in power.' Descalzo listened to me in amazement: 'Do you want power, Perón?' And I answered him: 'It is not a question of wanting or not wanting. It is a question of destiny.'

When the loneliness of my studies at the War College became unbearable, I began to look for a decent girl, from a good family, who would have sensitivity and social graces. I found those qualities in Aurelia Tizón, called Potota, which means 'precious' in the semi-language of children, because of her sweet nature. She was a teacher at a normal school, fond of painting and music. She played the guitar and the accordion, very gracefully. She also recited poetry by Juan de Dios Peza and Santos Chocano, with incredible expressiveness. I realized immediately that her temperament harmonized with mine. She encouraged me in my studies and with the greatest discretion always remained in the background. Since her family had excellent connections with the Radical Party, Potota conjoined the advantageous and the agreeable. I asked for her hand in March 1928. We were planning to marry in October, but my father's arteriosclerosis worsened and we lost the poor old man on 10 November. His mind gradually grew dimmer and dimmer and he died without a murmur.

Because I was in mourning we postponed our wedding until January. I have never had a good memory for domestic details, which are ordinarily a better source for trivial anecdotes than for learning really to know a person. And all I care to remember about Potota is this: the noble love she offered me for almost ten years of married life.

We have left your wife ageless. López interrupts his reading, there in the cloister, and breathes on his glasses to wipe them clean, misting them over again. Pubescent? Prepubescent, a Lolita? I have a handful of dates here that are completely confused, General. There are those who say she wasn't yet twenty when she married; others say seventeen. A local boss of the Radical Party in Palermo,

Julián Sancerni, has lent me these photographs. Take a look at them: 1912. Your wife as a little girl. Standing on the left is Sancerni, with a rosette in his lapel. She is hiding in the middle row, the sixth one from the right, in a gray dress with a white collar. As early in life as that she already had the trace of a Gioconda smile and in her eyes there was – can you see it? – the reflection of a waning moon, the sign of premature death. Neither she nor Sancerni was over nine years old. Let's say, then, that she was born in 1903. You must be right, López. That must be it. Look at that expression on the girl's face: so distant, so dark, as though she'd never met me. Was that her then: Potota? She was never willing to call me by my first name. She called me Perón. Even at moments that were appreciably more relaxed, I was always Perón.

When we returned from our honeymoon in Bariloche my appointment as an officer attached to the General Staff had already been announced. I also found out that, through the intercession of Lieutenant-Colonel Descalzo, I was about to be awarded the chair of Military History in the Graduate War College. I felt like the master of the world.

My thesis on the battle of the Masurian Lakes appeared in the Biblioteca del Oficial. All the ideas that I have been setting forth in the course of my life are already clearly expressed in it. I waved the flag of 'The Nation under Arms', which simply means the subordination of the industries, services and energies of the country to the objective of national defense. In it I also argued, following Schlieffen, that every army, however vigorous it may be, declines, reaches old age and dies with its leader.

The General emerges from his drowsiness. He pushes the lap robe aside and sits up. Don't leave that phrase there, López Rega. Put in its place instead: An organized army survives intact, even after the death of its leader. The secretary is disturbed. Move the phrase? That's not wise, sir. Since it comes from Schlieffen, I don't advise it. Instead, I suggest completing its meaning. Tell me, how does this strike you? 'Every army might well reach old age and die along with its leader if it did not have a leader to take his place, an heir, a power that arrives on the scene anointed by the power that is departing.' Period, new paragraph.

Don't turn my orders upside down, López. Do as I say. Correct that dreadful mistake this instant.

. . . that every organized army survives intact even after the death of its leader. In it I maintained, *ad nauseum*, that success is not improvised but is, rather, carefully prepared. 'The leader must seek victory to the very end, bearing like a man the blows of fate.' I dedicated that work to the man who deserved it: 'To Lieutenant-Colonel Don Bartolomé Descalzo, as a small payment toward my great debt of gratitude.'

The country, meanwhile, was having a very hard time of it. I shared everyone's shattered hopes. My sympathies for Lisandro de la Torre vanished in 1923, when he opposed the purchase of arms desperately sought by Colonel Augustín P. Justo, at that time the Minister of War. Later on I was disturbed by the ambitions of Hipólito Yrigoyen, who, at the age of seventy-six, when he was already visibly suffering from senility and unfit for office, sought re-election as President.

Underline all this for me, López. At the age of seventy-seven I am returning to my country with a lucid mind and without ambitions. I want this difference to be clear.

And although Yrigoyen won with sixty per cent of the votes in the 1928 elections, rebellion in the army was sharply on the rise. One of the stories most widely circulated in the officers' clubs was that, pressured by superior officers, Agustín P. Justo, who had just been promoted, would head a movement of national salvation with a cabinet of Alvearists. There was so much talk about it making the rounds that Justo had to publish a letter denying it as a false rumor.

The army was divided into two clearly defined camps. We might call one of them the 'evolutionist' element. It maintained that we Argentines must kick out Yrigoyen and his many cohorts and put an end to the cult of personality that had grown up around him, but go no farther than that. That meant that if the army meddled in politics it would do so only to preserve the country's traditional structures and to call for elections as soon as possible. The aim of the other camp, which had a definite 'reformist' orientation, was to change the organization of the State from top to bottom, adapting it to the models of peace and order forcefully promoted by Mussolini and Primo de Rivera. Each of the two factions had its natural leaders. The pacesetter for the evolutionists was Justo; the one for the reformists, José Félix Uriburu, a general who had clean hands and good intentions, even when he was hatching a conspiracy.

No officer with good sense could remain on the sidelines. In every revolution some twenty per cent proves to be for it, some twenty per cent against, and the rest don't have strong opinions one way or the other. They wait and then join the winning side.

Yrigoyen had only to take over as President for bad luck to overtake us. The prices of meat and wheat dropped. The unemployed, drifters, bums wandered aimlessly about the cities. The only businesses that prospered were prostitution and the renting of tenements, which were owned by Jews

I was a mere captain, and as such lived somewhat on the sidelines of those high-level dramas. On the sidelines, but not insensitive. I remember the 1930 carnival, the parade down the Avenida de Mayo, people's feigned joyousness. In the past, masked merrymakers would spray everyone with perfumed water; amorous passes were made; strangers embraced. That year I saw many people by themselves, indifferently throwing confetti on the street musicians as though it were a duty. A giant appeared, disguised as the King of Madness. And no one paid any attention to him. Two other captains and I used to go to the movies on the fashionable days, to the late afternoon matinee. There were always hordes of beggars loitering around the entrances. They congregated in clusters, covered with pimples, coughing.

I foresaw the worst. Nevertheless, I did not fully realize what dire misfortune awaited us.

I was among the first to join the movement that would throw Yrigoyen out of office on 6 September 1930. I came prepared to give my life for that ideal. But I asked myself: Is Yrigoyen worth it? Isn't he a man naturally inclined to avoid trouble, who will most likely flee when he hears the first shot?

I had my first meeting with General Uriburu in June 1930. In the course of it, I promised to talk things over with Descalzo and persuade him to join the conspiracy. My mentor was as concerned as I was by the inroads made by anarchism. Soviets had been formed in the linotypists' workshops and in the firehouses. The gangrene was spreading.

At the beginning of August, even the Minister of War knew the details of the military conspiracy. Nobody, however, showed any interest in putting a stop to it. There were many who believed, amid that chaos, that Hipólito Yrigoyen himself wanted to be overthrown, so as to be able to go home and rest. When anyone spoke to him about revolution, the President answered: 'Nothing is going to happen. This is temporary political unrest.' Temporary! On 6 September 1930, one Argentina died and another took its place. History will decide which was better. But that day was like the line that Pizarro the conquistador drew in the sand, on his march to Peru. The line of no return. Never again would we be the way we were.

Even Vice-President Enrique Martínez had his own plans for the coup. The poor man thought that we army officers were going to reward him with a promotion. But when he realized that we weren't to be played around with, he was one of those most in a hurry to leave the House of Government.

Yrigoyen, who had been in bed for several days with a serious pulmonary congestion, had strength and energy enough at least to get up out of bed and seek help. The revolution won out by a miracle because, up until the very last minute, the majority of the conspirators were still undecided. They feared that the story would end differently, and that instead of a victory parade through the Plaza de Mayo, the fiesta would end up in Ushuaia penitentiary. Or are we going simply to forget that early on the morning of Saturday 6 September, when General Uriburu began the march on the Capital, he was accompanied only by the Military Academy and the School of Communications? Most of the army was waiting for orders, though no one knew from whom. The forces of the Campo de Mayo and Palermo joined the coup only after Yrigoyen was overthrown. A civilian – a pitiful social climber – took over the Ministry of War. Yet the army still hesitated. Divided, disorganized, overcome by fear and bewilderment, the army came out in force, thinking that it would be defeated. A miracle saved it. What miracle? The anxiety of civilians, the voracious appetite for change, the enthusiasm for new pleasures that so rapidly takes hold among Argentines. We had grown tired of Yrigoyen. We wanted to see what things would be like for us with Uriburu. Around ten in the morning, I remember, the siren of the daily *Crítica* jubilantly greeted the revolution. At five in the afternoon, Government House stood abandoned. The people of Buenos Aires poured out into the streets and applauded the army troops as they paraded past. Without that civilian strength behind us we would have lost. We were being brought to power bodily, borne on the shoulders of civilians. When it entered the Avenida Callao, Uriburu's car was showered with flowers.

Yrigoyen was defenseless. The mob threatened to attack his house. A few loyal supporters took him to the local Palace of Government, in La Plata, at the risk of his dying on their hands en route. With dark circles under his eyes, emaciated, the President wandered through several freezing reception rooms. In that alien, invented, well-nigh imaginary city, everything was completely unfamiliar to him. He must have been afraid. Someone thrust a pen into his hand and placed before him a paper with his resignation written out on it. Yrigoyen signed. It was a brief text. It said that he was leaving power 'completely', as though it were possible to leave it partly. And he underlined the word: 'completely'. To the very end, Yrigoyen showed how disoriented he was in the face of reality.

I have always regarded that resignation as a symbol. To Argentines it was the first sign of the abdication of civilian power. With that document, the future was now marked out for us.

Let's look more closely. It was not addressed to the Congress, as would have been proper, or even to the triumphant General José Félix Uriburu, but to the head of the armed forces of the city of La Plata, as if the President hadn't even the vaguest idea of the importance of his gesture. That on handing over power to just any officer he was surrendering not to the institution known as the army but to brute force. Up until that point, we military officers had been afraid to take power. Yrigoyen's gesture freed us of that fear forever. And gave civilians the idea that by the mere fact that he wears a uniform, a military officer was empowered to do anything and everything: take over a trade union, lay down laws, run a school, receive the resignation of a president.

This was so obviously the case that even the Supreme Court came over to our side. On 10 September, four days after the coup, the judges solemnly declared that force was a sufficient guarantee of the order and security of the populace.

Since your 1930 memoirs end here – López said, wide-eyed with exhilaration, in the dim light of the cloister – I have noted down a number of observations in the margin. All of it can be emended when we have time. Listen to this, General: the story you put out for publication barely three years ago. When you told Tomás Eloy Martínez that you had joined the revolution of 1930 as just another army officer, with no guilt feelings, simply obeying orders. Remember Martínez, the reporter from *Panorama* magazine? Let me play you the whole recording.

From the cassettes classified under the label 'Memoirs for Eloy, part 2', López takes out the second one. He adjusts the volume of the tape recorder. The General's voice invades the cloister, older and rougher:

'The second administration of . . .'

Turn the volume down, López, the General says uneasily. And pointing his finger toward the ceiling, he murmurs: Let us show respect. Never forget the dead woman.

The voice comes back on, less loudly:

'The second administration of Don Hipólito Yrigoyen was not as good as the first one. The man was already well along in years by then and his revolutionary fervor had died away. A court of shysters and police hirelings had him under their thumb. He was kept in confinement in his own office. When a minister wanted to see him he was told that the President was very busy. And when Yrigoyen asked after the minister, they lied to him and told him that he was off on a trip to the interior. They made bishops and admirals wait for hours in the antechambers (those famous endless waits!). More often than not they went off without having been able to see him, because his entourage let pensioners and spongers who amused him in first.

'The army was not insensitive to such calamities, and of course a violent reaction ensued. The chiefs expressed their concern. Descalzo talked things over with me and I agreed to go along. I was simply one among the many who were involved . . . It was above all *esprit de corps* that motivated me. But it was the oligarchy that reaped the benefits. It sensed that it could take the government by assault, and did so.'

Do you realize, General? López turns off the tape recorder. It's easy to lose one's sense of direction trying to follow all that zigzagging. On the one hand, you say you were one of the first to join the coup. On the other hand, it's not at all clear whether you were a revolutionary by deliberate choice or by chance, whether President Yrigoyen aroused your compassion or your respect. I have also found out that Eloy Martínez is threatening to publish a photograph of you taken on 6 September 1930, arriving at Government House on the running board of Uriburu's car, with a triumphant smile. Martínez isn't a problem. We'll give him a good scare and that'll be the end of that. The documents can disappear, can be destroyed. That doesn't cause me any concern. What I want is for you to choose just one version of the facts. Just one: any one will do.

The General now lets out a guffaw. Set your mind at ease, man. Was that all that was bothering you? Let's see what's what. If I've become a leading figure in history at different times, it was because I contradicted myself. You've already heard what Schlieffen's strategy was. One must change plans several times a day and put them forward one at a time, when we have need of them. The socialist fatherland? I invented it. The conservative fatherland? I'm keeping it alive. I have to turn with the wind, in every direction, like a weathercock. And never retract a statement, but instead put various pronouncements together. What seems inappropriate to us today may serve us tomorrow. Mud and gold, mud and gold . . . You know very well that I don't use dirty words, but for history there's only one. History's a whore, López. She always goes off with the one who pays the most. And the more legends people add to my life, the richer I am and the more weapons I can count on to defend myself. Leave everything exactly as it is. What I'm aiming at isn't a statue but something greater. Getting the upper hand over history. Grabbing it by the ass.

What kind of vulgar language is that? Isabel says knocking at the door of the cloister. And opening it, but not coming in, she protests, with her arms akimbo. Here you two gentlemen are, having a high old time up here telling each other your macho stories while I'm being driven out of my mind downstairs, not knowing how to answer all the phone calls. They're telephoning from all over. Cámpora, asking whether you're coming. What should I tell him? From El Pardo Palace, I don't know how many times: asking if the General would rather bid the Caudillo farewell at La Moncloa or at Barajas. One of Cámpora's ministers, I don't even know which one, asking about the schedule for tomorrow. And I haven't been able to sit down for one second to choose what shoes I'm going to wear to Buenos Aires. Everyone else's suitcases are all packed, but mine are a mess.

Just don't take any more calls, my girl. Poor thing! If only they'd leave us alone for a while. I still have all this work to do and I've fallen far behind. And what are the men on guard duty doing? Have one of them sit next to the telephone and say there's nobody here in the house. The General has left. López – close the door. Put the blanket over me. My legs are cold from the drafts from downstairs. Keep reading, man. Get on with it, go on to the next year . . .

A great deal of nonsense has been written about what I did on that 6 September. That I accompanied Descalzo to the Grenadiers' barracks, roused them to rebellion and marched on Government House with them. That's rubbish. The one thing that's true is that I spent two days without seeing my family, shaving myself with a chipped razor so as to be presentable.

There's hermeneutics here, and the texts must therefore be revised. Descalzo, my mentor, had been posted to the Infantry School. I didn't want to let him go off by himself. Once again, he arranged for my transfer. When he got it for me, we toasted the new army and the new fatherland. We were falling into disgrace, but didn't know it yet.

In the very first weeks of the revolution, Generals Uriburu and Justo were involved in a fight for power that made all of us suspect. Loyalties were punished. Descalzo, who enjoyed Justo's complete confidence, was removed from his post at the Infantry School and assigned to a border district in Formosa. I was luckier. I was placed on special duty. And in order to keep me from just standing around with folded arms, they invented a job for me as a member of a geographical survey team in the far north. They unwittingly did me a favor. Riding on horseback through the ravines of Salta and Jujuy, the country got into my blood as never before. My senses caught fire.

Terrible years began for the people. I was the only one of all the military officers who did not disappoint the people. I claim no other merit for myself save that of having looked and fought. What my eyes showed me set my heart to beating.

In the Chaco, in Formosa or in Misiones there were thousands of men who had never worn even rope sandals and were terrified at the sight of an automobile. In the port of Buenos Aires drifters erected overnight shantytowns built of tin cans and sheets of cardboard, that tourists came to see as if they were a bit of picturesque folklore. In Avellaneda Alberto

Barcelo's conservative clan gave away sacks of potatoes and maté to poor people who gathered in crowds at the committee's doors. But at the same time they ran, with an iron fist, a chain of gambling dens and brothels.

Even Carlos Gardel, who was a great man, suffered from the confusion of those years. He made friends with a certain Ruggiero, a bodyguard of Barcelo's, and on Sunday afternoons, after the racetrack let out, he agreed to sing at parties in Avellaneda. They were such close friends that Don Alberto got Gardel the fake passport he used all the rest of his life. Out of gratitude, when he left the all-night parties, Gardel would sing Barcelo's favorite waltz as his last song: 'Alas, Aurora you have gone away and left me./I who loved you more than I can say . . .'

High-ranking officers used to turn up at these parties, and if you received an invitation to one there was no possible excuse for not going. I was obliged to attend a number of them and I even had a chance to talk with Gardel. He was a very unassuming, good-hearted man, with more sensitivity than intelligence. One day he wanted to know what my favorite piece was so as to include it in his repertory. I told him it was 'Where is there a handy handle, old Obregón/They've cleaned them all up with a pumice stone.' Those verses alarmed him. Like all artists, Gardel was a wary creature. Fearful that someone had overheard, he led me off to a corner, looking about in all directions. 'You must realize, Captain,' he said to me (I was a major by then), that I can't sing a song like that here . . . It would offend our hosts . . .'

I took advantage of my temporary ostracism to gather together in a book the lectures that I'd given at the War College. That was how my *Notes on Military History* came into being. I went on using the theories of Clausewitz and Count Schlieffen as authoritative sources, but this time I set forth other ideas with greater clarity. The doctrine of the Nation under Arms, for example, and also that of a joint command for all the armed forces, in peacetime and in wartime. The two would later be the cornerstone of Peronist organization.

In 1934 I published, in collaboration with Lieutenant-Colonel Enrique Rottjer, the two-volume *The Russo-Japanese War*. A certain general dared to accuse us of plagiarism and we were court-martialed. The trial was rigged and naturally they found against us, but we were obliged only to apologize. Envy – it was nothing but envy.

When Justo was elected President of the Republic, I was recognized as a man of the future. One of the most upright leaders the army had, General Manual A. Rodríguez, was named Minister of War. He immediately sent for me. 'Perón,' he said: 'I have read your books carefully. I believe that we share many ideas. From tomorrow on, you will be my right-hand man, my aide-de-camp.'

By order of the minister, a commission under Colonel Francisco Fasola Castaño went out on an expedition to re-connoiter the border regions of the Andes, between Las Coloradas and Villa La Angostura, south of Neuquén. I was second-in-command of the expedition. The beauty of the landscape took our breath away. At night the air turned phosphorescent. At dawn we would hear wild boar grunting beneath the poplars and birches. Amid such splendor, the Indians who lived in those backlands were dying by the age of twenty of epidemics and neglect. Fearing that they were all going to go out like a match, I wanted to save the last remaining traces of their culture at least. I spent days questioning them, with the help of interpreters, and even though I forgot their tribal legends I rescued the words, so that other soldiers would be able to use them when they returned to those environs. I composed a bilingual dictionary of them: *Place Names of Araucanian Origin in Patagonia*.

Once back in Buenos Aires I noticed that Minister Rodríguez didn't look at all well. He was the target of countless political phobias. Every time he submitted a plan to buy military equipment, the Socialists sank their claws into him. At the worst stage of his illness he had to appear before Congress. He gave an unforgettable speech before it. 'The army is not always the source of militarism,' he declared. 'Militarism is more often an evil to which politicians give rise when they use the army for the wrong purposes.'

A man like that was doomed to die young. They say he died of cancer. I believe he died, rather, of disgust. The country was corrupt. Even the aristocrats became criminals. Without the least shame they involved themselves in scandalous deals in meat, streetcars, electric power, railroads. President Justo, meanwhile, gave signs of utter indifference. From Yrigoyen's last years on, the House of Government was a foredoomed, accursed place.

In October 1935, Rodríguez, already dying, received me at his home. 'General,' I said to him, 'I want to leave here. I have served you for three years. Thanks to you I have pecked through my shell and need to test my strength in the world.' And that man who never smiled, parted his lips paternally. 'Very well. Be on your way,' he ordered me.

I began the new year with a heavy heart. One day in February I was told that I was to be the new military attaché in Chile. General Rodríguez lay on his deathbed. I gathered my gear together and prepared to cross the Andes in a voiturette.

And at this point, interrupted López, I wanted to reach the apogee, the culmination. I portrayed you in letters of flesh and bone.

I have often been tempted by fate. Move here, more there, fate said to me, offering me chances on a platter. I allowed those temptations to draw closer to me, but I did not allow them to hold sway over me. I will go where I please, I answered them. Each time fate knocked at my door, it was my will that went to answer. I have been a ruminant of chance. I have chewed it and chewed it to make it obey me. There are men who allow themselves to be led by fate and by others. I allowed myself to be led only by fate and by myself.

And like an actress on stage, Isabel waits for the conversation to die away before calling from a bend in the stairway. Lunchtime, General! Daniel, Cámpora is here! What shall I tell him? Perón sighs. Show him in, my girl, show him in! He removes the blanket from his legs and shakes it, in case a memory might have fallen onto it and some stranger might pick it up. Beneath his flock of muscles, he is aware of a body that no longer has anything to do with him and moves as in dreams. He lifts that body up and, turning to López, repeats his complaint of that morning: What drama is coming next? What misfortunes will the next chapter bring me?

10 *The Eyes of the Fly*

The leader of the coup d'état that overthrew me in September 1955 was Eduardo Lonardi, a drunken general who had already double-crossed me in Chile twenty years before, and whom I pardoned out of compassion. He remained in power for only a few months. He was replaced by a general who had been a student of mine at the Graduate War College, whose name was Pedro Eugenio Aramburu. He was a man who was inept at everything except perversity. Cirrhosis finished off the first one. He met the sad end he deserved. The people will take care of the second one some day. The people will not leave the damage this bastard did us unavenged. Aramburu handed the country over to foreign interests, shot to death without mercy patriots who rebelled against him and ordered Evita's dead body hidden or destroyed so that the people would be unable to venerate it. Such crimes never remain unpunished.

Juan Perón to the author, 29 June 1966

I

'I killed General Pedro Eugenio Aramburu.'

Zamora has often remembered the proud face that spoke those words in the haze of the Café Gijón, Madrid, two years ago now. And now that he sees it again, walking along the Beltway, now that the lightning bolt of that unique face penetrated him like a laser beam (the deep dimple in the chin, the red hair), he hears clearly the scars that each syllable has left in his memory: I killed him and you will never be able to write that. If you did, Zamora, it would be the end of you. You'd be left without a family. Your story would be over. I executed that man. It is not all that difficult to understand why.

Things take place in two ways: either they all happen at the same time, or none of them happen. How to cover every last scattered entrail of reality and not get lost? Emiliano Zamora, special correspondent of *Horizonte*, the weekly magazine, suddenly feels small and defenseless. His Renault 12 makes its way through the cobwebs of the crowd, against the current. What to do? Simply tell the story of times and places as they break a path through the dense undergrowth of conscious awareness? How? With the sheep of reason or with the dire chaos of the senses?

Who would not feel dizzied by the crush of so many people? Even the muddy shortcuts along the highway teem with thousands of bodies on pilgrimage to Perón's dais at Ezeiza. A battalion of drums crosses the Federal Firing Range, in Santa Catalina. Near the Monte Grande station the kiosks, torn down and used as barricades, block traffic. Zamora has kept his Renault bearing left, so as to reach downtown Buenos Aires. (Where has he read that by always turning left a person will inevitably reach the midpoint of any labyrinth?)

As he seeks out calm spots in the stream, with the car tilting – almost overturned – into the roadside ditch, Zamora turns the radio on and off, incredulous at the excesses of imagination that keep bringing the announcers, between one samba and the next, back to the sacred word: General.

A fly lands on the outside mirror of the car. A fly on the wing in this cold? It has a blue back, wings black with soot, and avid eyes: compound eyes, each with four thousand facets. Truth divided into four thousand pieces.

Let's see then. I am Emiliano Zamora, tall, bald, with scraggy teeth and a scrawny frame, stained bones, a man who chainsmokes Parisiennes. I am unhappily married. I am driving back, feeling hopelessly abandoned, from Ezeiza to Buenos Aires.

In the mirror of the Renault, below the fly, there is room for the whole postcard of Peronism: the headbands, the bell-bottomed jeans, the T-shirts trumpeting that Perón is Returning in Triumph. And all of a sudden, the dimpled chin. Nun Antezana.

I killed him, Zamora. I executed General Aramburu.

What a crush of people. Nun is leading an endless column of guerrillas: in dark glasses and with a crook in his hand, like a bishop's crosier. A thin, vehement, red-headed girl is shepherding the vanguard of the flock. I have seen that imperious face, that hair the color of shed blood, somewhere before. In Córdoba, perhaps, in a house on the Calle Artigas. I saw her in May '69, taking a police patrol prisoner and holding it captive for two hours. The patrol consisted of a deputy commissioner and five officers – hostages, I heard her say, of the battle plan, of trade unionism prepared to fight, of popular power. The patrol taken as hostages during the revolt in Córdoba. Ana, Diana? She was a Jewish girl, I remember. And now she's gone over to the other side. She's not a

Trotskyite any more. She's a guerrilla. She's a follower of Nun Antezana's. Or maybe today, 20 June, everything is still the same.

What shit. I thought that the morning would glide calmly by, that at the end of this oceanic labor of mine, 'Perón: His Life Story – The Man, The Leader, Documents and Accounts of a Hundred Witnesses', a breeze of a truce would be blowing. In the lobby of the international hotel, still belching from the breakfast I devoured sitting next to the General's cousins and his former sister-in-law, I, Emiliano Zamora, dozed off. I saw (or rather, sensed) María Amelia Frene with a rapt expression on her face, listening to an opera on the radio. I saw Captain Santiago Trafelatti discreetly leafing through a copy of *Horizonte*. I vaguely heard that Señorita María Tizón would write the story of her sister Potota's marriage and read it at the afternoon press conference. I closed my eyes. At that point in the workings of chance, the editor-in-chief of *Horizonte* telephoned me.

'Zamora?' His s's crackled on the line. He sowed his words with so many s's that even though I understood everything, I felt as though I were lost in a courtyard paved with Rosetta stones, immersed in the music of another era. 'Do you know how far behind schedule the plane from Madrid is? Two or three hours. Don't take it into your head that you're going to just stand around scratching your balls. Put those old-timers on a bus. Take them on an outing. Where to? You ought to know the answer to that one. Along the runways, through the woods, it doesn't matter where. Show them a good time. There won't be many planes landing at Ezeiza today. As a matter of fact, there'll only be one. Have Osinde arrange it for you. Tell him it's for me: we'll see if for once he pays me back the favors he owes me. What do you mean, it isn't possible? Relatives of Perón's, childhood companions? Hey, have you gone soft? So what? They're all gaga anyway! You've already interviewed them, haven't you? Well then, what the hell do you care? Come back to the editorial room. Yes, this minute. You have to make the piece on Perón's *risorgimento* longer. I want the General's whole life story, Part Two. Put him in slippers, killing ants in his garden, watching a cowboy serial on TV. Decipher him, Zamora. And on top of everything else I have to tell you how? You'd be a nobody without me. Look up Tomás Eloy Martínez; say I sent you. Phone him at *La Opinión*. If he won't lend you a hand, tell him to remember what I did for him when he hadn't had a decent meal in weeks.

I did as I was told. My servility is a reflex by now. Half an hour later a young man with a vacant look, a pimply face, and thinning hair arrived at the hotel. He was walking all bent over. His pistol made a bulge underneath his jacket. I made a guess: a 9-mm Walther. Osinde had sent him. He wasn't one to waste words: a bus was waiting outside for my witnesses, he said. He would drive them around the side runways of the airport; they'd visit the hangars. Three police officers in civvies would keep an eye on the bus.

I asked that they should not wear their sidearms. The passengers were old people, I said. They're relics, I explained. They belong to Perón's most distant past. The man with the vacant look parted his lips, whether out of sarcasm or amazement I'll never know. He held his hand out to me. It felt warm and sticky.

'You can depend on me. My name is Arcángelo Gobbi.'

I saw the eyewitnesses of my story disappear inside a bus decked out in Argentine flags. And sick with presentiment, I climbed into the Renault 12. I made my way behind the hangars, heading for Route 205. I saw a group of photographers on the Avenida Fair, around a log fire, eating. I ran across Bishop Jerónimo Podestá, who had renounced the pomp and ceremony of his diocese because he could not conceive of service to the Lord except by couples. He was walking hand in hand with the valiant woman who loved him.

I saw my friend Silvia Rudni, eating an apple and caressing the fresh air. She looked diaphanous, free. Her eyes were aglow with the bliss of those who never have given a thought to death.

I noticed Noé Jitrik and León Rozitchner, both of them poets, watching from a balcony on the Avenida Santa Catalina, engaged in one of their skeptical arguments. Standing between the two, Tununa Mercado was singing 'Oh, solitude!' as she rocked a baby.

On a wall, I read, scrawled in chalk, the endless litany repeating Perón's name. PRAY FOR PERON, HOORAY FOR PERON. ROW ON, PERON. DROWN, PERON.

The fly took off into the cold.

I looked through the window and the cloud of smoke of the Café Gijón, in Madrid, leapt to my eye.

II

Zamora plunged into the haze of the Café Gijón without knowing whose voice it was that had awakened him at the hotel, at two in the morning. 'I'm going to tell you who killed General Aramburu. And where Evita's dead body is.'

Someone would be waiting for him between ten and eleven that night at a table next to the window. Had it been a lie? No. He recognized the smut of falsehood in people's voices. So then?

He guessed the answer when Nun Antezana walked over to meet him.

'I'm not going to ask you how you are because I know, Zamora. We saw you in Paris – at six p.m., day before yesterday, in the Café Bonaparte. And we saw you last week in Gstaad, with Nahum Goldman. Are you about to write another glorification of the Jews?'

'I'm just passing through Madrid, Antezana. And I can't stay long. Arrange a meeting with Perón for me.'

Nun shook his head with a smile.

'Perón's gone off to the Guadarramas. Those damned polyps of his are bothering him again. He almost can't pee. I'm offering you something better. You've already heard: what I told you over the phone.'

'It's too big a story, Nun. I don't want it. And whatever it is, I don't believe it. If it's the truth, it's priceless. So it's a lie.'

Outside, the heat was shrinking the scrawny trees. A white-haired editor, with a beard but no mustache and wearing a black cape, let out a sinister burst of laughter to attract attention. A woman applauded. Everybody was smoking.

Nun took out a sheaf of papers. He let him see the title: 'Report to General Perón on the Pindapoy Operation/Juan José Valle Commando Unit.' And he deciphered several signatures for him: Fernando Abal Medina, Carlos Gustavo Ramus, Abelardo Antezana.

'It's a story about justice,' he said. 'It ought to interest you.'

'What's the price?' Zamora asked.

The editor in the black cape brandished a curved cigarette holder and challenged the café with another guffaw. Nun half closed his eyes.

'There's no price. That's the whole point. I'm here to keep the story from turning into merchandise. Your drama, Zamora, is that you know only part of what's happened. That makes you dangerous. You're not going to be satisfied till you know more.'

Someone turned out several of the lights in the bar, behind Nun. Faces were swallowed up by the semidarkness. Only the smoke could be seen.

'You're wrong, Antezana. I know everything I need to know.' Zamora's voice was tense, without a trace of boastfulness. 'I know where they hid Evita's dead body. I followed a trail I discovered, by sheer chance, in Gstaad. I went to Bonn. I looked for the body where they'd told me to: in a coal shed at the Argentine embassy. There was no such coal shed, just a garden. I presumed that the body was there, somewhere in the tulip beds, buried standing up. But it wasn't. I had a chance to look through some back files. I found out that around 1957 an oak box, full of old books and papers, had arrived in Bonn, and that nobody had taken the trouble to open it. A rectangular box. It lay forgotten in a corner of the coal shed: behind the embassy, in the place where the garden is now. In the summer of '58, that discarded oak box was taken out of Germany in a truck. I made inquiries and learned that when it crossed the border three men were guarding it: one of them was an Argentine Army officer. Such precaution struck me as excessive. Nobody dumps papers in a corner for that long a time and then, without having read them, sends them off under heavy guard. I had no doubt of it. It was the body.'

'And what are you going to do now, Zamora? You've had a red-hot coal fall into your hand. Publish the news? Have yourself a fame bath?'

'See Perón. Offer him the story. Ask him how he would write it if he were in my shoes.'

'That's why I phoned you, Zamora. So you wouldn't waste time. The General knows what you're going to tell him, down to the very last word. That the body was turned over to the Vatican. That it was buried in Plot 86 of Campo Verano cemetery, in Rome. That story is false. We've already looked for the body there. There's no such plot.'

Zamora rose slowly to his feet. His face showed neither disappointment nor surprise. He simply stood up till his head disappeared in the cloud of smoke.

'Well then, we've said all there is to say. Why go on talking?'

The editor with the beard but no mustache enveloped the two women in his cape and took them out into the street. A gust of insects made its way into the café beyond the lightbulbs. The waiters were dripping with sweat.

'Sit down,' Nun ordered. 'Half of what you already know will be the death of you. Now you have to know all of it so as to go on living.'

'I'm not an enemy,' Zamora said.

'No,' Nun conceded. 'You're worse. You might be an informer.'

The voices at the tables fell silent, as though they were open drawers and an idle hand were closing them. Words shorn of all light, of all taste or form that corresponded to the conventions of the senses, began to reach Zamora's ears. What he heard was little by little tattooed on his inner organs, like a Siamese twin that he would be obliged to take everywhere with him. And that he could never show to anyone.

'I killed General Aramburu,' Nun said. 'I killed him and you aren't going to write that. If you did, Zamora, it would be the end of you. You'd be left with no wife, no father, no children. You'd see them fall one after the other and you'd beg to be allowed to fall too. Your story would be over. And I can't do anything to keep that from happening. Listen now, because you're condemned to silence . . .'

III

The bus stops for the second time in front of a hangar. Maria Tizón, who has sat motionless in her seat polishing the reminiscences that she will read that afternoon at the press conference, goes over the text:

> My sister Potota possessed a tact beyond her years and was prepared to be the devoted companion and diligent collaborator of a man as studious and as full of ideals as Perón.
>
> She had a great vocation for culture and loved the arts. She was fascinated by painting and above all else by music. She studied piano to some extent and the guitar intensively. In the paintings she tried her hand at, her portrait of her husband was her best work.

Standing next to the steering wheel of the bus, Arcángelo Gobbi sniffs at the writing with his lizard's head. Señorita Tizón feels an ice-cold alarm signal blow across the nape of her neck. She is not afraid of the man. She is terrified only by the gaze, like a great empty lake, that has alighted on her reminiscences. Through the bus window she spies Benita Escudero de Toledo. She sees her come toward her, her face contorted with pain, obviously suffering from aching feet. 'Keep me company, Benita. Let's chat together.'

But this sister possessed of such infectious happiness was vulnerable when forced to confront the loss of those she loved. The death of her mother broke her heart. Potota survived her by only two years. Later, faced with the suspicion that she too would soon be leaving this life, she once again became a courageous woman. After the two months of cruel suffering that she underwent, lent strength by the Communion that she took each day and by the hope of a better life, she left this world with resignation. She died in Buenos Aires. Perón truly mourned for her. There are those who say that she was his great love.

The bus goes on through desolate pastures, alongside the airport runways. Captain Trafelatti tells of his adventures as a taxidermist. José Artemio talks of certain sedentary birds that nest and mate even in winter. Helicopters take off in pairs.

María Tizón would like to know how much of Potota's secret life has ended up in Benita's hands. What confessions and sorrows. But she doesn't know how to begin, or where. She says: Doesn't it seem to you that having known her is a gift from heaven? And Benita answers: A gift from heaven. They fall silent. Cousin Julio dozes off. On lowering her voice, María finally discovers the tone at which her memory coincides with Benita's. They whisper together, little by little beginning to share confidences.

Did you perhaps foresee that poor Potota would suffer that much?

Of course I did, Señorita María. From the beginning I saw that a bad fate was pinned to her face. We told each other everything. We were like sisters, if you'll excuse the expression. One day when she fell into a melancholy mood she said to me: Do you know where I met Juan, Benita? In the Capitol movie theater on the Calle Santa Fe. We were attending a benefit performance and chance seated us next to each other.

Of course: I remember! You saw *The Son of the Sheik*. Potota came back home trembling. Mama asked her if she was ill and she said no, not at all. It was sheer emotion. That night I went to her room to feel her forehead. She had a fever. She was lovesick, Benita. The few flattering phrases that Perón had said to her perturbed her. How old was she? Let's see . . . she was born on 18 March 1908 . . . she must have been nineteen.

Did her face turn red, Señorita Tizón?

Of course, Benita, the least little thing made her blush! When she played pieces by Albéniz on the guitar, she did it so well we all came out of our rooms to give her a kiss. And you know what she would do? Turn as red as a carnation! A week later, Perón asked her permission to visit her. He began to come to the house every Saturday. They used to stroll down the street together and we'd watch them from the balcony. What a precious couple! He was a big man, with an athlete's physique. And she so tiny and frail. One night, after they had decided to marry, Potota came to my room and hugged me: Oh, María! she said. I'm so afraid of being left all by myself! I tried to reassure her: What do you mean, all by myself, sister dear? You love Perón, don't you? Because if you love him, you will fill your life with love alone. I love him very much, she said to me. But his mind is always somewhere else, not on me. He's an army officer and can think only of things that have to do with his career. Mama came in, and between the two of us we little by little consoled her. I ran my hand through her hair, poor little thing, and Mama said to her: That is a woman's fate, Potota.

To be left alone. A man must go off to his work and a woman must wait for him. Then, with God's help, children come. And that's the end of the waiting. My sister blushed. But as you know, no children came.

I remember those months before the wedding well . . . María. I remember clearly the death of Don Mario Tomás and the mourning. The Peróns left the street door ajar to receive visitors' condolences and would not allow any music. Potota sold her guitar. She spent her days reciting the rosary with Aunt Juana. What shall I do, Benita? she used to ask me. I don't want to get married like this, when he's still in mourning.

She told us the same thing, until Mama convinced her. Men, she told her, mustn't be made to wait. A private marriage ceremony was arranged, at home, without a wedding party. And when they came back from their honeymoon, what poor Potota had foreseen came about. She was left all by herself.

A greenish fly alights on the briefcase where María Tizón has hidden from the shameless gaze of Arcángelo Gobbi the little memo book with her notes and a couple of family photographs.

Look, Benita – a fly, in this cold!

The avid eyes of the fly pass by like a gust of wind: compound eyes, each with four thousand facets. The truth divided into four thousand pieces.

IV

'There were thirteen of us who made up the first cell of Montoneros,' Nun goes on in the Café Gijón. 'Ten of us were in on Aramburu's kidnapping. Six of us sentenced him to death. The day Perón returns to Buenos Aires the numbers won't be the same. There will be talk of twelve founders, not thirteen. Of five judges. My name will be left out. I will remain forever apart from that judgment. I appear only in the role that I have explained to you,

Zamora. And now I must do away with it. That's how the General has planned it.

'Comrade Rodolfo Walsh has given a very clear account of the reasons that led us to the execution. I'll read you what he wrote: *Aramburu was executed at seven in the morning on 1 June 1970. His dead body appeared forty-five days later in the south of the province of Buenos Aires. Four serious charges were brought against him: the overthrow of Perón's constitutional government in September 1955 and the permanent banning of the Peronist movement; the killing of twenty-seven Argentines without trial or justified cause in June 1956; the clandestine operation that took from Perón the body of his deceased wife Evita, mutilating it and sending it out of the country; the fateful beginning of economic violence. Aramburu's rule served as the model for a second infamous decade. The Argentine Republic, which had annually transferred abroad just one dollar per inhabitant, began to negotiate the sort of loans that benefit only the lender, to invest our national savings in foreign capital enterprises and to accumulate that debt that today encumbers twenty-five per cent of our exports. A single decree, number 13,125, robbed the country of two billion dollars in nationalized bank deposits and placed them at the disposal of the international bank that will now be able to control credit and strangle small industry.'*

'Even so,' Zamora says, 'there was no need to kill him.'

'Then you don't understand what happened,' Nun says in surprise.

'I never understand death.'

'It was something more than death. Something more important, and also more definitive.'

Nun has spread out a neat line of papers on top of the café table. From a distance they looked like portraits in an album. Zamora envelops them in a cloud of smoke. The heat refuses to let up. It is still there, holding fast to the night, like a sentinel.

'We needed to survive,' Nun says, 'and so we needed to kill an enemy. The more impressive that sacrifice was, the more intense our existence would be. It's a Nietzschean idea. Every new creation has a greater need for enemies than for friends. For an enemy numbering well over a hundred. We had one: Aramburu. Another election was out of the question. In May 1970, before kidnapping Aramburu, I wrote Perón asking for advice. The General once again washed his hands of the whole thing. You doubtless know what you're doing, Antezana. In all likelihood you've already weighed the grave consequences. And when it was all over, I came here to give him this report: "Operation Pindapoy/Juan José Valle Commando Unit." The General laughed at the name: Pindapoy, a brand of oranges.

'You may be sure, Zamora, that he read each one of these pages more than once. The fate that Evita's dead body had met with was an exasperating mystery to the General. In the first interrogation sessions, Aramburu stubbornly refused to discuss the matter. A question of honor (he said) forbade him to do so. We finally dragged a partial confession out of him. The corpse had been turned over to the Vatican and was in a cemetery in Rome. He gave us the number of the plot. As you already know, there was no such plot.

'On 1 June, around four in the morning, we withdrew to deliberate. There were six of us and we wanted justice to be done, even in Aramburu's case. Fernando Abal Medina read the charges. I took over the defense. I separated ethics from politics. I argued that the man's crimes had been committed a long time before and that we could find some way to pardon him. Shortly before dawn, each one of us wrote his verdict on a piece of paper. Six times I read: death.

'We stayed outside together for a little while, smoking. We were in Timote, on a vast stretch of pampas, five leagues east of Carlos Tejedor. Among some big rusty copper frying pans, I found a phosphorescent bone. Alongside me, Carlos Gustavo Ramus was saddling a horse.

'On the horizon I saw the reddish line of dawn. I stood up and said: We'll shoot him at seven. We must inform the condemned man so that he can prepare himself.

'When he saw me coming, Aramburu turned pale. What have all of you decided? he asked. I spoke gravely: The tribunal has sentenced you to death, General. You are going to be executed in half an hour. Someone, I don't remember who, tied his hands behind his back. Forcing himself to keep calm, Aramburu asked for a shave. We don't have anything to shave you with, General, I said to him. And I touched my face. To my surprise, I noted that I too had stubble on my cheeks.

'We walked through one of the inside corridors of the house and went into the basement. I posted a sentinel next to the door. Outside in the yard, two of us went on working with carpenter's tools, so as to drown out the sound of the rifle shots.

'Aramburu halted on the way downstairs. He asked when the confessor would be arriving. You'll have to make your confession to God, General, I answered him. The roads are blocked off and we can't bring anybody in. He went the rest of the way down the rickety stairway. He turned his back to us and recited the "Forgive me, Father, for I have sinned". Midway through the prayer, he broke off: What's going to happen to my family? he asked. Nothing, Fernando answered him. We'll return everything that belongs to you to your wife.

'We stuffed a handkerchief in his mouth to muffle his death moans. We stood him up against the wall. I unholstered my 9-mm Walther and released the safety catch. I saw him shudder.

'We're about to proceed, General, Abal Medina announced.

'He closed his eyes. At that instant, I fired a shot at him. The bullet went straight to his heart.

'A month later, when I brought the report on the operation to Madrid, Perón noticed a curious mistake that Fernando had made when he recounted the story, perhaps to enhance the stature of our enemy. Here is that version, Zamora. You may read it.'

Abal Medina took the task of executing the condemned man upon himself. To us, the leader is the one who must assume the greatest responsibility.

'We're about to proceed, General,' Fernando says.

'Proceed,' was the last word Aramburu uttered.

'That word is impossible. *Proceed*, Perón said to me. Has anyone ever heard a man speak with a handkerchief stuffed into his mouth?'

Two flamenco dancers noisily enter the café. Zamora wipes the sweat from his face, and he is the one who smiles this time.

'So at the gates of death Aramburu pulled a fast one on them. He kept his word of honor and didn't reveal where Eva is buried.'

'It was the only thing he didn't reveal,' Nun concedes. 'And I think that that's the reason why I too voted in favour of his death. There's just one more story. I had to stay in Madrid all that summer. I returned to Buenos Aires on 8 September 1970. The previous afternoon a police patrol killed Ramus and Abal Medina in a pizza parlor on William Morris. I decided to leave Fernando's account just as it is. I'm not going to be the one who corrects the final words he put in Aramburu's mouth. That "Proceed" that never existed will remain forever.'

'It's my turn now.' Zamora puts a hand on Nun's shoulder. 'I know who has Evita. And where.'

'I know you know,' Nun says. 'If you've come it's because you're going to tell me.'

V

When Perón's seven childhood companions reach the tar-lined ditches that encircle Ezeiza airport, the windows to the bus they are riding in open onto images of an endless fiesta, whose episodes keep repeating themselves at regular intervals.

They see a spiderweb of pilgrims who are singing as they march along the shortcuts of a thicket of eucalyptus. The women are wearing white kerchiefs on their heads and carrying children in their arms. The men are holding placards aloft with a portrait of Evita in all the splendor of her beauty: in profile, her hair in a chignon, her lips parted.

A line of trucks goes slowly past, all of them packed with families who have come from a long way away. A number of trucks have the name of their distant cities on them: Aguilares, Monteros, Concepción, Choromoro. And on top of the cab, Eva again, her smile smudged by the journey, but not a hair of her chignon out of place.

To the rear, a van with loudspeakers is broadcasting a record of 'Evita capitana'. And all of a sudden Eva comes on with her voice of another time, hoarse, scratchy, riding roughshod over the air: *Fanaticism is the wisdom of the spirit.* A silence ensues. And then: *Dear comrades, fanaticism is the wisdom of the spirit.*

Women follow along after, with white kerchiefs on their heads and children in their arms. Some of them are laughing whole-heartedly. They are bathed in sunlight. A breath of a breeze is blowing.

'We have to go back to the hotel,' Arcángelo Gobbi, at the wheel of the bus, decides. 'This road has been taken over by the leftists.'

'Go back already?' Captain Trafelatti says querulously. 'When you come down to it, we haven't seen anything.'

Arcángelo doesn't answer. He slowly moves his lizard's head, sizing up the movements of the crowd on the horizon.

Several times the bus has ended up in the tar-lined ditches at the edge of the airport. The passengers have pointed out, in surprise, a swarm of flies swirling about above the scrub. Flies, in this cold? And they have seen lines of trucks that keep coming past, marked with the same names of prehistoric cities each time: Famaillá,

Burruyaca, El Chañar, Atahona. Can it be like at the opera? María Amelia has wondered. Is there just one backdrop that they keep making go round and round?

Remaining apart from the group, María Tizón and Benita are the only ones who, by allowing themselves to be carried away by their memories, have managed to get somewhere. They have scarcely budged from the past. Lowering their voices, as they enter together those mansions of memories that both, separately, have shared with Potota, a hunger to share confidences has gradually come over them.

Let us pick up the thread again then. Benita has recounted:

They hadn't yet been married a year when Perón decided that they would move to an apartment on the corner of Santa Fe and Canning. It was there that Potota felt the loneliest. I once dropped by to ask her to go with me to the movies. How can you think of such a thing, Benita? she said, refusing. What if Perón comes back and doesn't find me here? She began to pass the time by writing me letters.

María: She wouldn't even let me phone her. She was always afraid that the least little noise would distract Perón from his studies.

Benita: It all started with that feverish urge of hers to have a baby. When her period was a day late, Potota would get all excited and start talking a blue streak. And then when it eventually came, the whole thing ended in a flood of tears. 'What's happening to me, Benita, what's happening to me?'

María: That's how it was, all right. Without realizing it, Mama upset her even more by constantly asking: Well, Pototita? When is it going to be?

Benita: I noticed how upset she was in one of the first letters she wrote me. See, María? Read it. Just look how she bore her cross all by herself so as not to bother anybody else.

Dear Benita:

First off, I do hope that the two of you are enjoying good health . . . and a good bank balance. We're fine, thank the Good Lord!

Every day lately, I've been intending to visit you, but several times on account of the rain, and at other times on account of the festivities we've been having, to celebrate the Revolution, the days have gone by without my visiting you as I have so often said I would and so eagerly wished to do.

Benita, I also wished to see you and visit you so that you would give me the *needle* for picking up dropped stitches in stockings. I have several pairs of them that I don't wear because I don't want to ruin them by mending them, so you can imagine how eager I am to go see you or have you come see me. Benita, even though I have a lot more spare time than you, I'd be so happy if you'd come here, for even though Perón always comes home at a late hour, it nonetheless gives me an odd feeling to leave him by himself, because even though he shuts himself up all by himself, every so often he asks me for something.

Come visit me soon, *even if you've lost the needle*. You know that it's not out of self-interest, for I've kept asking you to come, just as I have Artemio.

And how is your family? We received a letter from the family in the Chubut. They are all very well and are expecting a visit from us this summer. When you come, we'll have a little talk together about everything and above all about *children*; maybe you already have news for me.

It's still the same as ever with me: it seems as if there's no way . . . Patience! Perhaps some day . . .

Benita, phone me as soon as you get this letter, because I want to know when I can come to your house or when you can come here.

Well, Benita, I hope all of you are well; best wishes to your family and especially to Artemio, from me and from Juan.

A fond embrace,

Potota

Buenos Aires, 10.9.1931.

In case you've lost it, the telephone number is 1053 Palermo (71).

María: Once, in summer, my sister Dora and I arrived on a visit. Potota's apartment struck me as being unbearably gloomy. She had a piano she never played. We sat talking for a while, she clutched my hands tightly in hers: María dear, she said. Have you noticed how any woman can get pregnant and I can't? We were worried about her when we left. My sister Dora began to phone her often to cheer her up: Mama is asking about you, Potota. She wants you to come here to spend time embroidering together. A very nice serial novel has come out in *El Hogar* and she wants to lend it to you. And things like that. Dora finally persuaded her that the two of them should go see a gynecologist together. Hoping for a miracle, Potota's mood changed.

Benita: Perón had his own worries as well, María. After he'd been appointed secretary to the Minister of War he heard that Aunt Juana and a farm hand, Marcelino Canosa, had fallen in love and were living together. That was terrible! But Potota convinced him that he should get the two of them to marry each other before the army learned of their affair. And that was what happened. Perón went to the Chubut and got his mother to remarry.

María: It was at that point that my sister Dora went with Potota to the gynecologist, taking advantage of the fact that Perón was away.

Benita: That week I received another letter. It was the last one.

Dear Benita:

I hope that God gives you and Artemio every blessing you

deserve. I don't know what to tell you about myself, Benita. I have endured many sufferings, undergoing all sorts of analyses and examinations, hoping to be able to get pregnant. I'll have definite word today. Thus far the doctor assures me that he doesn't find anything, that in other words I'm normal. I pray that he's right! But I've also been overtaken by certain very grave concerns, Benita, for if it's true that there isn't anything wrong with me and I'm able to get pregnant, I can't imagine why so much time has gone by without anything happening.

Benita: I hope I needn't remind you to bring the little bibs you promised me when you have time. I'm waiting for Perón to come back at any moment from his trip to the Chubut, so please phone me before you come.

Special greetings from me to Artemio. And for you, Benita, a hug from

Potota

Buenos Aires, 10.3.1934.

María: What sad days! When she was given the results of the examinations, Potota wouldn't answer the phone or see anyone. Imagine how she must have grieved, Benita. At out house we didn't know what to do. What was more, my sister Dora wouldn't say a word either. She said that the diagnosis was uncertain. One night I screwed up my courage, went to her room, and confronted her: Are you trying to drive us all out of our minds, Dora? Potota shut up in that apartment that's like a tomb, and you here keeping everything to yourself. Come on, what's going on? Can't she have children? Well then, she must resign herself, period. It's worse than that, Dora said. She can have children. The one who can't is Perón. And Potota won't ever tell him so.

Benita: She did the right thing, María. I would have done the same. One should never offend a husband's amour-propre.

María: As always happens, one misfortune led to others. A little while after that, Mama died. We all were grief-stricken, but Potota especially. Her hair turned white. She crocheted little doilies, and she spent hours cleaning the apartment. By afternoon she'd forgotten which baseboard she'd cleaned that morning and would scrub the whole apartment again.

Benita: Those weren't doilies she crocheted, María. They were baby booties.

How long has it been that the bus has been parked at the door of the hotel with them still inside, whispering together? When they get out, they are amazed at the changes. The arcades are now full of stern-faced, potbellied men, armed to the teeth. They are wearing white armbands. Mules have strayed into the parking lots, and the men are running after them, chasing them away by beating them with lengths of chain.

In the hotel salon, large portraits of Perón, Isabelita and Eva hang suspended from the ceiling. The corridors smell of flowers.

It's so unfair, María wails. They've left Potota completely out of all this. And taking Benita by the arm, she shares another confidence with her: How much Perón changed when he married Eva! With my sister he was a pleasant, well-mannered man. Later on he became vulgar, a boor. Some people say it was a pose, so as to appear to be more in touch with the people. I know that isn't so. That he did it on account of Eva. So she wouldn't seem so out of place.

In the shadows of the entry, Arcángelo has hidden behind a pair of dark glasses. An enormous, grotesque pistol protrudes from his hand. He is listening, with profound respect, to a man with dark brown hair and a vacant look in his eyes.

'There's no more time to be lost. The Lieutenant-Colonel needs you. Get going this minute, Arcángelo.'

'This minute, Lito,' he repeats. And immediately corrects himself: 'I'm on my way, sir.'

VI

It's my turn now. I know who has Evita, and where.

These sentences no longer interest anyone. When Zamora let them fall in the Café Gijón two years ago, in front of Nun Antenaza, they might well have driven history out of its mind. Now, 20 June 1973, nobody will lift a finger to pick them up. Everyone knows now what places Evita's dead body wandered to and who gave it repose. Let's think about tomorrow. In a little while, Zamora has written, this country will no longer have a past. The past is something unreal here, like a movie screen. At every moment, a new (and worse) kind of reality takes its place. It's not even oblivion.

It is past eleven-thirty when Zamora finally manages to cross the Riachuelo and enter Buenos Aires. At eleven he was to come by an apartment on the Calle Arenales to pick up a personal diary. She, the woman who has promised it to him, may not be there now. She may not have waited for him.

The streets of Barracas are deserted. The air is full of flies and pieces of paper. The sun, as cold as a medal, is dying out above the buildings. Near Constitución, two boys are washing a bar down. The soapy water licks the blinds and dumps a river of dead cigarettes out onto the sidewalk.

Zamora hears some flamenco dancers laugh as they enter the haze of the Café Gijón, puts his hand on Nun's shoulder again and hears himself say:

'I'll tell you what's become of the corpse. As you already know, I found some papers at the Argentine embassy in Bonn that described the transit of a certain rectangular oak box through Mannheim, Fribourg and Basel, Switzerland. I checked and found out that, as it crossed the border, it was accompanied by three men who were guarding it. One of them was an Argentine army officer. My suspicions were aroused on discovering that so many precautions had been taken for the disposal of some old papers, and I had no doubts. It was the corpse. I presumed that the person the box was being sent to would have the key. The addressee was a certain Giorgio de Magistris, via Cerésio 86-41, Milan. I took the first plane. The address was that of the Monumentale cemetery, near the Porta Garibaldi train station. You can imagine how on edge I was when I went in. I wasn't expecting a grave marked: *Eva Perón. Qui giace.* But I was expecting some sort of vague marker.

'It was in Milan, then, not in Rome,' Nun smiled.

'Milan, via Cerésio. I searched through the cemetery all one afternoon and then I had to come back the next day. An enormous gate, a ring of columns. I walked amid the imposing tombs. I entered the pantheon of heroes, the *Famedio*, where Manzoni's remains lie. As darkness was about to fall, I questioned the guards. I mentioned the name Magistris to them, gave them all the numbers written on the paper from the embassy. *Ottanta-sei!* one of the men exclaimed. *Ecco lo qua!* And he took me to the far end, to an austere building: the *Tempio di Cremazione*. I felt dizzy, apprehensive. It was a lost moment, as in a dream. Eighty-six because they ask – used to ask – 86 lire for the right to visit it.'

Zamora saw Nun shiver. The flamenco dancers, each with a glass of sherry in her hand, were signaling him from the bar.

'Those bastards cremated her!' Nun said. 'Why didn't you inform on them?'

'Because I'm not certain. There's not one proof. If I'd told the story, people would still be laughing at me. A thousand lies have been written about the corpse. I didn't want to add another one.'

The vast Avenida 9 de Julio opens before Zamora, completely empty. In the distance, beyond the Obelisk, he sees a truck decked with flags driving along. He feels the warmth of his own body in the Renault, safe from ridicule. Safe for how long? In Buenos Aires, ridicule dawns before the sun, every day. Three months after this meeting with Nun, General Lanusse's ambassador handed

Evita's corpse over to Perón, in Madrid. And the pieces of the puzzle suddenly fit together. Once again the phone rang at two in the morning, but this time at his house in Buenos Aires. It was Nun.

'Zamora? Have you realized what stupid jerks we were? It's my fault for not having seen things through to the end.'

'It's my fault,' Zamora said, hanging up after hearing the story.

Everything had passed through their hands: the numbers, the name, the places. For many years Eva Perón had lain in Milan under the name María de Magistris. Her gravestone was clearly marked: *Giorgio de Magistris, a sua sposa carissima.* The location of the grave matched: it was in garden site 41 of plot 86. The name of the cemetery was different: Musocco and not Monumentale, in the via Garagnano, not Cerésio.

He feels devastated, useless, and doesn't understand where this sudden anguish is coming from. He avidly smokes a cigarette so as to pluck up his courage and leaves the car in front of the door of the person who may be waiting for him. Hasn't Señora Mercedes promised to let him read the diary she kept in Santiago de Chile, between January and April 1938, when she and her husband were on intimate terms – or almost – with Potota and Perón? Hasn't she already told him on the phone, in a confidential tone of voice, about the hardships of the train trip over the Andes, the arrival at the apartment houses in the Nuñoa district. Potota's sudden decline before cancer killed her? You ring the bell and it is she who answers the door, Zamora: Señora Mercedes, the widow of the man who overthrew Perón in 1955. Mecha Villada Achával de Lonardi.

VII

Come on, boys, come on, be careful with the placards, don't let them show. If we give the game away now they'll smash us to bits.

Start singing! What's the matter with you? Have your throats gotten drowsy? Come on and sing, it's cold. *Perón, Evita/the Socialist fatherland. There's only one Evita, you know quite well/So why bust your balls for Isabel?* Look at that blowfly, Nun. Even the flies have come out in winter to hear the Old Man. A glorious day, right? Look at that bright sun. When I was a girl, an aunt of mine used to take me to the Parque Centenario. The boys would yank at my braids, say mean things to me, because of my hair and my freckles. But at the merry-go-round there was a boy who was sweet on me. A six o'clock in the evening face, he'd say to me. A rust face. A setting sun face. And instead of making me happy it made me sad.

What are you doing, boys? Come on! And that drum? Hey, have you lost your voice? When I was a kid, I used to think: I want to be like Rosa Luxemburg, like La Pasionaria, like Isadora Duncan. I want to be Krupskaya, reading Lenin a story by Jack London before he dies. When I grew up I realized that I was dreaming of a love being born at the same time as history – in the middle of the action, among the masses. A love that refuses to stop, understand what I mean? Like fire. Burning with passion in bed and militancy. And finally I said to myself: Evita is all that.

Watch out for that cordon of men there in that school, boys: the ones with the green armbands! Don't let yourself be provoked. Osinde and the sorcerer López Rega have brought in provocateurs from all over. But listen, don't shut up! Break their eardrums: *Perón, we want you to know/That sorcerer has to go! If Evita hadn't died/She'd be on the Montoneros' side!* Do you understand what I'm trying to tell you, Nun? I began to ask myself: Diana, doesn't a woman feel a deeper love when she's in the thick of the action? Can't sex and history be combined? And I answered myself: It's very easy, Diana. You have to live love as something normal in the midst of abnormality, let love be your very breath, your dream when you're wide awake. Share your love the way Evita did:

meeting the General from three to five in the morning, a marriage between secret lovers. Be – how shall I put it? – the pharos of your phallus. You like the sound of that, right? My pharos, your phallus, they'll never fail us. How's that? I'm crazy. I'm in love. I'm a woman. That word sounds better than ever today. I'm a woman.

Another step forward, girls! Sing the march, put your soul into it. Louder! Let's hear you. Put your soul into it. That's it, that's it! *Off to war with Perón/the people's war . . .*

Nun runs his hand across her shoulder, strokes the untamable mop of red hair and feels, without a thought, with a sheer necessity born of desire, the clamor of that body. He remembers that on returning the night before from a tour of the bonfires of the Montoneros from Cañuelas, Berisso and Florencio Virile, on entering Diana's lips, chapped from the winter cold (she says it's from life), Nun longed for the whole thing to be already over and be there with her again, caressing her, without his fire ever going out. He remembers that he stared at her with that fixed gaze that only darkness allows and said to her:

'I don't want you ever to go away, Diana.'

And, laughing, she began skilfully to loosen the knots that were still left inside him, to set each hidden tenderness of his veins free, to rescue the shipwreck victims of his feelings. With her fingers she slowly traced a body that would serve only hers now, and allowing him to enter the gentle warmth of her sea, answered him with the hoarse, impetuous words that had once belonged to Evita:

'I would only want to go away so as to be able to come back. I will return and I will be millions.'

Then he saw her fall asleep. He felt the burning sensations of insomnia moving once again through his blood whose fire was quenched. He had a cigarette, and the smoke left an undertow of moss and beetles on his tongue. He sniffed at his arms, so that the fragrance of sex would envelop him. And returning to the pages of the impossible rag, *Horizonte*, 'Perón: His Life Story – The Man,

The Leader – Documents and Accounts of a Hundred Witnesses',
he fell into the mud of another chapter.

'5. We shall never again be as we were. "One Sunday in 1922 . . ." '

VIII

At four p.m. the General makes out from the window of the plane
the dark brown craters of empty, open country. The sight of the
desert suffocates him. Where a river has contracted green streaks
have opened out in the earth. Trees, scrub? What desolation. Is
this the country I'm coming back to? the General will say later that
night. To this endless pampas, plundered, squeezed dry? I don't
recognize it. It's not mine. It was here that I always wanted to die,
and now I don't know. Does any of all this belong to me? And
what do I belong to?

López Rega distracts him with a cup of tea.

'It's almost time,' he says.

Isabel strokes Perón's hair.

'Is that true? It's almost time?'

Sitting down on the arm of the seat next to the General, López
unfolds another batch of papers scribbled full of countless figures
and endless hieroglyphics.

'I ordered comrade Norma Kennedy to read a press bulletin
from you. She got to work immediately and rounded up fifteen or
twenty people on the first floor of the international hotel. She has
told them that, despite the shooting and the imperialist plots,
General Perón will arrive in our country today, for good. She has
passed on the news that the plane is an hour late. And to
discourage any disorder, she has confirmed that you will come
to the dais at Bridge Twelve and address the masses.'

'Norma . . . what a good girl!' the General murmurs.

'But we won't be landing at Ezeiza,' López explains.

'Then where are you taking me?'

'To the military base at Morón, for reasons of security. Solano Lima, the Vice-President, has approved of our plan. We've asked him and the commanders of the three branches of the armed services to proceed to Morón immediately . . .'

Flashes of lightning interrupt him. The plane has turned on its lights and at the same time has entered a stretch of yellow clouds. The General is suddenly ill at ease.

'What's going to happen now to those poor people who are waiting for me, López? There are three million of them, do they say? Two and a half million? Heaven only knows what hell they've gone through to come see me. I don't like the idea of disappointing them so badly. What immense gesture will I be obliged to make now in order to satisfy them?'

'None,' López answers. 'It's an act of divine justice. What did they do during the eighteen years that you were out of the country? Nobody sacrificed himself. Nobody lifted a finger. You've done everything by yourself.'

'You and Daniel,' the señora smiles.

A fly lands on the General's stiff, liver-spotted hand. It has a blue back, transparent wings, avid eyes.

'A housefly,' the General notes as he chases it away. 'Flies here, this high up?'

They see it fly toward the lights in the ceiling and then land. It rubs its legs together.

'Oh, my,' the señora sighs.

'Look at it.' The General points. 'Look at those eyes. They cover almost its entire head. They're very strange eyes, with four thousand facets. Each one of those eyes sees four thousand different pieces of reality. My grandmother Dominga was very impressed by them. Juan, she used to say to me, what does a fly see? Does it see four thousand truths, or just one truth divided into four thousand pieces? And I never knew what to answer her . . .'

11 *Zigzag*

. . . The aforementioned personal effects of Abelardo Antezana
(a.k.a. 'Nun') and Diana Bronstein (a.k.a. 'Skinny,' 'Red,' 'Freckle-
Face') are accompanied by clippings from the weekly magazine
Horizonte, special edition dated 20 June 1973, article entitled Perón:
His Life Story – The Man, The Leader – Documents and
Accounts of a Hundred Witnesses, with handwritten annotations
by the two persons named above. All these effects were seized in
the raid that took place at 16:00 hours on this date at the villa
named 'Playa de la Noche', located on the Avenida de la Noria,
district of Esteban Echeverría, province of Buenos Aires . . .

5 *We Shall Never Be Again As We Were*

One Sunday in 1922, as he was returning from a visit to his
grandmother Dominga, First Lieutenant Perón bought, at a

newsstand in Retiro station, a certain poorly printed pamphlet, which appeared to be just another of the cheap serial novels that were so popular in that era. The cover showed, in washed-out colors, a crown of laurels. Inside were one hundred fifteen maxims by Napoleon on the art of war. Juan Domingo flung himself upon those maxims with the voracity of a love that has been waiting for too long. They gave rise in him to an unknown need for . . . what, exactly, he did not know.

One of the maxims went with him each morning to the firing range and could be heard each afternoon when he blew his whistle:

In war, nothing is more important than a single command. The army must be a single army, actions must have a sole aim, there can be but one leader.

Another maxim became so commingled with his dreams that, when he awoke, the odor of it still clung to his memory:

The great actions of a great general are not the result of fate or destiny. They are the result of planning and of genius.

That was it exactly: Perón wanted to plan the future, to get ahead of it, to intuit it.

In the officers' clubs there was secret, reverential talk of the General San Martín Lodge, which seemed to have imposed Colonel Agustín P. Justo as Minister of War, and on the blacklists of which the names of many Yrigoyenist officers appeared. Perón wanted to know at all costs what the officers in those inaccessible circles thought of him and sought out the only officer who could tell him: his protector, Bartolomé Descalzo. He found him in an irritated mood.

'I heard a lieutenant-colonel complain about you, Perón. He's one of the bigwigs of the Lodge and that man's unfavorable opinion could ruin your career. Be careful, you hear?'

'I'll do whatever you order me to, sir. How am I going to keep from being the victim of injustice?'

'If it were a matter of injustice I wouldn't have told you about it. That lieutenant-colonel has said that you while your time away going in for sports. And that he doesn't understand how, when you're almost thirty, you don't seem to be at all concerned about settling down. The Lodge is mistrustful of unmarried officers.'

Perón accepted the criticism. He spent several months mulling over the idea of marrying. In his philandering he had known only loud-mouthed, unpresentable sluts, who lolled about on sofas with their legs apart and spat on the floor. He asked Descalzo to help him to find a decent candidate.

'It so happens,' his protector said, 'that my wife and I have had our eye on three or four young ladies who are right for you. We'll introduce you to them at the first opportunity.'

But misfortune overtook the Perón family at just that time. Juan Domingo was expecting it. From the time he was a little boy, his mother had taught him that the workings of destiny are cyclical, and that fate obeys a law of compensation: every stroke of good fortune is paid for, sooner or later, by a run of bad luck. It never occurred to Perón, who had taken great care never to allow his feelings to become more than lukewarm in order to avoid that fate, that success also had its reverse side. He was the army's champion fencer, a physical education teacher, the author of a textbook on hygiene and morality for NCO candidates. A year after being promoted to the rank of captain, he was accepted for admission to the Graduate War College. Too much good luck in too short a time. Toward the end of March 1926, a telegram came from his mother: 'Papa very frail. Please meet us Monday Bahía Blanca train station.'

He barely recognized his father. Don Mario Tomás had tremors, was nothing but skin and bones dragging himself along, and stammered words with such a thick tongue that only Doña Juana was able to tell what he had said. He was suffering from arteriosclerosis, and in the backlands of the Chubut they could find no treatment that helped him.

They stayed for several days in Granny Dominga's new house, near the Flores train station. Then, thanks to a subsidy providentially granted Juan Domingo by the army, they bought a rambling old house on the Calle Lobos in which he had a room of his own in which to keep the maps and banners accumulated over fifteen years of living the life of a barracks nomad.

Doña Juana kept herself busy raising chickens and preparing noodles. In the afternoons she would bring the easy chairs out onto the sidewalk and deposit Don Mario Tomás there while she exchanged gossip with the neighboring women. Juan would come on weekends, wearing a straw hat and a suit, always of one dark color or another. And when open-air concerts in the Parque Chacabuco were announced, he would put on his dress uniform and go arm in arm with his proud mother for a stroll from one pergola to another.

Shortly before the spring of 1926, he interrupted his tracing of some Napoleonic maps to answer a phone call from Lieutenant-Colonel Descalzo.

'Meet me at ten o'clock tomorrow morning at the entrance to the Capitol movie theater,' his mentor said. 'And be prepared, Perón. My wife and I already have what you're looking for.'

He left two hours before ten, on the dot. He wanted to show himself as he was – impeccable, likable, self-assured – and dazzle the candidate, but never once did he wonder what she was like. If Descalzo recommended her, why waste the time? He had always disdained the useless expenditures of energy that ordinary men waste on sentiments instead of applying those same energies to attaining power or doing the work assigned them. He needed to marry, and Descalzo would introduce him to the right person. Nothing could be simpler.

From the window of a café, Juan Domingo saw the lieutenant-colonel's wife arrive with a short, slight girl, who spoke without raising her eyes and hid her mouth behind her hand when she laughed. Before they were even introduced to each other, he knew, without the slightest doubt, that she would accept him as her fiancé.

The movie theater was full of young officers and ladies decked out in cloche hats and ribbons at their hips. Perón pretended to follow with interest the complicated conversation centered on layers of ruffles, pleated skirts, boyish bobs and V necks that Descalzo's wife started. In the seat next to him, the candidate expressed her admiration of him with modest flutterings of her eyelashes. As soon as the house lights went down and the pianist reeled off an overture that had pretensions to being Oriental, Juan Domingo discreetly leaned over to her: 'Señorita Tizón, may I call you Aurelia?'

'Potota,' the girl corrected him, looking at him for the first time.

'Potota. I beg you never to keep your eyes lowered again. You have such a profound gaze that it makes a person shiver.'

'Shiver? Please forgive me, Captain. I am truly sorry.'

'Ah, no. Not Captain. Call me Perón.'

Toward the end of the film, when the sheik in love with the dancer turned back to rescue her from a deadly sandstorm, Juan Domingo, screwing up his courage, murmured: 'I thank you for coming. I have long wanted to meet a young . . . friend . . . such as yourself. Will you allow me to visit you? I hope I haven't arrived in your life too late.'

She did not take her eyes off the film. She hesitated between putting a stop to the captain's daring and, discreetly, giving it wings. An encouraging nudge in the ribs from Señora Descalzo made her decide:

'For me, anything that happens will happen early in my life. I'm eighteen years old.'

Perón dazzled her, in the darkness of the movie theater, with a schoolboy smile, mingled with melancholy.

'I shall soon be thirty-one. That comes as a sad surprise to you, isn't that so?'

The pianist electrocuted the audience with a tremolo. The sheik sighed lasciviously into one of the dancer's ears. Then he brazenly licked her cheek. Scandalized throat-clearings were heard.

Two weeks later, when they returned to the same movie palace with the Tizón sisters and saw from the same seats that daring simulated kiss, Juan Domingo brushed for the first time, with the tips of his fingers, Potota's gloved hands.

For two years to the day after they were engaged to be married, she believed that she was loved madly; that is to say, with respect, unfailing visits and formal thank-you letters. But on the last day of their honeymoon, he introduced her to such an impenetrable routine that the signs of love became totally confused.

Sometimes – she would recount many years later – I would go to Perón seeking affection and he would rebuff me without wounding my feelings, though with fearsome firmness. You and your childish ways, he would say to me. Don't you realize that you're a married woman?

And though he left her by herself almost all day long, even her most banal reasons for leaving the house were a matter of concern to him. He didn't like her to speak with anyone, not even with her sisters, as though he feared that caprices and false hopes would breed in Potota, and he would then be obliged to set things straight. His possessiveness reached such extremes that one afternoon, when he was most absorbed in his work, writing up some notes on the military plot of 1930, she left the house on tiptoe and went to the greengrocer's, and on turning around unexpectedly to pick out some tomatoes, she discovered Perón spying on her from behind a lamp post.

Only after their sixth year of marriage was Potota able to thank him for a sign of tenderness. It was the work of chance. Her mother, Doña Tomasa Erostarbe, had died of cancer. Taking time off from his duties at the Ministry of War, Major Perón remained with the family during the night of the wake, attended the prayers for the dead at the cemetery, but disappeared immediately afterward. During the novenas and memorial masses that followed he was not present. He came home to bed at a late hour and arose so early that Potota never managed to have breakfast with him. So as not to bother him, she kept her complaints to herself.

The rare occasions on which Perón telephoned her to tell her he'd be home for dinner, Potota refreshed her eyes with cotton pads and put just a bit of rouge on her cheeks – the maximum permitted a woman in mourning – to show that she was happy and carefree.

The Major once forgot some maps at home and had to come by in a hurry to pick them up. When he opened the front door, the silence and the darkness surprised him. He stole inside, entertaining in his mind the most terrible suspicions. All of a sudden, he heard a forlorn wail coming from the bedroom, that sounded at once like a litany of nuns and the awakening of a tomcat. He abruptly pushed the door open and turned the light on. He saw Potota lying face down on the bed, weeping, a tear-stained photo of Doña Tomasa in her hand.

Such grief finally softened his heart. He offered her his handkerchief and gave her a kiss on the forehead. She waited for the lump in her throat to dissolve, ceased all her sobbing by an effort of will and with eyes lowered in embarrassment as in days long past, said to him: 'Forgive me, Perón. This is foolish of me.'

The Major smiled faintly. 'It is of no importance. Those sorrows women suffer from will pass. Now allow me to go look for some maps. I must be off.'

Perhaps so much zigzagging in the life of our hero will disorient the reader. Inasmuch as events of a military (or perhaps political?) nature are approaching in the story – floods in which waters of the most varied sorts will merge – it might be prudent to halt and recall certain details of interest.

1926: The hero moves with his parents into an old house at number 3529 on the Calle Lobos (now Gregorio de Laferrère, between Quirno and San Pedrito) and becomes engaged to Aurelia Tizón, the daughter of a well-known photographer in Palermo, with ties to the Radical Party.

1928: In November, Don Mario Tomás Perón dies after a long and cruel illness. Our hero must postpone the wedding date to January 1929. When they return from their honeymoon, the newlyweds live with the Tizóns, at Zapata 315.

1930: Seeking privacy, they move to a spacious third-floor apartment at 346 Avenida Santa Fe. They furnish the bedroom with a Louis XIV-style armoire, a bed with a very high headboard and footboard and a dressing room. It has a pair of mirrors, six feet tall, that face each other, multiplying their bodies to infinity. In the dining room, the principal piece of furniture is a sideboard whose highest shelves can be reached only with the aid of a stepladder; the legs of the table rest on lions' heads. The floral centerpiece is a ceramic Saint Bernard with a Tyrolese peasant girl riding astride it.

In the living room there drowses a piano that Potota will never play.

1933: A mission on the border takes our hero back to the imposing settings of his honeymoon. His wife accompanies him on an excursion to Lanín volcano.

1935: Doña Tomasa Erostarbe de Tizón passes on. At the end of the year, our hero leaves to take up his post as military attaché in Santiago, Chile. On the eve of the journey, José Artemio Toledo visits him: he admires the red voiturette in which the couple will cross the Andes and praises Potota's courage: she will carry in her bag a .22-caliber pistol, prepared for any emergency.

1936: After arriving abroad our hero receives the news that General Francisco Fasola Castaño, who had been his superior on the Army General Staff, has been dismissed from active service for having circulated an open letter against 'the exotic ideologies that are endeavouring to muddy our own ideology and perhaps besmirch it.' Burning with patriotism, he sent him a note expressing his solidarity: 'My dear General . . . I have faith in your star and in your person, as a destiny and as a man. Nothing more is needed in order to triumph.'

A new zigzag. Early in 1930, Captain Perón was more an officer confined to a desk than a man of action. Infighting over blind hierarchical ranking in the barracks attracted him less now than did convoluted intrigues in the halls of government. He never went to sleep without reading a page or two by Count Schlieffen and reciting aloud a maxim by Napoleon, like someone praying. The subject of almost all his conversations was a book by the German general, Colman von der Goltz, *The Nation Under Arms*, which had just been translated in the Biblioteca del Oficial series, forty years after its original publication.

He taught Military History, and the more he discussed his favorite authors in class, the more submissively he accepted the truths of all of them as dogmas of a faith. 'There is no worse crime against the spirit than allowing an opportunity to go by,' he explained to his students. 'When a strategist of genius proposes in writing a new formula for an offense, why does he do so? So that other strategists will imitate him! And if he serves us up such a possibility on a platter, why fail to take advantage of it? Both in war and in politics there is just one morality: that of the useful. And only idiots have in hand what is useful and allow it to fly away.'

He recited Napoleon's maxims as though they were the Credo. Schieffen, on the other hand, was his Saint Thomas Aquinas: the translation of all supernatural enigmas into the light of the natural order. On invoking Napoleon, he recreated him. He took a key phrase as his point of departure and turned it every which way: *Man is everything, principles nothing./When principles are everything man is nothing./A man is everything, all men are nothing.* Schieffen's ideas, however, held such a great attraction for him that instead of modifying them, he chose to forget whose ideas they were. In the beginning he set them in quotation marks when he copied them; later on he underlined them; later still he hinted that they might be attributable to Xenophon, Plutarch, Livy, creatures who little by little were retreating into the night of time and finally were summed up in Perón.

The reader will allow us one last quick zigzag. In the spring of 1970, almost forty years after the facts that we are about to recount, the poet César Fernández Moreno and the aspiring novelist Tomás Eloy Martínez questioned General Perón in Madrid about the barracks coup that toppled the democratic government of Hipólito Yrigoyen in Argentina and brought on a series of military protectorates.

The Civil guards at the entrance to the villa, the little poodles, the dovecote, the ash tree: you are all familiar with the setting by now. The General's hoarse voice inviting visitors to come in, López Rega setting up the tape recorders, Isabel offering the gentlemen a demitasse: we will spare the reader all that. We will retain only the naked dialogue in which the voices intermingle and re-establish the past (that particular past) as it was.

The visitors arrived well equipped, with excerpts of speeches, opinions that Perón had let fall through the years and even the huge scholarly volume of a gringo professor, the vowels of whose name the General persisted in changing. The master of the house had no other weapon at hand except his memory, but in it was a lively ferment of experiences long pondered.

'Allow us to say, General, that at the beginning of '30, even if you were an obscure officer still, you enjoyed the respect of your superiors. You showed yourself to be discreet, obliging, trust-worthy, you had a punishing capacity for work, and in those times of such excessive appetites for power, your political talent was like a baby tooth. You therefore did not appear to be dangerous. President Yrigoyen's years were weighing heavily upon him. He spoke little, listened less, and a circle of fawning admirers kept him so far removed for reality that he began to mistrust even his senses that were still intact: he didn't believe what he saw. In 1930, the terrifying silence that descended from the seat of power set a number of military officers to thinking. Since nobody is issuing orders, why don't we who know what's going on begin doing so ourselves? A cast of elderly colonels had scruples: these officers were out to shed the blood of conscripts – the blood of civilians – in order to topple a legitimate government, thereby violating the regulations and codes that they had sworn to respect. The lieuten-ants and captains, on the other hand, were champing at the bit. They were going to take part in the first dress rehearsal for coups d'état. These coups would permit them, if only for a moment, to see themselves in the mirror of power. You, Juan Domingo Perón, would come across these officers many times on the way: Ossorio Arana, Julio Lagos, Francisco Imaz, Bengoa, all those lieutenants and cadets of 1930 would later turn against you. The moves they plotted were like large-scale training maneuvers for doing battle with historical reason.'

'Not true. I refused to get involved in them. I was among the last to learn what was going on. On the very eve of the coup, on 5 September, I had asked to be transferred to Uspallata because I didn't want to have anything to do with those betrayers of the Constitution.'

'How, then, could you write, in the notes that you entrusted to Lieutenant-Colonel Sarobe, who was among the first, that José Félix Uriburu, the leader of the army uprising, organized it in June 1930? Uriburu announced – you write – his intention to replace democracy with a corporative state. Since he was a captain, you did not have the courage to oppose him. But you offered to involve other prestigious leaders in the conspiracy, rallying them round a single tendency and orientation.'

'That was always my greatest concern: organizing. In 1943 things came off well because by then we were organized. But in '30 . . .'

'You were made a member of the revolutionary General Staff, Operations Section. You were asked to do certain minor tasks. Despite your efforts, General, that coup d'état was chaos.'

'As was the country, boys. All of Argentina was falling to pieces. Having a president that old aged all of us. We were poor, but people didn't feel sorry for us the way they do now. More than thirty per cent of the peasants who were examined for military service turned out to be suffering from tuberculosis. Everybody was living on handouts, touching people for money, as we used to say in those days. Every sponger staked out a café or a restaurant to make his pitch in, as beggars do in the atrium of churches. They closed the whorehouses and a new business came into being, that of taking johns to hotel rooms rented by the hour. For two pesos, a manicurist gave you the whole treatment: they didn't leave a single nail untouched. Young men from good families took up the habit of making their debut with poor servant girls. Every day trains arrived at Retiro station filled with girls ready to offer any service, including being taken to bed, for twenty pesos a month, and if they refused to give in to the demands of the man of the house, or the sons – so long, girlie. The only diversion those unfortunate girls had was going to the zoo on Sundays and listening to Nick Vermicelli on the radio. Yrigoyen was popular, of course, but he was already far gone in years. His revolutionary ardor had been dampened. There was nothing to do but overthrow him. But who overthrew him? The army? No! It was the oligarchy, that had been ousted from power in 1916 and was just waiting for its chance to hit back.'

'Nonetheless, General, listen to what you said on 8 April 1953; let yourself go back to your past and listen: "It wasn't the revolution that brought Yrigoyen down; it was his own supporters. Those going around making speeches today: they're the ones who double-crossed him . . ."'

'Don't you see, boys? The poor old man was overthrown by the oligarchy in cahoots with the radicals. Even Alvear, who was like a son to Yrigoyen, toasted his downfall in champagne when they brought him the news! Human gratitude is like a bird flying by: it leaves no memento of its passage except its droppings.'

'You admired him, then?'

'Yrigoyen? Of course I admired him! He thought the same way I did!'

'Why did you join the coup, then?'

'Because they hoodwinked me, boys. They told me that the Government stole, that such and such a minister kept a mistress with the money he got from selling railroad sleeping cars and that another one did a good business selling the pencils belonging to the National Board of Education. And never a peep out of the

Government: it said nothing at all. What else could I, a crummy captain, have done?'

'You described the many things you did. You told how, at nightfall on that 6 September, you made your way through the city in an armored car, following the squadrons of grenadiers. You said that people all around you were leaping for joy and tossing flowers from the balconies. Long live the fatherland! Death to Yrigoyen! You told how, when you reached the Plaza de Mayo, you saw a tablecloth fluttering like a flag of truce on the rooftop terrace of the Casa Rosada.'

'That was so, boys. And I heard Enrique Martínez, the Vice-President, beg Uriburu to kill him. The poor man, backed into a corner, became hysterical. I won't resign, General! Kill me if you like! Do you know why I saw him? Because I left the grenadiers around five-thirty that evening, walked as far as the Calle Victoria and caught up with General Uriburu's car there. I stood on the running board and entered Government House with him.'

End of the zigzag. A new chapter is beginning, to the tune of the tango that Discépolo was to write five years later: 'Cambalache' ('The Swap Shop').

. . . Below are notes made by Diana Bronstein in the margins of the copy of *Horizonte* confiscated from her.

Note of the official presenting the indictment: The phrases below are conclusive proof of the extremist ideology that rules among the accused ringleaders. Submit them to the authorities as a source of further information.

> *The Old Man had a Napoleonic sense of smell.*
> *He had a big schnozzle. A nosy nozzle.*
> *'Never again will we be the way we were.' A quote stolen from* The Wings of the Dove, *Henry James, last sentence.*

Zigzag. Zagzig.

Fasola Castaño, also known as Fa Sol La No-Dough From Mi, precursor of the national-Fasolist fatherland.

Pass me a fasofag for a drag, Nun. Pass me an I love you.

12 *Cambalache*

Zamora has imagined her as she no longer is. He expected to find the fragile, imperial face that appeared in the 1955 photographs. It hasn't occurred to him that time might make her more beautiful. When Mercedes Villada Achával de Lonardi answers the door, Zamora wonders whether he might not have come to the wrong place. Time has gradually moved the woman's beauty to the inside of her body, as though she had been embarrassed to show it and her body were now nothing but the transparent chrysalis that shelters it. She has been a widow for over fifteen years. The men who succeeded her husband in power have been ungrateful to her. Strangely enough, their ingratitude has suited her: it has shed a dim, autumnal light on a demeanor that must once have been too haughty. It is plain to see that she hasn't slept. Underneath her big black eyes lie violet valleys.

'Weren't you expecting me at this hour?' Zamora apologizes.

She remains in the shadow, on the defensive.

'I never expect anyone.' And yet, as she shows him in, she shakes Zamora's hand warmly. 'I have forebodings. It's only natural on a day like today. Sit down, sit down. Would you like some tea?' She rises to her feet, obviously tense. 'Listen: the silence. They have left this whole section of the city deserted. A moment ago, when I went out onto the balcony and saw the streets, I felt that a tragedy was about to befall us. You may have heard, Zamora, what people are saying: that the masses are going to burn down the northern section of Buenos Aires once Perón sets foot in the city. A family that lives downstairs in this building went off to Mar del Plata. They took their jewelry, their paintings, their pets with them. They were panic-stricken.'

'You mustn't worry,' Zamora consoles her, he too rising to his feet. 'Perón will see to it himself that nothing happens . . . He has stated that he is coming as an earnest of peace and I don't think he's lying. And he's going to die soon. It's in his interest to enter history with clean hands.'

As his eyes gradually accommodate to the darkness, Zamora notices that the apartment is untidy, and it is obvious that Doña Villada Archával de Lonardi has hesitated for several hours between leaving and staying on. In one corner of the living room there are two little trunks with the lids open and nothing in them. Hanging behind them, presiding over a horizon of furniture covered with dust sheets, is a portrait in oils of General Eduardo Lonardi, with his ceremonial staff and wearing the presidential sash. Clouds of steam emanate from a silver samovar.

'History, history . . . ' She shakes her head dubiously.

'Nothing of what's happening can be seen from here. It may be that there are people in the Plaza de Mayo; I don't know. But the outskirts of the city, señora: a river. It took me more than an hour to drive from Lanús to downtown. When I left Monte Grande, my car was held up by a drum corps that was over a mile and a half long. With buses, trucks, dilapidated vans strewn all over the streets, any which way, blocking traffic. It's as though the entire country were hypnotized.'

'The eve of the Millennium . . .' she suggests.

'That's it exactly. Argentina peering into the abyss of the end of the world. Have you been listening to the radio?'

'I prefer not to,' she answers as she pours tea. 'Radio depresses me.'

'On one news bulletin it said that Admiral Rojas has set booby traps in his house, to defend it against an attack by the masses. He is sitting in an easy chair, facing the front door, six-shooter in hand. If the attackers manage to break through his defenses, he will shoot off the first five bullets and then kill himself (they're saying) with the last one. He has given out several very pompous statements, brimming over with rage.' Zamora consults a grimy notebook. 'Listen, this is a word-for-word quotation from one of them: "The tyrant who is returning today to defame the country is acting out the farce of the prodigal son, bring with him new errors and even more nefarious plans in the depths of his fathomless perversity . . ." '

'What atrocious style,' Doña Mercedes blurts out. And as though the invective had suddenly awakened her to another reality, she transfixes Zamora with a penetrating gaze. 'What is it you're after? Tell me the truth. What are you going to do with whatever I may be able to tell you?'

He has been waiting for that question. 'And you? What will you tell me? Will you remain silent, fearing Perón's vengeance? I'm asking you: Are you one of those people who would rather have the story write itself?'

'It's of no importance any more. But General Lonardi is sacred. Nobody lays a finger on him if I can help it. So many reporters have recounted things that didn't happen, so many have put history together and torn it apart in bad faith, that I no longer know, I don't know . . . I find it hard to believe that you'll be different.'

'I have to be different, señora. I'm not writing a biography, the way the others are. I'm not searching for explanations. I'm not passing judgment on anyone. Who am I to say that this or that person did good or evil? What I'm trying to do is simpler: it is causes, not consequences that interest me: the forces that brought events to pass. Have a look at this special edition of *Horizonte*. There's an enormous gap. The title promises an account of Perón's whole life, and it isn't his whole life: it's only part. The General hangs suspended at the height of his glory, ascending to paradise with Evita. You will not see him there in that article, with dark circles under his eyes, in a panic, waiting, almost ten years later, in a Paraguayan gunboat, for Lonardi to take pity on him. Do you know why I never got to the end? Because I was lacking the beginning. Read these paragraphs in the magazine: there's not one line on the Greek tragedy that your husband and Perón acted out on 2 April 1938, in Chile. At that point there's just a blank.'

'The enemy brothers,' Doña Mercedes sighs, overcome with fatigue, sitting down.

'That's the key I'm interested in playing,' Zamora explains. 'Cain and Abel. Romulus murdering Remus so that the city (history) will bear the mark of his name. The red Asvin and the black Asvin of the Vedas galloping side by side, one in the light and the other in the dark, as though the chariot they are driving were running along the eternal edge of twilight . . .'

'Tell me what you've written, Zamora. I want to understand where you're going, what you're trying to accomplish in this piece.'

Zamora hands her a copy of the magazine. She hesitates. She feels a fog of anxiety within, but on the outside she gives off only an air of calm.

'May I turn on the television, señora? Just for a moment. Ezeiza is boiling over now. And we'll be able to see the dais from close up . . .'

Doña Mercedes shrugs.

'Watch if you like. I'm not going to. And kindly excuse me now. I'm going to turn my back.'

She walks over to the writing desk, in the shadow. She puts her glasses on, takes refuge beneath the light of an antique oil lamp wired for electricity, and reads in *Horizonte*:

Following the 1930 coup the military were suddenly all the rage. Almost every Saturday young ladies in society gave a ball in honor of the heroic cadets who had saved them from the rabble. A sign that uniforms softened even the most conservative hearts was the marriage entered into by Mercedes Villada Achával and Artillery Lieutenant Eduardo Lonardi, the son of an Italian musician who played at open-air concerts in small towns.

But behind the scenes, the contagion of power was wreaking havoc in the army. Eager to satisfy General Justo's appetites, President Uriburu designated him Commander-in-Chief. For several weeks both pretended that they were enjoying a honeymoon. Justo placed his most trusted men in command posts and handed in his resignation, biding his time. Captain Perón, who was still tacking from one faction to the other, was assigned to the Secretariat of War. For a few months he was given important missions. Then he fell into disgrace. Descalzo, his mentor, had been removed from the scene: he was head of a remote military district, in Formosa. Sarobe, another lieutenant-colonel who had treated him kindly, was posted to the embassy in Tokyo.

As Uriburu's prestige rapidly declined, Perón began showing his brand-new sympathies for Justo with greater self-assurance. In May 1931, he was relieved of his post at the Secretariat of War and sent to investigate whether everything was well on the country's borders. As though that were as easy as stepping outside to see if it's raining.

He proceeded on foot from Formosa to Orán amid swamps that devoured animals by night and turned into fields of pestilential flowers by day. He went on muleback from La Quiaca to San Antonio de los Cobres, through milk-white deserts whose inhabitants wore guanaco skins and spoke in a language of gargles interspersed with snuffles.

One dreadfully hot morning he was told that he had been promoted to major, which meant something more than simply an advancement in rank. From that moment on, he was a leader: he would be obliged to command rather than to obey . . .

Doña Mercedes leapt over the barrier of several pages abounding in descriptions of Patagonian landscapes and in rhetorical reflections on the 'Siamese warp and woof' weaving together, according to Perón, the destinies of the army and of the fatherland. She lingered over the references to Chile. They were a mere parenthesis within a very long chronology:

1937: Our hero has conquered Chile. The military attachés of a hundred countries elect him to represent them before the head of state, Arturo Alessandri, at the Independence celebrations. His eloquent speech wins him an ovation. The President of the Republic invites him to a private banquet that he hosts two days later. In the course of it, Perón wins Alessandri's eternal friendship. At dessert, he sings, off key, but with profound feeling, the tango 'Cambalache', which he describes as the ethical rhapsody of the Argentine soul. The Chilean civil servant Luis Villalobos, who made the acquaintance of our hero at that dinner, remembers that at the end of the tango he got the words mixed up but that Dr Alessandri politely pointed out to him the mistake he had made. To the accompaniment of an accordion played by Potota, our hero is reported to have sung:

> Twentieth century, a swap shop
> Full of problems and feverish work . . .
> He who doesn't shed tears doesn't get to suckle
> And he who doesn't suckle is a jerk!

(And the President pointed out to him that the right words were: *He who doesn't knuckle down is a jerk.*)

The genuinely warm ties that Perón – who now holds the rank of lieutenant-colonel – forms in Santiago become evident in March of . . .

1938: when innumerable dinners in his honor are given on the occasion of his return to Buenos Aires, where the Minister of War has a momentous destiny laid out for him . . .

'This isn't serious writing, Zamora.' Doña Mercedes turns around, taking her glasses off. 'And is it your intention to involve Lonardi in gossip-column banalities of that sort?'

Zamora doesn't hear her. He has discreetly reduced the volume of the television set to a minimum. Even so tumultuous sounds, which could be the chants of the crowd or the booming voice of the TV announcer, can be heard.

The camera prowls amid the crowd, as though it had lost its bearings: it crosses several deserted pastures, flies across fields of letters as though it were following the trails of an anthill, freezes on the unfinished photograph of Isabelita that a number of workers are hurrying to fill in: she still is missing a shoulder, a bit of ear, the chignon of her coiffure. Alongside the dais, several trucks unload baskets full of doves. The musicians of the symphony orchestra endeavor to tune their instruments. Zamora? Doña Mercedes repeats, and this time he looks at her, in astonishment, as though he were coming ashore from a forbidden sea. *C'est fini?* she asks, angrily. *Fini, la mascarade dégoûtante?* And from the circle of shadow around the lamp she holds a sheaf of handwritten pages out to him.

'Here, Zamora, take them,' she orders, waving the sheets of paper. 'Here you have the story that Eduardo and I shared with the Peróns in Chile, thirty-five years ago. I spent all last night copying it from my personal notebooks. There is more there than you were expecting.'

She rises to her feet and walks into the light, poised and elegant. For a moment, she seems remote from her body, as though the chrysalis of her beauty had broken apart and the light of bygone days had begun to take wing.

'I'll publish your story exactly as you've written it down, line for line.'

'Not so fast, Zamora. Till very late last night, my children advised me not to hand anything over to you. Why to that man, why to him all of a sudden? Marta, my eldest daughter, who's writing a book in honor of her father, said to me. And to tell the truth, I didn't know either: why to you, Zamora. Just now, as I was reading that filthy rag, I had a revelation. Because you know the other side of the story, Cain's side. Because if you've called on me, it was for a purpose. God is just, remember? God is just: the sign and countersign with which Eduardo overthrew Perón.'

Her angry language advances calmly, as though it were a trained mastiff being held on a leash, until something gives her away: she picks up the cup of tea and a drop spills on her immaculate skirt. At that point, she and Zamora hear a low road of thunder in the Plaza San Martín, two blocks away. The thought of a prophetic rain has crossed both their minds, though they do not say so: the red rain of the end of the world. Doña Mercedes goes over to the window and parts the curtains. The sun is shining. The thunder rumbles again with the sluggishness of a dying animal.

Now it is intermingled with a monotonous buzz, gives a locust leap, becomes a voice, caws with the unmistakable melody, how great you are, Perón, Perón.

Zamora is prepared for the exchange. He has brought a folder full of old clippings and opens it.

'I'm not going to tell you the other side. I'm going to show it to you to surprise you. You will very seldom hear so many contradictory passions given expression in a single drama. Begin here. Read this report from the correspondents of *Horizonte*.'

ACT I. Perón arrived in Santiago in March 1936, via Uspallata. Until December 1937 he lived in the Providencia district – and not in Nuñoa, as is usually said – possibly in the Calle Diego de Almagro. He began his day's work at seven in the morning, in a little office in the Pasaje Matte, the windows of which at that time overlooked the private gardens of the Argentine ambassador. It is worth describing this setting where the drama that sealed the destinies of Perón and of Lonardi will be played out. It is located opposite the Plaza de Armas. Its four exits lead to Huérfanos, Ahumada, Compañia, and Estado Streets respectively. Dampness oozes from the shops. Their musty show windows display craft objects from the provinces: copper frying pans, leather reins, earthenware ashtrays. All the offices of the Argentine embassy were grouped together there, on the fifth floor of that building on the Calle Ahumada.

Outside lay a wretchedly poor city, slowed down to a torpor by phalanxes of beggars. Roberto Arlt, who passed through Santiago in 1937, described it to his mother in these words:

This is worse than Africa. People have almost nothing to eat. To us Argentines who have money with us, living is cheap; to those who live here it is extremely expensive. Statistics show that a Chilean eats less than two-tenths of an ounce of meat a day. Two-thirds of the capital consists of tenements dating from colonial days. Tenements a block long, with roof tiles going back to the era of San Martín . . .

For the military attachés of that time it was their routine assignment – both in Santiago and in Buenos Aires – to secure plans, maps, statistics, reports of maneuvers and strategic documents of the other country. They played at war, espionage, patriotism. The President of Chile, Arturo Alessandri, a leftist, did not accept these swaps of information good-humoredly. From the beginning of 1935 the army and the navy besieged him with pleas for money to modernize the country's armaments. They needed pretexts: an illusory enemy, an incautious spy, the shadow play of a war projected upon the defenseless state. Perón, who foresaw those threats, wove his spiderweb in the semidarkness, retreating a number of times when the moment came to act. In all innocence, Lonardi wanted to earn praise and he took the hook that Perón baited.

There are three versions of the story, and all three show no mercy to Lonardi. The daily papers of the time do not mention Perón. They tell how (the details must not be lost sight of) the Chilean military intelligence services had been tailing, for at least a year, a former army officer, Carlos Leopoldo Haniez, who was believed to be interested in selling secret documents.

The head of the intelligence services, Colonel Francisco Japke, laid a series of traps. He ordered two of Haniez's old army buddies to renew their friendship with him and pretend to be his accomplices. There were – the weekly *Ercilla* recounts – 'wonderful wines, festive dinners, endless toasts'.

The documents were to be sold through Guido Arzeno, an Argentine who represented the interests of United Artists in Chile. Arzeno lived in apartment 311 in the Pasaje Matte. Japke ordered his telephone tapped and microphones hidden in living room.

Encouraged by his buddies, Haniez loosened his tongue. The military attaché of a neighboring country, he said, was interested in buying useless documents at a price that equaled their weight in gold. He was offering seventy-five thousand pesos for the Chilean Army's mobilization plan and twenty-five thousand more for a secret report on the army's most recent maneuvers. A captain earned two hundred pesos a month. The Argentines would hand over a fortune to them in return for something that had cost them no effort.

Haniez's friends pretended to be having moral scruples. They finally said yes. They agreed to meet on Saturday, 2 April, at eight p.m. in Arzeno's apartment.

Here it is necessary to stop and recapitulate. The one who had made the attractive offer to Haniez was Perón. In the middle of March, Perón returned to Buenos Aires. In a final rendezvous with Haniez, he supposedly told him: 'Don't worry, man. My successor, Lonardi, has orders to go through with the deal. Wherever you go with the documents, he'll bring the suitcase with the money.'

On the night of Friday, the 1st, the traitorous officer received a false set of maps and statistics, forged by Japke. The next day a police patrol suddenly appeared in the Pasaje Matte. Lonardi was caught photographing the papers with a Contax. At his feet was the suitcase full of money. The detectives seized sixty-seven thousand pesos.

Three days later, the Argentine Government ordered the military attaché to return immediately and arranged for him to be tried by court martial. Arzeno and his wife were expelled from Chile. Haniez served two or three years of his sentence in a military prison. Someone saw him in Lima in 1941, dressed like a fashion plate, coming out of a night club.

ACT II. *Statements by Señora María Teresa Quintana, the daughter of the man who had been the Argentine ambassador during these events.*

I was a close friend of Perón's. My father, Federico Máximo Quintana, gave signs of an immediate affection for him, and invited him to banquets and lunches several times a week. I still have a vivid memory of him, as though it were yesterday. He was a brilliant man, extremely refined. He arrived in Santiago in the first months after he became a widower and comported himself with exceptional Catholic devotion. When he was ordered to return to Argentina, he was given an unusual farewell banquet at the embassy, attended by the Chilean chancellor himself.

The new military attaché, Major Lonardi, arrived at about that time. He was not as brilliant as Perón and I have only a vague memory of what he looked like. Out of innocence or slow-wittedness, he found himself involved almost immediately in a story of espionage that deeply affected Papa . . .

ACT III. *Statements by Doña Enriqueta Ortiz de Rosas de Ezcurra, the wife of the man who was consul-general in Santiago between 1933 and 1942.*

Perón? Of course! Certainly I remember him! The day I was introduced to him I remarked to my husband, Andrés: Did you see that fellow? He thinks he can ride roughshod over everybody. He thinks he's everybody's superior.

At that time the embassy was like a club of good friends. Among its members were Ludovico Lóizaga, Tulio de la Rúa, Adolfo Béccar and Federico, the ambassador, who was involuntarily involved in a disgraceful incident brought about by Perón a week after his arrival.

Federico invited him to dinner. We women were all dressed in evening gowns. Perón's wife – poor thing! – was a disaster. She was – how shall I put it? – a mere nobody. Out of sheer curiosity, I asked Perón what impression he had formed of our diplomatic corps. His answer was shockingly rude. He said that our husbands were sent abroad more on account of their names and their connections than on account of any real expertise. There are a whole lot of asses running around loose, he said. I'd round them up and set them straight with a month of military instruction.

You can imagine what ensued: an icy silence! With an elegant gesture, Federico hinted to us that we should ignore Perón's outrageous remarks. I heard later that the ambassador's wife, deeply upset, said that if he repeated his rude behavior, she herself would send him away from the table.

Perón must have been aware that he was ostracized because he turned up at receptions at the embassy only occasionally. I was told that he kept company with Chilean officers and that he even tried to con one of them into taking part in some sort of mysterious spy game.

ACT IV. *Statements by Carlos Morales Salazar, author of* An Exegesis of the Peronist Doctrine.

The Chilean press took little notice of the case. We all know that military attachés have no other function except spying: when they go to a country, it is for that sole purpose. What other reason would bring them there? Only spying and procuring arms. Perón offered Lonardi a peeled fig on a platter and Lonardi let himself be taken in. Was Perón to blame? No! Lonardi had only his own stupidity to blame. It is perfectly understandable that Lonardi never forgot his terrible blunder and blamed the person who was his brother officer but turned out to be his worst enemy.

Perón is very cunning, very clever. If he was guilty of anything, nobody was ever able to pin it on him. And Chilean history has long since declared him innocent. The proof is that when he came on a presidential visit, my country received him with all sorts of honors and nobody so much as mentioned the unfortunate episode in 1938.

'Good heavens!' Doña Mercedes sighs, covering her neck with one hand. 'So you journalists write history using rags and tatters like that?' She rises to her feet. The dark circles under her eyes have made their gaze look older.

'Using indecencies of that sort? I am going to be the loser in the exchange with you, Zamora. I ought to have foreseen it. I'll be giving you the truth in exchange for a pack of lies. It's not your fault, not really. How could I blame you? It's Perón who's to blame. Everything that has passed through his hands has become contaminated. The men, the army and this country full of – ' she is about to say 'shit'. The word fades away to a low hum and does not escape her lips. '. . . this wretched country. And now we are giving him a second chance. Imagine . . .'

She turns away sadly and looks at the television screen. A flag flutters. A ring of men in ponchos, wearing dark glasses, slowly ascends the esplanade and heads for the dais, at Ezeiza. The camera slowly moves in for a closeup of Perón, who is dressed in severely tailored civilian clothes. His eyes light up with an ironic gleam.

'They've finished Isabel's photo in time,' Zamora discovers. 'They've put her elbow in. And, look, they're draping her in flags.'

Doña Mercedes isn't listening to him. Her hand is still on her neck, as if to defend herself from the darkness that is now tattooing the silences of the air from countless directions.

'No one has ever had a second chance here. Neither San Martín nor Rosas nor Lonardi. This country is cruel. It is foolish. It's only riffraff who get a second chance.'

* * *

From the papers that Zamora has been given there emanates an almost physical malaise, an ailment that must have hung all night like an albatross about his neck and that is only now slowly going away. They are papers that have felt a great deal and have been convalescing from their feelings. It is noticeable. On the first page of Doña Mercedes's diary the words are interrupted by a rough sketch – the profile of a woman, a city seen from above? – and above the last two of them are flaking funeral mementos: the card with the photograph of Potota commemorating her death, and the funeral notice in the daily *El Mundo*. As Zamora leafs through the papers, the uncontainable gluttony of gossipmongers comes over him. He would like to sink his teeth into them at this very moment.

'May I?' he says, and immediately is confused and embarrassed. What am I doing here in the middle of all of this? Nothing belongs to me, I've sneaked into this story like an intruder. He murmurs a clumsy apology. 'I'm sorry.'

'There's not enough light here,' Doña Mercedes advises him, with her hands on her skirt, hiding the tiny tea stain. 'You'd best go over to the window.'

Zamora reads:

Santiago, Santiago: Cordillera, bleak highland, mountain pass. Good heavens, what a long journey. How terrible if we were traveling through these environs by night. Highlands, passes. I envy Eduardo, my husband. Such trust in fate. In these vast expanses, these towering mountain ranges, I have no trust. God help us. I have no trust.

Bells ring, in the distance.

'Bells ringing at this hour, on this day? How odd! They're coming from the church in Socorro.' Zamora hurries over toward the TV set. 'Can it be the plane, arriving this soon?'

'If you're worried, listen to the news,' Doña Mercedes invites him from an armchair, in the shadow. She is sitting with her back turned to the windows and the images, but she gives the impression, rather, that she has turned her back on everything.

Helicopters zoom above the crowd. The television issues an asthmatic appeal: 'Let us rehearse . . . Just a moment, comrades. Let's see, let's see . . . How are we going to welcome our General when he arrives? Let's rehearse . . . One, two . . . Three! Peronistaaaa lads . . .' The voice grows hoarse.

Zamora understands. The bells too have committed a faux pas, shown a sudden discourtesy. Faced with the morning's silence, so spasmodic, so cavernous, they don't know what to do. He turns the set off and goes back to reading Doña Mercedes's diary.

Sketches: circles, arrows. A city or a mountain? The journey was very tiring. Something ridiculous, but awful at the same time, happened. My littlest daughter lost her pacifier. I crossed the mountain range shut up in the lavatory, so that the other passengers wouldn't have to put up with her crying.

Arriving at the Santiago station was a relief. We forgot all our troubles when we set foot on Chilean soil. My husband and I were full of false hopes. The post as military attaché would mean an entirely different life. For a couple of years we would be more or less well off financially: a parenthesis in that routine of counting pennies and continually limiting our expenditures.

From mid-'37, Eduardo – who was now a major – hoped that he would be sent on a mission abroad. He was first chosen for a study tour of Germany. It was the usual waiting room for those who, on their return, would teach at the Graduate War College. But certain influences were brought to bear against him and he was sent instead to Chile.

Perón was waiting for us on the platform with Potota, his

wife. I had never met them. They made a most favorable impression on me. They were likable, and most kind. They had already secured an apartment for us, in the Lerner Residence in the Pasaje Subercaseaux, and they themselves, in order to make us feel less alone in the first months in Santiago, had given up their apartment in the Providencia district and moved in there. They had seen to everything so as to give us a warm welcome: the living room full of flowers, and chilled fruits for my little ones.

Our husbands worked together. Potota and I were neighbors. In the afternoons we went out in Perón's car to visit the city. He had just traded his voiturette in for a new Packard and was very insistent that we should not miss out on the bargain prices available to the diplomatic corps and buy ourselves a car. 'Go ahead and buy one; it'll be practically a gift,' he kept telling us. On Saturday nights, we went out dancing, with Eduardo always my partner on the dance floor. It was understandable, then, that we ended up forming fraternal ties of friendship.

I noted immediately that the Peróns were a couple who were very close to each other. Every time Potota mentioned him, her voice was filled with pride. One afternoon, I remember, the two of us were walking along together behind our husbands. They were both in uniform. They were impressive. Potota said to me, her eyes sparkling: Look what fine figures they cut. What good lads they are. Keep an eye on Eduardo. Chilean women are eagles. Intelligent, attractive. And above all, very forward. Potota was extremely jealous! And Perón too. Both of them enjoyed home life. She cooked and did the housework; he spent his time reading documents.

Eduardo and I saw very few people in those days. Since we were newcomers, we knew almost no one at the embassy. We made friends with two married couples, the Ezcurras and the Lóizagas and, of course, with the ambassador, Federico

Quintana, whose wife, Clementina Achával, was a relative of mine. Living in the same building as the Peróns, and their kindness to us, naturally made us more and more intimate friends. We saw each other every day.

I am rereading my diary entries of those days and skipping a whole string of trivial anecdotes. To whom could they be of the least importance? I see here a note I wrote on 7 February. 'Potota has complained of often not feeling well. Female disorders. What do the doctors tell you? I ask. Bah, they never find anything wrong with me. We spoke of the Quintanas. According to Potota, they detest military attachés. She says: Every time they are about to give a party my head starts aching. From the bedrooms, on the upstairs floors of the Residence, the kids throw shoes and papers down at us. Their parents have taught them to show us how much they dislike us. I calm her down – it's nothing to get so upset about, Potota.'

Eduardo was rather surprised when Perón told him that he had received orders to stay on for two more months in Santiago. It was not at all what usually happened: an officer was ordinarily expected to hand over his post almost immediately to the officer who was taking his place. It struck us as a trivial detail. In just a few weeks Justo would be passing his office as President on to his successor, Roberto M. Ortiz. I thought the whole thing was merely a matter of protocol.

It was not. Though we didn't know it, Eduardo and I were headed for a terrible disaster.

One night we all went out dancing. It was hot. Our husbands trusted our discretion and spoke freely in our presence. Eduardo was worried about Alessandri's ideological balancing acts, for he managed to stay on the best of terms with both the conservatives and the Popular Front. Perón found these maneuvers most diverting. He drew arrows on tablecloths to show what

Alessandri's tactics and his strategy were aimed at. I don't know at what point the conversation got sidetracked.

'I've discovered something very serious,' Perón said. 'The Chilean Government is interested in provoking a border incident with Argentina. If they manage it, troops will be called up. The Parliament here has refused to grant more money for an arms purchase. But if it is confronted with the prospect of an imminent war, it will have to give in. Someone has offered to sell me all the documents for a song: the plan for the border incident, the steps for mobilization. Naturally the Argentine General Staff is well informed of all these developments. We have already begun negotiations for the arms purchase.'

He asked Eduardo what orders he had received from the Minister of War, General Basilio Pertiné.

'To collaborate with you on everything,' my husband answered.

'I'm going to put you in touch with an Argentine who's a real gaucho. His name is Guido Arzeno,' Perón said. 'We'll pull off the whole operation with him.'

We lingered on together till late that night as Perón and my husband went on talking together. I had the impression that Perón wasn't at all pleased to be relieved of his post. He had embarked on a difficult spy mission and was surely eager to see it through himself. Our arrival was a nuisance to him. Eduardo tried to persuade me differently. He told me not to be ungrateful. To remember the many favors the Peróns had done us, the friendship they had shown us. But he was suspicious of the ease with which his predecessor had come by the plans. 'Mightn't it be a trap?' he said to me. He was ill at ease because Perón had involved a civilian in a delicate matter that compromised the country's security.

On 20 February, Roberto M. Ortiz took office as President. Pertiné was replaced as Minister of War by General Carlos

Márquez. One afternoon, we went for a walk on the Plaza de Armas. We dropped by a café.

'I've been ordered to return to Buenos Aires,' Perón suddenly announced. 'We'll be leaving in the Packard on 5 or 6 March.'

'What's that? And what about that matter of the documents?' Eduardo asked worriedly.

'I've left everything all ready. The only thing you have to do is open your hands and the documents will fall into them like a peeled fig. You have the dough, and Arzeno will let you know when the time is right. What I strongly recommend is that you do not use the embassy for the operation. Use Arzeno's place.'

A man always receives warnings from his conscience: don't do this or that. Some people call them premonitions. Others, scruples. Eduardo had a heavy heart. He thoroughly disliked the prospect of being entangled in that spiderweb, but at the same time he didn't want to be taken for a coward. On top of everything else, we found out around that time that, on the pretext of keeping check on security at the embassy, Perón was going through the papers that the embassy personnel discarded in the wastebaskets.

We felt a certain relief when he left. Goodbyes were said by all with feigned cordiality, but we no longer spoke together with the same mutual trust; nothing was the same now between the Peróns and us. I felt sorry for Potota, who looked more haggard by the day. Shortly before they left, she said to me:

'I'm bleeding all the time, Mecha. And no doctor can find anything wrong with me.'

'They'll be able to cure you completely in Buenos Aires – just wait and see,' I consoled her. 'You're the way you are out of pure melancholy.'

Everybody knows what happened after that. On 2 April, at eight at night, Eduardo was arrested by Chilean intelligence officers as he was photographing the plans that a former lieutenant, named Haniez, had offered Perón. The Arzenos fell into the trap too. Our apartment was broken into. They removed from a strongbox the fifteen thousand Argentine pesos with which the job was to be paid for. The next afternoon Eduardo received a telegram from Buenos Aires. We were to return immediately. The journey was over.

A woman must seldom feel, as I did, that all her hopes have been dashed so unjustly. We had been in Chile only a little over two months. Eduardo had behaved most discreetly and most honorably. And yet now we would be forced to leave, with our heads bowed in shame.

I am not one of those women who allow themselves to be easily defeated. I resolved to meet with the Quintanas by myself and ask them for help.

'My husband has done his duty,' I told them. 'But the Chilean Government has gone too far. My apartment was broken into. It is only right that you present a diplomatic protest.'

Federico looked at me in astonishment, as though I were mad.

'Don't tell me that, Mecha. How could they have broken into your apartment? Think carefully. Might you not have dreamed it? Sometimes, in times of crisis, a person's imagination gets out of hand . . .'

I left in despair. The next morning. I found the answer in *El Mercurio*. The Chilean Foreign Ministry would not present a diplomatic protest in Buenos Aires. And Buenos Aires, for its part, would say nothing. The deal had been made at the cost of my happiness and Eduardo's.

My husband was kept under house arrest at the Savoy Hotel in Buenos Aires for two weeks. My brother Clemente was told that Eduardo would be discharged from the army. Once again, I made up my mind to act. If this whole horrible story began with Perón, it ought to end with him. God (I told myself once again) is just.

It was raining buckets. The streets of Buenos Aires were flooded. I took a taxi and went to the apartment where the Peróns were living at the time, on the Calle Arredondo near the corner of Obligado. Perón answered the door with ill-disguised surprise. I shall never forget it. He was wearing a polka-dotted dressing gown and two-toned slippers, white and brown. I broke down and contained my sobs with the greatest of difficulty.

'You are the only one who can save Eduardo,' I told him. 'Tell the truth in the General Staff. Inform them that you and my husband were obeying orders from Pertiné. That it was you who set up the operation: you spoke with Haniez, secured the money and made the contact with Arzeno. That you left Eduardo with everything all ready to go, so that the documents would fall into his hands like a peeled fig. Do you remember?'

'I've nothing to do with all that,' he answered me curtly. He was standing, and so was I, soaking wet from the rain. 'If your husband ruined everything, it's not my fault. I warned him in no uncertain terms not to photograph those documents anywhere outside the embassy.'

Such cynicism came as a surprise to me:

'Perón! How can you talk like that. I was right there when you advised Eduardo not to get the embassy mixed up in this. For the security of our country, you told him. And there was no mistaking your tone of voice: you were giving him an order.'

'Don't get things all confused, Mecha. I never said any such thing. And now, for your own good, clear out of here. Women must not meddle in affairs of state.'

'You won't do anything, then?'

'Clear out of here,' he repeated. And I, fool that I was, summoned up strength from somewhere as I left and asked him:

'How is Potota?'

That same afternoon I saw Eduardo at the Hotel Savoy. I

found him very depressed. And the steps that I had taken behind his back made him feel even worse. He gently reprimanded me. Then he tortured himself by thinking about what he would have liked to tell Perón when he made that threat: Clear out of here, for your own good. *For his own good*. My husband very seldom lost his temper. But that afternoon, his anger slowly mounted to his face. It seemed to me that his body was filling up with ashes: he was Eduardo, but all there was inside him was ashes. He scared me. He got up from his chair and looked through the window. It was raining torrents. I felt frozen to the bone. Eduardo shook his fist at the sky of Buenos Aires.

'God will make him eat his words,' he said, between clenched teeth. 'God will make him pay the price for them, one by one.'

A friend, Benjamín Rattenbach, interceded with the Minister of War on Eduardo's behalf and saved his career. With time our anger gradually subsided. In September, I learned by way of a death notice that Potota had passed away. I went in silence to her grave and took her flowers. I stayed there for a long time, praying and meditating. I left, bathed without my realizing it, in a flood of tears.

Mementos, daisy pollen, yellow clippings: the memoirs that Doña Mercedes has copied arrive at the last pages with their tongue hanging out. There are rough drafts whose lines bend like trees, with a river of words or weeping willows below.

Her back is still turned. She is sitting all hunched over so that her whole body will find refuge in the shadows, and only her hands come and go, exposed beneath the lamp, leafing through the photographs in *Horizonte*. Her body has totally dissociated itself from what her hands are touching, as though she were afraid that someone else's memories – Perón's memories – might sink their sharp barbed proboscis like a tick's into her blood.

Zamora buries the papers in the leather pockets of the folder that he has brought with him, and turns around toward the television set for the last time. What he now sees disappoints him: tiresome welcoming placards.

TO THE GREAT CREATOR OF NATIONAL REUNION/
THE STATE PETROLEUM WORKERS' UNION HAILS THE
SYMBOL OF UNITY/
THE PEOPLE'S KANGAROO COOPERATIVE JOYOUSLY GREETS
THE GENERAL OF ARGENTINE AND LATIN AMERICAN
LIBERATION/
FATHER AND MASTER OF OUR LILY-BEARING NATIVE SOIL,
MAGICAL
PATRIMONY OF THE CELESTIAL///NATIONAL///BARQUE
HOMAGE FROM ROT-AR AUTOMOTIVE CORPORATION

It is a few minutes after noon. Nothing is happening at Ezeiza.

13 *Nomad Cycles*

If the Lieutenant-Colonel draws a red line on the blackboard and orders that the reds cannot go past it, they don't get past and that's the end of it. Otherwise, what's the dais for, I ask you? For us to guard with our very blood, I say. The Lieutenant-Colonel asks us one by one for an estimate of the situation. And you, Arcángelo, how do you thee it? he lisps (I can't get used to that: the fact that he lisps). I find it easy to see, I say. I see it as absolutely under control.

He shouldn't have arrived late at the meeting, but at least he's arrived. How much too late, I don't know. The explanation of the operation has already begun, but the Lieutenant-Colonel repeats it for me because he knows I have an iron will, he has blind faith in me. I sit down in the back, next to the door. The room has immediately filled with smoke but we can't even open the windows. Top secret. There's not a single room in the international hotel that's not contaminated forever; the stink of cigarette smoke has clung to the curtains, to the rugs, to everything. How much nicotine floating around! A smoker's throat (Daniel used to say, I remember) is like a nest of cockroaches. The twelve of us who are called the Elect are all here. Lito, who has arrived after me, seats himself at the head of the table, presiding, to the left of the Lieutenant-Colonel. To his right is a nervous comrade, past her prime but full of stamina, biting her fingernails. She's the only broad Lito Coba takes his hat off to. Norma risked her neck in the resistance, he's told me more than once. She's got a pair of balls that big.

Lito is one cool cat, a real buddy; when I see him I feel . . . I don't know, something like sweat in my heart. He was sort of rough on me at first, but with the experience I have now I realize that tough initiations like that are necessary for a man; they temper a person, teach him to be more self-confident. When he came in he winked at me and handed me a little sketch showing the layout of the airport, and underneath it the words: *Athí eth Etheitha, Athiethe the itna* – 'That's Ezeiza': if you lisp, it's a palindrome. And I sit there laughing to myself, because the Lieutenant-Colonel never just says Ezeiza, period. Always the litany, That'th Etheitha. And I've just now caught on that maybe it's a secret password.

The dais is neatly drawn on the blackboard, with the exits clearly marked and the weak points where the leftists can sneak past us circled in red chalk. From the dais the entire crowd can be seen, spread out like a fan. By three p.m. there are going to be two and a half million people here, the Lieutenant-Colonel calculates. Pay the closest possible attention now, he says to us. And I copy down:

'Let uth thituate ourthelveths on the daith. To the rear of it there ith nothing: it ith a rethtricted area of a mile with three thecurity cordonth clothing it off. Impenetrable. Let uth take a clothe look at the right flank: two hundred yardth from it ith Boarding Thchool Number 1 –'

(Green circle: that stronghold is ours.)

'– that ith is now therving as a thupply thone. Mealth, firtht aid thenter, arthenal, everything ith all here. If thomeone hath the mithfortune of getting wounded, he retreath to the little thcoolhouth. Here it ith, alongthide the ethplanade –'

(More green circles and a straight line.)

'– the way ith blocked by an ambulanth. There are no doctorth inside. There are fifteen heavyweight noncomth who come burthting out at the thlightetht dithturbanth. They are what we call a dithuathive forthe. They have no weaponth. Jutht piethes of hothe filled with lead. Thee thith line I've drawn? It'th a cordon of militanth in ponchoth, wearing green badgeth. Underneath their ponchoth they're carrying a complete thet of hardware . . .'

(To the left it's the same: a wall of steel. We have an armored Dodge, a truck we can use as a movable firing platform, a guard of Falcons armed with double-barreled shotguns, and in the danger zone – the famous three hundred yards that we must guard with our lives – barriers of barbed wire and cables have already been strung up so that the mechanics' unions, the butchers' unions, and the thugs of the Metal Workers' Union can be posted there. The nerve center, as the Lieutenant-Colonel again stresses, is the dais. That's where everything will be at stake.'

'That'th Etheitha, boyth. When we thee it on the blackboard it theems to uth that we have it under control. But we don't. We're going to be confronted with a high-caliber enemy. Gobbi ith the one rethponthible for the daith. Around two o'clock, a column of thirty thouthand leftith will try to thurround the front rankth of the demonthtratorth by moving in on them from the flankth. You already know the redth' rallying cry: The Thothialitht fatherland. They will advanth from behind the daith in a pinther movement . . .'

(The Lieutenant-Colonel draws several red arrows that penetrate the green defenses.)

Someone asks: 'And how are they going to get behind the dais if things have been planned so that they can't get that far?'

'That'th Etheitha. By letting them into that area we'll avoid premature bloodthed. We'll trap them inthide our thircle. Onthe inthide, we'll know they're redth and be able to neutralithe them more eathily. We'll be uthing the thame thtrategy ath Hannibal at the battle of Cannae . . . They can mount the daith only at the prithe of death. They mutht be repelled with chainth, with hotheth, with pickactheth . . . Dithtract them by letting loothe the doveth and the balloonth. And fire on them only if nethethary. We mutht not run out of ammunition. I've now given you a more or leth complete picture. Quethtionth, anyone, doubth? . . .'

(No one speaks up.)

'. . . How about you, Gobbi?' the Lieutenant-Colonel asks.

'It's all clear to me. I can see everything quite easily,' I say.

The middle-aged woman gets to her feet. 'Let's set to work, then. Giving our life for Perón!'

That's right. Our life for Perón. There is no other. I wonder what the leftists are after. For me the thing is to go back to 1955, period. The Peronist fatherland. One people, one leader. With the General in command, in less than a year Argentina will again be a great power. That's why the leftists really bug me. What's the point of trying to cozy up to Fidel Castro and Salvador Allende? This whole business of Socialism may sit right with underdeveloped peoples who are starving to death, but not with us Argentines who eat meat every day. I'd give them something besides doves and balloons. Some lead. Clip their wings. This country can be set to rights only with an iron hand. Gallows. A stake in the middle and every last leftist burnt at it, going up in smoke. Cleansing. Purification. How did the General put it? The day the people start hanging, I'll be on the side of the ones doing the hanging. That's right. For friends, everything. For enemies, not even justice. Lito has told me: You're being asked to be merciless, Arcángelo. When the time comes to beat our enemies to a pulp, show no pity for a single one of them. If need be, not even for me. Not even for you, Lito? How can you talk like that?

And my heart started sweating again.

Tonight, no matter what happens, Evita's body will remain empty for all eternity. When the hour of Universal Resurrection comes, she'll be different, the Lord will call her by another name, the musical notes of her astrological sign will have changed. Her body will still be empty, but its appearance will not have changed. The same river of formaldehyde and nitrate of potassium that keeps her uncorrupted will repose in her veins, her heart will awaken at the same place in her body each morning of history, nothing will sully the beatitude of her face. But tonight, without fail, her soul must enter Isabel's.

Everything is now ready in the sanctuary. Before dawn breaks, Taurus will find repose in the house of Aquarius. The Moon is propitious. Uranus and Mercury, the ruling planets, will be in perfect conjunction. The bodies must remain oriented north-northeast. The hour of transit, the astrolabes say, will occur at the midpoint between sunset and sunrise: eleven minutes before one a.m., 19 June 1973. Of the seven words that must be uttered, López knows four; one in Bengali, one in Persian, one in Egyptian and one in Aramaic. He still does not know the Chinese and the Sumerian ones. The seventh – he knows – is formed by combining *ad infinitum* the sounds of Eva: Vea, Vaé, Ave; he need determine only the order in which he will substitute one letter for another.

It is necessary, therefore, to change the General's plans: make him skip his afternoon nap, cause him to absorb himself in the Memoirs until nightfall, and then distract him with visitors he can't get out of receiving. At eleven, after the news broadcast, López will give him a cup of tea and put him to bed. He will need a blind and deaf accomplice – someone who will suspect nothing and won't ask any questions. He has already found him: nobody fits the bill better than Cámpora.

The secretary goes down the stairs from the cloister with the agility of a bear, practically hanging suspended from the hand railing, descending more swiftly than the painful calluses on the soles of his feet. As he goes past the kitchen, he orders lunch not to be served immediately. (I'll snap my fingers when we're ready.) And now, in the study, he comes upon Cámpora: standing up, his hair slicked down with pomade. Effusively, López takes him by the arm.

How are we going to allow the General to leave without a little meeting alone with his closest friends? He's been hoping for one for days and doesn't dare to ask for it. Surprise him, Mr President . . .)

(Mr President? Cámpora raises his eyebrows. López, who has entered the Cabinet as Minister of Social Welfare, has never before deigned to address him in that way.) I'll make the complicated domestic arrangements. Don't worry on that score. Phone Doña Pilar Franco. Inform Ambassador Campano . . .

(Cámpora clenches his fists, on his guard. He has a feeling nothing good will come of this. Why all this courtesy from the secretary after a week of icy relations and rude disregard of his authority as head of state? He had best keep his distance. He has an ironclad excuse.)

Not today, Lopecito. Let's have it tomorrow, the night before the flight. Or have you forgotten that the General and I have accepted Franco's invitation to a farewell dinner at Moncloa at nine-thirty p.m. tonight? We can't fail to show up. It would be a terrible slight.

Mr President, we've already called the Pardo to present our apologies for not coming. They understood. The Spanish chief of protocol spoke with me and said, it seems to us entirely reasonable that General Perón prefers not to go out. A sick leader is a sick state. May Our Lord God grant him a rapid recovery. Imagine, Cámpora. The truth is that the General woke up again today with a fever of over 101. He's nearly eighty years old. We forget that. Go to the celebration for him at Moncloa; it's the only thing you can do. But send Doña Pilar, Don Licio Gelli, Valori and his mama here to me . . . And tell your sons to come, Cámpora. They haven't yet paid their respects to the General.

The President is disarmed. Both my sons?

Certainly. They're reliable. Give them instructions to take the guests somewhere else around ten o'clock. We'd best put the General to bed early tonight. I'll hide the orchestra. If Doña Pilarica hears flamenco music there's no stopping her. That woman is dynamite. Tomorrow, when I have more time, I'll attend a couple of ceremonies with you. As a minister it's the proper thing for me to do, right? Just last night the General said to me: López, why have you left Cámpora on his own so often? Seeing that I'm ill, you go with him. What a time you've chosen to come give me orders: when there's only one day left before we leave!

Deeply touched, the President is no longer hesitant. Something has happened. The mood of the house, so unfriendly up until yesterday, has suddenly shifted in his favor. His eyes grow damp and he squeezes one of the secretary's shoulders. I know that you have done a great deal. I thank you from the bottom of my heart!

Once again, everything happens at once, as in a stage play. The secretary snaps his fingers. Isabelita pounds on the dining-room door and calls out: Lunch! It's time for lunch. You'll stay, won't you, Cámpora? And the General's voice comes drifting down from the bedrooms, addressing him: What's become of you, man? We've lost sight of you for almost a day. We missed you . . . Have another place set at the table, Chabela.

Ah, no, sir. I can't possibly stay. (The President's chin is trembling.) If it were up to me, I'd rather be here than anywhere else. You know that. But they keep me running all over, affixing my signature to cancellations of treaties and letters of collaboration that the military regime signed before our victory. I merely came by for a little emergency consultation. How is protocol going to deal with our departure from Barajas? You hold power, General, but you have no official rank or title. How should General Franco address you? I've sent a confidential note asking that you be accorded the precedence given a head of state. And where I'm concerned, they can do as they please. As everyone knows, I am a servant. But they're very punctilious here. All the consultations have made me dizzy, and once again I've been obliged to have recourse to your serenity, sir. What path am I to follow?

At three in the afternoon, seated among the snouts of his Memoirs and his other huge tomes, alone in the cloister, with the lap robe rucked around his legs to keep them warm (a few varicose veins in them have suddenly turned blue, as if unexpectedly affected by early cold weather in Buenos Aires), the General sympathizes with his poor deputy who is now exposed to the worst of the storm. You decide, Cámpora. Pretend to observe whatever protocol you please. What do I have to do with these infections of power? My mind is elsewhere. Age is paying off my debt. I've even retired from exile. Wrestle with the Caudillo's incense-bearers yourself. And leave me out of it. It's enough that they're taking me to the place. It's more than enough. I don't expect anything from Buenos Aires except work and suffering.

He opens one of the folders of Memoirs at random and the shock of war appears before his eyes. He reads:

When I returned from Chile there was tension in the air everywhere. It was evident that the planet was about to explode at any moment . . .

My destiny adamantly observed nomad cycles. I emigrated, history retreated. I was becoming accustomed to this. If I went to bed a river, I prepared myself to wake up a lake next morning. Am I talking nonsense? Let's see what the page just before says.

... and in the last letters I sent to Lieutenant-Colonel Enrique I. Rottjer I informed him of my eagerness to circle the country on foot, to reconnoiter the desert from Lake Vilama to the salt flats of Arizaro, then follow the crest line of the high mountain range through the lake district, and on reaching Cabo Vírgenes, to cross the Strait of Magellan on one of our navy transports. Then widowhood struck me. The project was postponed.

I'm becoming confused. What was after that, what before? Now that I think of the many times I went into the cemeteries in Milan when Eva hadn't yet been buried there, time reels within me. Why doesn't all of eternity happen in an instant? Why is what is to happen tomorrow not already something over and done with? Or is that how things happen, in bursts: is everything already past without our being aware of it?

I had been a widower for a month. It was October 1938. The Minister of War ordered me to go on a reconnaissance mission through southern Patagonia. Colonel Juan Sanguinetti, who had just completed a three-year tour of duty at the embassy in Berlin, was in charge of the expedition. We disembarked in Comodoro Rivadavia and proceeded overland to Lake Argentino, in dilapidated automobiles. Hitler had deeply impressed Sanguinetti: he's a volcano, he said. He'll lay everything to waste. Hannibal? Napoleon? They're mere apprentices compared to him. He hasn't studied strategy: he was born knowing it. He's the Pentecost of politics: he doesn't know any other language besides German, and yet a Japanese can understand him. We talked and talked as we made our way through narrow passes and across glaciers. I imagined that Hitler was a hero six and a half feet tall: a colossus of Thebes. His physical appearance is unfortunate, Sanguinetti told me. He's a short little fellow. But the minute he opens his mouth he grows in stature.

Why can López Rega have suppressed the sinister fermentations of that time? Let's see, let's see. Where can they have they gone?

The Minister of War, General Carlos Márquez, one of the best military officers that I have ever known, called me into his office at the beginning of 1938. We were fairly close friends. In my days as a cadet, he had been an instructor at the Military Academy, and later on he was my professor at the War College.

'Look, Perón,' he said to me. 'A world war is about to overtake us. There is no human power that can stop it. We have made all our calculations, but the intelligence we have at our disposal is quite inadequate. The military attachés keep us more or less informed of what is happening in their sphere, but when hostilities break out, ninety-nine per cent of what happens will be a political phenomenon: a matter of peoples rather than of armies. You are a professor of Strategy, Total War and Military History. There is no one more qualified to send me the intelligence I need. Choose a place to go to.'

Germany or Italy: there were no other options. I asked for twenty-four hours to think it over. Let's see, I said to myself. Hitler had turned the Reich into a perfect piece of clockwork. In less than five years, public works and the war industry had been enough to wipe out unemployment, to increase the country's reserves of foreign currency and to get heavy industry under way again. I had read *Mein Kampf* at least twice and was acquainted with other good books on Hitler and his doctrine. In Italy, after the occupation of Abyssinia, the Duce was preparing to invade Albania. His popularity and his charisma kindled the imagination of all of Europe. Hitler himself admitted that Mussolini was his teacher.

But what made me opt for Italy was the fact that I spoke the language fluently. Since my duties would involve making contact with the people, I would not be of much use in Germany. I speak Italian as well as I do Spanish, and if I'm hard pressed, even better.

My first assignment landed me in Merano, where in a few months I learned the secrets of Alpine combat. After that I took several courses in pure sciences in Turin and applied sciences in Milan. Many concepts became clear to me and many of my prejudices, especially with regard to political economy, faded away.

It was all intensely exciting to me. My every impression was dazzling. I felt I was living at the heart of a historic experience as important as the fall of the Bastille. Perhaps even more so. The model of society that was taking shape in Italy was completely new: a national Socialism. Let us see how this came about.

The Soviet revolution had had a profound influence in Europe. Lenin and Trotsky, its agents, would have liked the fuse that had been lighted in Moscow to set off immediate explosions in Berlin and Madrid. But it did not. Bolshevik ideas were faced with an insurmountable wall on the borders of Western Europe. What happened on the other side of it, however, was the Socialism of Lasalle and Marx, though with features characteristic of Italy, France and Germany. It is precisely there that the true cause of the Second World War is to be found: in the accelerated pace of events provoked by the ideological movements of the West. I could already see the storm clouds gathering as the Munich Pact was signed. This is just a parenthesis, I told myself. The marathon runners have halted to catch their breath. There is worse to come, and in the near future. And that is exactly what happened.

A few months after my arrival, the Duce invaded Albania and

the Germans signed a non-aggression pact with the Soviets. War broke out almost immediately. I took advantage of this opportunity to study the Eastern front. I traveled to Berlin by train. The German people were working together and Hitler's enemies, who later on were so numerous, were nowhere to be seen. The officers of the Wehrmacht were very kind to me. I conversed with them a little in French, and a bit in Italian as well. Now and again I grunted something in broken German, but only Germans and the devil can speak that language.

They took me to the Loebtzen line, in east Prussia. At the front, the Russians were holding the Kovno-Grodno line. The commanding officers of the two forces were friends with each other and I went from one side to the other with the greatest of ease. I went quite far inside the Soviet Union in military vehicles.

On my return to Berlin, I read a number of hostile commentaries published in the United States by American correspondents. They described Fascism and National Socialism as tyrannical systems – which may have been true, but they did not take the time to notice the magnitude of the social change that these systems were producing.

In Italy I made it my task to take the process apart and see how the pieces were being fitted together. I discovered a very interesting phenomenon. Until Mussolini's rise to power, the Italian nation was going one way and the worker another. They had nothing to do with each other. The Duce gathered all the scattered forces together and got them to moving in the same direction. Medieval corporations reappeared, but as authentic motive forces of the community this time. The sacrifices of the people were not in vain: they worked in an orderly way, at the service of a perfectly organized state. And I thought to myself: this is what Marx and Engels were searching for, but they chose the wrong paths. Here, in a more realistic and thorough way, the utopias of Owen and Fourier are coming into being. This is true popular democracy: the liberty, equality, and fraternity of the nineteenth century.

At that time I did not know about the concentration camps in which Hitler tamed, with a certain cruelty, the rebellious minorities of the East. But in Italy, where everybody is like we are – sentimental and always in a dither – these Teutonic rigors were not necessary.

I lived that golden experience for almost two years. I saw Spain devastated by the famines of civil war. And I stayed for some time in Portugal, which at that time was a focal point of espionage. But I couldn't leave Europe without having a talk with Mussolini.

On 10 June 1940, Italy formally entered the war. Several battalions of *bersaglieri* marched into France. The Duce spoke from a balcony of the Palazzo Venezia to announce the news. I listened to him, just one of thousands in the huge crowd. I saw Calabrian peasants with their eyes riveted on that great man, as though he were a passing comet. I saw women of the people embracing and weeping with enthusiasm, all at the same time. I heard the crowd sing 'Giovinezza', roar out cheers for the fatherland, the Empire and the Duce. Carried away by those feverish outbursts of joy, I too sang a few verses: 'eia, eia, alalà'.

The following day, through the Argentine embassy, I asked for an audience. They could not arrange one for me before 3 July, when the Duce came back from a tour of inspection on the Western front. I went directly into his office. The room was almost dark. A lamp shone straight down on his imposing shaved head. He was writing. For a moment he did not raise his eyes. Then he saw me and came to meet me with his hand outstretched. He asked me about the morale of the Alpine troops. I told him the truth: there there was no army better prepared to fight in the mountains. 'E vero, è vero,' he smiled.

'Sono bravissimi i miei Alpini.' I felt like embracing him, but the solemnity of the place held me back. I clicked my heels, and for the only time in my life, instead of saluting him, I bade him goodbye with my right arm upraised, in the Fascist manner. Today this gesture would be misinterpreted. I did not make it with any political intent in mind, and I could leave it out of this account if I wished, for there were no witnesses. But it is important to me to acknowledge it as a mark of respect from a military officer to a militant, from a novice to a master.

I expended a great deal of saliva explaining, when I returned to Buenos Aires, the complex system that ruled all those hurricanes. In a lecture I gave on Christmas Eve, 1940, I resorted to the metaphor of water. Peoples – I said – advance like water: using the same tactic. Once water finds the line with the greatest downward angle, it flows. If a dike is built, it tries to seep through it. If the base of the dike keeps it from advancing, the water then rises and overflows its walls. If it can do nothing else, it pounds. It bores holes and pounds, until one day it destroys the whole thing. When Germany lost the war, it was as though the dike had burst. The water poured out all over Europe. And now the tide is bringing it our way. This is the era that it is our lot to live in.

What's making you so restless, López? Why all that hustle and bustle in the sanctuary? I was hoping to be alone. What is it you're doing now, squatting on your heels all by yourself up there?

Nothing, General. I'm just putting everything in order before we leave. I'm dusting, checking the fuses, inspecting the roof for leaks. Excuse me if I'm making noise. However lightly a person steps, the spiral staircase persists in creaking. And these flat feet of mine are a constant nuisance.

You smell of maté, López. Of cinnamon. And what are those streamers you're carrying? Let me see: the other one, the purple one. What's this written on the edge, in such tiny letters. It sounds like a Brazilian jungle chant: 'Saravá Oxalá/Saravá Oxum Maré/ Que assim seja!' Moroccan, is it? Galician?

I don't know, General. They're ribbons that the maids keep leaving around when they clean up. They strew them all over the house. How's your reading going? It's past three already.

Something is missing in these Memoirs, López. I don't know what it can be. The recollections dating back to the Second War aren't mine. I read them and it seems to me that they're going on living on their own. Look at this, for example: who am I here, saying this?

In 1941 I had several secret meetings to inform the higher-ranking officers of the changes that were in the offing. The new Minister of War, Juan Tonazzi, understood me immediately, but the Neanderthal generals who supported him accused me of being a Communist.

They tried to take me out of circulation. Without realizing it, they did me a favor. I ended up at the Montaña Training Center, in Mendoza. The country was rotting to pieces, but I, meanwhile, by remaining on the sidelines, kept my prestige intact.

Corruption was tearing the army apart. One faction of nationalist officers wanted to start an uprising, but the conspiracy collapsed all by itself, a victim of its lethargy. The entire country seemed to be asleep, snoring like lazy provincial Catamarcans. It woke up only to engage in immoral acts and fraud. Our sacred uniform had fallen so low that several cadets at the Military Academy were caught in a dragnet set up to haul in homosexuals. It was a very serious scandal. The Academy covered it up as best it could, but the institution came out of the affair with one wing damaged.

My preaching began to bear fruit in the summer of '41. Ten or twelve young colonels who had heard my most recent secret lecture presented themselves to me in Mendoza and offered me their support.

'We haven't wasted any time,' they told me. 'We have already organized a power bloc within the army. If you like, we can take the country over in twenty-four hours.' It was the initial nucleus of the GOU, the Group of Officers for Unity or the Group for Organizing Unification, as it also called itself. Because of its idealism, its purity, its altruistic views, that group of men working together could found an indestructible, rigorously just Argentina, able to suffice unto itself for a thousand years. We were counting on an advantage that would not present itself again: there were neither civilian mentors nor civilian allies among our number. And therefore, we enjoyed order, discretion, and a strict chain of command. It was the cornerstone of military power in the soundest sense of those latter two words: power is that which sets something in motion; the word 'military' comes from 'militaris': that which pertains to war. That was the goal we sought: reviving the idea of the Nation under Arms.

López? Enough of that, man. Come down from the sanctuary. What's all that commotion I hear? What's that music? Don't calm me down with gargles at this hour, you're keeping me from concentrating on my reading. Don't you see? You've even made me lose track of what I was saying. The señora is in peace. Let her rest. She's already been made to endure countless comings and goings in her short eternity. Eva, poor little thing. What is she telling you? What is she saying? I'm coming, General. I'm finishing up now and I'll be right down.

> OGUN CHEQUELA UNDE
> CHEQUELE
> CHEQUELE UNDE
> OGUM BRAGADA E A

Let's see your hand, López. You've hurt yourself. Look at all the blood.

The people imagined her as being blonde and blue-eyed but Evita Duarte was not like the woman who ran the grocery store in Santa Lucía when she arrived in Buenos Aires in 1935: she didn't sing like a nightingale, she didn't reflect the glory of the day. She was nothing (they say), or less than nothing: a sparrow, at an outdoor laundry sink, a caramel bitten into, so skinny it was pitiful. She began to make herself pretty with passion, memory and death. She wove herself a chrysalis of beauty, little by little hatching a queen – who would ever have believed it?

Such a thought never went through my head, even though I was on such close terms with her, said the actress Pierina Dealessi, who took her into her theatrical company, taught her how to walk, polished her diction. When I met her she had black hair, pearly skin and eyes that were so lively and so filled with astonishment that that is why people don't remember what they looked like – their gaze was so intense, so profound that you couldn't see their color. But Evita's other facial features weren't at all attractive: her nose was coarse, a bit on the heavy side, and her teeth stuck out a ways. Though she was flat-chested, she had quite a good figure. But she had thick ankles about which she had a complex. A pretty girl, but nothing out of this world. Today, when I realize how high she flew, I say to myself: where did that frail little thing learn to handle power, how did she manage to come by such self-assurance and such a way with words, where did she get the force to touch people's hearts where it hurt? What dream can have fallen inside her dreams, what lamb's bleating can have so stirred her blood as to turn her overnight into what she was: a queen?

That is the woman that López Rega wants to place inside Isabel's body now, 19 July, at eleven minutes to one. He wants one soul to occupy the other. But it isn't all that simple. They are unequal souls: how can the ocean be made to fit inside a river? And then too, not all of Evita's turbulences ought to pass over into Isabel. If they did, López wouldn't be able to handle her. The gift for languages, the mighty outpouring of love of the dead woman would be of no use to him. He would be putting a hurricane in motion, but one that would not obey his will.

López has been preparing himself all his life for this supreme challenge to the laws of providence. Again and again he has repeated to himself that, despite more than a sufficient store of knowledge, he has lacked the opportunity. Evita is now lying defenseless, in an oak coffin, in the light of six red lamps shaped like torches. In the attic that serves her as a tomb, to which Isabel has given the name sanctuary, no sounds enter, nor are there changes of temperature, or incursions of the darkness of night. The light is always uniform, the seasons do not come or go: the air that the purifiers deposit there knows that it is doomed to be air from nowhere. At the head of the coffin of the deceased, López has ordered that a wooden crucifix with metal rays be set up, identical to the one that was in the funeral chapel of the Ministry of Labor twenty years before. On the outside the imitation is admirable: inside it is plastic.

Now, when the moment for making the leap and savoring his triumph has almost come, López hesitates. Couldn't the celestial powers have deceived me and I am where I am not? Isn't it possible that only my desires come upstairs to the sanctuary? And even if this fake alchemy of souls were real, what will happen to me if Evita's spirit refuses to be transplanted? There are so many inharmonious substances in nature: olives and cucumbers, mangoes and rice, oil and water! The same thing might very well happen with these two creatures who are so unlike: the one who arose out of nothing and ended up being everything, the other who might have been everything yet is ending up as nothing. López pinches himself. I am here. Here. It doesn't hurt anywhere. So then, am I dreaming?

He has shared the secret of his excitement with the thugs who guard him. I'm going to have my golem, boys. Everything that Isabel says from now on will come out of my head. When you hear her talk, watch how my lips are moving. I am going to be her ventriloquist. The thugs nod. With great difficulty they have finally got it into their heads that the master, already powerful, will now become invulnerable.

At the foot of the coffin, in a basin, lies the decapitated hummingbird that López has sacrificed that afternoon, as the General was reading his Memoirs. He has already checked and seen that when a pin is driven into the crop of these tiny birds, blood comes pouring out as swiftly as a match flames when struck. He must be very careful, because only a half a thimbleful can be caught. Another hummingbird, a live one, is awaiting its turn in a cage, its legs trussed. At midnight, López summoned Isabel to the sanctuary. Have a cup of tea, señora, and dispel your fear with a few hypnosis drops. Put on a silk dressing gown, make your thoughts descend to your profound self, sit erect and pray. You are well aware that we will suffer the most terrible setbacks in Buenos Aires, that Perón will die there and when we are his widow and widower the vultures will fall upon us. Let us prepare ourselves. We need the help of a sacrosanct soul to escape from danger unharmed. Lie down on the couch, señora, alongside the coffin of the deceased, and try to sleep. Be careful as you take your rest. Dreams here are very fragile and a false step can shatter them.

When he feels that Isabel is relaxed, he pierces the throat of the other hummingbird and daubs the fresh blood on the eyelids of the sleeping woman. He wets Evita's lips with a trace of blood. And he sits down to await the hour. He has left his own body in several places at once. Through the window of the señora's bedroom he deciphers the signs in the heavens, he hears the heart of Sirius beating, Mars yawning and stretching, senses the colossal death throes of Betelgeuse: everything presages death and return, ark and ascent, deluge and life. Standing next to the General's bed, he keeps watch over him as he sleeps. Fortunately, the visitors have left early. And here, in the sanctuary, you smell the odors of your anxiety, López Rega, you wipe away your terrible fear of failure. If you are simply dreaming, if you are merely clothing fathomless forms in a beautiful outer garment, your performance will soon come to a disastrous end, López; people will chase you offstage with jeers and catcalls on every hand.

I have no time left. I concentrate now. In what order will I make Evita's moira flow into the other body, how to pass on to the ignorant Isabel the trees of soma, the joys of Kinvat? Sink deeper, dream on, sink deeper: learn to be, like the dead woman, a bridge between the General and the descamisados, the standard bearer of hierarchical order.

At five minutes to one López chants the first invocation: 'BA', in ancient Egyptian, the long vowel, the consonant with a breath, in the middle so as not to break off, BA, that is to say the sixth order of angelic power of a soul that is returning to empty itself inside a new appearance, BA, I am your body, Isabel, I fill you. The disciple frowns in her sleep, breathes out a yellow breath: it is the pain of the needles that are sewing up her soul.

López continues: his left palm on Eva's forehead, his right on Isabel's heart, the medium, the copper cord, López the cord of water proceeds to recite in Sumerian An – An, in Aramaic bájar, in Bengali samsara, in Chinese dóongo, in Persian Fravasi, angels of heaven and earth, sacred phalluses of the universe, watch this elect meet the end of her successive existences, hear her, impregnate yourselves with her music of a muse, tomorrow the masses will sing: *Isabel Evita the fatherland is Peronist/Evita Isabel Perón/one heart and one alone.*

At exactly one a.m., the blood of the hummingbird has dried. López inhales the breath of the dead woman and exhales it onto the lips of the live one. Evita's expression has never been more diaphanous. Isabel's face, however, is now full of scratches and red spots that twitch. The tension of her dreams is apparent. She is like a guitar.

Suddenly López writhes and draws his head down inside his trunk. Only the malevolent green of his little eyes, like a lizard's, is visible. He lifts his neck up again. And draws it down again. He is silent for a moment. He stands up. He stretches his arms out and slowly envelops the two women in Umbanda ritual prayers, shrouds them in the hynotized butterflies of a Candomblé litany, *salve Shangó, salve Oshalá*, the daub of blood on Isabel's eyelids is evaporating, *salve a lei de quimbanda, salve os caboclos de maiorá, ogum maré ogum*, the trace of blood suddenly disappears from Evita's lips. *Que assim seja!*

At noon the following day, López slowly approaches Isabel in the bedroom on the first floor. Outside the dogs are barking. The sun is rushing into the windows. Off by himself somewhere in the house in a world beyond, the General is still reading the Memoirs. Isabel is busily rummaging about in some drawers. Everything is in a mess. Strips of tissue paper, creeping vines of clothing, bowls of cosmetics hang from everywhere.

In that sleepy commotion, López utters the final invocation still lodged in his throat, the definitive one, the one that will prove for all eternity how much of Evita's immortal soul is now implanted in Isabel. She will need only to answer *Que assim seja!*, and then there will at last be no question as to whether the two spirits are one.

'Eva?' López calls to her. 'Ave, vaé a e, aev a, la morte è vita, Evita. Ah?'

Isabel turns to him.

'What's that you say, Daniel? Come here just a second, man. Help me. I can't find my pink slippers anywhere.'

14 *First Person*

I have told this story many times, Zamora, but never in the first person. I don't know what obscure defensive instinct has caused me to take my distance from myself, to speak of myself as though I were another. The time has now come to show myself as I am, to expose my weaknesses to the elements. Look at these photographs. Here are Perón and I, on a spring day in Madrid, talking together. Read these manuscripts corrected by the General's own hand. Take a look at this unctuous correspondence with Trujillo, Pérez Jiménez and Somoza which happened to come into my hands. Note the vocatives that Perón uses to address this most holy trinity of heads of state: Illustrious Son of America, Bolivarian Hero, Honored Benefactor. Listen to him speak out in one passage against the conspiracies of international Communism, and in another fawn upon Castro and Che Guevara. The General is an endless contradiction of nature, the body of a bear with the face of an owl, a harvest of wheat in mid-ocean. There is no definite pattern to him. He's a man made of mercury. I think I know him well and yet after more than ten years I have no idea who he is.

(Zamora listens. It is shortly after one o'clock in the afternoon. On the top floor of the daily, *La Opinión*, it is as quiet as a tomb. Claps of thunder are heard. Tomás Eloy Martínez stops talking. Is it going to rain? He remembers that outside there is not a cloud in the sky, the air is crystal-clear, winter is gently approaching. Perhaps it's the sound of drums. Any noise, these days, is an omen. And even more so today, 20 June 1973; if sounds are coming out of their caves, it's because they're hinting at something. Martínez feels exposed. I wish – he says – that my friends were a little closer. And my children. They live a long way from here. I'd like it so much today if I knew that they were waiting in the next room for me to get up and come kiss them. None of them is here. I miss them.)

I'm going to go on telling you everything in the first person because it's time for the masqueraders to lower their guard, Zamora. Journalism is an accursed profession. One lives through, feels with, writes for, others. Like actors: playing the part of a Gay Nineties dandy yesterday and Perón the day before yesterday. Period; new paragraph. For once I'm going to be the main character in my life. I don't know how. I want to recount what hasn't been written, cleanse myself of what hasn't been told, disarm myself of history so as to be able at last to arm myself with the truth. And as I can already see, Zamora, I don't even know where to begin.

In June of 1966 a magazine that no longer exists sent me to Spain to describe how that country was faring thirty years after the Civil War. I wandered through the dead towns of Andalusia, I went to a bullfight in Toledo, I spent my nights drinking bottle after bottle of dry sherry with a poet from Extremadura who had lost an arm in the battle of Guadalajara. On 28 June I arrived in

Madrid. Late that night, I was sent the news from Buenos Aires that Arturo Illia, the constitutional President, had been overthrown by the military. My magazine wanted me to interview Perón.

I met with him the following day. He received me in the offices of his friend Jorge Antonio, near the Plaza de Castelar. On the desk was a memento, a large portrait photo of Che Guevara.

Did Perón say anything about Che? Zamora wanted to know.

Very little, and as far as I know, nothing that was true. Che, he said, was a lawbreaker who had failed to register as a draftee, a deserter. If he fell into the hands of the police, he was going to be made to serve four years in the navy or two in the army. As they were about to nab him, the boys in the Peronist resistance passed the word on to him. He immediately bought a motorcycle and took off to Chile. How odd, General, I said to him. That version doesn't accord with history at all. With what history? he broke in. The one that Che recounts. What do you mean it doesn't accord with it? he said. It has to.

We were alone together for a little over two hours. In the beginning, I felt intimidated. I suppose my hands were trembling. It was like stepping into a photograph outside of time. Everything surprised me: his trousers pulled up high, hiding his pot belly, his two-tone brown and white shoes, the Saratogas he lighted with wax Ranchera matches. It suddenly seemed to me that I was seeing him on a movie screen, speaking in the voice of Pedro López Lagar and Arturo de Córdova. I heard inside myself a tango by María Elena Walsh:

> Do you remember, brother
> The year 1945
> When the man I told you about
> Came out on the balcony?

These details may seem trivial to you, Zamora. They weren't for me. I was smoking a Saratoga with The Man I Told You About. For the first time in my life I could shake hands with a drawing by Levene or Grosso, sense that a historical figure was something more than a text. Don't get the idea that I was all that naive. Before that I had met Martin Buber, Fellini, Gagarin. But what was coexisting with me inside a room in Madrid, all by ourselves, went by the name of Perón. It wasn't just a man. It was twenty years of Argentina, for or against. I saw the liver spots on his face, the cunning in his little eyes; I heard his cracked voice. My entire country passed by way of his body: Borges's hatred, the executions by firing squad of the ringleaders of the Liberation Revolution, the leftist unions, the trade union bureaucracy, and even though I didn't know it then, the dead of Trelew also passed that way. I thought: Here is the man to whom millions of Argentines offered their lives in the rituals of the Plaza de Mayo, remember? Perón or death; the colonel with whom Evita fell so madly in love that she called him 'my sun, my heaven, my mission in life'. How is it possible to bear as heavy a weight as that? I asked myself.

Then I moved closer to him. I heard him say exactly what I expected him to say. I sensed that he always intuited how the other person saw him; that he hastened to incarnate that image. He had already been the leader, the General, the Old Man, the deposed dictator, the macho, the man I told you about, the tyrant on the run, the ringleader of the GOU, the First Worker, Eva Perón's widower, the exile, the man who had a piano in Caracas. Who could say what other things he might be tomorrow. I saw so many faces of his that I felt let down. All of a sudden, he ceased to be a myth. I finally told myself: he's nobody. He's just Perón.

We drank tea and orange juice. He asked me to be discreet about any statements he made. He was living in Madrid as a political refugee, subject to very strict rules. He was not allowed to speak publicly about politics. I turned on the tape recorder.

What I sent to Buenos Aires that night wasn't an article; it was a scrupulously exact repetition of what he had said. You can imagine how upset I was when a French reporter phoned me at my hotel at two in the morning to tell me that Perón had denied that the interview had taken place. What would you have done, Zamora? Produced the tapes, right? Belied his lie. As a matter of fact, I had no other recourse. A couple of hours later the news agencies listened to my tapes and in office number 20 reconstructed the facts that they had revealed in office number 5 and then denied in number 10. The feeling of historical reason stuck in my throat. My notions concerning the truth turned into a lump. I caught my breath again at Atocha station, as I boarded a train that was going somewhere or other.

With time, I gradually tied the loose ends together, Zamora. On the day of the military coup against Illia, the General needed to make a show of force in the Buenos Aires press. He was confident that the insurgents would call for immediate elections and hand over the reins of government to the lawful winner. I was on hand and he used me as his mouthpiece. But he couldn't violate the Spanish laws governing asylum. So he lied in his teeth about the interview with me. He knew that out of professional arrogance I would make the tapes public. That his statements would end up being read in Argentina the way he wanted them to be. Political morality is always the polar opposite of poetic morality. It is in that abyss that men badly misunderstand each other: it is there that Stalin the politician cannot understand the poet Trotsky, or Fidel Castro Che, or the Fascist Uriburu the Fascist Lugones. If Eva hadn't died when she did, she too would have violently disagreed with Perón. They were birds of a different feather.

Let me get back to the story. Little by little I discovered that on that night in June, seven years ago, I had been a minor piece in a major power play. That as the General spoke precisely the words that the others had been hoping to hear from him, he for his part was making the others act exactly as he wanted them to.

It was not a hidden strategy. Perón himself frankly informed me of it, once when we were speaking of Evita: 'I used her, of course, as I do everyone who can be used and is valuable.' To him, a leader was the ultimate incarnation of Providence. Are you laughing, Zamora? I laughed too when I heard him say that he manipulated Providence. I thought it was a joke. But very odd things began happening to me, and I laughed no more.

In March 1970, I phoned the General from Paris and asked him for an interview. I was surprised when he agreed. I was mistrustful. I asked him if I could bring a friend along. He said yes.

The night before leaving I wandered aimlessly through the labyrinths of the Latin Quarter. When I went past the cathedral of Notre-Dame I heard shouts, saw terrified nuns running, came upon a cordon of frantic police officers. An old man had just committed suicide by throwing himself from the top of the towers. When he hit the ground, he had crushed to death a couple on their honeymoon. The bad omen haunted my dreams. I had nightmares. Red spots broke out on my back, as on Perón's.

I made the trip to Madrid by car with a wonderful friend who has the gift of turning everything he touches into poems. Finding a haystack in a needle is not something that surprises him. It fills him with joy. We crossed the frozen peaks of the Pyrenees without incident. But then at a certain moment the wind blew into the car and began to buzz. It's not the wind, it's flies, my friend said. The buzz became insistent. We opened the windows. It was worse. We felt piercing little stabs in the neck. We had to stop to wipe away the blood. My friend had had enough, so he recited a magic formula to ward off the evil eye. At that very instant the wind went away. As we took to the road again, both our shirts tore down the front. My friend said: It's Perón.

We reached the Villa 17 de Octubre one Friday afternoon

around three. The General was in the garden, sprinkling powdered ant poison on the rose bushes. He went off to wash his hands and embraced us. As he was helping my friend out of his overcoat, he told him that a man and his overcoat fight an eternal battle with each other, and that if no one comes to the man's aid, he is doomed to defeat. We laughed. My friend remarked to him: That could be a poem, a haiku. Did you think of it just now, General? Yes, Perón replied. Parables and allegories come pouring out of me like that all the time. But later on we read the same phrase in an interview dating from the year before, and one from seven years before.

We sat down. I unthinkingly happened to mention Vandor, the leader of the Metal Workers' Union, who was Perón's enemy. Months before, Vandor had been mowed down in the lair of his own union: two shots in his chest, and three in his lower back as he was falling.

There you have food for thought, he said to us. The poor man had to come to a bad end. He was an intelligent, clever sort, but he flew very close to the ground. When he tried to fly really high, he got smashed to smithereens, like Simon the Magician.

Another parable, my friend commented. Simon Magus – the one who thought he was God. He appears in the Acts of the Apostles and in Gnostic writings of the third century.

That is where my simile came from: it goes back to the Gnostics, the General said. But to go on. In 1968, Vandor wanted to see me. I agreed to meet him in Irún, in the north, near France. He confessed his errors to me. He had sold out to the Argentine military government and the US embassy. Be careful, Vandor, I advised him. Stick to the rules. I forgive everybody. But you've gotten yourself in bad trouble. They're going to kill you. You're between the devil and the deep blue sea. Whatever you do, they're going to kill you. If you keep up your contacts with the US embassy, the Peronist movement will settle accounts with you. If, on the other hand, you repent and try to back out, the CIA will do the job of wiping you out. Vandor looked me in the eye and burst into tears. What shall I do now, General? he said to me. Save me! I told him not to be an idiot. If he'd gotten himself in as big a mess as that, even God himself wouldn't be able to save him. He went back to Buenos Aires, and as you know, he was bumped off almost immediately. I don't know who the persons were who fired the shots. I don't need to know, because I know who gave the order to shoot. In any event there was a great deal of money involved, of course, many dirty hands. It wasn't a question of being clever. It was a question of being decent. And Vandor wasn't.

Ah, Zamora. I felt myself levitating within a story whose signs my mind couldn't grasp. I had never heard anyone describe the violent death of someone close to him with such a lack of emotion, such aloofness. I played dumb. I asked the General if that death had grieved him.

A soldier looks upon death as the most natural thing in the world, he told me. Sooner or later, all our lives end up the same way.

I shall skip the conversations that followed: all during that Friday afternoon till nightfall, and on Saturday morning. Nor is it worth telling about the mishaps that occurred on the way back, Zamora: the rain of birds we saw in Soria and the accident we had as we entered Paris. I turned paranoid. I began to imagine that my misfortunes obeyed a plan devised by Perón. I calmed down when I read in a book by Américo Barrios that the General's store of knowledge concerning Simon the Magician didn't come from Gnostic treatises but from a Jack Palance film.

I only want you to know what our last meeting, two years later, was like. It was summer. Night was falling. We walked through the garden to the door of the villa. We talked about dogs and trees. All of a sudden, Perón stopped. He stared into my eyes, as though he had finally noticed me and I was the last survivor in the universe. Tomás, he said to me. You have the same name as my grandfather. I too should have been named Tomás.

I didn't know what to say. I came out with some banal phrase. Then, for no reason at all, I explained that I was not a Peronist. He smiled. He asked me what Peronism meant to me. What I remembered of all that past.

The only thing I remember is what I didn't see, I answered. Something I will never be able to see. I remember you spreading your arms wide and greeting the multitude in the Plaza de Mayo. I see the banners fluttering, the workers chanting *Perón, Perón*, in unison, over and over, as you go on waving to them, for a long time. Finally your hand puts an end to the clamor. Nobody breathes. Thousands and thousands of people raise their eyes in ecstasy to where you are standing, on a balcony of the Casa Rosada. Your voice makes its way into the emptiness at the heart of that tremendous silence: Comraaades! I hear that one word from you and then cheers again, shouts. My memory is something that I saw in movie theaters, that I heard over the radio. Nothing that has been a part of my reality.

I saw him smile again. The images enveloped me and at that instant the General was fifty years old again.

Everything can be recovered, he said to me. Listen to the shouting in the plaza.

I heard it. I heard the multitude grow excited, setting the city afire like a torrent of lava. The incandescent ashes rained down on my memory.

Darkness fell over the garden. The General spread his arms wide and exclaimed: Comraaade! His voice was hoarse and young, the voice of long ago.

I clasped his hands. And I left there, like someone bleeding to death.

15 *The Escape*

I can never get anywhere. The phrase falls off Zamora like a shirt button. He has left the Renault 12 at the door of *La Opinión* so as not to repeat the tribulations of the return from Ezeiza on this trip. He has taken a taxi that is charging triple fare to get him 'as close as possible', and he now discovers that the closest possible is right there: just on the ramp of the expressway, six miles south of the dais. Trucks, barricades of kiosks and drum corps saturate the horizon. Not even a glimmer of light can be seen in the distance: only a pit of human darkness.

Inch your way ahead, he suggests to the taxi driver. Put the pass that says Access to all Areas Permitted on the windshield. We'll get there sometime.

If we ever do, the man says resignedly.

We have to get there, Zamora says. And leans back in the

corner of the seat, smoking. A very old Zen poem suddenly starts going round and round in his head:

> I wandered all over for twenty years,
> I went to the east and to the west.
> I returned at last to Seiken.
> I hadn't moved at all.

Like Perón: twenty years to end up in the same place.

All things considered, the trip to *La Opinión* has borne fruit. After hesitating for a long time, Martínez has entrusted him with a few scattered pages that reconstruct the General's years in Europe. They consist of maps with holes burned in them, fragments of a monograph on war in winter in the Alps, bits and pieces of an unfinished article, and stories recounted by a lieutenant-colonel, Augusto Maidana, who shared quarters with Perón in 1939 and 1942.

Zamora takes a look:

1 *Portrait, Seen Through Maidana's Eyes*

Transcribed from a tape recording. Check on the meaning of bunraku, *providing the word is written correctly.*

He didn't look like a man. Perón was an automaton, a golem, what the Japanese call a *bunraku*. Several times I saw him with his mind distracted. This is something that almost no one has experienced: seeing Perón distracted. He was a hollow, soulless figure. Then, as his mind returned to the reality at hand, he gradually filled up with the feelings and the desires of others, with things that needed to be done. You would go out to look for a horse, and Perón was already coming with it, all saddled up. You would find a refuge in the snow and he would be there inside waiting for you. When his mind was distracted, he showed no sign of hatred or sadness or happiness or weariness or enthusiasm. The only thing you could see in him was emptiness. When his mind was focused, yes: then other people's feelings were reflected in him, as though he had a mirror in place of a body.

2 *Diary Entries*

Christmas Eve, Tucumán, 1971. Someone, on meeting me on the street, addressed me not as Tomás but Nucho, the name my father went by. This upset me. Can it be possible that a person's name changes down through the years?

Today I found someone who knew Perón a long time ago, when as yet he had no history and acted without giving a thought as to whether or not he was in the public eye. I am quite certain that he was able to see in that past what the present cannot yet show us: that he had deciphered in 1941 the enigma that we Argentines still have not learned to decipher thirty years later.

He is a friend of my parents. I talked with him in the afternoon, in the yard. His name is Augusto Maidana. When he speaks he twirls words round and round, as though they were a hat in his hand.

When he left, I stood there thinking of Kurt Gödel's theorem. How to translate Gödel's mathematical formulas into words? Let's have a try at this impossible undertaking. Let's see.

In every system of mathematical logic . . .

No. That's not the way to go about it.

Every truth, however evident it may be, always involves something that cannot be proved.

That's better. The fact that a man has ears, nails, a nose and walks does not necessarily mean that he has ears and walks. However, what Gödel means is more complicated still.

After having thought it over carefully, I discussed the theorem with Perón, in April of last year. I asked him: Has it ever crossed your mind, General, what history might have been like without you? Imagine. That everything is the same as it is now: Madrid, the sky, the death of García Elorrio, run over by a car, Franco's avowal that he is disappointed by his ex-Minister Fraga, the poodles, the dovecotes. That everything is happening, but that you have never happened. He answered me: A man who thinks that would have to get outside himself and jump out the window.

That is precisely what Gödel's theorem is.

3 *Notes For a Note*

Work in progress: A dead work? All the sources have been provided by Lieutenant-Colonel Maidana. Look for others. In the tourist guide that he lent me there are marginal notes written by Perón. One line in it is underscored (I translate): 'The bus trip to Tyrol (altitude: 1835 feet) takes half an hour and another twenty minutes to reach the Castle.' In the margin I read: Andare! *One of the maps, of the city of Trent, has a burn on it, from a cigarette? Sparks have landed on the Adige River, filling it with charred islands. There where there was an arrow pointing to the Piazza Dante, the letters, half eaten away – pia Da te – are all that is left now.*

At the end of May 1939, when he arrived in Merano, Perón moved into a small house on the via dei Portici: three bedrooms, a hallway, a living room with a fireplace. The windows overlooked the Duomo.

Spring was late. Monte Benedetto still had a few patches of snow showing, and the waters of the Passirio River often swept dogs and frozen birds along with them. The Milan radio broadcast alarming news. In Birmingham Chamberlain declared that England should prepare for the worst. In Berlin Ciano signed the ironclad pact with Germany. In the Tridentine Division, whose troops Perón reviewed, Inspector Ottavio Zoppi ordered an edict posted that the officers interpreted as an advance declaration of war: *Da questo momento, secondo l'articolo del Patto Bipartito, l'Italia è legata al destino del Terzo Reich.*

Lieutenant-Colonel Perón decided to hone his intelligence, train his senses. They arrived at the firing range half an hour ahead of schedule in order to practice handling heavy Hotchkiss machine-guns and learn the effect of Brandt mortars on fixed targets.

Captain Maidana turned up in the middle of June. Perón gave him the room farthest from the street, to isolate him from the noise outside. His new comrade helped allay his sadness at being left a widower, which had so depressed him at the beginning of his tour of duty. There was still a touch of loneliness prowling about the house, but it was no longer as overwhelming as before.

The air turned warmer. Perón began to wear the white silk uniform of an Alpine officer. He learned a great deal by keeping his eye on the Duce's plans to turn the beaches of poverty-stricken Albania into a showcase for his brand-new imperial grandeur. 'The hour of utopians has arrived,' Perón predicted in a lecture before the General Staff of the Tridentine Division. 'An ordinary man accepts his fate. A utopian invents it, and then succeeds in making fate obey him.'

Merano was suddenly overrun with tourists and with Tyrolean bands that made a terrible din in the public squares till daybreak. Foreseeing war, they all wanted to drink life down in one gulp. Maidana and Perón strolled at dusk along the Corso del Principe Umberto. They made their way back home only at the hour when the matrons, feeling drowsy, left their balconies and went inside to digest tangles of spaghetti alongside their radios.

They became inseparable. The Lieutenant-Colonel taught the Captain the ruses of diplomacy by telling him how he had escaped the intelligence officers in Chile who kept tailing him.

'I put sand down on the terrace of my apartment and in the hallway outside my office,' Perón said. 'I left a little piece of thread of a different color each day on the documents to check to see if, despite my precautions, somebody was taking a look at them. Two intruders tried to get in to search my apartment one morning. My wife heard their footfalls in the sand and chased them away with a broom. I sent my intelligence reports to Buenos Aires in a diplomatic pouch with a false bottom. In a personal letter to our Minister of War, I once wrote that the Commander-in-Chief of the Chilean Army was tougher than a Galician's shoe. I had had cordial relations with that general, but after I sent the letter I found him surly. He avoided me whenever possible. I realized that he had got his hands on my correspondence. I made up my mind to confront him. At a reception I said to him: 'The opinions I expressed about you in the diplomatic pouch were lies, General. The truth went to Buenos Aires in another pouch.' The man just stood there staring at me, dumbfounded. Do you remember a chorus that the organ grinders played all over the barrios? The one that went: Never mind/if fortune proves unkind./No Argentine's a dummy/Even if he's crummy? Well, that's how things are in diplomacy, Maidana. If a person doesn't have a clever trick up his sleeve, he invents one.'

Reality flew by so swiftly that no one could follow it. In July, the two of them traveled to Rome to learn their new destinies. At the embassy they were promised an interview with the Duce, but they had to be content with no more than a public audience with Count Ciano, at which the latter arrived late and with his mind distracted. They heard a few empty phrases about the war that was now inevitable, a trap (he said) that Italy would not fall into. Ciano disappeared amid photographers' flashes before they realized it. They didn't even have a chance to ask him any questions.

During the ten days that he remained in Rome, the Lieutenant-Colonel didn't once wear his uniform. He went about dressed in golf knickers buckled at the ankle and gray wool socks, unheard of in such hot weather. After beating about the bush for some time, Maidana worked up his nerve to tell him that this struck him as being very odd.

'It's so they'll mistake me for an Englishman,' Perón said. 'And I come by much more accurate information about what's going on.'

'How can that be, if you don't speak English?' his friend said in surprise.

'I don't speak it, but I make English gestures, and nobody catches me out.'

After that they went their separate ways. Perón returned to Merano, and Maidana was stationed at Bassano del Grappa, some twenty miles north of Venice. They had no sooner accustomed themselves to the oxygen of one city when they were distracted by the folklore of another, as if the eve of war meant no more than drifting about and getting drunk. At the end of November 1939, Perón had to move to Pinerolo, near Turin. Three months later he crossed the peninsula and settled in Chietti. Those irrational kangaroo hops through an unknown geography did not train him for anything other than pure and simple movement. To keep himself occupied he devoted his time to utterly pointless activities. He translated Italian army regulations into Spanish and then translated them back into Italian just so as to be able to translate them yet again later on. He made terrible mistakes in both languages, confusing for instance the ardor of the *Arditi* with the ardent zeal of the *Alpini*, what interested him, however, was not perfection but the alertness of his senses.

In the middle of spring he was transferred to a battalion in Aosta. He felt that that gloomy city, with ruins everywhere, was the crossroads at the end of the world. Every so often, as he walked from the arch of the Emperor Augustus to the Collegiata de San Orso, he stopped at the tomb of Count Tomaso of Savoy, telling himself repeatedly that all that pastoral calm would soon be broken and flailed by the approaching storm. The triumphant tanks of the Reich were progressively closing in all around at a lightning speed. To get himself in the proper mood, Perón reread, tirelessly, *The Nation under Arms.*

Von der Goltz's book now spoke to him in the Duce's voice. It repeated that a divided people, unwilling to commit sacrifices, badly governed by wretched political hacks, incapable of creating a war industry for itself, was a people of vassals. Only the authority of the father, of the military officer, of the leader could save it: only the power of a chief who had trained himself for power, the command of one who knows how to command, the providential will of one who was provident.

He supposed that the hand of God had been placed on his shoulder when he received a call from Rome. Darkness was now descending over Europe to eye level. Soon it would keep people from breathing and all the foreign observers would be forced to leave. On 14 May 1940, Hitler's armies crossed the Meuse and advanced on Amiens. France was being crushed underfoot like a piece of spoiled fruit. Elated, the Duce wanted to occupy the provinces in the South of France immediately. Several generals tried to hold him back: *'Non siamo pronti. Il popolo italiano non vuole questa guerra.'*

The Duce would demonstrate that a single will was sufficient to drive thousands to any abyss. The demonstration took place on 10 June. Maidana and Perón, dressed in their Argentine officers' uniforms, mingled with the crowd in the Piazza Venezia and attended, in disbelief, a ceremony that bordered on the religious. At dusk, the Duce appeared on the balcony of a palace. He looked to the right and to the left. He possessed the disorderly crowd with the imperious thrust of his jaw. He imbued it with a sense of security; he set it alight. He began to hold a dialogue with it and little by little dissipated the fear and the shock that his words unleashed. He spoke of death and the multitude answered *Viva!* Maidana felt his friend levitate, take in the spectacle with all his senses, and learn once and for all that the art of leadership lay not only in what was said but in how: a simple, straightforward manner was stronger than all rational arguments put together.

They stayed in Rome for almost three months. Food was rationed, but as diplomats they had cards entitling them to double rations. Every so often they ventured into the labyrinths of the black market in search of cigarettes and liquor. They spent most of the day bent over maps, plotting safe routes for getting across the border, reaching a neutral country and returning to Buenos Aires on a passenger boat across an Atlantic teeming with enemy fleets.

Italian troops invaded Greece and Libya. They advanced to be humiliated, with no other respite save that of their continual defeats. In November, Perón learned that his friends in the Tridentine Division were being annihilated. He did not have time to pity them. He was obliged to leave the war, without having seen it. He left in a convoy from Genoa, armed with open sesames and safe conduct passes. He crossed the border at Ventimiglia and followed the arc of the Riviera to Marseilles. For two weeks Perón lived through vicissitudes and scares until, on the first morning in December, he entered Barcelona.

E via dicendo. *'That was Perón's entire European experience, except for the escape that I haven't yet told about,'* Maidana summed up.

And the visions of Berlin that he recounted to at least three visitors? And the trip to the Masurian Lakes that he gave a detailed account of to two others? And the meeting with the Duce that he bragged about at such length to Pérez Jiménez and Trujillo?

None of that happened, Maidana said. And yet Perón wasn't lying when he told those stories. They were lies, I grant, but he told them so many times that he ended up believing them.

Anchored in Ezeiza

We aren't getting anywhere, Zamora says dejectedly when the taxi, stranded on one shoulder of the expressway, finally finds it impossible to go any farther. The shield of trucks that was ahead of it in close formation has stopped in front of the highrise buildings of the Workers' Housing Project: on strike, endlessly delayed, suffering cardiac arrest.

The order we have is to wait it out here, and here's where we're gonna wait it out, one of the truck drivers announces, brooking no arguments, an image of Perón stamped over the heart of his T-shirt attesting to his authority.

Tune into another station, Zamora cries, his head spinning from the endless tangos the taxi driver has been listening to. Colonia. Rivadavia . . . See if there's a newscast on Belgrano. Maybe Perón has already landed and we'll miss his speech. Hear that? The national anthem. They're playing the national anthem over the loudspeakers!

On the left of the dial is an apotheosis of tangos. On the right, a chorus of national and popular greetings welcoming the Great Man. And in the middle, Leonardo Favio is giving out with a tearful 'Fuiste mía un verano'. All of a sudden, a solemn voice is heard across the dial:

'. . . And considering the seriousness of the events that have occurred in the place set for the reception of our greatest leader, the highest government authorities are studying the possibility of diverting the aircraft in which General Perón is traveling to an alternate military terminal. More news in a few minutes . . .'

Zamora lights another cigarette.

Shall I try to find a detour? the taxi driver asks.

Stay here. Traffic will clear any minute now. We're not the only ones who won't be getting anywhere today.

It's all the same to me, the man answers. After all, you're the one who's paying.

A gray light falls on the last pages that Zamora has rescued.

4 *The Escape, According to Maidana*

Transcribed from a tape recording. Literal. Except for the syntactical betrayals.

Finally we went to unload the baggage. It fell to me to go with Perón. Whew, a long hard job. After that it was left to me to explain that we would be traveling by train, bus and truck, but not our baggage – it would go by boat, direct from Genoa. We spent the entire day there. Perón would say: 'Bonell's crate! It's falling!' If we heard the sound of glass breaking: 'Maidana's losing everything he owns!' And the crane disemboweled my trunk full of clothes.

We must have stayed in Barcelona for less than a week. From there on we were free to do as we chose. I stuck with Perón, who had proved to be both sensible and shrewd in the face of the challenges of the journey. We went to Madrid by train, via Zaragoza. We saw nothing but the ruins of war and bullet-riddled bell towers. Hunger. We ate in secret, so as not to expose ourselves to people's desire for food. In Guadalajara a bunch of armless beggars with shaved heads and swarms of flies in their wounds, tried to take the train by assault. The Civil Guards came and fired on the beggars to drive them away. Perón said: What we saw in Italy was terrible. But this conflict that has ended in Spain must have been much worse. Hatred is never as great as when it's between blood brothers.

So then: we headed for Lisbon from that same station in Madrid. And once there, just wait. Two weeks, three, whatever fate decreed, in wartime, everything is a matter of patience and death. Death so that patience rests in peace or patience so as finally to end up dead. Finally, we secured passage on a little Portuguese boat, the *Zarpa Pinto*. And set out. There were musicians on board. But the heavy seas didn't even give them a chance to play. It took us two days to reach Madeira, and during that time there wasn't a soul to be seen. All the passengers had retreated to their cabins, waiting to get over being seasick. All at once the rough seas died down. Then people came up on deck again, with dark circles under the eyes. Not Perón: as elegantly turned out as always. A storm? he asked. I didn't have time to notice it! I've been hard at work.

A sly fox, that one. In the infirmary we were told that the bucking and rearing of the water had addled his brain. That his liver had been left in a terrible state. And his stomach as hard as a rock from having vomited so much.

I saw him again in Mendoza. The summer of 1941 was coming to an end. He was on the General Staff at the Montaña Training Center, and the open air rejuvenated him. I sensed that something in him was changing. I found him less tense, more inclined to live life to the full. In Europe he had lived like an ascetic. Now he was catching up. In the afternoons he could be found drinking orangeade in the Colón Café, invariably surrounded by young girls. He described to them the invisible cities that Hitler had built, according to him, in the occupied countries. He told them of secret meetings in which the Duce asked his advice. I believe that his detours from reality go back to those years, when he went about with an overwrought imagination. They tell me that he keeps saying to those who come to visit him in Madrid nowadays that reality is the only truth. In those days, however, he was fond of saying that for every man there is one truth, and that he knew of no two truths that were alike.

Once, near Uspallata, an old highlander handed his daughter over to him to rear. In all likelihood the girl wasn't yet fourteen, and malicious gossip had it that Perón began living with her there and then. She might have been the same girl who turned up with him in Buenos Aires, the one he introduced as his goddaughter. I couldn't say for certain. What I do remember is that both girls went by the name of Piraña.

I know about things like that because back in 1942 he often asked me to go with him to the Cabaret Tibidabo, on the corner of Cangallo and Carlos Pellegrini. He was altogether at home there. He was a friend of the owner. He would give the girls the once-over, single out two or three who were to his liking, and ask the owner what such livestock was like when it came to braying. There was nothing he liked better than to sleep with a girl's feet in his ear.

He latched on to me as his confidant. He dreamed of reviving the General San Martín Lodge, which had been so powerful in other eras, but Justo had the army under his thumb at that time and no one did anything without his permission. If Justo had lived a couple of years more, there wouldn't have been a Perón. Who knows where any one of us would be today. But fate forgets what we might have been. It clings only to what we were. A colonel by that time, Perón began to be more and more self-confident. We worked together as troop inspectors at

Montaña. The moment day dawned, he began to talk on and on. He was a word-machine.

We drifted apart because of a stupid thing that happened between us. He had taken it into his head never to allow anyone to pay the check for him, thereby making us his toadies. One night, at the Tibidabo, I answered back. I didn't want him to keep me in his debt by paying for a couple of drinks I'd had. I'm paying, I said. He wouldn't let me. You're not paying, he said, trying to order me around. Nobody pays for Colonel Perón's vices. Much less Major Maidana. I turned my back on him, put my money on the counter and walked off. I never went back to the Tibidabo again. I chose to cross the street and stay the way I still am today.

A Last Reflection by Zamora

That damned Zen poem refuses to leave me in peace. It goes on buzzing in my head:

> The moon is the same old moon
> The flowers are still the same as they were
> I have come to be what is left
> Of all the things I see.

That's what my Gödel's theorem is right now. The only movement possible is getting outside myself and jumping out a window. Leaving the taxi and falling into my life. But even by doing that I won't get there.

16 *The Face of the Enemy*

What can the Old Man have been like in bed? Diana Bronstein asked when she and Nun got back to the gloomy villa on the Beltway, close to midnight, on 3 June. They laid a burlap mattress down on the floor, Nun lighted the stove, Diana spread out the yellow-flowered sheets, and looking at each other's vulnerable bodies, they felt love and pity for each other, sought warmth in the fires that were flaming up from their every pore, embraced and imbibed each other until dawn fell upon them. Outside, just for a change, the trees gave off mist.

(Now the roosters are breaking the day with other gullets. At the head of the southern column, Diana and Nun advance holding hands amid the eucalyptus trees. The excited crowd that is following them has left behind the last houses on Monte Grande and covers all the wide ocean of Route 205, that ends at the altar of the dais, in Ezeiza. The crowd numbers more than twenty thousand

and keeps getting bigger. At the crossroads mudslides, islets, springs, tributaries of all kinds rain down on them. They sing, they fly in the light of the bass drums, they allow their happiness to surface wherever it pleases. And you are a different person, Diana. Not the one who asked that question.)

What can Perón have been like in bed? I don't mean in these last few years, of course, hey, you dummy with the ground-glass face, to tease you I'm putting the tip of my tongue in your belly button. I mean before that, when he was in the prime of life. Who had he hooked up with then? That one, Nun, the one who had a really sensual nickname. That's it – Piraña. Heaven only knows why she was called Piraña. She must have had a big greedy mouth yawning open between her legs.

But that doesn't give you the right to touch me. Lie still. I'm going to anoint you with cold chocolate and melt it for you. Well, look what's happened to you down there. A person can't even talk with you. Wait a sec. Have you ever thought of the Old Man that way, horny, caressing, floating with his tongue? What do you expect? Those are luxuries that even the most miserable wretch can offer himself, but not a historical figure. It's only their virtue that ever gets written about. On that score books don't remember Freud, as though sex was shit, Nun. Wrong, all wrong. Without libido you don't get anywhere.

That's the way, you frustrated soldier. Stroke me, nice and slow. Thank heaven you're frustrated. If you were a soldier who'd realized his potential I'd be dying of boredom. When I used to dream about hell, I was a soldier's wife. I kept polishing swords all day long, I mean all dream long, just to console myself. Or was the wife of a historian, one dressed in academic robes, scratching the ultimate truth with his fingernail. I was a little rat with a liberty cap and sat in the doorway of truth shouting: Nobody gets in, because my husband's inside and the truth can't be shared. And I, willing to share anything except you, used to wake up in a cold sweat. There, touch me there. Don't move from that place. Come. Now.

At three in the morning, the odor of sex aroused Nun again, and since Diana was now lying back on the torpors of her red lava, curling up into a ball inside the long long threads of her lava, Nun licked her ear and kept exciting her with a cunning whisper: I don't think anything special happened with the old man in bed. Which was enough to put Diana in a sudden amorous mood, with her senses pricked up, and lazily wake from her desire beneath Nun's more and more tender fronds, that's right, take care of me. Well, go ahead and go mad, that's it, don't go away yet, not now, not yet, stay till it gets light.

Diana intended to be alert and remember how happiness kept moving ahead in her, but when she reached port she had nothing to remember, the limit of happiness was a river, a forgetfulness of self, a shore of oblivion, a levitation to her own depths. And when she began to come to again, the only thing she heard were little verses of the sort on caramel wrappers and in tango lyrics. Stupid things like: *May the sun not rise again, nor there be light from the moon,/If a tyrant like this one sows more misfortune.*

She licked the bad thoughts like a cat, and sitting against the wall with her arms crossed, frowned menacingly, returning to the charge:

But you told me that feet had an erotic effect on the Old Man, and that's already a sign of imagination. That he fell into the habit of sleeping with Piraña with his feet in her face and vice-versa. Do you think he did the same thing with Evita? Hey, wake up. What do you think?

How should I know? It depends. Maybe Evita didn't have pretty feet.

They were perfect, Diana decided. There was nothing about Evita that wasn't perfect.

They stayed awake all night, sailing on and on with their

caravels alight, entered and left their mutual seas regretting that they still had so much left to explore, that Nun had lost Diana's Seven Cities and she Nun's White Caesar, that you don't touch my El Dorado a little bit more, that you haven't drunk the last drop of the Fountain of Eternal Youth.

When dawn came they took a bath together. Nun soaped Diana's feet and surfaced with a bubble on the tip of his nose. She sighed, beating the copper of the hair melted by the water: Lucky we're not national heroes of the War of Independence. Where would we end up if the history books condemned us to the sex of an angel like Manuel Belgrano, to die virgins like Paso and Moreno, to have kids by an oversight on nature's part as happened to poor San Martín . . .

(In the distance, Vicki Pertini and Bighead Iriarte appear, with flags unfurled, in the vanguard of a fleet of Leylands. To the rear, above the dry expanses of the Las Ortegas Arroyo, the roar of another tempestuous multitude is heard, the sky is still blue, the truth in a pure state has not been corrupted by the falseness of documents, life is beginning, I feel such great elation that even the urge to smoke has vanished from my mind. Everything has gone away on me except you, Nun, you staring blockhead, you sewer-cat.)

Let's go see the face of the enemy.

There are two helicopters prepared for action in the military sector of the airport, with their motors warmed up. Around them, a guard of infantrymen paces back and forth in the sun. The orders from the walkie-talkies intermingle and overlap in the air where gasoline rains down intermittently, and the smoke grates on people's minds.

Tholdier, path the word along that we're about to leave. The Lieutenant-Colonel climbs into the helicopter that has the best firepower. The guard fans out. The blades begin rotating with a hair-rumpling blast. In one leap Lito Coba gets in and sits down next to the chief. Behind the seats are boxes of tear-gas grenades, ammunition, several Ithacas, two Magnums.

War, Lito murmurs.

The helicopter takes off.

They're the oneth that want it. The one thought that enterth a leftith's mind ith war.

The moment they are airborne, the wind keeps driving them toward the dais. The Lieutenant-Colonel is making the flight in his parade uniform: a jacket with wide lapels and a tie with a horse motif. His cuirass of pomade is so rigid that not even the hurricane of the helicopter blades has dared muss his hair.

At the sight of the crowd, the pilot is unable to contain himself: Good Lord, there are millions of them!

A river of pilgrims is running through the fields. What a fever! A crowd that big has never been seen driving along the enormous riverbed of the expressway, wading through the streams with their shoes on top of their heads. The words inscribed on the banners no longer upset the Lieutenant-Colonel: held on high, they intermingle and cancel each other out. From his armored tabernacle, Perón will be able to read only a whirlpool of letters. And the acoustics of the choruses will commingle with Leonardo Favio's melodious baton. This very minute, there can be heard, over the loudspeakers down below, the drumrolls of the master of ceremonies: *You were mine, boys/united we will triumph one summer.*

Swelled by the wind, the few tents that still have not been taken down dance. From the food stands patches of smoke rise in the air. The smell of sausages mounts heavenward, body and soul. On the horizon of the broad river a fleet of trucks blocks traffic. To the rear, caravans of desperate taxis tear up the hard-shoulder of the expressway in search of an exit. Impossible to move.

Lito has been carefully noting each suspicious buzz in the swarm. With the aid of his binoculars, he has identified beneath the placards of the Montoneros a rowdy chorus from Berazategui, the Blue Rivulet, which is disrupting the harmony of the main contingent with refrains hostile to the deceased General Aramburu. And he knows that at the foot of the dais, alongside the music stands of the members of the symphony orchestra, a small group from Lanús, the Golden Throats, has been harassing the cordons of the Labor Union Youth Movement for some time. Let them sing. They are already doomed. They are swans with dying plumage. Surrounded on all sides, they are pouring their slogans into an acoustic pocket. Nobody can hear them. It is not these opponents who alarm Lito. The enemy he fears is the one that is invisible: the leftists lying snugly in ambush at the bottom of the ditches, the ones who are doubtless digging trenches between the roots of the eucalyptus trees, the ones who are preparing to leap out from who knows what propitious hollow to attack the dais.

They are now flying over the low, unlighted houses that border the fields from Tapiales to Llavallol. There seems to be nothing out of the ordinary. They detect only little outbreaks of harmless people walking along, with balloons held on high, children on their shoulders, portable radios. And yet (Lito thinks) the invisible ones must already be very close. It is nearly one-thirty. The General will land shortly before four. The leftists have only a couple of hours left now to capture the first three hundred yards and take a firm stand in the redoubts they've won. If they allow them to. Because once they penetrate the red zone, inside the cordons, an iron corset will smother them. The problem will be what to do with them. Simply dissuade them? Throw a scare into them so they go away? That's no longer possible. It is several days too late. They have no other recourse left now (Lito thinks) except to annihilate: with everything they have and a blow straight to the head, as the General orders.

Inside the helicopter, the vibrations of the engine drill into their eardrums. They speak to each other only in signs, with their thumbs and forefingers. Since they've lost their hearing, the only human sense they have left is sight. They are eagles, seagulls, predatory crows. As they fly over the dais, Lito makes a quick inventory of their forces. The ambulances, the armored Dodge, the cordons of ponchos, the guard of hawks with double-barreled shotguns: everything is in place, beaks razor-sharp, talons out. To the left, he glimpses wicker baskets with eighteen thousand doves, all ready now for the fabulous release, a thousand doves in the wind for each one of the years of exile that the Great Man has suffered. Even Leonardo Favio is saying what he has been programmed to say at this precise moment: 'Never has anyone, in the entire history of humanity, ever become the object of an act of homage such as this. Neither Julius Caesar nor Alexander the Great, nor Pedro de Mendoza when he discovered Buenos Aires. Nobody. Only Perón.' From the anthill of the dais a shadow separates itself, an ugly, neckless shape. They see it salute the helicopter, with Ithaca raised. Lito identifies it with the binoculars: it is Arcángelo Gobbi. How imprudent. And the Lieutenant-Colonel shouts: Too bad!

The aircraft veers off to the west. It raises the angle of its blades, scrutinizes the groves of eucalyptus from the muddy banks of the Matanza River to the buildings of the Atomic Commission. No sign of the enemy. The gurgles of the engine split the afternoon in two. All of a sudden, to the right, Lito perceives a flash of darkness on the horizon. A sinister serpent is coming their way. A serpent? The leftith, the Lieutenant-Colonel points out.

They see a compact vapor advancing, a hippopotamus. The dark brown animal is swaying down the Avenida Fair, pointing its snout toward the Esteban Echeverría district. It has already gone past all the security cordons. It is approaching the little schoolhouse, where traffic is blocked off by double barriers. But before it gets that far, its snout turns aside, its legs sink in the swamps of the district, its haunches blend into the dry pastures. There are more than twenty thousand of them: not as many as the Lieutenant-Colonel had calculated. And yet, wait. Lito discovers three or four thousand more who are advancing along the sides of the Olympic swimming pools, beneath the narrow windows of the hotels and the vacation camps, where the metal workers have left replacement troops. But let them advance, we're coming – Lito clenches his fists – let them fall into the eye of the storm. It'th them, the Lieutenant-Colonel rejoices. Look. They are walking along in thilenthe, ath though they were thneaking in, timidly, a bundle of nerveth. They are carrying their flagth lowered. They know we're following them and want to trick uth by being ditharmed.

The Thothialist fatherland: there we have it. The Lieutenant-Colonel goes on marking them with the branding iron of his binoculars: Nun, Iriarte, Red, Juáreth, that Pertini. And he relaxes in his seat. They're thpoiling for a fight. I can thmell them. I know them. We're going to give them the pleathure. Hurry up, let'th go down for a landing. The thothialist fatherland.

He rubs his eyes. He tosses his head back and guffaws, till the tortoise's shell of hair cream peels off his head from his explosive laughter. The pilot laughs too, not knowing why. And Lito, with his jaws clenched, his nostrils pounding, becomes tense. He shouts: Look at them, sir! They're heading straight into the trap.

Yeth, thtrait into it. Five to one: there won't be a thingle one left.

Hey, look, how incredible, Diana says exultantly, and yet it's perfectly credible that Pepe Juárez and Bighead Iriarte should appear there, in the shadow of the water tower, on the Calle Almafuerte. But she keeps going on about how incredible it is. She lets go of Nun's hand and runs to kiss them as though she hadn't seen them for centuries – where in the devil have you been, just look at you, you're in bad shape, what a pair of miserable wretches.

She scratches Pepe's neck, tries to get her arms around Bighead and can't, I never can manage to hug you, kid, you're a baobab. Vicki Pertini sticks her Egyptian profile out the window of a Leyland. A mist of nervous tics runs through her. Come on, what are you waiting for, she breaks in. She claps her hands. The revolution begins today or never. The phrase has been the object of a great deal of thought. Vicki is always surprising people with these efflorescences of her brain.

She's getting skinnier by the day. She wakes up wrinkled and dwarfed every morning. When she's in a bad temper, Diana says that Vicki sleeps inside a bottle of nicotine and kerosene. Since she's nothing but skin and bones now, her nerves are flowering from exposure to the elements, mingled with her hair. She has a pointed nose, lips permanently pursed from the hollow trace of a cigarette. She breathes only when she moves. Staying still suffocates her. She gets out of the Leyland in one leap and gives a helping hand to the shanty dwellers feverishly preparing the big placards. She chews her words. Nice and slow, boys. Unfold the cloth carefully. Make the letters look as though they were starched when the General sees them.

Diana, on the other hand, never stops kissing and embracing. She sows chaos. The pilgrims take the water tower by assault, as in the Crusades. The tower has battlements, simulacra of cloisters, medieval plumbing. When they open the faucets, the water drains down through the gutters. The shanty dwellers are exhausted, filthy from the sausages with mustard that they've eaten on the road. Leaning against the tower, Bighead makes no attempt to hide his dejection. He feels strange. His one consolation is Vicki's presence nearby, though she gives him no hope. He looks at her with his dark, tearful cow eyes. For her, the only sun is Nun. Fatties don't appeal to her. And Bighead Iriarte is hopelessly fat.

In the spring of 1970, when Bighead decided to join the group, Nun told him: Watch those depressions of yours, you hear? A person who's depressed can't take this. And even though sudden fits of melancholy overtook him every five minutes, Bighead didn't back down. He was available for any and every mission. He cured himself. Shutting himself up in the garage, he got rid of his fits of depression by cleaning carburetors and differentials. When he surfaced again, there wasn't even a scar left.

His father had been a bar pianist in Bahía Blanca. The year after Evita's death, he was taken to Buenos Aires to provide the music for a party at the presidential villa. He met Perón, and it changed his life. It must have been ten o'clock that night when the General came over to him to say good night. At that moment, Bighead's father was playing 'La Morocha'.

I congratulate you, Iriarte, Perón said. I've never heard anybody bang out that music so well.

Bighead's father didn't know how to thank him.

Well, then, sir, I'm going to beat the world record for a continuous performance of the same piano piece by playing 'La Morocha' in your honor.

Perón took him at his word and offered him the Palais de Glace for his try for the record. The father trained obsessively. Finally, one day in October he declared that he was ready. He played 'La Morocha' for one hundred and eighty-four hours, varying the rhythm so as not to fall asleep. In the beginning there was a big audience. A couple of ladies gave Bighead lollipops and boxes of hard candy. But on the fourth day, the visitors began to thin out. The only ones left were his mother and the official observers. They set up a cot for Bighead on the platform, alongside the piano. The news that the father had established a world record came out in the papers. One of the ministers received him and offered him a medal in Perón's name. That summer, they spent two free weeks at a vacation camp in Claromecó. It was a time of spectacular good luck for them.

Soon after that, the General was overthrown, and the father

found himself out of work. His name was on the blacklist in all the bars. He had to play piano in brothels. For several years they lived like nomads in towns south of Buenos Aires. Bighead could never finish a grade in the same school. Finally, he was hired as an apprentice in a car repair shop. As he cleaned carburetors, he had more than enough time to think. One day, he told himself that if he had known happiness with Perón as a child, Perón was the only one who could bring him back that happiness. He saved every last centavo he earned so as to make the journey to Madrid and meet him. He survived on leftovers from pizza parlors. He put on weight. One Saturday night in the car repair shop, somebody knocked him out with a club and took all the dough he had on him, sewn inside the cuff of his pants. He spent a week convalescing, devastated. When he got out of bed, he decided to go look for work in Buenos Aires.

He was lucky. He was taken on immediately, near Retiro. After a month, Pepe Juárez introduced him to Nun. Then he met Vicki. Bighead was as sedentary as a cow and the beelike frenzy with which she occupied any and every space dazzled him at first sight. He began to dream of her. He would wake up with his jockey shorts soaking wet from desire. Pepe advised him to bed Vicki without bothering his head about it so much. Any activity would do so long as it kept her awake. But Bighead felt abashed and invited her to the movies instead. He tried to stroke her hands. Vicki irately withdrew them and kept her eyes riveted on the screen. As they left, she said to him: Don't try to make out with me again, Bighead. The next time I'm going to smack you one.

When Diana appeared on the horizon and became the center of gravity of the group, Vicki began to spend her days scrubbing the basic units and sewing clothes with the shantytown women. Bighead, ever faithful, tried again. In vain. To her it was a matter of principle: she could go to bed with any man who came along.

But nobody was going to fuck her around with a bunch of crap about love.

In one of the tape recordings that Nun brought back from Madrid, the General told the tale of the dogs and the cats. They all found it cynical and enjoyed it. It made Bighead fall into a gloomy silence though. The General said:

'People are made up of ninety per cent materialists and ten per cent idealists. Materialists are like cats. If a person tries to beat them, they run away and can't be caught. And when they're cornered, cats put themselves on their guard and take a stand. They react out of desperation. Idealists are like dogs. They react out of instinct. If someone gives them a good swift kick, they retreat and then come right back to lick the hand of the person who kicked them. The only way to get an idealist off your hands is to kill him. And even then a dog may very well thank you. But just look at cats. It's not that they have nine lives. It's that they have a profound love of the one and only life they have. I'm fonder of dogs, but it's cats I admire.'

Bighead became aware of how unfortunate it is to be a dog one Saturday, when Vicki stayed with him until almost dawn, drinking maté by candlelight. It was cold. Gray flowers hung from the ceiling, cobwebs of dampness. They had only one blanket and she covered him up. Come on, cuddle up close. We can be together, but platonically, OK? He felt uncomfortable because his roly-poly body was a big round ball of affection and he didn't know how to separate one thing from the other, what corner to hide his affection in. She asked him what role Nun would play in the reorganization of cadres within the popular government, and Bighead, licking her with his cow's eyes, offered her a minutely detailed organization chart, tried to get on more intimate terms with her by way of pronouns: first it was *they* and then *you*, and finally he braided her in with a *we*, but Vicki kept her distance, logarithmically. She insisted on knowing how Nun would dissolve the structures of the movement that had already been infiltrated by Lópezreguism, enveloped the poor boa with her toad froth, gradually surrounded him with her jargon straight out of a manual on revolution, until the baobab saw the light and realized that Vicki wasn't in that sordid room to listen to him but to gather echoes of Nun from his lips, leftovers of Nun that had stuck to his lips. And even though he was outraged, even though he felt shat on and badly treated, the poor boa reproached her for nothing: he stood up, said that he was too sleepy to stay awake another minute, and as he left emphasized that his heart demanded that he stay – but I can't, Vicki, all this platonic cuddling up together only makes me suffer.

Now they are together, at the foot of the water tower and on the shores of death, as though they did not have a story in common and were losing their last chance to have one: Vicki submerged in her obsessions about order, her forehead already neatly bound in a blue and white headband declaring her credo, MONTONEROS, lining the shantytown volunteers in brigades of twelve, all arm in arm, determined – let us hold the placards aloft and march.

The ominous helicopter flies past again. From the bell tower of the church, a couple of blocks away, the wind wrests several peals. Nun orders them to hide their hardware in their backpacks and forward march, boys. His beard has grown out. At his side, Diana leaps ahead like a canoe, her eyes fresh and ardent, heaven only knows where she won't go, how many deaths will be saved from life now.

When they veer off toward the little public square of the district they discover a big old rambling house with flaking walls on the balconies of which a bunch of fearless youngsters in gray uniforms appears. Orphans, Bighead murmurs. And he remembers the moldy flowers that were falling from the ceiling as he was drinking maté with Vicki. Orphans, Diana says. Who's brought them here? The kids are waving little national flags. Some nuns are peeking out behind them, in the shelter of the shadows. All this makes me uneasy, Nun growls.

The helicopter has disappeared. The sky, however, is full of spots. Balloons, smoke, sparrows: a bit of night is passing by up there. Come on, boys, let's strike up a tune, Nun says to lift his spirits. The din in the distance calms him. Nobody can guess that the tongue of the hippopotamus will split in two when it reaches the dais. That Pepe Juárez's brigades and Vicki's will lick the right kidney, and Nun's and Diana's the liver. Bighead, in command of the squadron of shantyowners, will stay behind, in the tonsils, covering them if there is a retreat and unfurling above the expressway, in the forbidden area, an enormous placard of welcome from the guerrilla movement.

The Lord sheds his light upon us. The hour is at hand. From the railings of the dais Arcángelo Gobbi sees the face of the enemy approaching, in a slow-motion shot. And he feels invincible, historic, thirsty to be this minute what he will be tomorrow, a hero of a martyr, Perón or death. At his back, the cortege of Elect is on guard, Ithacas in hand, with a stash of sharp lengths of chain at the foot of the armored tabernacle. Overhead, like a new bird, the jubilant photo of Isabel allows the deluge of her protection to fall on Arca. She is coming closer. They are all coming. And this time it is not a dream.

17 *If Evita Had Lived*

Fate is unjust, Perón says. Eva stayed in Madrid only seven days and they showered honors on her. I have lived here for thirteen years and have been able to leave only the trace of my name on a street.

Under cover of the ashen twilight, hidden between several large chests that blocked off the windows of the Mercedes, the General has managed to vanish from the villa without being seen. What he had thought would be difficult was easy. In the dining room he found Lucas, the Moroccan gardener, and asked him: I want to go out. Do you feel like driving the car? That was all. The mass of journalists and photographers outside paid no attention to them. Who would have predicted the obvious? It was unthinkable to anyone that the General, officially ill, would risk going out of doors. Even to Lucas. Disconcerted, the gardener wanted to have López's permission for them to leave the house. But he couldn't find him anywhere.

At the intersection of the road to El Pardo and the La Coruña expressway, Lucas stopped the car so as to stow the chests away. Relieved at last of his cover device, Perón can relax as he bids Madrid farewell.

The streets smell of pious women. A greasy chill of night is falling, like wax from a candle. In the labyrinths leading to the Reservoir, a number of old people dressed in black, wearing hats, are bearing, with profound reverence, on portable platforms, several cemetery angels. The Mercedes turns into the Calle de Espronceda and heads north. The summer darkness falls torpidly, like a fly.

The General has two of the folders of Memoirs with him, lying on the seat beside him. He knows he won't even glance at them, but neither does he want to be separated from them.

Once I came back from Europe I felt the need for a revolution. I was impatient to set it off. No one was better prepared than I to take over Argentina, and yet my instinct told me that the grapes were not yet ripe and that my harvesting of them had to wait. I needed a general to take command for me. I then thought of my superior officer, Edelmiro J. Farrell, with whom I worked in the Troop Inspection Section in Montaña. He was a good man, a bit spineless, fond of the guitar and of animals. He was not particularly cultured or intelligent. He was made to measure for me. By way of a few chats I had with him over time, I brought him abreast of the responsibilities that would be placed on his shoulders, but I chose not to be really forthcoming with him, so as not to frighten him.

Into what lazy habits has his memory fallen? Not the memory of the folders, which by being turned into words has ceased to belong to him, but his own private one, the one that serves him to remember the person to whom he has sent this and promised that. That memory has gone sluggish and hard on him, like his prostate. And in the doctors' consulting rooms there is no one who knows how to resuscitate it with warm baths nor sweep out its clouds of smoke. His memory has always been faithful, but now it becomes distracted and every so often it gets lost. It would have been better to train it, to keep it on a leash. But is that possible, with such an erratic little animal? Because when a particular memory is old, then yes, it leaves deep traces in him: the General's head is a grille of moldy memories; in each square the faces are still clear. Even odors remain for years and years in the same frame. Not what has happened to him only a moment before, however; no, the memory of that flies away. Someone comes from Buenos Aires and embraces him: Thanks for what you did yesterday, General. And he doesn't know who is pressing against his body. You're welcome, son, you're welcome. He always answers the same thing, so as not to make a mistake. Immediate memories are smooth: a desert; distant ones, conversely, stick to him. Eva, for example. Eva's tour of Spain is a trip he hasn't experienced, and yet he can't rid his imagination of it. What a bother: the flour-and-water paste of someone else's memory.

I sent her here as my messenger, Lucas, twenty-five years ago. The people of Madrid haven't been able to forget her to this day. It was June, as it is now. She wore fur capes beneath a blazing sun. And even dressed like that, completely out of phase with the weather, Eva made them fall in love with her.

But I keep thinking – doesn't that glory belong to me? When I came to get her, after I'd been exiled, the Spaniards didn't want to give her to me. I waited for thirteen years. And nothing happened. I had my street: the Avenida del General Perón. It was my person that didn't exist. Franco didn't answer my letters. The ministers refused me audiences. Am I a pariah? That was what I wanted to know. But I got nowhere: deafness in the halls of government. I was gradually acquiring a new body in my country, where I no longer was, and here in this one I became ghostly. López says that by being a ghost I've lived longer. That that way, since I'm mere fog in Madrid, neither illnesses nor misfortunes have been able to catch me.

Look, Lucas: that's the street they've given me. Stumpy, gloomy, on the edge of a soccer field. So that the shouting of the fans will torment me in the next world. And so that the gassy masses, when they come out of this sheepfold, will paw my name over. Malicious things that Franco has done to me, pushing out the turds of his ingratitude and his envy. Have you seen the district of the city that he's put me in? Chamartín. A mockery of our sainted liberator and of my exiled person. Che San Martín, they call you. It's wicked. I'm the only Argentine of consequence who has resigned himself to vegetating here in this godforsaken backwater of Europe. The liberator had the good sense to go off to the Pas de Calais to die. And the last years of poverty of our estimable national leader Rosas were more bearable for him because he didn't budge from Southampton Bay. In 1940, when I passed through this far-from-capital city, they took me to Chamartín. It was nothing but brothels and swamps. Franco caught a glimpse of them and yanked out of there the skull-and-bones convents that my avenue is now crawling with, Lucas. Stop up your ears: in this heat all you can hear are the bowel rumblings of novenas. I predicted as much in my Memoirs: that we Argentines should turn the lights out in Madrid and not come back. But I came back. We all did. Even Eva, poor thing, followed in my footsteps.

War changed the nature of the human race. It made men eager and effervescent. I was one of the few who kept a cool head. In 1942, the oven wasn't yet ready to bake buns. General Justo wanted to succeed Castillo as constitutionally elected President, and in order that his ambition would not be frustrated, he put a stop to the army's attempts at conspiracy. The majority of the officers wanted Argentina to remain neutral in the war, and Justo was a rabid Alliedophile, for reasons of political convenience. The people didn't care one way or the other which side won.

In the first months of autumn 1942 the horizon was dark. The army had been discredited. There were irregularities in the Directorate of Military Supply. An indictment was brought that had scandalous repercussions. And then there was the episode of the homosexual cadets. I felt the need to join a lodge of colonels capable of stanching the moral wound. We should prepare ourselves. The country required a leader with an iron hand, who would force landowners with large holdings to reinvest their profits in industry. We were eager for peace, and if we wanted to keep it, we had to be ready for war. The next president could only be a military officer. The boys insisted that I should be the one. But what ambitions could a person have in a country where two sharks with Pantagruelian appetites were fighting over the school of fish? Providence, as usual, sent me signs: at the end of March 1942, the first of the two, Don Marcelo de Alvear died; on 11 January 1943, the other, General Agustín P. Justo, suffered a sudden fatal hemorrhage. Almost immediately, President Castillo stuck out his paws to push the candidacy of Robustiano Patrón Costas, a feudal hoodlum for hire, from Salta, whose language stank like an English backside. Ah, I said to myself, I'm not going to let this one get one step farther. And then I called the boys who had been looking for me. Do you want a revolution? I asked them. Well then, the moment has come. Let's contact the officers, and we'll throw anyone who gets out of line or plays the fool out the window, OK? That's how it all began.

At the end of February, we began to hold secret meetings at my place. By March we were organized and could count on a strict code of discipline that consecrated us as apostles of a new military doctrine, strongly opposed to traditional politicians and to Communism. There were nineteen of us, and among ourselves we called each other the brothers of the GOU. It is common knowledge that both many different meanings and many different intentions were attributed to those initials. I for my part am quite satisfied with GOU: it is a forceful onomatopoeia, like the 'eia, eia, alalà' of the Alpine troops.

I went ahead without notifying Farrell of our plans. I kept him as a figure in reserve. The one who committed himself to our cause was the Minister of War, General Pedro Pablo Ramírez, whom we called 'Palito' – Stick Man – both because he was as skinny as a bean pole and because he downed whiskey till he was stiff as a stick. In the preludes to the revolution, Ramírez put our men in posts where they were in command and freed them from administrative tasks.

We intended to put off staging our coup until September, but before Patrón Costas won the presidency through election fraud. An alternative that would save the situation and avoid bloodshed then occurred to me. If Ramírez were the army's candidate, he should be summoned and told straight out to present his ticket and his platform too. When they got wind of the idea, the radicals, who were nosing about like a dog on a bowling green, grabbed me by the coattails and told me that if Ramírez was the man, they'd support him. We had several meetings. The Minister of War dodged the issue. He didn't know what to do. He knocked back all the whiskey I had in the house, but went on flirting around with us like a pretty girl.

The one who decided matters (unintentionally) was Castillo. Somebody went to him with the story that Ramírez was throwing a wrench in the plans to keep Patrón Costas from winning, and the President flew into a rage. He asked Ramírez for his resignation. We sensed the danger and forbade Ramírez to sign anything. 'Well,' Palito said. 'I'm not going to take a stand against all of you, but neither am I going to take one in your favor. Go find yourselves another general.' One of our boys, inexperienced and ambitious, made a deal with the commander of the cavalry, Arturo Rawson. Rawson wasn't to my liking, and if I let him move ahead, I told myself it wouldn't be for long.

On 4 June, as day dawned it was drizzling. I got up feeling dead tired, because all the day before I had had to go about getting officers who hadn't yet decided one way or the other whether or not to join the coup. The best part of all was that this time civilians didn't stick their noses in. We had the moral support of philosophers such as Nimio de Anquín and Jordán Bruno Genta, but that was all. It was a movement that hadn't compromised itself: the Nation under Arms.

At about five a.m. I went to the Círculo Militar and got Farrell out of bed. 'You can't miss out on this revolution,' I said to him. 'What revolution?' The poor man didn't have a clue. 'Yours, General. Ah,' he said in surprise. 'In that case I'll get dressed right away.'

The march began at seven, beginning at the intersection of San Martín and General Paz. We marched without incident as far as the Navy School of Mechanics. There they opened fire on us and we answered with artillery and mortar fire. The head of the guard and several enlisted men were hit. The opposition immediately surrendered.

When he saw what an easy victory it had been, Rawson donned his musketeer's cape and placed himself at the head of the troops. By six p.m., he was comfortably installed in the President's seat and the office was ours. That night he double-crossed us. He went out to dinner with two civilians and offered them cabinet posts.

The revolution was the work of the colonels, and since I had been the one at the forefront my comrades had every reason to come to me and ask: 'Hey, what are we going to do with Rawson now? Let's see if you can come up with an idea.' I calmed them down. 'This can easily be settled, boys. I'm going to go to his office and ask him for his resignation. If he refuses to give it to me, I'll throw him out the window.'

And it was as easy as I'd said. Several colonels, six or seven of us I think, entered Government House with .45s under our capes. We found Rawson in the President's office, doodling. 'You're leaving here this minute,' I said to him. Rawson tried to put us off, seeking to protect himself through his friendship with General Ramírez. 'Let me think it over till morning, boys. That suits you and it suits me.' I stood firm: 'It doesn't suit us one damned bit! This presidential seat is ours, and we will see to who's going to sit in it. In any case, it's not going to be you.' He then gave in. 'And what do I do now? Where do I go?' It occurred to me that the best thing to do would be to send him off somewhere as ambassador. 'What country suits you?' I asked him. 'The closest possible one,' he answered. 'Start packing, because next week you'll be leaving for Brazil,' I promised him.

The boys insisted that I should stay on as President. But I wasn't stupid. I made them sit through a history lesson: 'Every revolution devours its children. And I'm too raw. I don't want the revolution to get indigestion. Let's hunt up Palito Ramírez.' I had him brought to Government House and put the presidential sash on him. 'We'll accompany you tomorrow when you go to take the oath of office,' I told him. 'On what conditions?' he wanted to know. I answered that he could appoint only one civilian as a minister and that he must give Farrell the portfolio of Minister of War. He accepted then and there.

I had to face a few attacks by sly enemies, jealous of the influence that the GOU was acquiring within the Government. They tried to get me out a couple of times, but didn't succeed. On the contrary, the GOU's patriotic ideas were winning new disciples each day among the young officers. In September, 1943, fed up with intrigues, I asked Ramírez to appoint me head of the Labor Department.

'What are you saying, Perón!' he exclaimed in surprise. 'That's not a post for a man of your stature.' At that time the department was insignificant, and fulfilled bureaucratic functions almost exclusively, directing timid demands from the labor unions toward the Government's ever-deaf ears.

'You're mistaken, General,' I said to him. 'From there I can make the Communist agitators toe the line and create a broader base for the revolution.'

When I arrived at the department, I ran into a drove of odd-job government clerks who weren't even familiar with the labor laws. I put them to work getting the files in order and dusting off the folders. And I brought with me a state planner worth his weight in gold: the Catalan José Figuerola. He was an expert who had made in-depth studies of corporate organizations in Italy and was now undergoing a baptism of fire in revolutionary governments such as that of General Primo de Rivera in Spain. 'Go to it, Figuerola,' I said to him. 'Analyze the plans for the economy and for labor of previous governments and put before me the reforms that are needed.' After a week he came to me, flabbergasted. 'There aren't any plans!' he exclaimed. 'What do you mean there aren't any plans? The one plan that existed in this country was Alberdi's *Bases* and it's now useless,' he said.

It was another sign from Providence. I had started a revolution, but in an amorphous country without an identity, with too many paths and no goal. Fourteen million Argentines were drifting along from one day to the next. I then said to myself: I shall give a destiny to this land without a destiny. I myself. Is it made of cartilage? Then I shall give it my bones. I shall be its workings of chance, its necessity, its prophecy.

*   *   *

Why do these lapses of memory happen after many long years, Lucas? Stop the car. Look at those sordid balconies, draped in mourning. And those grilles on the left. Everything clothed in darkness, in perpetual death throes. That is what Madrid has been for me, Lucas. A monastic little censer-capital. God has delivered me from dampness, but at the same time he has slowly been suffocating me in the smoke of age. I have had too many droughts. My prostate has dried up, I suffer from ice-cold feet and a head that's stifling hot. I have cramps in the joints of my fingers. And not one of Franco's petty bureaucrats has shown any interest in my health. They spent on Eva all the light they owed to me. Do you know what that was like, Lucas?

The gardener shakes his curls. No, sir. And keeps his olive-colored eyes riveted on the statue of Cybele.

Well, with Eva it was the opposite, Lucas. I gave her memory training. When she came to Madrid, in 1947, she found this gloomy Calle de José Antonio all gaily decorated. Thunderous applause and carnations rained down from the balconies. It was almost ten at night, the same hour as now. Dead Spain came back to life. They hid the pious ladies. They turned on the fire hydrants in the general frolicking in the public squares. When Eva passed beneath the arch of Alcalá, the mayor caught up with her and set her aglow with flowers. She received two decorations that night, not to mention the keys to the city, honors from the Moorish guard and hand kissing from the crowd of people who prostrated themselves to offer their thanks to her: to her, for the favors that I, the one who wasn't there, had authorized. The festivities were so extravagant that, before retiring to her apartments fit for a princess, in El Pardo, Eva thought it best to speak on the radio. She avowed that she was overwhelmed, intoxicated with happiness. A bit abruptly, she mentioned me at the end. 'I am merely the messenger,' she said. The next day she telephoned me to apologize. 'I don't deserve you,' she kept saying. 'I don't deserve you.' I didn't attribute any importance to it at the time. But now it weighs heavily on me. Why is Eva disturbing today this farewell that is mine alone? Everything is making my head spin now. I don't know if I'm going or coming. If she is the one who is going away from me and I'm the one who's staying behind with her.

I met her amid the mad chaos of the earthquake in San Juan. The catastrophe happened on Saturday, 15 January 1944. The following day I mobilized the entire country to lend its aid to the devastated city. By that time my office had become a powerful ministry. I was the Secretary of Labor and Social Security.

I sent planes and trains to help, chartered trucks to bring in food supplies and tents, organized charity committees that went all over the country to raise funds. It was a terrible disaster. Eight thousand people were dead amid the ruins.

Various performers offered their help from the start. Many of them just to make an impression. Others, wanting sincerely to help, stayed on to work. Eva was the most fervent of them. On the Saturday following the earthquake, a benefit performance to aid the victims was held in Luna Park. Someone seated her alongside me. She fixed her deep brown eyes on me, and said to me, in a soft, sweet voice: 'Colonel . . .'

'What is it, young lady?'

'Thanks for existing.'

Thanks for existing. That phrase threw my soul into confusion. I wanted to go on talking with her, but the commotion of the moment did not permit it. I looked at her for the first time, intently. On stage, Libertad Lamarque was singing 'Madreselva'. Eva was pale and nervous. She was always on the alert, on edge. I was struck by her delicate, tapering hands. Her feet were the same, like filigree. She had long hair and feverish eyes. She didn't have a good figure: she was one of those typical Argentine girls, thin, with skinny legs and thick ankles. Her physical features were not what attracted me. It was her kindness.

I asked her where she worked.

'At Yankelevich's station. Radio Belgrano. I'm in a troupe of second-rank actors there.'

She always denigrated herself with that one little phrase: 'I'm not an artist. I'm a second-rank actress.' But the truth is that she was fulfilling a noble educational mission. On her program they acted out the lives of famous women such as Lola Montes and Madama Lynch, and Eva played their parts with deep conviction, as if she foresaw that in real life she would outdo them all.

The following week I dropped in at the radio station. I called the magazines and asked them to take some photos of us together. Yankelevich, a Russian, didn't treat her well, and I wanted to give him to understand that, if he got out of line, he would have me to deal with.

Evita proved to be most grateful. She came to see me at the Department of Labor, so as to go on lending a helping hand to the victims of San Juan. I gave her carte blanche. She then took an ambulance plane, went all through the ruined city, and came back with a list of needs to be taken care of immediately.

She was so intelligent and sensitive that I couldn't get her out of my mind. The power of a waterfall radiated from her. Even among the men who backed me there was no one to equal her. I said to myself: 'I must work uncut stone, turn it into a pure diamond.'

And that's what happened. Eva Perón is a product of mine. She had an enormous heart and a noble imagination. When a man knows how to cultivate those qualities, the woman learns to serve him better than the most sophisticated of tools. It is also necessary, of course, to give her a bit of polish, and with Eva it wasn't easy. She rejected everything that smelled of varnish.

When we became friends, I asked her:

'Why don't you come to the Department of Labor and help us a little?'

She accepted immediately, working without pay and laying down no conditions. I gave her a small office and appointed her secretary of women's affairs. Although we soon began to be on intimate terms, we both agreed that what was political and social must come first. And when there was time left over, all the rest. For Eva, her new mission was a matter of life or death. She didn't dress up often. Only when we had a party with poor people: then yes, she would spend hours in front of the mirror and deck herself out in her fanciest outfits. 'I want to show that a woman of the people also has a right to dress in luxury,' she would explain. She didn't make herself look glamorous out of vanity. She did it to make others feel proud.

I was interested in clearing the Communists out of the trade union movement. The Communists infected all of it. And Eva turned out to be an invaluable collaborator. On one occasion a bank employee who proclaimed himself a Socialist introduced himself to us. It was a cover. The minute he opened his mouth the hammer and sickle gleamed in his teeth. It fell to Eva to deal with him. The man saw her as weak and it aroused his ardor; she tossed him out of her office by whacking him with her handbag. I came out of my office in alarm. I had never heard a rosary of swear words of such caliber. When she wanted to, Eva had a honeyed tongue. But anyone who provoked her had to be careful. When that nest was stirred up, wasps with very venomous stings poured out.

She was a special woman. With no other one could so much have been accomplished. With her I practiced in depth the art of leadership. Sometimes I became disheartened, because her indomitable will left no room for restraint or good sense. If Evita had been alive on 16 June 1955, when the first reactionary sedition took place, she would have been merciless. For her the only fate a rebel deserved was the firing squad. She was always like that, a sectarian Peronist; incapable of giving in to anything that was not Peronist. I for my part had great difficulty calming her down. In politics, sectarianism is negative. It lessens people's sympathies. This didn't matter to Eva. She was who she was, and for all she cared the world could come tumbling down.

Shortly after we met, there was no longer any reason to put up a false front. We began living together. Ramírez had been a failure, and I had to replace him with Farrell. Since the army had little confidence in their new commanding general's genius, it obliged me to accept the Vice-Presidency of the Republic and the Ministry of War. I was more interested in the Department of Labor and remained head of it as well.

Soon envy sank its claws in us. Men in the military are frightened when they see a woman running around loose. They want females to be tied down and have a broken leg. Eva wasn't that sort of woman. They came to me with the most idiotic arguments. That a military officer who weighed as many carats as I did couldn't get involved with a chorus girl. And they stuffed my head full of filthy gossip. I had to stop them dead. One day I got them all together at the ministry and said to them: 'I'm not a hypocrite. I've always liked women and I always will. I don't see anything immoral about that. But if I liked men, that would be immoral!'

Fate is unjust, Perón says. I was the one who made her, but she is the one who kept the best part of my glory for herself. Misfortunes of a man who doesn't die young, Lucas. In people's memory, Eva will always be outward bound. They will remember her for what she was capable of doing, not for what she did. Look at me though. I'm homeward bound. The time that's going by is time that's losing me. Get me out of here. Take me to the Palacio de Oriente. They received Eva there as though she were a queen. I on the other hand have never been able to get inside.

I don't know if I really fell in love. In my day, men didn't stoop to saying 'I love you.' Intimacies came about or they didn't, with no need for cloying sweet talk. I only know that when a woman loves us a great deal, the way Eva loved me, there is no way to resist.

In the chaotic weeks following the San Juan earthquake I was living in a three-room apartment, opposite the Palermo beer garden. My job responsibilities kept me out until midnight. And always, when I came home, Eva was standing outside, leaning on the door jamb, waiting for me. What could I say? I would invite her in, we would drink a vermouth together and sit there talking.

Little by little she started putting woman's face cream in the bathroom. One night she brought a toothbrush, and the next she filled the bathroom cabinet with La Sancy cosmetics. After a week I had to turn a closet over to her to give her a place to hang up the silk negligees, the cotton frocks and those tailored suits that actresses wore in those days.

For a couple of years a young girl from Mendoza had been looking after my clothes and making my meals. Piraña? Yes, I suppose I was the one who gave her that nickname, to tease her about her big teeth that spoiled her looks. But that I had a love affair with her, no. That's a lie. How could I have had one, if she was my goddaughter? Her father, a penniless cowhand from Uspallata, placed her in my care when the poor thing was so little she was still wetting the bed. Within limits, I'm a man of strong instincts, I grant you. But degeneracy doesn't suit my temperament. It's true that Piraña sometimes went with me to Luna Park. We greatly enjoyed watching fights by Lovell, the black boxer. People saw that we were happy together and that was enough to cause the worst sort of gossip to make the rounds. It didn't bother me in the least. I was beyond good and evil. And she, Piraña, didn't realize. What apprehensions could a little kid from the backlands with only two years of schooling have? And yet those malicious stories sneaked into history books. We go through life without being aware of the weight of the little things we do, and forget them. But suddenly it's the future and there all those things are, lined up in a row, belonging to us again.

One afternoon when I came back from the Ministry Piraña was nowhere to be found. I went to her little cubbyhole, and didn't even see her bed. Her clothes, her dolls, the Columbine costume I'd given her: all of that was gone.

'I packed her off to Mendoza,' Eva said to me. 'One woman is enough, more than enough, to take care of one man.'

Whether for good or ill, Eva was stubborn, fierce. When she got an idea into her head, she would vent her feelings with no thought of the consequences. That may be why many men were afraid of her. I wasn't, because with me she kept her rage to herself.

In her scrawny, ivory-colored body, there was more inflammable phosphorus than flesh. A man who didn't know how to handle her got burned.

The Plaza de Oriente has seldom been darker than on that summer evening. The waning moon goes dim behind the storm clouds. Bad weather has always been a bad omen in the General's life. It was raining when Lonardi swore to take his revenge on him. And on the morning when he was overthrown a deluge fell. What was it like? 'The sky of Buenos Aires, low and overcast, pressed down on the roofs of the houses. There wasn't a single sign of life anywhere about' (as is true in Madrid right now) . . .

'Shall we go back?' Lucas, the Moroccan, asks, drowsing at the wheel of the Mercedes.

'Just take it easy, my boy. Let me wander about.'

Over there are the arches of the Palacio Real, in the idleness of the night. Eva once described to him the gleaming stairway decorated with lions and castles, where she had herself photographed with Franco's ministers. She marveled at the marbles, the stones from Colmenar, and Venetian glass. She walked about as though in a dream through thirty salons of the palace, having her guides tell her over and over the stories of Trajan, Hercules and the Good Angel depicted in the Gobelin tapestries. Then, in the West Gallery, she turned to Doña Carmen Polo, the Caudillo's wife, and asked her out of the blue:

'Tell me, how many war orphans are there in Spain still?'

'Two hundred thousand, I'd say. Perhaps a few more.'

'And why, with as many empty rooms as you have here, don't you offer them a decent home?'

Doña Carmen was struck speechless.

'Don't wait any longer, you two. Transform this into a vacation camp. If not, what's the use of our being heads of state?'

When Eva came to Spain – was the General told about it or did he see it at the movies, twenty-five years ago? – there was a feverishly excited crowd in that plaza that is now so deeply shrouded in darkness, so deserted. Filled with emotion, Franco, in dress uniform, offered her his arm to help her out of a gilded carriage. In the throne room he decorated her with the Grand Cross of Queen Isabella. The weather was muggy, as hot as lava. With majestic self-possession, Eva sweated buckets without blinking an eye, beneath a sable coat and a hat with ostrich feathers. After the speeches, she took off the coat and came out onto the balcony. A hurricane of applause swept over the plaza. The men knelt. The children from the orphan asylums waved little flags. Remembering the theater, Eva greeted the multitude with a bow and lowered head. Hysterical cheers were heard. A number of peasant women dressed in black burst into tears. 'I have never seen such enthusiasm,' Franco said in her ear. Eva paid no attention to him. 'Thank you!' she shouted into the microphone. 'Thank you, my people of Madrid . . .' She drew herself up, stiff as a rod, and saluted with her right arm held high, Falangist style. Then she disappeared from the balcony.

It was more than two months before she returned to Buenos Aires. Her triumphant image appeared on the cover of *Time* on 14 July 1947, and the next day the Argentine dailies joyously proclaimed their good news: 'It is not just because of her. It is also because of him.'

'It's because of me,' the General admitted. Now, amid the somber statues in the Plaza de Oriente, he knows that it was because of her, not because of him. And the chill of jealousy bites into his soul.

One Sunday morning in the middle of the tour, Eva telephoned him from Lisbon and told him between sobs that she needed him, that she missed him, that happiness, without him, had no meaning. After he'd hung up the phone, the General sat there thinking, and finally decided to see what the issue of *Time* had to say. He read the translation that an amanuensis had prepared for him.

Last week, on the broad imperial Avenida Alvear in Buenos Aires, municipal workers were erecting an enormous platform. 'And what is that for?' a journalist asked 'To celebrate Independence Day or perhaps for the visit of the president of Chile?'

'It's to welcome the señora,' one of the workers answered. 'Her tour has impressed the entire world. In Europe no one talks of anything but her. A miracle, isn't that so?' Yes, it's a miracle.

*   *   *

We can't fête her less than foreigners have, the General decided. We'll offer her a welcome of mythic proportions. And he said to the ministers: My wife's glory belongs to all of us. She is Argentina.

Even though it was winter, Buenos Aires prepared to receive Evita with a rain of flowers. When the boat of the river steamship line that was bringing her from Montevideo docked, all the other vessels set off their sirens. Around three in the afternoon, the General spied her among the wisps of mist. She was on the deck of the steamship, decked with jewels, imposing.

She waved her handkerchief at him, as in the movies, and blew him a kiss. He leapt impatiently onto the pier before the crew had finished lowering the gangplank. The crowd immediately swallowed her up. She felt that she was being tugged bodily back and forth. The General, who had failed to meet up with her, was nowhere in sight. What's become of you, Perón? she asked, in tears. Finally she spotted him. Feeling dizzy, she fell into his arms. The photographers raced to capture the image of the immortal queen who had suddenly turned into a defenseless adolescent.

I am nobody without you, Perón, Evita said to him when night fell and they were alone at last in the official residence on the Calle Austria. Wherever I go, without you I am incomplete.

The General had sat down a good way away from her. He was ill at ease, tense. He was wearing the waistband of his trousers higher up than usual. Seeing his wife walking about the house again, talking without stopping, disconcerted him. She was different, everybody said so: she had come back metamorphosed into a goddess. Chain-smoking, the General put off the moment of going to bed.

'You must rest now, Eva,' he said. 'Having your routine so badly upset is going to kill you.'

'How can I rest if I'm the only one who can help you?'

Overwhelmed by the fury of that insatiable love, the General did not know what to do with himself to calm Evita down.

Has something come between us, Perón? Have I hurt you in some way? What harm could I have done you, if we were never apart for a single moment? Come on, don't hold back. What's making you feel bad, tell me? What I was once? I no longer deserve your mistrust. I'm yours. You've made me. I'm yours.

It was true. I made her. I redeemed her. Evita had suffered a great deal because of the misfortunes that had overtaken her family. When she was a baby, just a year old, the father, a rancher named Juan Duarte, abandoned his five children and went to live in Chivilcoy with another woman. Before Eva began school, her father was killed in a car accident. The fatherless children turned up at his wake. They were received with contempt. That terrible snub left its mark on Eva. I'm a waif, she used to say to me, a poor little waif from the country. Whenever she remembered those days she was racked with heartbreaking sobs. She had nightmares and woke up in a cold sweat. I calmed her down: don't talk about that any more now. Bury your past forever. Yes, yes, she would promise me. But at one moment or another, as she was putting on a tailored suit or opening a drawer, those bad memories would come looking for her again.

Eva finished sixth grade in 1934, when she was fifteen. Doña Juana, an enterprising woman, had turned part of their home in Junín into an eating-house so as to support the family. The older daughters one by one married respectable attorneys and army officers who dined there. Eva, however, had no desire to live a humdrum life. She wanted to be an actress. She once told me that next to the house in Junín she invented a circus beneath some tall paradise trees. She leapt from branch to branch as though they were trapezes and recited film dialogue for her brother and sisters. Her favorite actress was Norma Shearer. She saw her more than ten times in *Marie Antoinette*, and invariably left the movie theater in tears.

She was so bent on becoming an artist that finally there was nothing her mother could do but take her to a radio station in Buenos Aires. At the station they had her recite poetry, as a tryout. Eva moved everyone with verses by Amado Nervo that, after we were married, she used to recite over and over at night, as she was taking a bath. 'Where do the dead go, Lord, where do they go.'

But that was only the beginning. She went through some very hard years. There was no lack of riffraff who tried to take advantage of her lack of experience and her innocence. Eva found clever ways to evade them and drove her hurts into her memory like nails, so as to get her own back for them some day. Unlike me, she harbored grudges; she was one of those women who never forgive.

The first night she stayed over at my place, she looked at me intently with her big brown eyes.

'They're going to tell you very nasty things about me,' she said. 'Nothing they'll say is true. Everything they tell you about me will be a despicable lie.'

'It doesn't matter in the least to me, Chinita. Not in the least,' I calmed her.

In the beginning she had fits of melancholy. She would curl up against my chest, weeping, and beg my forgiveness.

'I'm going to go on loving you even after I die,' she used to say to me. 'Everything that's mine, even what was bad, belongs to you.' She would smile sadly then and envelop me once again in the sweetness of her most unforgettable phrase: 'Thanks for existing, Colonel.'

*   *   *

Now, with his back to the old Teatro Real, next to the statue of Philip IV astride a rearing horse, Perón sees her again as she was when they woke up together that first time: her dark curly hair; her translucent hands, traversed by undulating veins. In those days Evita didn't like her body. I have, she used to say, a disobedient body: my nerves are rebellious; they raise terrible rumpuses underneath my skin. Don't look at me in the morning, Perón. When I don't have makeup on, you can see the dark circles under my eyes. I'm prettier on the inside. And happier. It isn't fair for just one woman to be so happy.

One night, when they had moved to adjoining apartments in the Calle Posadas, she whispered in the General's ear what would later be proclaimed to the four winds, in public squares and over the radio: 'There was a time when I didn't know how to see misfortune, adversity, poverty. The blinder I was, the more injustice surrounded me. At last you came into my life, Perón, and opened my eyes. From that day on I have loved you so much I can't tell you. I feel you here at my side, my fairytale prince, and think I'm dreaming. And since I have nothing to offer you except my soul, I give all of it to you. To belong to you is a grace of God.'

She so badly wanted to deny her past that before the General said 'I made her', she said 'Perón made me.' It wasn't true. Everyone is, at each instant, a different person. But how could they be different persons if, deep down, they didn't go on being the same one? Eva was already Eva when Perón met her.

At the time she was living in the Calle Carlos Pellegrini, a few yards from the Avenida del Libertador. In the mornings, when she left for the radio station, on the stairs of the Pasaje Seaver she often used to run into a bunch of monstrous children, runaways from institutions. She would stroke their matted locks and look at them sadly.

She once said to them: 'Don't you have a home? What do you eat?' And discovered that they were all mutes. That day she was to play the role of Lola Montes. She did so distractedly, without conviction. A nervous cough cut off her voice in the middle of a love scene. She left the radio station almost at a run, in search of her friend Pierina Dealessi.

'I want to rent a room for those poor children,' she said to her. 'To pay for their food. The neglect they experience makes it impossible for me to sleep with a clear conscience.'

Pierina knew of a boarding house in the Bajo district, where musicians from the provinces holed up. She was sure that the owner would care for the orphans for a modest sum. Evita closed the deal that very afternoon.

When Pierina arrived at the Pasaje Seaver with her friend and saw the freaks of nature picking nits out of each other's hair, she couldn't keep from feeling sick to her stomach. They weren't children but wizened albino dwarfs, dressed in burlap sacks and covered with scabies.

She tried to dissuade Eva. She argued that her protégés would be less happy in the boarding house than if they were left to the savagery of the elements. It was useless. With the unyielding stubbornness of a Samaritan, Eva spent nearly half her pay on anti-scabies medications, mattresses and dwarf-size clothes, and a morning never went by without her visiting them in their new home. She treated their blisters, she kept an eye on their weight, she taught them to eat with a spoon, and to shout. That especially: to shout. She never lost hope that their voices would come bursting forth at any moment. She went out onto the balconies with them and ordered: 'Shout, kids! Come on: shout so Evita can hear you. A-e-i-o-u! A-a-a-a-a!' The mutes strained their throats, tensed their necks, turned red in the face, but nothing came out. They had been born without vocal cords.

She was so proud of the slight progress her freaks made that as soon as she met the General, Eva took him to the attic in the boarding house so he could see them. It was a disaster. When they opened the door, they found them naked from the waist down, amid the snow-white, newly starched bedspreads, dirtying the walls with scrawls of fresh shit.

The General retched violently.

'With so many orphans without a family, Evita, why do you waste your time with ones that can't be cured?'

An army truck picked the mutes up that night to take them to an asylum in Tandil. The NCO who was taking them got distracted at a truck stop in Las Flores where he stopped for a pizza. It was there perhaps that they disappeared. The cornstalks in the fields were tall, and though several brigades tried their best to find them, the monsters were lost forever.

Eva was impossible. She went at everything hell bent for leather. Once she began to work at the Social Aid Foundation she slipped from my grasp. We would meet every once in a while, for a very short time, as though we lived in different cities. She liked working at night. She would come back home as dawn was breaking. As a long-time military man, I had habits that were precisely the opposite: I left for Government House at six in the morning. Sometimes our paths crossed at the door of the residence. She always boasted of how dead tired she was.

Among the many deeds she is known for there are two that still move me. One is like a tango. It happened in winter. It was raining for a change in Buenos Aires. It was dawn. After having worked all night, displeased with what she had accomplished, Evita was being driven down the deserted streets, on her way home. At the doors of the Güemes Gallery she saw a haggard woman, barely sheltered from the downpour, with three little girls clinging to her skirt. Eva had her chauffeur stop the car along the curb and stuck her head out the window: 'Where would you like me to take you, señora?'

Because of the darkness or the fog, the woman didn't recognize who it was talking to her. She carried the children to the car, got in and sat down next to the driver. With her head drooping she unburdened herself there and then of the story of her misfortunes. Her husband was in jail, the few belongings of any value that she had left had fallen into the talons of her creditors, and only one hope sustained her: seeing the Señora and awaiting her compassion. She sobbed into a filthy handkerchief. The little ones coughed. Even Evaristo Carriego couldn't have thought up a more pathetic scene.

Then the miracle happened. Eva tapped the chauffeur's shoulder, and with her face lit up by a sudden burst of energy, she ordered: 'Let's go back to the Foundation. I must take care of this.'

The woman heard that unmistakable voice, and dropped her handkerchief, speechless and spellbound: 'Dear God!' she exclaimed, hugging her little girls.

She was given, there and then, a job as a monitor in a school for orphans, enabling her to save enough money to buy a little house.

The other story also happened as dawn was breaking. For months Eva had been sleeping only a few hours a night. When her assistants insisted that she rest, she was offended and sent them packing. The endless line of humble people at the doors of her office kept her wide awake all night long. It was as if time, as it passed, set her aflame. Around four in the morning there crept into her office a woman straight out of a nightmare: her head was joined to a prehistoric, sawtoothed hump, and as though that were not enough, she had little parasitic arms hanging down from her armpits, short stumps ending in curled-up fingers. Eva, who was always so poised, was upset by that infernal monster. One of her aides heard her murmur: 'It's them . . . The ones who are coming back . . .'

She hesitated. The thought no doubt went through her mind: who could love such a freak of nature, who could possibly bear its presence? And feeling that such a thing was beyond even her powers, she yanked off a magnificent pair of diamond earrings.

'Here. Begin a new life,' she said as she gave them to her.

That may be why they loved her so.

To allow her to distract herself a little I sent her to Europe. That was the origin of her famous tour. I wanted to save her from the exhaustion that was bringing her close to collapse. The invitation of the Spanish government was extended to me, not to her. Soon Italy too wanted me to come on a visit. Both countries were greatly in my debt. Toward the end of World War II, the Allies resolved to isolate Spain, and there was only one ambassador left there: mine. I saved the Italians from famine in 1947 by sending them half a million tons of grain as a gift. Why wouldn't they have begged me to come? But it wasn't possible. Important domestic problems required my presence in Buenos Aires. Then the thought came to me: if I send Eva, I'll kill two birds with one stone. I'll satisfy the countries that want to honor me, and I'll make her take the vacation that she needs so badly. And that was what happened. Eva was a most capable woman and represented me to perfection. From Rome, it seems to me – or perhaps it was from Lisbon? – she sent me a moving letter thanking me. Her life was spent thanking me.

'Let's go now, Lucas,' the General murmurs, suddenly downcast. 'I don't want them to miss us at the house.'

Anxious to avoid the traffic in the Plaza de España, Lucas inadvertently heads the Mercedes into the pitch-black darkness of the Rosaleda. It is midnight and Madrid smells, as usual, of fried food. In the distance a torchlight procession is moving slowly along. Gentlemen wearing ruffs and black garments are strolling amid the trees, flanked by a guard of halberdiers. Once again the city has allowed itself to fall into the past, and if it were not for the fact that the poplars are gleaming with all their greenness intact, if vague live heads did not appear at the windows, the General would feel that Madrid, this last refuge of his old age, was disappearing in the maelstrom of time; that Madrid was retreating to the hollows of history, carrying him on its back. I am this city, Perón says. Suddenly vultures of cold swoop down on him. He clasps the folders of Memoirs to his chest, and, with great difficulty, bundles himself up.

That next to last night before his departure, the General dreams once again of the expedition to the Pole. He is ill at ease as he ventures forth in his dream, because thanks to the anchor of good sense that keeps him yoked to reality – always, even when he sleeps – he knows that claiming the center of the expanses of ice as a conquest is a meaningless feat now. Other Argentine infantrymen have done the same thing for him before, in the summer of 1965. They made their way – he has read – across plateaus bristling with towers and caverns, hearing at each step the lamentations of their dead forebears. At the entrance to the Pole they saw no volcanoes, only illusions of nature: burning-hot white flies buzzing over a blinding pampas.

Even so, the General dashes, in his sleep, across Weddell Sea, coughing. And walks on and on. Once again, his body floats on the rigid foam of the narrow gorges and is rent by stalactites. Finally, sticky with blood and amniotic dribbles of saliva, he makes out in the distance the volcano of the Pole: the sign that nobody but he knows. His instruments suddenly rise up in rebellion. Compass and theodolites show him that there is no volcano there, but rather, an immense erect vagina looming up. At the summit, his mother is on guard duty, with her braids undone and a man's poncho on her ceremonial staff. But who is that at her side? It is

López, wearing the dress trimmed in grosgrain and lace that Granny Dominga used to don for evenings at the opera. López shields himself behind Perón's mother and warns him off:

'Go back, Perón, go back to Weddell Sea! You can't come in here!'

And as he tries to protest, panting for breath: 'Just for a moment, please, Mama . . .' the grandmother-secretary drives him away with psalms from hell, *Pe pe orupandé/Oxum maré coroo Ogum te*, scatters his bones throughout the confines of those frozen penances, *salve Shangó/salve Oshalá*.

Sweating, the General opens his eyes. It is already daylight. From the foot of the bed López, in a kimono and thong sandals, hands him a glass of water and a couple of aspirins. For once he has sensed the General's desires before the fact: he is rescuing him from the iron bandages that are squeezing his head. He now helps him out of bed. He tests the temperature of the water in the bathtub: lukewarm. And then, from the other side of the curtains, he hands him a big bath towel.

'What would become of me without you, López,' the General thanks him.

'And without the señora, who watches over the two of us.'

'That's right. What would become of us without Chabela.'

Once he finished his breakfast – nothing but strong coffee and a water biscuit – the General feels much better, eager to get to work. The memories of what he is about to read play across his face: a past that has gone before he could enjoy it, like that of children, woven of the ephemeral threads of what I will do tomorrow, I will be tomorrow.

'We'll be leaving here without having corrected even half the Memoirs, López, do you realize that?' he says, breathing heavily as he slowly climbs the stairs to the cloister. 'That makes me feel uneasy . . . How will we go about things then, in Buenos Aires, so as to have one or two hours by ourselves?'

'You put your soul into them, General, and I'll put my body. You'll see. There'll be time for everything.'

Upstairs, on the prie-dieus, López has laid out copies of the 'Projects for the Nation' that the General wrote in draft from thirty years before: in one of them are the reforms of the Labor Laws and the lists of Suitable Individuals chosen to carry them out; in another, the maps with the Changes in Nomenclature, and the Almanac of New National Anniversaries; hanging on the wall, the Chart of Deadlines and Goals; and on the little table, among the photographs of Eva, the scrolls of Mnemonic Exercises for classroom use. Now, at the sight of the herbariums that have turned to dust before he could use them, the General is moved:

'Handle those mementos very carefully, López. On the outside, they've been reduced to ashes but on the inside they are alive. Anything a person leaves unfinished is to be feared. It bites. It's best to leave sleeping dogs lie. Open that folder instead. What do you find in it? Is it damp? Perhaps the night air creeps up even to the top floors of the house . . . Read it to me, what does it tell us?'

In Argentina all men are what they are but very seldom are they what they appear to be. Our country cannot be known through visible powers but only through the wellsprings – invariably underground and hidden – that feed those powers. In 1943, the revolution that overthrew Castillo was embodied in a lodge, the GOU. And the GOU was the army. Of the three thousand officers who made up the institution, only an extremely small group of Alliedophiles wanted us to mortgage the country's destiny by going to war. The rest of us were neutralists. We felt united by a blood pact. On drafting the basic regulations of the GOU it was decided that each officer, on joining our ranks, was to sign an unconditional and undated request to resign as insurance against his conduct and his honor. I kept these resignations in my office at the War Ministry, where I was

Under-Secretary and where they would be at the disposal of Farrell, the Minister, and of the President of the Republic. It is common knowledge that the master of paradise is not God but the one who has the keys to it: Saint Peter. At that time, I was the Saint Peter of the army.

In October of 1943, when the revolution still lacked deep roots, the Treasury Minister Jorge Santamarina, made several imprudent public statements that checkmated neutrality. I telephoned President Ramírez in indignation and warned him that if he didn't boot Santamarina out in a hurry, the army would do so with no qualms. Ramírez not only acknowledged the complaint. He also wanted me to choose Santamarina's replacement.

Several names kept running through my mind. I found I had reservations about all of them. I decided to give my imagination a rest and went to lunch with some reporters at Scafidi's, a restaurant in the Calle 25 de Mayo. I was halfway through my steak when I saw the light. How many Argentines do you know who have built up a fortune starting from nothing? I asked them. They couldn't say. One of the journalists went to the back files of La Razón and brought me a list. What do you want it for? he asked in surprise. Very simple, I told him. Someone who's been clever enough to make money for himself can't fail to make money for the country.

When I read the name at the top of the list, I gave a start. I know that man very well! I laughed to myself. It was thanks to me that he earned the first thousand pesos he ever made in his life.

How did it happen? Allow me to go back twenty years. One Sunday in 1924, as I was going up the Calle Viamonte, on my way to my grandmother's, I came across a wretched little store, black with coal soot, that one could sense was about to go broke. It gave off an odor so sweetish and so strong that it seemed to be waiting like a hawk for people passing by to catch the scent. It surprised me to see behind the counter not the typical little old man and his wife who keep their store open on Sundays but an edgy, dark-skinned young man with bright, alert eyes. I stopped, out of curiosity and pity, and bought fifty centavos' worth of pipe tobacco. I sampled the mixture.

'It's Turkish tobacco,' I diagnosed.

'It's Greek, from Smyrna.'

It didn't take the talent of a Sherlock Holmes to deduce, from those four words, the young man's entire life story. From his accent he was Greek; from the geographical reference, a patriot, since Smyrna had fallen under Turkish rule the year before; from his fear, a refugee without papers; from his manners, a shopkeeper from a good family. I told him what I had deduced. And since I was right on the mark on every point, he insisted on filling out the rest of the story for me.

He was twenty-three years old. A fugitive from the atrocities of Mustafa Kemal, he had hopped from Trieste to Naples and from there to Buenos Aires, with a fake passport. He worked by the hour for the River Plate Telephone Company and lived on stale bread. In an effort to help him, his father, with heaven only knows how many sacrifices, had sent him a small shipment of tobacco. In order to get it out of customs, the young man had to spend a year's savings. And now he didn't know how to sell the shipment.

'Nobody goes into business in this country unless he has connections,' I told him. 'I'm going to recommend you to someone.'

One of the managers of the Piccardo factory owed me favors. Then and there, on a piece of brown wrapping paper, I wrote him a brief letter of introduction.

'What's your name, young man?' I asked.

'*Pos me léne?*' he answered me in Greek.

At that point we became involved in an odd and comical misunderstanding. I thought that he was asking me if his *melena*, his long hair, would pass muster for the interview with the manager, and I answered him that he should leave it just the way it was: with a little pomade it would be perfect. But he simply kept asking me in Greek, as before: do you want to know my name? Finally he said to me:

'Aristotle Onassis.'

Months later he came to the barracks to see me, by this time wearing gaiters and a wing collar. He had become a naturalized Argentine citizen. He was selling thousands and thousands of dollars' worth of tobacco. He discussed prices directly with the owner of Piccardo. 'Simple ideas are always the best ones,' he thanked me. 'Like Columbus's egg.'

Fate had marked him for business, not for politics. Everyone in his family had mythological names: one of his uncles was called Hermes; his older sister, Artemis; his father Socrates Ulysses; his mother Penelope. No one can escape the tricks of fate, especially when it has so many of them.

In 1943, my telegram offering him the position of Treasury Minister found him in New York. I received a kind and generous reply: 'Count on me for anything except to govern. Ari the Argentine.'

I thought I would lose sight of him forever. But it was not to be. In 1946 he telephoned me and asked me who in Buenos Aires could sell him ships. I put him in touch with Alberto Dodero, who had an enormous fleet, and with Fritz Mandl, an arms manufacturer who had taken refuge in Argentina to escape from his wife, the actress Hedy Lamarr. They never came to an agreement, I believe, but the three men sealed a firm friendship. On that occasion, Onassis visited me at Government House. I reminded him of the way he'd given me the slip in 1943.

'And who did you finally put in my place?' he asked me.

'It wasn't a man. It was a philosophy. All the ministers I have now started from zero, the way you yourself did.'

I noted that he had dark circles under his eyes and a gloomy look about him. Great wealth had turned him into a collector of celebrities. Historic figures came and went in his life, on the closest terms with him. When Eva went to Europe, Dodero was a member of her entourage. Through him, Onassis chased after her so persistently that my wife ended up inviting him to lunch in a villa on the Italian Riviera, where she had taken refuge, fed up with protocol.

Onassis arrived punctually, looking impeccable, with a bouquet of orchids. Eva, who had put on a cook's apron, showed him into the kitchen. She herself was preparing breaded veal cutlets.

'A person who gives as much as you, señora, has a right to ask for a great deal more,' he remarked, flirting with her. 'Order me to do whatever you please. I am at your feet.'

My wife, who told me the story later, feared that he had an amorous adventure with her in mind, and with great elegance she stopped him in his tracks: 'I'm easy to please. Make me out a check for ten thousand dollars for the orphans of Argentina.'

Every time I think of the way Onassis must have winced at that, I can't help laughing.

'You see? I'm still laughing at the memory, López. We were talking about the GOU and heaven only knows how we ended up chatting about such trivialities. Mischievous tricks of memory. We should take them out, don't you think? They'd spoil my image, wouldn't they? No, leave them. If it weren't for the little things in life, we'd die of pathos. In the cold of the heights, a man can only live by thwarting his feelings. He enjoys power, but nothing else. And life slips through our fingers like water. When a person wants to find out what other things are like, it's too late. There's no time left to get to know them. That's why it's a good idea to sit down on top of memories of no importance and let oneself be gradually enveloped by them. In days gone by, I never used to get out of bed in the morning without doing a few memory exercises so as to wake myself up. Nowadays I've even forgotten to do that.'

One of the clocks in the cloister, which only occasionally strikes, is doing so this time: an obscure ding, a bad omen. Nine-thirty.

'Cámpora is already in the study, General, waiting for us. He's come to get the final instructions for governing. And then, just as you ordered me to do, I will have to accompany him to the floral ceremonies they've involved him in this morning: flowers for San Martín in the Parque del Oeste, for Columbus in the Museo de América, flowers for those executed by firing squad in 1808. What a sacrifice, General. It's going to take me several days to rid myself of the pollen.'

'Have him come upstairs, López. Tell him to come up.'

'Here to the cloister?' the secretary asks in surprise.

'Yes, let him see these old trappings of government. If he didn't learn about them before, when Evita was his teacher, maybe he can learn about them now. Even as dense as he is, in the cloister he'll open the pores of his wits.'

President Cámpora arrives better turned out than usual. Before he has set foot on the stairway, the high polish of his shoes, his pinstripe trousers, his helmet of hair cream, his Paco Rabanne toilet water are already upstairs. He appears with wide-open but reverent arms, held out to the General in a gesture signifying submission rather than affectionate embrace.

'How inexpressibly happy you made the reporters this morning, General. Mounting guard for so many days in order to see you, worried about your health, and suddenly, with no prior notice, you come to the door twice, hale and hearty . . .'

'I came to the door?' the General says, puzzled.

'Yes,' López says reassuringly. 'Your body . . . They saw it and so they had something to write about.'

'The boys at Télam have asked me to show you today's news

bulletins. They want you to approve them before they send them off to Buenos Aires. Let's see what you think of them, General: "7:30 a.m.: On arising, Perón had his usual breakfast of black coffee and a water biscuit." '

'That wasn't how it was this time,' López breaks in. 'Correct them to read: "Feeling better, the General had tea with toast and marmalade for breakfast today." '

Cámpora goes on reading:

8:00 a.m.: The Peronist leader appears in the distance, some twenty meters from the gate at the entry to the villa (the correspondents cannot get inside from there). He seats himself in a lounge chair and remains there meditating for some time. He is wearing a beige shirt, a yellow jacket, light gray pants and sports shoes. On his head is a Pochito cap (like those that became popular during his administration), a red one with black stripes.

'Aren't those the clothes I was wearing last night, López?' the General, still in his pajamas and dressing gown, says in surprise.

The secretary's little eyes perceive a cloud of uneasiness in the air of the cloister. The early-morning hustle and bustle have dismantled his intelligence. His defenses are lowered. He feels himself. His toes, sticking halfway out of his thong sandals, have turned hostile. His kimono is gaping farther open than it should be. And even his hair, ordinarily so docile, has blossomed out in cowlicks.

'You know how bodies are, General. A person can put other clothes on them, but they go on wearing whatever ones they please. And now' – he lowers his head – 'please excuse me, sirs. I must go get dressed, accompany the President and be back before noon. The señora will be asking for me when she wakes up . . .'

Cámpora, in a relaxed mood, closes the door:

'The news agencies and the television networks want us to be photographed in the midst of the boxes and trunks you'll be traveling with, General. So that viewers will see us in Spain as though we were already in Ezeiza. It's not a bad idea, it seems to me. It would be an encouragement for the million people doing their best to get to the airport.'

'Stop worrying about other people's problems. Let them solve them themselves. Think of yourself.' The General collapses in his armchair, as though he had gone blind from the lack of air. 'Come closer. Have you been training your memory lately? How many speeches can you deliver without reading them?'

'Only sentences, sir. I haven't been as well endowed by nature as you have.'

'And what about the Peronist doctrine? Have you continued to make it the prayer you say every night?'

'I haven't missed one, General, except when they took us to the prisons in the south and the liberation revolutionaries read our lips even when we were sleeping. I know the Peronist doctrine backwards and forwards.'

'That's the trouble, Cámpora. Some of the Peronist boys get confused and recite it backwards. Sit down here. Open those scrolls. Aha. The Mnemonic Exercises. What do you see?'

'A face, General. I think it's Figuerola's face. It looks rain-streaked, like in the movies. And a caption underneath. Yes, that's who it is: "The people will never forget Perón, not because he governed well but because the others governed worse. Signed: José Miguel Figuerola." '

A brief cackle escapes from the General's lips. 'That's a brilliant maxim. Do you remember Figuerola?'

'Of course I do, sir. The Galician. He was a genius.'

'The best state planner in the world. He invented the Five-Year Plan; the Memory Scrolls; a Game of Dice that foretold revolutions; the New Almanac of National Holidays; the Wheel of

Fortune of Military Promotions. If I had kept him at my side, nobody could have overthrown me . . .'

'That's perfectly true, General. I absolutely agree. I shall never forget Figuerola's efforts to hide his Catalan accent when he read the Five-Year Plan in Congress. It fell from his molars.'

'His gums, Cámpora. You, as a dentist, ought to have noticed the difference. In those days, Figuerola already had false teeth. He had his dentures made at the same time I did so as not to be outdone. They alienated us through intrigues, because he was a Spaniard. As though one blood or the other made any difference . . . But let's get back to business. I want to ask you a favor.'

'I don't do you favors, General. You give me orders.'

'Close your eyes and recite the Peronist doctrine the way it should be recited. Do you remember that, according to Figuerola's recommendations, the best way to learn a doctrine was to look for a simile for each precept: an object, an image? Tell me: what did you use to practice?'

The President has lowered his large eyelids. He gnaws his thumb.

'I used radio commercials, sir. I chose the most popular ones.'

'Recite the first precept then. Everybody knows that one.'

Cámpora raises his hands to his forehead. He hesitates.

'Have you forgotten it?'

'No, General. I'm in the habit of repeating it more than once a day. But I've never been able to keep it separate from the advertising slogan that I used to learn it in the old days.'

'Recite it then, man.'

'I feel embarrassed.'

'Recite it.'

' "Take your pleasure when you can. Smoke Caravan." Our party is a mass party, an indestructible union of Argentines, which acts as an institution prepared to sacrifice everything with the aim of being useful to General Perón.'

'But that's a really easy one. Let's see how you do with precept sixteen.'

' "Don't say hi or hello or hola. Say O-la-vi-na." General Perón is the supreme commander. The inspirer, the creator, the fulfiller and the leader. He can modify or rescind decisions of the authorities of the Party, as well as examine them, intervene in them, or replace them . . .'

The General nods wearily. The entire morning, which has only just begun, is falling heavily on his shoulders.

'You needn't worry, Cámpora. You did very well. You've got what it takes and we didn't recognize it at the time. We did later. Nobody knows when the right time has come. Not the opportune time, but the right one. For a representative of mine, such as is the case with you, the most important precepts are the first and the sixteenth. But remind your boys of number seventy-seven.'

'It's the one I never forget, General. Do you know how it comes back to my mind? "Your clothes don't tear if it's Roveda you wear." I remember it exactly. And the minute I do, the precept pops up. Whatever the circumstances, a Peronist must firmly maintain that every decision by a Peronist government is the best possible one. He will never tolerate the slightest criticism or entertain the slightest doubt.'

'Are you aware of the difference in style? The others are the work of Figuerola, a civilian. The last one can only be the work of an army officer. It is mine.' The General wraps his dressing gown around him and makes as if to rise to his feet. All of a sudden he lets his arms fall. 'Pay attention, Cámpora. Before we lose sight of each other in Buenos Aires . . .'

'How can you think of such a thing, sir? I'll come see you every day. I'll be available around the clock . . .'

'But I don't know whether I'll be available. I'm taking many things to think about with me . . .'

'You aren't intending to leave me to govern by myself, are you, General? If you give up power, so will I.'

Perón looks at the President in bewilderment. He can't understand why he doesn't understand.

'How can you think of such a thing, man? I couldn't give up my power even if I wanted to. I carry power about with me, the way these legs go wherever I go. Stop worrying and listen to me. Have a monument erected to Figuerola.'

'Yes, sir.'

'And have them inscribe beneath it: "The best state planner in the world. Not because he was good, but because the others were worse." Note it down.'

'Very well, sir. I will order it engraved in the marble exactly that way.'

'And have the doctrine taught every day in the basic units of the Peronist Youth Movement, but after the Galician's exercises.'

'I understand.'

'One last instruction. Bring those almanacs.'

Devoutly, trying not to brush against the prie-dieu, Cámpora unrolls the huge maps of Argentine cities not yet founded, which Figuerola was in the habit of naming after defeats.

'Which one shall we begin with, General?'

'It doesn't matter. In this case, what counts is the philosophy of history. Figuerola once warned me that we Argentines are addicted to death. He used an odd word – thanatophiles. There's the fact that we celebrate San Martín's anniversary not in February, when he was born, but on 17 August. And that it's also not the births but the deaths of Belgrano, Sarmiento, Evita and Gardel that we commemorate. We make children in the first grade repeat the last words of our national heroes. We are cultivators of cadavers. Figuerola thought we shouldn't suffer from our defects, but rather, reap the benefit of them. He was right. I want the names of the streets changed, Cámpora. Were you thinking of naming them Perón? Call them Vilcapugio, Ayohuma, Cancha Rayada, Curupaytí. So that we feel at every moment the goad of our defeats. Have the Malvinas painted black on the maps. If we lose them, have them wear mourning. And invent a colossal statue to Lonardi. And have it say at the foot of it: "Honor to the man who overthrew Perón." '

Cámpora feels that he is being dragged toward heaven only knows what abyss by a violent will that smells of death. He trembles: 'Is that what you want, General? Are you certain?'

'Nobody has ever been more certain.'

At that moment, the soccer player Omar Sívori and the boxer Goyo Peralta are walking toward the doors of the villa. For years they have shared Sunday barbecues with the General. They have sung one tango or another out of tune together. An officer of the Guardia Civil bars their way: 'No, sirs,' he says to them. 'There's an order out to leave him in peace. The General cannot receive anyone now.'

All of a sudden, one of the doors opens a crack. Among the swarms of photographers Peralta makes out Perón, in the background, on the porch, meditating in a lounge chair, wearing a yellow jacket. On tiptoe, he shouts:

'It's Sívori and Goyo, General! We've come to say goodbye to you!'

A sad, blank face turns toward them. And smiling at them with a smile that seemingly takes centuries to appear on his face, Perón says (or they sense that he says) in his unmistakable cavernous voice:

'Thanks, boys. Goodbye.'

18 *With the Past that is Returning*

I am afraid of the encounter with the past that is returning to meet my life.

ALFREDO LE PERA,
Volver

Specks of air have now taken all their places, have invaded even the disorientations of their thoughts. The seven companions of the General's early years no longer even have the illusion that they have returned to the hotel at Ezeiza for some purpose. No one is paying any attention to them. The man with the lizard's head who took them on the bus ride through the hangars and along the dead-end runways of the airport has disappeared, revolver in hand. Zamora, the journalist who seduced them into coming here with salaams and false promises, is lost in a burrow of silence. Señorita

Tizón and Benita de Toledo have tried to track him down by telephone, furious at first, and then very concerned about him. At his house, his wife has no idea where he is. At the editorial room of *Horizonte*, a compassionate woman calms them down. Be patient. Zamora will be along soon. It's odd that nobody from the magazine is there. The editor-in-chief isn't there either? Don't be alarmed. What reason would they have for disappearing at this very moment, just as the General's plane is landing?

But nobody comes. Not even they, the witnesses, feel that they're getting anywhere.

Outside, the airport arcades are filling up with stern-faced, potbellied men, armed as if for combat. They are wearing white armbands. When several unattended mules appear, wandering about loose in the parking lots, the men chase them off with barbed prods.

Artemio and Captain Trafelatti have tried several times to use the bathrooms on the ground floor. No, sirs, you can't go in there. They haven't allowed even Cousin Julio, whose urgent need is obvious, to relieve his bladder. A famous lieutenant-colonel is holding a court martial and has ordered all access to it barred. María Tizón has prowled about in search of a dressing table somewhere so as to put on new makeup. In vain. The area cordoned off by the security forces includes the bathrooms. All they have at their disposal is a repulsive latrine in the hallway. And even that is seldom unoccupied.

In the mirror in the lobby, filthy with patches of mildew, they note in terror that they look like ghosts. Benita's three-quarter-length fox coat has become disarranged: one of the shoulders, out of rebellion, has now slid down to her elbow; Don Alberto Robert's wad of tobacco that he was chewing has dribbled down onto his shirt; what's more, his flinty blue eyes are beginning to hurt. Señorita Tizón's fancy pink suit is spattered with grease and mud: the excursion to the hangars is to blame. The one who comes off worst that morning is Cousin Julio: the lack of rest has made him lose all control of his sphincters, and despite María Amelia's solicitude, his trousers are now dripping wet. Quite some time ago, his long socks too have become soaked through.

Shortly before two, they hear shouts and applause. Hordes of soldiers are running to the military area of the airport, and the potbellied men with the white armbands close ranks in the arcades, firearms at the ready. José Artemio pokes his head out and discovers, to his disappointment, that the reason for all the commotion is not the General, but merely the hustle and bustle of the welcome committee. He recognizes three silhouettes: that of the apostolic nuncio, Monsignor Lino Zanini, in full vestments, as for a wedding; that of Solano Lima, whom Cámpora has named acting President in his absence – he is moving forward, an athletic spring to his step, as pleased as punch at the salutes from the mob of soldiers; and one pace behind him, the ecclesiastical silhouette of Don Arturo Frondizi, a legislator set up as President fifteen years before by Perón, looking solemn, with the smile of a seminarian, come to pay him tribute. At his back the ministers are milling about, but José Artemio, buffeted about by a new swift-running current of guards, can no longer see them.

He hears Benita cluck excitedly. The radios are saying that the retinue of dignitaries has just lunched at an air base. And what about us? It's almost two o'clock and nobody has offered us so much as a sandwich. The potbellies with the armbands pay no attention to their complaints. They go straight past, as if the seven old people were ghosts of the General, cloacas of his past.

Then José Artemio announces a heroic decision: 'All these security agents have had lunch here. They smell of chicken. There is chicken somewhere, and soft drinks. I'm going to search around in the rooms upstairs.'

The tremulous voice of Cousin Julio pipes up from the depths of an armchair: 'And please, have a look and see if there's a bathroom on the way.'

Taking off his beret, José Artemio uses it to improvise a white armband that Benita fastens to his suit coat with a couple of pins. Señorita Tizón approves of the metamorphosis: standing with his chest out, without his muffler, Señor Toledo has the elegance of a middle-aged ladies' man; he could be mistaken for Pedro López Lagar. But the best part is the disdainful expression distorting his face. Along with the vacant look in his eyes, it makes him look like the potbellies.

Screwing up his courage, José Artemio heads straight for the elevator doors: they are the only ones which, because they are too noticeable, nobody is guarding. He goes up to the first floor. He takes a look through the peephole in the door. Impossible to leave the elevator. There is a whole bunch of men sitting in the hallway, amid submachine-guns, rolls of barbed wire, lengths of chain and cartridge clips. José Artemio shakes his head. It's a hotel, and it looks more like a run-down stable. A cramp of fear grips the nape of his neck. He goes on up, straight past them. Arriving at the second floor, he looks out. There are guards at the entrances to the stairways, but not in the hallway. He then opens the elevator door and steps out. He walks along as if there were no one in sight. When he was a little boy he thought that if a person doesn't see, he can't be seen. The tactic seldom failed, and it works now. He moves forward, his mind a blank, through the semidarkness. The only thing he feels is the shelter of the odd dampness that is gradually impregnating the hotel, yard by yard. How is that possible, if outside the sun is exploding and a dry, clean autumn breeze is blowing?

He discovers, at the far end, a door guarded by three men: hefty, swarthy-skinned, with tattooed hands. Turks or sons of Turks. It is necessary to efface himself immediately, to become a body that they overlook. In one glance, José Artemio sizes up the door handles, divines the state of the locks. Alongside the Turks, there is a room without a key. He slowly heads toward it, as though it were his fate, and enters.

He is in luck. There is no one inside. It is a small, shabby bedroom. The light is on. The blinds over the windows, which overlook the parking lots, have been lowered. On a night table are two unsharpened pencils and a memo book with notes in it. Someone has laid out on the double bed a pair of nylon hose, an Ithaca, several cartridge clips and a Magnum, one of those that can only be fired by using both hands. And next to the window is an open door leading to a clean bathroom, furnished with soap and toilet paper. With a smile, he imagines Cousin Julio Perón's relief.

Whiffs of food and cigarette smoke drift in from the room next door. José Artemio glues his ear to the wall. He hears distant voices. Maybe they're coming from the fortress being guarded by the Turks, at the end of the hallway. But there, next door, there is no one. His intuition tells him so. He has the instinct of an old poker player: he just knows. Slowly and cautiously, he creeps toward the door leading to the adjoining room. He tries the lock. He fears that they have slid the bolt of the door shut. He digs around with his penknife. There is no need: the door is unbolted.

He goes in. An overhead billiard lamp sheds a greenish light on the remains of a banquet. His rat's sense of smell has not failed him. He is about to pounce on the platters of meat when all of a sudden the voices he heard before speak again, loud and clear. He is paralyzed. He has miscalculated. They are close by: one room away. On the side of the room that he is in he sees that there is no door. An immeasurable feeling of vulnerability comes over him. It is as if his body were naked, beneath the overhead light, and someone, suddenly, were coming at him with a knife. He is terrified now at the thought of moving. He has trusted his luck too far. He retreats, barely moving, through strand after strand of air. And all of a sudden, against his will, against the warnings of his instincts ordering him to get out of there as fast as his legs will carry him, he hears:

'Enough of thith nonthenthe, Lito. The General cannot, mutht not land here. If he landth, the leftith will nab him. Without realithing, the Old Man, thwept along by the thlogans, will do what they want him to. If that happenth, we'll have to hightail it out. There are more of them than uth, far more.'

Now an icy voice that José Artemio immediately recognized leaps out. It is the voice of an obsequious, dark-haired man who met Arcángelo Gobbi when he came back from taking all of them on the bus excursion. The voice that said to him: 'There's no time to waste: the Lieutenant-Colonel needs you.' It now repeats:

'There's no time to waste, I agree. But look at the overall situation. We're waiting for them and they don't know it. Even though they come with firearms, they won't dare use them. If they do, they risk being blamed by the General afterwards for ruining the celebration for him. You must understand the mentality of those people, sir. The leftists believe that politics is moral. They suffer from the malady known as scruples. That dooms them. If what we're trying to do is to secure the first three hundred yards, then we can concentrate our forces. Those three hundred yards are already secured.'

'You're a jerk, Lito,' a woman's voice, hoarse from tobacco, breaks in.

'You're a jerk. What about the oneth who'll be yelling and thcreaming behind the three hundred yardth? Who can control thothe people? There are millionth of them. How do you per-thuade them not to call Cámpora Uncle?'

'And how about poor Isabelita?' the woman asks, siding with him.

'That'th right. They can't get Eva out of their mindth. They'll find thome way to thnub her. It'th a thure thing. The problem ithn't the leftith, Lito. The whole buthineth about the leftith ith for jerkth, for the little guyth in the army who are going to do the reprething. The problem ith the matheth. You have to know who you're going to team up with: with the needy or with the one who kneadth them into thape. And you can't make a mithtake. The one who doeth the kneading ith Daniel. Thay Daniel and you thay Perón.'

Moving without breathing, José Artemio has discovered a spot from which he can see the three shadows. The woman is gesticulating. Her movements are angular, hysterical. The man with a lisp is resting his hands on a desk, smoking. As for the one named Lito, he can make out his body only from the waist up: he is standing.

'Then there's nothing more to talk about,' Lito says. 'We need a provocateur to light the fuse.'

I have to get out of here, José Artemio thinks. And he repeats it a hundred times: I have to get out of here, I have to stop listening, I have to rid my mind of this bad memory. His hunger has been drained out of him. The food that he has before his eyes is plague and smoke.

'A leftist provocateur,' the woman laughs.

'The one we already have. The thame kid who thang like a canary and gave you the thtraight thcoop. The one who told you that the thouth column wath going to advance in a pinther movement and take the daith. Thend that kid word that when all hell breakth looth, he'th to take hith piethe and fire one bullet. Only one and no more. That will give uth a pretexth for thtarting the big brawl.'

'It has to be now,' the woman says.

'Now,' Lito repeats.

José Artemio gambles: all or nothing. He steals back to the door of the room where this nightmare began, pushes it open and enters. He sees once again, to his relief, the cartridge clips, the Ithaca and the nylon hose on the bed. He waits. He hears Lito give orders and run toward the stairs, with the Turks following behind. He hears the Lieutenant-Colonel talking things over with the woman, but he doesn't understand any of it now; he doesn't want to. He takes a deep breath and goes out into the hallway, once again without looking, as though a routine a thousand years old were weighing heavily on his shoulders. The elevator is still there. It goes down only two floors and it is an eternity: a long abyss.

In the lobby, everything has changed. It is teeming with police and soldiers protected by armbands now of different colors. At the entrance to the hotel there are two cordons impossible to get past. The copies of *Horizonte*, the tables, the armchairs have been taken away.

'Did you find any food?' Benita whines.

'There's no food. There's nothing.' José Artemio walks about, his muscles contracted, his eyes blank. 'Let's ask someone to have pity on us and take us back to Buenos Aires. Everything is over and done with here.'

'What do you mean? The General will be landing within an hour,' Captain Trafelatti wakes up and says. 'They said so on the radio.'

The elevator doors are thrown open, and a woman, followed by two guards, looks around. Her thin lips are drooping at the corners with nervousness or sarcasm:

'Coba!' she calls. 'Lito Coba!'

Suddenly she notices the seven companions of Perón's early years: standing there helpless, out of place in the pandemonium of the lobby. José Artemio feels a shiver run down his back. He thinks: the voice hoarse from tobacco, on the third floor. She's seen me.

'What are these old people doing here?' the woman shouts. 'Clear them out!'

'I'm Julio Perón.' The cousin stands straight and tall, in a bold show of dignity. He does not say: I'm the General's cousin.

'I'm the General's first cousin,' María Amelia says.

In the uproar, in the fever of the general hysteria, the woman doesn't hear them. 'Who the hell brought them? Get them out of here. Toss them in the fields.'

A horde of potbellies fling themselves on the old people. Benita sees, not believing her eyes, how they lift Señorita María up bodily, tearing her precious pink suit, then dump her on the asphalt of the parking lot. She sees how they drag Don Alberto outside and rip María Amelia's skirt. She herself feels an indecent hand grab her, and in a lightning flash of lucidity, hears herself fall onto the floor of a bus.

'. . . a long way from here, out in the middle of the countryside!' the woman says hoarsely.

'I understand the order, Señora Norma,' one of the potbellies replies, standing at attention.

Benita has ended up alongside María Tizón, in the last seat. One of the guards aims his revolver at them.

The sun is still pouring down. The air moves about, burning-hot. Amid the clumps of trees, people are marching along singing. The hangars, the runways now jam-packed with trucks and troops, the wire fences, the eucalyptus trees pass once again before the witnesses' eyes. The bus is – Benita and María notice simultaneously – the same one that took them on the excursion that morning. The remains of a copy of *Horizonte*, spattered with mud, in shreds, are lying underneath one of the seats. Benita sadly discovers, on a torn page, a photograph of herself as an adolescent. And tenderly, she picks up the tattered remnants of the story to give them shelter in her skirt.

The bus brakes to a stop in a scorched pasture.

'Here!' one of the potbellies yells. 'Your tickets are good only as far as here.'

They get out of the bus. Suddenly they feel the forlornness of this deserted expanse of open ground, the boundless emptiness of their lives. And walk on. Captain Trafelatti quickens his pace. As he wades through an irrigation ditch, he loses sight of them. Cousin Julio, his fists clenched, sobs. Benita and María stop to wet their swollen feet, full of scratches from burrs. To open her eyes to the truth about the past, Benita reads:

As fate would have it, Evita Duarte, who was endlessly fascinated by the role played by chance in parallel lives, had as obscure a family background as Juan Perón's. Her father and mother were not married when she was born in Los Toldos on 7 May 1919. They were never to marry. Before Eva was a year old, Don Juan Duarte, at the urging of his lawfully wedded wife who was waiting for him in Chivilcoy, left Los Toldos. Eva and her four older brothers and sisters grew up without a father, 'little waifs', as she was to say later.

Doña Juana Ibargüren, their mother, was a proud, beautiful country girl. In her family too the names were as mixed up and the degrees of relationship as incestuous as in Perón's mother's family. Instead of Toledo Sosa, on this side of the family the confusions of Núñezes and Valentis were such that the town gossips never managed to straighten them out.

Both fathers were justices of the peace at one time or another. Both mothers were enterprising, bold-spirited women, who never were concerned about the finger pointed at them by the neighbourhood women. But unlike what happened in Juan Domingo's case, Don Juan Duarte never recognized Evita. She had to found herself, invent herself a past, be the beginning and the end of her own lineage . . .

Torn page. Photograph of Evita as a child, in tatters and filthy with mud.

. . . at this point in the story there are discrepancies. When Evita was fifteen, did she run away from Junín with Agustín Magaldi, the tango singer? It does not seem likely. It is probably not true.

Magaldi sang in Junín at the end of 1934. Eva journeyed to Buenos Aires on 3 January 1935, with two letters of recommendation and the express consent of her mother. If one of the letters was written by Magaldi, it proved worthless to her. On 28 March 1935, when she began to work as a bit player in a theatrical company in which another woman named Eva played the female lead, she was living in a boarding house in the Congreso district and Magaldi had disappeared on another tour, headed for Santiago del Estero . . .

The darkness is making it difficult for Benita to see. The letters grow smaller and smaller inside the pupils of her eyes. The wind blows the page out of her hands.

The benefit performance that Colonel Perón had organized at Luna Park was to begin at nine, but President Ramírez's wife was delayed by domestic mishaps. The Ramírezes arrived at the stadium at ten-thirty.

It was one of those damp nights of unbreathable air that only summer in Buenos Aires can produce. The San Juan earthquake had hit just a week before: at the show put on to aid the victims grief and a festive mood were conjoined.

The stands were full. Evita looked radiant. The mother-of-pearl of her skin went very well with her black dress, her elbow-length gloves and her hat with a white feather. A friend, Colonel Anibal Imbert, got her a ringside seat in the second row, behind the President. Eva somehow managed, no one knows how, to get herself the seat next to Colonel Perón's.

At eleven p.m., people saw her weep when the Colonel spoke, ramrod-straight, haughty, luminous in his chalk-white uniform. Eva was already smitten with him when she heard him say: 'It is the poor who have suffered most in San Juan. It is the poor who suffer the most and sacrifice the most in this marvelous country. And as the working class expresses its solidarity generously, as it has done tonight, there are many potentates who live the good life at the country's expense and with their backs turned on our suffering.'

The Colonel came down from the platform, wiping his forehead with a handkerchief. The stands acclaimed him. He had to get up from his seat several times, with his arms upraised, to acknowledge the applause and ask for silence. Finally, he remained motionless for a moment alongside Evita, with his eagle eyes staring into space. Recovering her breath, she worked up the courage to brush the sleeve of his uniform with her fingertips.

'Colonel?' she said to him.

Perón looked at her for the first time. Until that very instant he saw nothing in her but a slender body whose heart had been touched, just another throat in the multitude. He answered her:

'What is it, young lady?'

Evita then let fall the phrase that would change the life of both of them forever.

'Thanks for existing – that was all – thanks for existing.'

Cousin Julio walks in a muddy ditch, his feet wet and numb with cold. A dew, which at first is pale and to which the night, little by little, will communicate its darkness, begins to fall. He does not know why he has kept a few bits and pieces of *Horizonte* in his trousers pocket. The paper is now sticking to his wet thighs. The letters dissolve, become unreadable.

8 *Thanks for Existing*

. . . not even the nucleus of seven officers who, together with Perón, created the Lodge in December of 1942, knows today what the initials GOU stood for. History textbooks decipher it as Group of Officers for Unification, Group to Organize and Unify . . . What does it matter?

They agreed to have no leader, they renounced personal ambitions beforehand, they pledged that the Lodge would serve no other interests save those of the army and the fatherland . . .

. . . Perlinger stood up. He was frantic. Perón didn't move a muscle.

'Have you ever thought about Severo Toranzo's letter to Uriburu? Have you ever had the guts to read it? It was written in 1932 and it could be written again tomorrow. Have a look at it.'

'I don't have the patience. There's no time now. Enough of that,' Perón said.

'Listen to it,' Perlinger said, barring Perón's way as he tried to leave. 'Even though it's the last thing I do in my life, I'm going to make you listen to it.'

Trembling, he put on his glasses. Perón, armed with infinite patience, gazed at the ceiling.

'Until 6 September 1930 we had an army that was the idol of Argentines. Heads of the government, even the worst of them, had not dared to use it as an instrument of oppression against the peop . . . You and your followers undermined its discipline, corrupting it with gifts and privileges . . . Today the Argentine army is execrated by the real people . . .'

The countryside has now fallen on the horizon. It is dark, overcast. Not even animals pass by. Señorita María, collapsing from exhaustion, has sat down in the ditch. In the distance, the multitude goes on down the highway in endless rivers. But now it is not leaving. It is returning.

. . . strange, but both stories took place the same day, had to do with the same individual. The train, covered with dust, left the salt marshes of Córdoba behind and entered the desert expanses of Santiago. It was early morning. The berths were crowded with women secretaries, census takers, heads of basic units. Unexpectedly, they all heard Evita. No one needed to say as much. They heard her. She was walking along the corridors in a long white gauze peignoir. She was wearing her hair loose. And a satin shawl.

'Am I a goddess or not? Am I or am I not?'

Around nine in the morning, the train stopped at the Frías station. It was teeming with poor people, all stooped over, like sad little animals. All they wanted was to touch her. Eva threw a shower of banknotes to them. The people didn't even bend down to pick them up. They kept their eyes riveted on her grand appearance, clinging to the light like moths.

An old woman with a bundle on her head managed to make her way through the crowd. She approached Eva and handed her offering to her. It was some pieces of fried chicken, covered with a napkin. Eva touched the woman's head and blessed her. Then she raised the chicken to her lips. In a low voice, one of the census takers tried to restrain her:

'Señora, don't even think of eating that!'

Eva ate with gusto. Then she disappeared for an instant. In the train compartment they heard her berate the census taker.

'A woman of the people cooked this for me, don't you realize that? God only knows how much love and respect she put into this dish. And you want me to throw her love in the trash? I've had enough of you! I don't want to see you again, do you hear? I don't want to see you!'

Central Intelligence Agency
Report No. FIR DB-312/04751-73

. . . once Eva became bedridden, Perón never once entered the room. Apparently, he stopped at the doorway and asked her from there how she was feeling. He tried to keep his distance. He was afraid that cancer was contagious.

The witnesses have stopped again to catch their breath. Taking refuge on José Artemio's bosom, Benita is weeping: brief, dejected sobs, like little matches that soon go out. Cousin Julio, fortunately, has fallen asleep in his sister María Amelia's lap. Will there be a telephone there on the outskirts of Ezeiza, a miserable first aid station, a compassionate nurse for that old man snoring in the throes of death?

Don Alberto Robert, who has fallen behind, is being held up in the darkness by a barbed-wire fence. Seeking support, groping about in empty space, he injures his hands once again. They touch paper serpents, free them from their barbed-wire prison and scatter them in the freezing-cold night air. Perhaps Don Alberto, peering out of the abyss of his blindness, with his senses perpetually on the alert, senses the meaning of the obscure phrase that the wind is now carrying away and that none of the other witnesses will ever read. The phrase that Perón uttered – when? Before whom? – the phrase that encompasses everything: the river-phrase into which the ocean flows.

I know nothing of doubt. A leader cannot doubt. Is it possible for you to imagine God doubting for a single instant? If God were to have doubts, we would all disappear.

19 *Don't Let the Sparrows Alight*

When the Chinese want to kill sparrows, they do not let them alight in the trees. They drive them off with sticks, do not let them alight, and thus make them lose their breath, until finally their hearts burst. With those who want to fly a lot, I do the same thing. I let them fly. But sooner or later they all fall, like the sparrows.

Perón, to the author, 29 June 1966

He has drunk so much water that his body feels inundated, and yet the fear has settled in his throat: the dryness, there, strains its tissues; his saliva is a cork. He shouldn't have any reason to worry. When all is said and done, he has been assigned the easiest job: waiting.

Meanwhile, Nun and Diana's column, its flag on high, continues to open breaches in the left flank of the opposing concentration of forces, penetrating it, entering, and as Vicki Pertini, at the head of another long tongue of militants, rips apart the security cordons on the right flank, he, Iriarte, the baobab, cow-eyes, has stayed behind to cover the rear guard, behind the dais, in the no-man's-land that is keeping the multitude isolated from the airport.

He would have preferred it if Diana or Nun had not taken it for granted that the maneuver would succeed: if they had asked themselves why no tribe of thugs had stopped the march when they moved out from the water tower to the blocked-off highway, to which only police vans are being allowed access; why no helicopter tried to halt the column when it divided in two, amid the underpinnings of the platform, and in a pincer movement went to fling itself on the multitude. Usually so alert, they too suspected nothing. Simply seeing the goal was enough to blind them.

Bighead Iriarte can take in the entire field at one glance. Behind him, in no-man's-land, the hordes of volunteers from the shantytowns are forming the double line that, as Perón approaches, will unfurl a huge welcome placard. In front of him, Diana and Vicki are digging their elbows into the ribs of the enemy concentration, and between the buttocks of the platform a row of ambulances and buses is drowsing, apparently empty, with engines turned off. As though nothing were happening.

He has drunk quarts of water. And yet his tongue is a dead toad. He is suffocating. At the top of the metal framework of the dais, some thirty-five feet above the ground, shadows leap about among the pipes, blend together. Will that frail skeleton hold up when the General appears? How many men, of the millions who are now roaring on the other side of the bridge, will resist the urge to run to him and embrace him, crushing it? Although all sounds intermingle in the deafening din, Bighead can hear the metal pipes breaking: a house of cards. The wind is blowing. On the flanks, the flags buck and rear.

He turns around. He surveys the empty field: the church with glazed tiles that he has just gone past, the run-down orphans' home, the crenelated tower. Three Ford Falcons glide like snakes through the empty streets, at full speed. They are coming toward him. He hears the squeal of the tires, not with his eardrums but with his belly. Sticking their torsos out of the windows, with their hands on the roof, men dressed in black bring out Ithacas, Beretta rifles. And take aim at him.

The Falcons cross a plank bridge, wade across a ditch. They are now on top of him. In the last car, Bighead makes out Lito Coba's icy smile.

To get up onto the platform set up for the symphony orchestra, like the lid of an enormous grand piano at the base of the dais, a trombone player who arrived late has to be hoisted up bodily by the crowd. A path has been opened up to allow two violinists to inch their way through, walking sideways, but they are not allowed to bring their instruments with them. Strings of mortadella, oxides, bird droppings rain down on the music stands every so often. And even though the scores are ruined, the musicians manage to go on tuning their instruments.

The press of bodies gives off thicker and thicker vapors. It is past two o'clock. Nobody has moved for half an hour. Anyone who goes away doesn't get back. Families with children have been chased back to the empty spaces at the rear. Here, in the first yards, the only ones still remaining are those who have steel elbows, cement feet and anesthetized sphincters.

At the foot of the platform, several drum corps are producing their thunder. Fireworks zoom about. A fat sweaty woman pushes her way forward, armpits in the air. Pretending not to notice, another giant of a woman trips her and knocks her down. They threaten each other. They tear each other's hair. Take it easy, girls. Cool it. This is a Peronist day.

Between the helicopters patrolling back and forth, a blue and white balloon, from the State Gas Company, appears. Two trapeze artists, released by a spring, pop out of the basket and fall through empty space. A rope stops them in midair. They are dummies. The moment of suspended reality has been enough for the pickpockets to celebrate their harvest, their June holiday, their flag day.

The booming voice of the official announcer, Edgardo Suárez, is heard above the din: 'There are more than two and a half million of us Argentines here waiting for the General!' Leonardo Favio grabs the microphone from him and corrects him: 'Take heart, comrades, there are three million of us!'

Favio tries to hide his alarm. He is watching fleeting disturbances break out alongside the dais. 'Let's rehearse, comrades!' he shouts, pushing back the pompom of his woolen cap. 'Let's tune up our throats in honor of our beloved General . . .'

It is useless. The cordons of the Labor Union Youth Movement close ranks, each comrade links his right arm with his neighbor's left arm, and, standing shoulder to shoulder, with their head and knees, they roll back the tide that washes over them. They stop only the first attack. At once, the wave forms again and charges. Diana and Nun have already torn down several barbed-wire barriers. Sweat pours down them. The irresistible force following behind them contracts for a moment and then pushes on again. Bodies are disemboweled, raped, as the tidal wave floods forward. A wooden fence falls, in splinters. From the dais one of the Elect blows his whistle: it is the order for the cordons to break up and take shelter behind the ambulances on the flanks.

All those at the head of the column hold their breath. Then they puff and pant like a woman giving birth. And fling themselves forward. When the two long tongues of the column finally meet, in front of the dais, a great shout goes up. Pepe Juárez and Nun raise the flags.

The enormous concentration of defending forces has given way and is scattering into the ditches. The husky lads with the green armbands, who have climbed up onto the labor unions' trucks, regroup their forces, four deep. They ready themselves. They wait for the signal. They bring out their lengths of hose filled with lead, put on their knuckledusters.

There are still some who are struggling, but it is so as to work themselves free and clear out. The Golden Throats have come forward and are singing:

> Rucci, you traitor,
> You're going to get
> What they gave Vandor,

while in the distance the Blue Rivulet chorus, pushed along by the avalanches, is dancing around the trucks, defying the union men:

> It's the end, just wait and see
> Of trade-union bureaucracy.

One of the engines roars, spits out smoke as it threatens to run them over. All the drum corps thunder in unison. Vicki, who doesn't know what to do with herself, leaps about and shouts: Come on, Pocho, Come on, Pocho! as though that would make the General's flight arrive sooner. As the sounds collide, they steam up the air.

Then a shot rings out, loud and clear. In the vortex, where no one can even hear himself breathing, everyone hears it: the first shot falls, and with it silence falls.

*   *   *

All that struggling so that we can enter the whirlwind as if it were made of butter? But what are you saying, Diana Bronstein? The worst hasn't even begun. On the dais, the Faschos are arming themselves as if for a war. I should have worn a head scarf. With this mop of red hair I stand out like a traffic light. Go on, raise the placards, boys! Hey, you, don't you have a bit of cloth you can lend me?

They shove them back and forth. They push and pull them. Every so often, they find an opening. We only have one body, and treating it like this wears it out. But what would become of our body otherwise, what would wear out on us if it weren't for our body?

And yet, it's odd that it's turned out to be this easy. Odd? You're a paranoid Jewish girl, Diana. Centuries of concentration camps have battered your hopes. This isn't the Warsaw ghetto. Who knows if it isn't worse? Take a look at the dais. Good god, what ugly mugs. A mural by Lombroso. The kapos may have cleared out of Auschwitz and Dachau but they're alive and kicking here. Do you see that Rigoletto, Nun? Do you see him, the one in the sweater rubbing his hands together with glee? No – the skinhead, the baldie, the hunchback who's moving around behind the cabin. That one, did you get a good look at him? He's been shooting at me with his eyes for quite a while now.

Able to breathe at last, sheltered beneath the placards, Diana discovers that there are hundreds of people nesting in the trees. In front of the little schoolhouse taken over by López Rega's hawks, families from the provinces have built platforms among the branches of the cedars and the walnut trees: towns in the air, just as in Jules Verne's novels. An elderly woman has lighted the brazier up there and is making maté. Doña Luisa? Isn't that the old lady from Villa Insuperable who told her two days ago: If you're going to be there, Diana, I am not going to miss it. And the man at her side, who's singing or talking to himself with a cigarette butt in his mouth, isn't that her rheumatic husband? Doña Luisa! Diana calls out to her, and the woman, her attention distracted from the brazier, gives a vague wave of her hands.

A pair of twins from Lanús, with guerrilla headbands, hail her from the top of a walnut tree. They have come on her account, following her. How the trees are flowering.

Farther on, in an ash-colored eucalyptus, a dark-skinned woman with a sweet face is nursing her baby. Sheltering her, three men are tuning their guitars. They too twirl their handkerchiefs and smile. Every so often, all heads lift up and scrutinize the signs in the sky: the trails left by the airplanes, the gut-rumblings of the helicopters. The General will be landing at any moment. An eclogue, Diana thinks: people whom one chooses to be near, earthbound figures that are one's equal.

We have only one body and there are times, brief moments, when we would like to love with two, eternities when we would like to forget this body that is afraid. And yet.

Going past the fence, in the area of the little schoolhouse now, some twenty men with light rifles, squatting on their heels, have positioned themselves on double-leveled platforms along the telegraph poles. They are aiming in all directions, as though they were getting ready to blow up the world.

The louder we shout the slogans, the more we'll feel that if we've come here it's to leave with our country rejuvenated, and the easier it will be for the General to throw his arms open and avow: As the people wish. National Socialism? As the people wish. I'm not going to shout myself hoarse right this minute though. Come on, boys, let's sing. It goes like this:

> We'll make a country that's Peronist
> But one that's Montonero and Socialist.

Right? right? Let's sing it again. Hey, what's the matter with you? Have you got a bone stuck in your throat?

'Comrades, put away the placards for a moment!' Leonardo Favio orders over the microphones on the dais. 'Just for a moment. Here alongside me are cameramen and photojournalists who have come from the farthest corners of the world to record this glorious spectacle. It is unheard of, comrades, an enthusiasm without equal in the history of America . . .' Each word must be carefully weighed. The General's name mentioned as often as possible. He is as immortal as the Andes, as hallowed as Pericles, as great as Napoleon. And his image coupled with Isabelita's. But Eva must not be mentioned. Nor the Uncle. The libretto is clear on that point. Watch it.

'Lower the placards for just a moment so the photographers can get a shot of this crown of laurels that we are placing today on the brow of our Great Leader, General Perón!' No one pays any attention. At Favio's every word, the placards are held higher, beating their wings. Nobody is listening any more. The sky is covering the earth with its mouth.

Behind the cabin where Perón will take refuge, Arcángelo Gobbi is waiting for the signal. He walks about. As he goes past the Elect, he repeats to them: Keep your ears pricked. Wait for the first shot. His hands are sweaty. He fears that they're so tense, so still, that they'll turn to water at the very moment he needs them. He is edgy. His back is killing him. An unexpected choking sensation descends as far as his belly and stays there puncturing it. It is like the shiver from masturbating, when he can't bear it a moment more and runs to the bathroom to relieve himself.

Something has fallen on the dais. A bottle? A piece of barbed wire? No, it's a violin with broken strings. All his senses are sharply honed.

He adjusts his dark glasses. And though he has told himself

many times that he mustn't, Arcángelo rivets his eyes on the young woman with flaming red hair. His sweaty hands tighten their grip on the pistol. The moment he hears the signal, he will erase that image that hurts him, he will blast to bits the woman in the depths of his thoughts. Because the green eyes, the freckles, the red hair of the enemy who is shouting beneath the placard of the Montonero Guerrilla Movement are the same ones that torture him in his dreams: the Virgin who comes looking for him each night is finally there. And now he must get rid of her. He must. What better offering to Isabel Perón, the true owner of that holy face?

It is rare for something to happen in the interval between two thoughts. But there's a gap now, Nun thinks, as the unbelievable Bighead climbs up the metal underpinning, holding a drawn Colt, and in that gap reality can be felt: to the right, inside the supply truck from Social Welfare, he senses guns at the ready; on the embankments he has spotted the web of wires and cables that is descending on him; he smells, behind him, the lightning flash of the truncheons that the thugs with green armbands are wielding. He would like to know for sure if it is he or someone else who is hearing this silence. The drums have stopped beating, the musicians have vanished into thin air, the loudspeakers are closing their eyelids. Favio is no longer there. The hot-air balloon enters a cloud. And precisely in this desert where things don't happen, Bighead Iriarte squeezes the trigger.

As Lito Coba leaves the metal framework of the dais behind him, zigzagging along the no-man's-land expressway, heading for the airport, through the astonished shanty dwellers who plod on, unable to understand how Bighead Iriarte could have gone up to bigwig Faschos like that and shaken their hands without feeling revolted – how a militant of the people could confer, on his own, for four to five minutes with the most bloodthirsty lieutenant of Lopezreguism – still open-mouthed with amazement, the shanty dwellers see Bighead abandon his post in the rear guard, make a mad dash, in his clumsy way, to the dais, climb up the pipes of the framework, aim the Colt .45 that Lito has just given him at one of the guards, shout 'Perón or death!' and fire, but in the air, any old way, the guerrilla headband shining like a beacon on his big head, and then light out, duck down, run hell for leather to the Olympic pools, Vicki Pertini trying to catch up with him but able only to send a stream of obscenities whizzing past him. What have you done to us, Bighead? What kind of a stinking mess are you trying to get us into? Words which the terrified baobab doesn't even manage to hear because at that very moment, from one of the telegraph poles, they have blown off the nape of his neck with a rifle that has a telescopic sight, have put to rest forever the troubled, solitary dreams of Bighead, who is breathing his last without explaining how it is possible that his loyalty has shattered so suddenly, what resentments he swallowed, which death he has to go to now, in what dark corner of the sky his ill-starred tenderness will be setting.

You were dying for a cigarette, Vicki Pertini. After all that struggling, you wanted to wet your head in any old puddle, catch your breath and warm your soul with a fag. Then, the shot. An unexpected door opened and *ciao*, you were already on the other side, exhaling the vapor of the cigarette that you will smoke tomorrow. The shot. You run, for a change. You shout something. And without any idea how, you go back to the eye of the whirlwind, the maelstrom sucks you in, your scrawny body marked for nothingness and evaporation isn't you any more, Vicki, the only thing you feel now is that Pepe Juárez is letting go of your hand, that you have lost sight of the Golden Throats, and that an animal strength is lifting you up by the hair to the dais, is dragging you underneath the giant photo of the General as other paws suffocate you with a piece of black plastic. And you don't know what corner of the nothingness to hide your body in, the little puff of smoke of a person that you are, how to get outside yourself so that they don't go on lacerating you with the blows from their lengths of chain.

As soon as Bighead collapses, a line of stretcher bearers runs toward him, but nobody cares about the bullet hole in the nape of his neck, the last flower of blood oozing out of it. Instead they lay the stretchers down all round the body and take shelter behind the parapet.

Alongside the embankment where they have shot him down is the rearguard of the Blue Rivulets, still singing. The only thing they have heard there is the thunder-crack of the telescopic rifle. They know what their eyes can see: that on this bank of the river is a comrade, wounded from behind, with his headband bloodied. One of the baritones, wearing a red neckerchief, infuriated by the incident, defiantly moves forward to recover the body. Heavy fire stops him. The stretcher bearers have opened the first aid kits, revealing among the bandages several flat Berettas, which sting before the report can be heard. If the trigger is skilfully handled, the bursts of fire, three to five shots, never miss. They have blown off the fingers of the baritone in the red neckerchief. They shatter the jaw of the contralto trying to cover him.

When he has let go of Vicki, Pepe Juárez feels his instincts abandon him, all of them except that of survival. If he doesn't retreat right now, he will endanger his men. Lowering the flags, at the head of a mass that fans out in wider and wider zigzags, Pepe manages to reach the eucalyptus grove. The moment he is safely ensconced in that providential refuge, he orders his men to take out their weapons: .22s, airguns, shotguns – any loud noise will help the unnerved, ragtag men in his rear guard save their necks as they disband.

Juárez is dumpy, very dark-skinned, with eyebrows that meet on the bridge of his nose. He has never thought of himself as being courageous, but he discovers now that the blindness of his muscles, his sudden disdain for any sort of future is precisely that, courage. He has an overwhelming urge to leap toward the trenches of the ditch, crawl round to the rear, and attack the stretcher bearers who have so viciously attacked the Blue Rivulet singers. How many of them could he save before he gets killed? Even though, on reflection, he isn't worried about getting killed – from what he has heard of these Faschos, what he is worried about is that they'll tear his tongue out and, afterwards, torture him to make him talk.

So he'll have to wait it out in the eucalyptus grove. López Rega's hawks control the entire field: the ambulances, the dais, the little schoolhouse, the unions' trucks, the Olympic pools. The only escape route is behind him, across the Matanza River.

The hail of gunfire has finally split up the main contingent. The men are scattering, groping their way through the scrub hoping to see no more, to hear no more until the hurricane blows itself out. Balloons have been released from the dais. The sky, idiotically, takes on a festive air. Lying face down on the platform the symphony orchestra players shield themselves under the forest of music stands.

Only Nun and Diana's column has held the positions won, shouting the slogans in unison as though nothing had happened, placards held on high. When the barrage grows heavier and two men behind Nun fall wounded, the tough guys in the column reach for their weapons. Sternly, without stressing the words, Diana orders: 'Hands off your weapons, comrades! Don't let yourselves be provoked.'

For a few minutes they stay there, trusting that their superior numbers will be enough to protect them. They hear Favio through the loudspeakers again: 'Calm, comrades, calm! Don't anybody move from where he is. There's no reason to panic.' But the bursts of automatic gunfire hit closer and closer, and even the veteran photographers move back from the line of fire.

> Hold out, hold out,
> The General will soon be here.

Diana encourages them. She is unable to finish the song. Two ambulances suddenly appear out of nowhere, ripping the vitals of the column with the fury of a wounded whale, crushing bodies, knocking flags down. The blood-chilling sirens are the worst of all.

Now shots are coming from all over the field. In shreds and tatters now, the column breaks into a run. Nun runs. He manages to slip in underneath the dais, between its metal underpinnings. He waits. He closes his eyes and breathes deeply.

When he opens them, he finds a miraculous breach in the labyrinth of pipes. He creeps through it. He finally comes out in no-man's-land, behind the stage, and crosses a bridge, reaches the edge of the Echeverría district. Only then does he discover something unreal, in his hand, an emptiness, like a memory that has said goodbye. And he realizes that Diana is not at his side. That in that sudden flash of eternity he has lost Diana.

Several times, even in the worst of the confusion, Arcángelo had Diana in the sights of his Beretta. And each time, the pleasure of feeling he had her at his mercy has made him lower his weapon. But he has not thought about the pleasure. What he has told himself is: If I shoot her from here, I'm going to lose sight of her. The leftists will take her away and I won't find her again. She won't leave me in peace. When I dream, I'll have her on top of me.

A fierce determination throws him into confusion. And his movements, which up until then have been slow and deliberate, stubborn, become as lightning-quick as a cockroach's.

'Bring the ambulances, right away!' he decides. 'I want three well armed men with me.'

It is not three men who come: it is seven. Following the orders that an Invisible Elect communicates to them with his whistle, the cordons with the green armbands rapidly open a breach in the guerrilla columns. It is at that moment that the ambulances leap forth from the embankment, their sirens wailing, and attack. The flanks of the column give way almost at once. Others have seen the attack and counterattack. Suicidally, they fling themselves between the tires driving gaffs and pikes into the vehicles, but the armor plating does not give, the ambulances don't stop. Arcángelo has clearly indicated, when they set out, who it is he is looking for.

The prey is in the most densely packed nucleus of a whirlwind that is defiantly singing *Hold out, hold out.* A swarm of women with Indian features and husky lads with bushy beards, yellow with mud, is defending her. In the excitement of the hunt, one of the ambulances turns its sirens on full blast. And attacks. Diana has deciphered the signal, correctly – she is the one who is the target of the attack. She gives a leap, breaks loose from the swarm and slipping through the cordons, takes cover next to the dais. Kneeling there, she confronts the Faschos. She defies them with the staff of a flag. She rams it into the radiator, the glass of the windows, until her hands are broken. Then she waits for them: let them run her over. Let them dare to kill her.

But the hunters play with her. Putting the ambulance in reverse, they block her escape. Three men bring her down, immobilize her, feed her into the ambulance, and closing the doors, they stuff a gag in her mouth.

Arcángelo is waiting for her dark interior. Avid to examine his prey he can do so at last: will she be an insect from another world? He scrutinizes the arch of Diana's red eyebrows, the desperation of her green eyes, the freckles on her bosom. And as though he were plunging his hands into a brazier, with infinite caution, he touches her. He feels the strange warmth of the perspiration on her lips, the flaring of her nostrils, the clamor of her breast.

The ambulances, with their hoarse sirens, go round the embankment and out onto the expressway, heading for the airport.

Arcángelo peers at the shadow that, outside, is slowly growing denser. He sees the silhouettes of some houses, a crenelated tower, a church that must once have been blue and now is black. He lays a damp paw on the driver's shoulder.

'Let's go back,' he orders. 'I want to shut this woman up there. In the chapel.'

20 *The Shortest Day of the Year*

Around three in the afternoon, as the shooting was finally dying down, Norma summoned the correspondents to an office in the international hotel and gave a press conference that was less neurasthenic than usual. The tensions of the day had left their mark in her that would not be effaced for some time: her shoulders fell as if on a toboggan slide, and her skinny, muscular legs began to tremble, out of control.

On her desk, the disorderly jumble of telexes, situation graphs and reports on what was happening on the General's plane – which was now on hold over Porto Alegre, in the silence of a cloudless sky – was replenished spasmodically by an entourage of radio operators and potbellied police officers. The Lieutenant-Colonel poked his head in once and then, screwing up his courage, went over to Norma and said in her ear:

'The leftith have thrown thtoneth and now they're conthealing

their hand. They're leaving the platform. Anyone who ithn't at
Etheitha ithn't there becauthe he doethn't want to rethieve the
General. Do you underthtand?'

Norma, who hated looking straight ahead, gave the army officer,
who in the past had more than once underestimated her political
savvy, a withering look out of the corner of her eye.

'I know what I'm doing. I know what I have to say.'

For some time now she had been trying her best to imitate
the General, placing words where others hoped they would be
found, but she was too nervous to determine which direction
others' people's desire was blowing in. This made it seem that
she was being unpleasant, which was unfair, because this un-
pleasantness was not a characteristic of her words but of her entire
nature.

She ordered coffee, would not allow photographs to be taken
and spoke in a voice that was so modest, so violent a contrast to
her manner, that she was obliged to repeat the first sentence more
than once:

'Some of you know that a few minutes ago the dais where we
were all waiting to receive our great leader was attacked. We have
already identified those who gave the order to fire. They represent
trade-union monopolistic and imperialist interests that are
opposed to the General's presence in our land. The hired assassins
are being dissuaded by the popular security forces . . .'

She noted with a start that she had left the 9 mm Walther on
the desk. She put it away in her briefcase.

'. . . popular forces,' she emphasized. 'The infiltrated elements
have no alternative except to abandon the area. Only the real
people will remain, then, to welcome General Perón. Our watchword on this glorious day is to fight for a Peronist fatherland.
Perón is the fatherland.'

She stood up. One of the journalists detained her:

'Do you believe, señora, that when the General learns of these serious incidents he will nonetheless come to the dais for the welcoming ceremony?'

'Yes, he will come.'

'If he should decide not to come, are any alternative airports standing by?'

An uncontrollable grimace clouded her face. She asked one of the potbellies, in a low voice, if the press conference was being broadcast over the radio. The man nodded: yes, broadcast live.

'There is no reason to consider alternative airports. The General will land at Ezeiza. That is certain fact.'

'You maintain, then, that the situation is under control?'

'Completely.'

'And what time do you estimate that the plane will arrive?'

'After nightfall. It is an hour behind schedule. Don't forget that today, 20 June, is the shortest day of the year.'

The answer to the news of the press conference, as had been foreseen, was a frantic attack by the south column. When Lito Coba returned to the area surrounding the dais, in a bulletproof Torino this time, he saw that the flags of the leftists were coming back to life amid the trees. A desperate roar was advancing, in seismic waves, from the farthest reaches of the concentration of forces to where the pilgrims from the northwest had retreated:

> What's happening, what's happening, what's
>   happening, General?
> The country is Socialist
> And they're trying to change it.

The chants were silenced by bursts of merciless gunfire from the ambulances and the dais, but the column reappeared each time by virtue of wondrously ingenious strategies: it was immediately preceded by deafening drum corps and squadrons of cripples

pushing their wheelchairs with one hand and waving flags of truce
with the other. The barricades of the eucalyptus grove had long
since been broken down by the onslaughts of Dodges and Falcons,
the trenches in the ditch were being cleaned out by sappers with
Turkish handlebar mustaches, but nobody knew by what tricks of
will this multitude without commanders or voices to rally them
picked up the wounded each time it was driven back, and persisted
in congregating in front of the dais, to repeat in unison the same
phrase: *What's happening, what's happening?*

Lito noticed that a few armed men had found refuge in the
platforms in the trees and were covering the column's advances
from there. It was one of those problems that the generals of
antiquity solved in a few words. He went up onto the dais and
resolutely seized the microphone. He blew into it. It was working.
He ordered the Elect to diminish their fire and aim their rifles at
the trees.

'I am going to deliver an ultimatum to you,' he announced,
passing his hand through his hair. 'All persons who have cravenly
hidden in the treetops must come down at once. I give you five
minutes to do so.'

There was a brief spark of silence that went out because
someone hammered out a series of pistol shots, immediately
followed by an earsplitting chorus of boos and jeers.

'You've heard the order,' Lito shouted. 'You have four and a half
minutes left.'

Defiantly, he leapt down from the dais and ran to the little grove
of walnut trees and cedars crowning the end of the embankment.
The order had had its effect and the women were coming down,
panic-stricken, with their children in their arms. There were no
sharpshooters in sight. They had now evaporated amid the mirages
of the afternoon. Maté kettles, braziers, dirty diapers and guitars,
however, were falling from the branches. As a number of towns-
women of Villa Insuperable held their arms out so that Doña

Luisa's rheumatic husband could climb down without going into spasms, she, his elderly wife, supported herself on the stumps of the branches along the trunk as she gracefully descended, until finally, as she placed her slipper on the hump of a root, her eyes met Lito Coba's.

That was the only instant on that short June day whose duration was not measured by clocks but by the taste of eternity that the present had: because Doña Luisa, whose gray hair was covered by a white kerchief and who had lost count of her wrinkles many years before, was now getting the better of the logic of time thanks to a marvelous pregnancy impossible to hide. She showed off her belly with such serenity, with such contagious conviction as to the sweetness of her fate, that the other crones of Villa Insuperable had begun to try their luck. They were all pregnant, like the old women in medieval engravings.

Disconcerted by the gentleness of those smiles that came from such a distant past, Lito Coba turned his back on them and set off toward the dais.

He had not walked more than two steps when Leonardo Favio hailed via the microphones the flight of the eighteen thousand doves that had hopped out the prison of their baskets and taken off toward the ashen sky.

'. . . a thousand doves of peace, Peronist comrades, for every year that our General had to spend in exile, a thousand emblems of peace for each year . . .'

As soon as he heard them take wing, the conditioned reflex that Inspector Almirón had ingrained in him in the little camp in Cañuelas was set off in Lito. Drawing his Beretta, he kicked a fence down, shouted 'Now!', and hearing the whirring of the doves in the air, shattered several beaks with a single, certain burst of fire.

Until the moment when he ended up in the little public square of the Esteban Echeverría district, Nun Antezana had obeyed the

General's favorite maxim as though it were a divine truth: *Situate yourself in the center as you walk along the side*. But now, when the law of gravitation ineluctably pushed him to the sides, he understood how dangerous it was for any man who was not the General to touch the center.

He rinsed his face in the public fountain and was amazed at his own image in the water, filthy with mud and burrs. He must find a refuge before dark. Once the distraction of the butchery was over, López Rega's men would go to great pains to scour the countryside in search of him. He felt the lightness of time going by. He saw looming up opposite him the absurd bulk of the glazed tile church, with its red roof tiles, its main door with the pointed arch, its belfry with four clocks each showing a different time. He reached the atrium at a run. He tried the door.

It allowed him in. A dim light filtered down through the Romanesque stained-glass windows in the wall. At the altar, the sacristan was polishing the crown of a statue. Two neon crosses were lit, and at the foot of saints, votive candles were melting down. There was no one inside. Outside, night was slowly falling.

He realized that he needed to think, but there was no place left in his body for thoughts. He could hear only one thing, and even that only halfway, as though one part of him were eavesdropping on the other.

The jarring wail of a siren, in front of the atrium, unthawed his nerves. He heard insults, orders. His first impulse was to crawl underneath the benches and hide amid the narrow planks, covering his eyes like a little animal. To his right, in a recess at the entrance, he spied a confessional. He managed to slip into it just as a gang of thugs burst into the church with an insane mixture of brutal violence and reverence. He peeked through the grating. He immediately recognized the hunchbacked movements of Arcángelo Gobbi. And was thunderstruck to see him bow before the main altar, crossing himself. What happened after that seemed to have

the texture of a dream, but the voices were real and the m̶
were acting with that burning zeal that is to be found only i̶
reality.

One of the thugs knocked the sacristan down with a blow of his
rifle butt and dragged him by the feet to the atrium, where two
others lifted him up bodily like a head of livestock and flung him
in the back of the ambulance. Arcángelo paid no attention to
them. He moved swiftly, from one side to the other, amid the
images of the stations of the cross, as though the humdrum
adornments of the chapel were a disappointment to him. Suddenly, alongside the confessional, he seemed to have found
something. Nun held his breath. Through the grating he saw him
kneel, disappear from sight, then appear again with the toylike
statue of a little Virgin carrying a plaster Infant Jesus in her arms.
He deposited the image in its place as carefully as a person would
cleanse a wound, and stood there for an instant with his hands
joined, adoring her.

Then Arcángelo unbuckled his belt and began to remove his
weapons. He left his Beretta on a kneeling bench, unburdened
himself of a Walther with a silencer and two grenades hidden in
the armholes of his jacket, slowly piled up between his knees the
thirty-round cartridge clips that were making his jacket bulge.
Finally, he pulled up one of the legs of his pants. He removed a
pair of tailor's shears from it and spread them open. He held them
up to the light and gauged the gleam of the blades. A cold smile
distorted his face.

Only then did Nun Antezana notice the bundle that Arcángelo
had put down underneath the holy water font as he came in. He
then saw the hunchback, allowing no one to help him, drag the
bundle and, puffing and panting, dump it amid the glow of
the candlesticks surrounding the dwarf-size statue of Our Lady. A
single gleam of light was sufficient. Beneath the bloody weals, the
gag, and through the tears in her blouse, Nun recognized Diana's

dy. Her eyes were frozen in an expression of horror. Her bosom was covered with dark scratches. And her lips, which used to get cracks in them with the first cold winter weather, did not have cracks but holes in them now.

Nun heard the snip of the shears. Then he saw Diana Bronstein's flaming red curls fall to the floor, still warm; he felt himself riveted to the darkness of the confessional by the blood-stained whiteness of that head that he had so many times heard pulse between his hands, and with that remote sense of surprise that belongs only to childhood, Nun found that his face was wet, that a flood of tears was forming on his face as though to remain there forever.

He waited for a long time until his senses regained their calm and his body became properly his once more. Then, cautiously, he left the church. Hugging the walls, he walked past the gloomy houses in which every so often he glimpsed the flicker of a television. The night was gradually becoming saturated with dampness. The lawns smelled of rot. Suddenly he saw Leonardo Favio gesticulating on one of the screens, looking very upset. He heard him say:

'A kid asked me to go to the international hotel because they were torturing people there. I went upstairs. A thug tried to stop me. I shook him off. I said to him: "Don't try to stop me because I'll start screaming to high heaven." I knocked on a door. They let me in. An NCO grabbed me by the arm: "Just leave without making a fuss. Don't worry, everything's OK here, Leonardo." But I'm not an idiot. There were lots of people lying on the floor, beaten almost to a pulp. The walls were covered with blood. What it must have been like – with the spatters going all the way up to the ceiling! Then I began to cry. I fell on my knees. That may make me a wimp, but I don't care. "I'm not going to inform on you, but I want you to guarantee that you won't take those lives," I pleaded. They promised me they'd call a doctor and stop the torture. Then I left. I copied down the names of the wounded on a little piece of paper, so as to calm their families' worries: José Tomás Almada, Alberto Formingo, Vicki Pertini, Luis Ernesto Pellizón . . .'

Images of the General, Isabel and López Rega with arms upraised, getting off the plane, traversed Nun, and his soul turned into a desert of such endless rancor, an emptiness so irremediable, that he abandoned the shelter of the houses and entered the darkness, like a sleepwalker.

On the morning of 21 June, at three a.m., a police patrol came upon Nun Antezana, motionless, out in the open, contemplating a eucalyptus from which three hanged men, whom no one knew, were dangling.

The General had imagined sadness, but not like that, amid the ravings of so many people. When *Betelgeuse* finally landed at the army airbase at Morón, at five in the afternoon, the first thing he saw through the passenger windows were the threatening strands of dampness hanging suspended, like ghosts, in the air.

He heard applause at the back of the plane, a discordant voice shouting: 'Long live the fatherland!' and at the same time discovered that, outside, ministers, commanders-in-chief, archbishops and bankers were also applauding.

López leaned over to him and said: 'Don't you see now that this way was better, General, more secure? With no uproar, no crush, no torches . . . You'll have only too many occasions for all that now . . .'

'Yes,' the General agreed. 'The poor people will want to see me too.'

The señora tidied her hairdo. She opened her compact, removed the shine from her nose and asked: 'Do I look all right? Now that I see the women outside, dripping with jewels, I regret not having brought my black tailored suit with me to put on.'

'You'll be fine in your winter coat,' the General eased her mind. 'And a rosette in your lapel. Today is Flag Day.'

'They should have brought us the doggies by now,' the señora fretted. 'The poor things threw up all during the flight. They're sick.'

'Daniel will bring them to you, Chabela. Daniel is taking care of everything.'

They had to remain aboard until the Vice-President had handed power back to Cámpora. Then, in the darkness, they came down the stairs. A few photographers lighted their way with flashes, from a distance. The General was upset that *Betelgeuse* had fallen so abruptly into the confusions of nighttime. They had been flying in daylight for eighteen hours, the number of years of his exile, and all of a sudden, on peering out the passenger window, he found a horizon with no twilight: there were only stars and a skeletal waning moon.

They paid him honors, with sabers unsheathed. The same people who had once ordered that the mere mention of his name in public be punished by a prison sentence and had forbidden his party to run in all the elections, were once again there, embracing him, thanking God for having kept him safe and sound, in shape to save the fatherland.

The General was eager to enter into the respite of routine as soon as possible. He felt, bodily, the urgent need of a house. He said as much. But López Rega took him by the arm and led him away to an office where the commanders-in-chief were awaiting him.

Paying little attention, he heard once more the details of the recent slaughter. They again told him the names of several of the guilty parties. The General forgot them immediately: his exhaustion turned those names to water in his mind.

'We will make their punishment a thundering one,' he said, with all the severity he could muster. Then, turning to López, he asked:

'Have you brought the folders with the Memoirs in your portfolio, my son? Tomorrow, when we get up we must go on correcting them. Everything that has begun must end sometime.'

One of the commanders insisted on reading aloud the official reports on the dead and wounded at Ezeiza. The General cut him short. He wanted to know where the pilgrims who had come from distant provinces to see him were being given shelter, so as to send them flowers and blankets.

'There aren't any flowers, General. It's winter,' President Cámpora said, spacing out the syllables. 'The best thing you can do for them is to speak to them.'

The señora stood up. She always had an anxious look in her eye, as though she were about to lose it at any moment. Now her anxiety had left her. The only thing that was left was the lost look.

'What about my doggies?' she asked. 'Why don't they bring them to me this minute, Daniel? Where have they taken my poor little rascals?'

My fate is sealed, Zamora said to himself again. I am seeing history through the keyhole. The only reality I know is the one I see on television.

At six p.m. the barrier of trucks that had blocked his taxi in front of the highrises of the Workers' Housing Project unexpectedly broke open, and the vehicles trapped at the entrance to the expressway retreated toward the depths of the city, in an incomprehensible, unanimous reversal of the migrations that had ruled the day. The once-deafening drum corps returned, but with no drumrolls now, beating out only a sporadic mournful tattoo. Along the shoulders of the highway, a silent multitude retraced in a few hours the path whose end it had taken it eighteen long years to reach.

Zamora was struck by how the silence remained motionless, floating like a planet above the endless lines of people. He had not imagined that they could make their way along like that, in silence, all together, without either they themselves or the silence breaking, especially since they were bearing that enormous weight of backpacks and sadness.

Once again, he felt cut off by a pane of glass from the things that were happening, and decided to leap out into the open. He paid the taxi driver the triple fare, and as he opened the door he was suddenly afraid. Writing about history is easy. Plunging headlong into it might cause the meridian of his feelings to shift. He got out. He was surprised to find that the night had neither an odor nor sounds, only those same myriad silences that he had discerned from inside the taxi. There was a hint of frost in the air.

He walked against the current. He no longer cared about how he was going to get back to downtown Buenos Aires, because now the center was here, in this blind spot in the mist. He broke a path for himself yard by yard, struggling against the crowd, but the effort slid down his body, as though instead of advancing it were allowing itself to fall on top of the others. At least I know where I am going, he said to himself. But he didn't know.

Finally he reached a house with peeling plaster, one with many rooms that people kept going into and coming out of. In one of the courtyards he saw men standing in a row urinating. He urinated too and began to prowl about the deserted areas of the house. He reached what must have been a dining room. Dogs and several saddled horses, with no one looking after them, were wandering about in the darkness.

He went out into another courtyard. It had a kitchen built of wooden planks. People were warming their hands over the burners of the stoves. The walls were dusty and full of cracks. Peasants with stiff gray ponchos were sleeping on the floor. No one said a word. Their eyes were all vaguely following some sort of gleam in the air, and if they were saying something it was only phrases spoken to themselves.

From the shadows, in the houses in the background, television screens, flickering like fireflies, multiplied the lines of downcast pilgrims along the highway, the national discouragement, the mortal depression that was slowly blanketing the city along with the thick fog.

Suddenly, Zamora heard a few scattered sentences rise out of the silence. He recognized the General's voice, stripped bare of all inflection, as though it were coming from a throat not his own:

'I don't know what dark fate has destined me to arrive in Buenos Aires after eighteen years in exile without my being able to give the Argentine people a symbolic embrace from the depths of my heart . . .'

The men awoke. Even the horses turned their heads toward the lighted television screens. The volume rose.

'. . . first of all, because we were already a little behind schedule when we left Madrid. And then because today, the twentieth of June, is the shortest day in the year. We made the journey in the usual way, but we have arrived outside of time . . .'

Zamora approached the knots of people, which were growing denser and denser. Finally, he managed to catch sight of the General, ramrod-straight, in tiptop condition, bearing no trace of the long flight. He had smoothed his hair down with a layer of hair cream. He was sitting in an Empire armchair, scarcely moving. López Rega, standing one step behind him, was leaning his hands on the back of the chair. President Cámpora, from an armchair alongside his, was listening, spellbound. The nation's coat of arms beamed down upon the scene.

Although the speech was delivered impromptu, López appeared to be following it with his lips with no difficulty. The General was saying:

'. . . in order to avoid disorders, I did not want a crowd to gather at night, in a dark area such as the airport. I did so most regretfully, thinking of the poor people who had come to Ezeiza from such a long distance away to bid me welcome . . .'

Something about the image, however, was outside the natural order of things, as though it were raining upward. The peasants and the horses grew nervous. Zamora paid even closer attention. The General said:

'I am to make a tour of the entire Republic . . .'

Then one of the men realized that López's lips were moving ahead of the General's speech.

'Just look at that,' he muttered. 'They're driving the General along.'

It happened again. On the secretary's lips could be read the words: '. . . and I shall enjoy seeing the people of Jujuy' a fraction of a second before the phrase came forth from the General's throat.

'. . . and the people of Salta,' the secretary's lips dictated.

'Salta,' Perón repeated.

Disappointment came over the crowd like an instantaneous illness. One of the women walked away from the television set in tears and went to lie down alongside the braziers. Others began to warm the children's food. The entire house remained suspended in that abyss that exists between indifference and a violent outburst, until one of the peasants finally rose to his feet and said, calmly, irrefutably:

'That man can't be Perón.'

'It can't be,' the women agreed.

'When Perón finds out what's happening, he'll come back,' the peasant said.

On the screen, the General gave a last faint, melancholy smile. Zamora turned his back on him and looked in the direction of the commotion the kids were making, so as to rest his eyes for a while. The shortest day of the year entered eternity, as they said. It reached its end. Zamora rose to his feet.

'Even if he returns, it's too late. We shall never be again as we were.'

Epilogue

Standing in the saddle, haranguing, he offered his hand to the dead, one by one. No one knows whether it's a good thing if he receives us or a good thing if he turns his back on us.

José Lezama Lima
Telón lento para arias breves

The women of Villa Insuperable moved forward toward the ocher mass of the Teatro Colón with a feeling in their bones that they wouldn't see the General this time either. A persistent rain was falling. They took shelter beneath oilcloth canopies, held up by broomsticks, that the wind kept blowing down, and took turns warming the newborn babies' nursing bottles in nearby cafés, at whose doors funeral wreaths were piled up.

They had marched with the columns of mourners just over

twenty blocks, from west to east, in the course of some fifteen hours. It was not easy to measure the time because they were already on the other shore, in the eternity of the funeral rites, where the tremendous death of the General rained down its contagion without regard for proprieties or limits.

Every so often, the radio stations came on the air and listed the telegrams of condolence or picked up the fits of weeping of the people in the long lines. The doors of houses were left ajar and the newspapers spoke only of the mourning.

At daybreak on Wednesday, 3 July 1974, the news broadcasts fired off a jumble of facts and opinions for the benefit of history, thereby placing the General even farther out of the reach of the women, as if a mirage had carried him off.

The Great Man's coffin was now in the Blue Room of Congress. One deputy proposed that it be left indefinitely on the rostrum of the meeting room so that his immortality would inspire the laws and decrees of the future.

The corpse was dressed in military uniform. Its intertwined fingers clutched a mother-of-pearl rosary. The presidential sash lay across its chest. The uniform – the reporter from Radio Rivadavia reflected – looked out of place on that body that had not been able to wear it for eighteen years and that had finally adapted itself to the freedom of civilian dress. Eight governments had forbidden the General the use of sun symbols on his epaulets, the curved saber and the cap with gold palm leaves that now gleamed on his chest.

The multitude waiting to see him must have numbered more than four hundred thousand people. No more than two thousand per hour managed to get as far as the coffin. Radio Belgrano said that no one might touch the General the way people had Evita. It was a wake for an old man, at which there were fewer tears and more philosophizing. A railing draped with a blue cloak separated the coffin from the crowd. The cloak was filthy with tears, mud, the flotsam awash in the streets, but the pilgrims kissed it just the same. Every fifteen minutes, the grenadiers brought a new cloak.

So, finally, Isabelita, the widow, was President of the Republic. She carried herself with studied dignity, so as to rise to the occasion. Every two or three hours she visited the funeral chapel, escorted by her military aides-de-camp. There, she would say an Our Father, smooth the hair of the deceased and wipe away his saliva with a little handkerchief.

The Radio Mitre announcer was surprised that López Rega came into the chapel every time Isabelita left it, and bending over the deceased, recited a few prayers in his ear. 'You can follow him on your screens,' the announcer said. 'Watch as the secretary brushes his chief's forehead with the tips of his little finger and his ring finger. Observe the fervent devotion with which he does so. He touches him once, twice, three times. And now he also steps back one pace.'

Before daybreak, Radio Continental's news broadcast announced that the mother of the Reverend Martin Luther King had been assassinated in Alabama or Kentucky as she was playing the organ in church. Doña Luisa, the old woman from Villa Insuperable whose pregnancy had frightened Lito Coba at Ezeiza, was nursing the baby when she heard the news. It gave her such a scare that she took her breast away from him, fearing that her milk had turned sour.

'The General laid the egg of death,' she told her husband. 'And when misfortunes like this begin, no one can put a stop to them.'

She suspected that the radios had thought the same thing because they used the word *death* with extreme caution. When they spoke of the people who had fainted and been left where they fell, they said: 'Seven thousand people fainted and are now back; one hundred and fourteen have been taken to hospitals. Twelve departed from heart failure: these latter will not return.'

On account of the humidity, Doña Luisa had been tormented

for hours by a bunion. The pain put forth branches, and at times even rooted itself in the pit of her stomach. Like the other Villa Insuperable women, she was wearing a shawl over her shoulders and a white kerchief on her head, but in that wet winter these articles of clothing were a burden to bear, not a protection against the weather.

The husbands were making maté. When dawn broke, the rain died down a little and the column of mourners left the sheltering bulk of the theater behind. Some bricklayers brought wicker chairs so that the women could suckle their babies in comfort. Different radio stations could be heard at different places all down the line of mourners, but all the voices on them were lugubrious and pompously formal; and when they broadcast music, it was church music.

The mobile unit of Radio del Plata announced that the women textile workers of Pergamino had decided to hold their wake for the General in the meeting hall of their union, before a large photograph of him. The correspondent reported in a grief-stricken voice: 'It is most moving to see how these women of the people have placed the venerated photograph on a lace pillowcase, adorning it with bands of crepe so that everyone will get used to the idea that here too, in Pergamino, the General is present in person, like Our Lord in each consecrated host.' After that, it was announced that the parishioners of San Luis and Catamarca were enveloping busts of Perón in shrouds so as to recite requiem masses for him.

'If that's so, we women here in Villa Insuperable can also hold a wake for him,' Doña Luisa decided.

They all agreed. It took them some time to walk with their bundles on their head through the muddy back streets of Bajo Belgrano. When they finally got close to home and smelled soup heating, they felt that the General would be better off there than exposed to the elements, together with people like himself and not with the authorities and their pomp.

Doña Luisa lived in a one-room house. The husbands removed the cots, the dining table, the cradle of the newborn baby, and used fruit crates to set up an altar. They ended up with a pyramid. This they covered with a cretonne bedspread and placed the television set at the apex. The image of the General was placed in the funeral chapel they had made for him. At intervals, the television cameras showed his rigid face, amid his womb-like shroud. Mourners were seen filing past almost at a run, and when someone tried to stay one second longer, soldiers dragged the person out bodily.

'You see,' Doña Luisa said again. 'The General is better off here than there.'

They lit two large tapers on either side of the television set and hung from the ceiling a crucifix put together from planks of scaffolding. They adorned the walls with black bows, and Doña Luisa made a lovely floral arrangement, with plastic carnations, for the foot of the pyramid. The news of the wake spread through all of Bajo Belgrano, and a long line formed at the entrance to Villa Insuperable. When they arrived in front of the television set, the mourners knelt, lovingly stroked the screen and walked away in silence. Every so often, Doña Luisa cleaned the image of the General with a little black handkerchief and touched his hair through the glass.

They saw Nun Antezana stand to attention before the deceased and salute him with his fist upraised. They saw how Arcángelo Gobbi held the señora up by the elbows when at dawn on 4 July, overcome with grief, she fell into a fit of weeping and looked as though she were about to faint.

Doña Luisa did not take her eyes from the television set until they closed the doors of Congress. The cameras zoomed in on the General for the last time and showed his face shrouded in the uterus of tulle. Something went wrong then, and snow fell on the image. The dead man slowly sank into the white depths until nothing was left on the screen but snowdrifts and ice volcanoes, like those at the Pole.

A voiceover accompanying the snow-covered image recounted how two hundred thousand persons had been left outside the Congress, unable to say their last farewell to the General. The lines of disappointed faithful stretched out for ninety-four blocks at that time, from the Calle Paraguay to the north to the Avenida San Juan to the south, and from Carlos Pellegrini to the east to the Calle Jujuy to the west.

At 9.15 on 4 July, the funeral procession left for the chapel of Nuestra Señora de la Merced, at the presidential residence in Olivos. The women of Villa Insuperable knelt before the image of the coffin, which was mounted on an army gun carriage draped with the flag. A drizzling rain was wetting it. Thousands of flowers fell from the balconies: carnations, gladioli, jasmine, orchids, frail summer insects that had left hothouses so as to live that one moment. The presidential guard beat kettledrums.

The women of Villa Insuperable burst into tears. Doña Luisa had the feeling that they too were dying in that oppressiveness at the end. She had a sudden knot in her throat. She realized that once the coffin disappeared from the screen they would all be orphans forever, and she was not a woman who readily resigned herself. She went up to the fruit-crate altar and gave the television set a strong embrace. The General's smile enveloped her in its omnipotent warmth then, and Doña Luisa thought that anything could happen, that a person needed only to say it for it to happen:

'Come back to life again, man! What'll it cost you?'

Acknowledgments

To César Fernández Moreno, in whose company the idea for this novel was born, as we crossed the Pyrenees in a car named Eolus because every gust of air blew straight through it.

To Cora and Manuel Sadosky, who lent me a corner of their house in Caracas so that I might write the first drafts.

To the Woodrow Wilson International Center for Scholars, in one of whose skyscrapers in Washington, DC my mountains of documents began to take on life. To Louis W. Goodman, who was concerned about the excessive length of the first version (nearly two thousand pages) and persuaded me to be briefer and have pity on my possible readers.

To the Seven Witnesses, who put their store of documents at my disposal and kindly put up with my endless questions. To Mercedes Villada Achával de Lonardi, who allowed me to copy her diary.

To Guillermo O'Donnell and to Leslie Manigat, for their confidence in me. To Carlos Fuentes, for his memorable counsel given me in the dining room of the Wilson Center.

To Susana, who read and discussed every page of the manuscript, even in the final weeks of writing, when we both decided that sleeping wasn't worth the trouble.